PRAISE FOR
THE DINOSAUR CLUB

"A wryly twisting, engaging tale. . . . Heffernan's suburban fantasy of betrayal, retribution and May/September romance above the 40th floor is a highly entertaining read." —*Publishers Weekly*

"Highly recommended. . . . Heffernan is masterly in examining the scruples of corporate downsizing with a discerning eye and blends levity in his cauldron of good and evil." —*Library Journal*

"Fun and amusing, Heffernan's book nonetheless mirrors a growing societal terror." —*Gannett News Service*

"A must read for those hit by downsizing. . . . If you prefer to wait for the movie, you shouldn't have to wait too long: Warner Bros. has already purchased the rights." —*San Antonio Express-News*

"An enormously entertaining yarn that puts the concept of human resources in an arresting new perspective." —*Kirkus Reviews*

"Funny." —*New York Daily News*

"Entertaining. . . . In his novel about corporate downsizing, William Heffernan lets the little guy win." —*Columbus Dispatch*

"A ripping good read. . . . Briskly written. . . . The Dinosaur Club fights back against the company poohbahs with some quite clever scheming." —*Poughkeepsie Journal*

Books by William Heffernan

BRODERICK

CAGING THE RAVEN

THE CORSICAN

ACTS OF CONTRITION

RITUAL

BLOOD ROSE

CORSICAN HONOR

SCARRED

TARNISHED BLUE

WINTER'S GOLD

THE DINOSAUR CLUB*

*Published by POCKET BOOKS

THE
DINOSAUR
CLUB

WILLIAM
HEFFERNAN

POCKET STAR BOOKS

New York   London   Toronto   Sydney   Tokyo   Singapore

This book is a work of fiction. Names, characters, places and incidents are products of the author's imagination or are used fictitiously. Any resemblance to actual events or locales or persons, living or dead, is entirely coincidental.

A Pocket Star Book published by
POCKET BOOKS, a division of Simon & Schuster Inc.
1230 Avenue of the Americas, New York, NY 10020

ISBN: 0-671-02099-4

First Pocket Books printing January 1999

10 9 8 7 6 5 4 3 2 1

POCKET STAR BOOKS and colophon are registered trademarks of Simon & Schuster Inc.

Cover art by Ben Perini

Printed in the U.S.A.

QB/✶

This book is for all the dinosaurs,
and for the lovely Stacie Blake, who married one.

ACKNOWLEDGMENTS

I would like to thank the many people who helped make this book possible. Liza Dawson and James O'Shea Wade, for their extraordinary editing talents and faith. Debra Weaver, for guiding me through the legal quagmire of case law. Peter Fleischman, for his equally valuable help in understanding pension abuses. Gloria Loomis, agent and friend, the woman who stirs the pot. And especially Dominic and Sue Mara, and all the *dinosaurs*, who took the time to share their own often painful experiences.

Surgeons must be very careful
When they take the knife!
Underneath their fine incisions
Stirs the Culprit—Life!

—EMILY DICKINSON

Oh roses for the flush of youth,
And laurel for the perfect prime;
But pluck an ivy branch for me
Grown old before my time.

—CHRISTINA GEORGINA ROSSETTI

THE
DINOSAUR
CLUB

1

JACK FALLON'S LIFE TOOK ANOTHER CAPRICIOUS TURN ON the Fourth of July weekend. He was holed up in the small, paneled study of his oversized suburban home, reading through sales reports that stared at him like harbingers of doom. Behind his desk, a steady drizzle patterned the window, the tiny droplets careening into erratic cascades of crisscrossing streams, forced together by a speck of dirt, or an irregularity in the glass, then pooling at the base before slipping off to form still other miniature estuaries that raced along the sill. Had Fallon been watching, he would have thought the small, irrationally formed rivers resembled his life, perhaps everyone's life, speeding along under the tyrannical force of gravity, until thrown off course by unseen obstacles, uncontrollable vicissitudes of fate. Fallon also failed to notice far-off rumbles of thunder that hinted at more serious rain to come. Had he heard, he would not have cared. He had intended to work throughout the holiday weekend, to struggle for his own tenuous survival, rather than celebrate his nation's birth with barbecues and beer.

Trisha, his wife of twenty-four years, entered the small room—dressed to the nines, as they used to say—

and perched on the very edge of a well-worn, leather club chair. He should have noticed the high heels, the carefully applied makeup, the gold earrings, the necklace, the stylish slacks and silk blouse. It was Saturday afternoon, when she'd normally have on a pair of shorts and a designer T-shirt. He also should have noticed her wedding ring was missing.

"I have to talk to you, Jack. I'm leaving," she said. His eyes didn't move from the report he was reading. "Jack?" she said again.

Fallon turned a page. "Great," he said. "But let's talk when you get back, okay? I'm really up to my ears. Maybe we can go to that restaurant you like. Chez . . . whatever." He glanced up.

"No, Jack. We have to talk now. I'm leaving *you*." Trisha's lips were tight and nervous; they moved awkwardly as if finding it difficult to surround the words. She readjusted herself on the edge of the chair, drawing her knees tightly together.

"I want a divorce, Jack. I've packed some things, and I'm leaving today." She paused a beat, swallowed, then hurried on, rushing the words. "It's not something I want to discuss. I think we're past that. You can stay in the house. We'll work something out later." She drew a breath, then pushed on again. "I've arranged for some people to come by and pack the things I want."

The initial words hit Fallon like a kick to the stomach, his mind clouding to much of what followed. Then it had clicked back with denial. This could be fixed, smoothed over. It was her final sentence that had got his attention, drove the denial away. People coming to pack. So well organized, something she had planned out. But that was how Trisha did things. When they were first married she even arranged the socks in his drawer according to color. Handkerchiefs and underwear set in neat little rows. Such a long time ago. The remembrance made him feel as though he'd been kicked again.

He shook his head, as if trying to clear it. "Wait a minute. You said you wanted to talk. Now you say we're past talking." He tried a smile; felt the misery of it on his face. Perhaps he could joke it away. "Hey, listen, we can't afford a divorce," he said. He pushed the smile again. "Believe me. We can't. I've seen our checkbook." He felt sweat begin to form in the palms of his hands and instantly hated it.

Trisha ignored the attempt, gritted her teeth against it. "I mean there's nothing we can say to each other that will change things, Jack. It's something I've thought out. Something I have to do. And I think it's best for us both." Her mouth seemed tight and awkward again, and she worked the words like some marionette whose strings were being pulled behind a curtain.

"Whoa, wait a minute, Trish." Fallon held up both hands; tried another weak smile; failed with it again. "We've been married half our damn lives. We've got two kids. I think I'm entitled to more than that."

Trisha lowered her head; closed her eyes. When she looked at him again her mouth seemed even tighter. "Jack, I have to do something for *me* if I'm going to be happy." She drew out the final word; twisted ever so slightly on the chair. "I can't do that here with you. I've tried and it just doesn't work anymore. I've talked to my therapist about this, and she agrees with me. There just isn't much more I can tell you right now."

"Are you talking about getting a job? Going back to school? If that's what we're talking about, those are things we can work with." He raised his hands again; shook his head; wondered if he looked as bewildered as he suddenly felt.

She let out an impatient breath. "It's some of that," she said. "I'm not sure I can really explain it, or if I even want to. Just accept that I have to leave. *Am* leaving."

Fallon fought against the hollowness in his gut. "Are you moving in with someone else, Trish? Is that it?" He watched her eyes blink and his stomach twisted again. "Who? Howard? Has it gone that far beyond just flirting?"

Trisha's mouth became a small circle; her eyes widened, blinked twice. Then she got hold of herself. "I'm surprised you noticed."

The admission hit like another blow to the stomach. Howard. The dentist. The friendly neighbor with whom they occasionally played tennis. Doubles with Howard and his wife—silly, eager to please, slightly overweight Marge—the four of them prancing around the courts at that ridiculously upscale tennis club Trish had been so desperate to join. Then, later, all of them sharing a meal at a local restaurant.

"I noticed, Trish. How could I help it? I just didn't realize it had gone beyond an occasional giggle and flirt, that you'd actually started screwing him." His voice had hardened and it seemed to startle her. He immediately softened it, hoping to hide the sudden rush of bitterness he felt. He forced a small smile, failed with it. "Jesus, Trish. A goddamned dentist? What the hell is this?" He stared across the desk, his eyes a mix of hurt and anger. He wished he could laugh in her face, desperately wanted to, but found he couldn't.

"Don't be crude, Jack." Her face took on a pink hue, and her well-shaped rump twisted uncomfortably in the chair. "Howard appreciates me." She raised her chin slightly, emphasizing the words. "Something *you* stopped doing a long time ago." She stared at him, looking past the hurt in his eyes. She had thought about it for months, convinced herself the accusation was true, and now she hurried on, wanting to justify it. "Howard wants me for what I am, Jack. What I can be. We aren't just *screwing*." She threw the final word out like another challenge, perhaps even an assault.

Fallon pressed a thumb and index finger into his eyes. "I thought you were leaving to find out what that was. Apparently Howard's already told you." He added the last sarcastically, then released the pressure on his eyes, shook his head for emphasis. He knew he was blowing any chance he had, but right now he didn't care. He leaned against the chair, forcing it to tilt back . . . away from her. Then he noticed his fingers; how they gripped the arms—some terrified airline passenger on his first flight. His face flushed with anger. "No, Trish, you've been screwing him, and now you're leaving. So where the hell does Howard think you'll find yourself? On the second floor of Bergdorf Goodman?" He had snapped it out, the acrimony unconcealed, and each word seemed to hit her with a physical force, but she recovered quickly.

"Have it the way you want, Jack." She stood abruptly and looked down at him. "This is exactly what our problem is. What it's always been."

Fallon blinked. *This* is the problem? You're off screwing someone else, but this is it? He pushed the chair away from his desk, lowered his gaze, and stared at his shoes. On the way his eyes passed the slightly bulging midsection that had developed over the past decade. It hadn't been there when he'd turned forty. It had crept up on him. Now, at forty-nine, there it was, firmly—or not so firmly—in place. Howard was trim. Inexplicably, he suddenly realized he couldn't recall the man's last name. Howard . . . The dentist . . . A man who had literally franchised himself, turned himself into a flaming HMO—four offices, with other dentists working for him, glossy brochures, even television ads. Fallon gritted his teeth. And you, you're about to be tossed out of the only job you've ever had.

Fallon had intended to stand, to face her. Now he remained seated. "What about Marge?" he asked. "Howard's still married to her, isn't he?" He looked up at Trisha again, still standing over him. Even at forty-five she was beautiful. Trim and sexy—at least to him.

And, obviously, to Howard. But she was more than that. Twenty-four years more. He let out a breath, took in the blond hair that hung to her shoulders, and suddenly realized it was cut differently. He didn't know when she had changed it. Hadn't noticed. Maybe she was right. Maybe he had stopped appreciating her. No, not that. Maybe he had just stopped showing it, had been too overwhelmed by his own problems to even think about it. He drew a deep breath, suddenly angry at his willingness to blame himself. Maybe Howard noticed those things. Maybe the world wasn't coming down around Howard's ears, and he had time for personal observation.

"Howard left his wife. We're moving into a condo in Manhattan. Close to Howard's main office. I'll be working there. Running it for him. He values my ideas, Jack. He values my values." There was a tinge of pride in her voice.

Fallon blinked. "I thought you didn't want a job. That you wanted to stay with your volunteer work—the homeless, pregnant teenagers . . ." He tried to recall what the other cause was, failed, and added a quick "whatever." The look on Trisha's face told him the final word had been a mistake. In recent years she had complained that he never asked what she did with her time, her energy, and especially the nights she spent taking the odd course toward a distant MSW degree and an empty-nest career. And her complaints had been justified; he had become like so many men, imprisoned by his work and that constant, gnawing anxiety that was so much a part of it. He wondered now if her complaints had been a warning he had failed to recognize. Suddenly he wanted to tell her that she had always done everything competently, including being a wife and mother. But the words wouldn't form. His own hurt and anger were too deep.

Trisha continued to stare at him, lips tight. "It's not

enough anymore, Jack. I have to think about my future. I have to make it what I want it to be."

Her words brought him back, hit him again. Fallon remembered Howard saying that his main office was on the Upper East Side. Sixty-third Street, he thought. From the glitter in Trisha's bright blue eyes, he was certain it was. She had always wanted to live there, all the way back to the early years of their marriage. In those days it would have been a big step up from their beat-up first apartment in the East Village. Two cramped rooms on the fifth floor with a bathtub in the kitchen, which, with a sheet of plywood laid across it, doubled as a countertop and table. He glanced around his well-appointed study, felt the deep carpet beneath his feet; thought about the rest of the house, how they now lived. They were far away from those early days—in more than just years. But maybe not far enough.

"Have you told the kids?" Fallon asked. A picture of their children flashed through his mind. Both were away at college in Vermont. Liz, their first, was a junior at Bennington; Mike, a freshman at Middlebury. Both had small partial scholarships, but even with that, their tuition, room, and board totaled nearly three months of his gross annual salary, or thirty-six thousand three hundred dollars a year. He knew it to the last damned penny, because it scared the hell out of him that he might not be able to pay it much longer.

"I planned to call them tonight. I wanted to tell you first."

"That was decent of you." The sarcasm passed her, producing only a small tic at the corner of her mouth. "What are you going to tell them about their tuition? They might not ask, but they'll be worried about it."

Trish straightened her shoulders, causing her small, still-trim breasts to jut out slightly. "I plan to tell them that you'll continue to take care of it."

A sardonic smile played across Fallon's lips. He ran

the fingers of one hand through his still dark hair, then reached down and picked up the sales reports that lay atop the old mahogany partner's desk he had inherited from his father. He held them up to her, as though they explained everything. The reports showed a sharp drop in the company's most vital area, its newer lines of fiber optic cable. Now, with rumors of downsizing rife, the sales figures, combined with his age, made him a perfect candidate for the street. "I may be out of a job soon," he said. "You're aware of that, right?"

Trisha drew a breath. "I'm very aware. And it's not as though you haven't seen it coming, Jack. Everyone else did. We talked about that, about your need to reposition yourself."

The words stung, and he stared at her. *Reposition* himself. Like she was now doing, he supposed she meant. Or like Howard had. Howard the one-man HMO. The man of the nineties. Was that it? he wondered. Did she see him as hopelessly out of date, someone whose personal values were set in the seventies, a sinking ship that had to be abandoned? She had been warning him for months that he was about to lose the only job he had ever had—and the one-fifty in base salary it brought in each year, a bit more with bonuses. He had tried to convince her it would be all right. But he had seen it coming, damn it. He had simply chosen to ignore it, to fight it through. You just didn't walk away from a company you had helped build from its inception. At least he didn't. His eyes fell on a three-month-old copy of *Cosmopolitan* lying atop a stack of papers on the corner of his desk. The cover touted one of the issue's lead articles; the one Trisha had suggested he read. "The Top 10 Ways to Reposition Yourself in Corporate America." He had read the article and had marveled at its advice. It had been slanted toward thirty-year-olds, as if people over forty didn't exist or— even more depressing—were simply beyond help. He let Trisha's words slide by, unchallenged. Right now there were more pressing facts she had to consider.

"I'm not going to argue with you about this. I'm sure you paid attention each time we sat down and reviewed our money market, our IRAs, and the few stocks we own. I sure have. I look at those figures every week—because they terrify me. It's not a helluva lot to carry us—I'm sorry, to carry *me*—if I'm out of work for six months or more. Because our twenty-five-hundred-dollar-a-month mortgage isn't going to go away. Neither are the five grand a year in taxes, or the insurance bills, or the rest of the monthly nut. And with college costs for two kids added in, and without my present comfortable salary . . ." He ended the sentence with a snort.

"I know all that, Jack." She pushed it away and went on blithely. "But obviously we'll sell the house sometime in the near future. And you'll have your half. And you'll be getting a settlement from the company. If the worst happens. I'm sure it will be enough to handle the tuition and other expenses." She paused a beat. He suddenly realized she expected him to carry all the financial burdens alone—with or without a job. He was smiling at her and shaking his head. She continued quickly, "Look, I know this is a bad time for you. But things aren't going to get any better. Not for you; not for us. It wouldn't have done any good to wait."

Fallon bit down hard. "No, I guess not," he said. "You better get going." He forced a smile that didn't quite work, wasn't really intended to. "You'll be taking the car, I suppose."

Trisha looked momentarily surprised. "Yes," she said. There was hesitation in her voice, and her mouth seemed tight and awkward again. "It's mine. It's registered in my name. And you still have your company car."

Fallon nodded, thought about the baby-blue Mustang convertible. Trisha's favorite color. "That's right. It was an anniversary present, wasn't it?" He had said it sarcastically, but she hadn't seemed to notice. It had been an extravagant *gift*—one really intended for both of them. He shuddered inwardly.

Trisha drew a long breath, preparing herself to leave. She looked very beautiful, Fallon thought.

She was holding a small purse in her left hand, and her now empty ring finger seemed surprisingly naked. It was the first time he had seen her without her wedding band. The thought jarred him. He wondered if she had worn it when she was with Howard. Trisha preferred the left side of the bed. And when they had made love, she had always turned on her right side, then used her left hand to stroke him. She had liked that, had once told him it gave her a sense of power to be able to get him so hard, so quickly. "You better get going," he said again. "Howard will be waiting."

Trisha stared at him for a moment. "I guess I thought you'd be more upset." There was a flicker of something in her eyes. Disappointment, Fallon thought.

"Good-bye, Trish."

Trisha drew a breath. "Good-bye, Jack." She turned quickly and walked out of the room.

Fallon watched her leave. She moved nicely in the slacks she had chosen. He turned his head away, not wanting to watch any longer. His stomach was sitting in his throat, choking him. He fought it; closed his eyes. Jesus, he thought.

The telephone jarred him awake before the alarm clock. Then the alarm went off, the two sounds beating at him. Fallon rarely drank, an occasional beer or glass of wine with dinner, but the previous night he had put a serious dent in a bottle of bourbon. Now his head felt like an overripe melon, his mouth as though a cat had been living there.

He grabbed the alarm; shut it off, then stared through

blurred eyes at the digital readout: 7:00 A.M. He swung his legs out and the photo album he had taken to bed went crashing to the floor. A picture of Trisha stared up at him, and he was hit with a sudden sense of self-disgust; wondered if that was what the future held: becoming a maudlin drunk. The phone rang again, hurting his head, and he picked it up, fumbled with it. "Yeah," he said. His voice sounded like a croak.

"Daddy? Are you okay?"

His daughter's voice came across the line, sounding small, worried.

"Yeah, baby. I'm fine. Whatsup?" The final word came out slurred, sounded more like *catsup.*

His daughter hesitated, then blurted her message out. "Mom called last night. She told me she'd left, and I worried about you. She called Mike, too. He's on the extension."

Fallon's mind froze. At first he thought she meant his son was there, at home, on another extension in the house. Then he realized she meant he was at the apartment she rented in Bennington.

"Hi, Dad. You sure you're okay?"

His son's voice came across fuzzy, like his sister's. Because they were both on the same line, he thought. "I'm fine, Mike," he said. "Not great, but I'm okay. How come you're in Bennington? Were you down visiting Liz?"

"He came down because we were worried. And we thought it would be better to talk to you together." It was Liz again, answering for her brother. Just as she'd been doing since she first learned to talk.

Fallon envisioned his children sitting in the second-floor apartment, just off the Bennington campus. Liz: tall and slim and beautiful, just like her mother. But even more so, he thought. With her mother's blond hair and blue eyes—a younger, even lovelier version. Mike: built like his father—or like his father had once been.

Six feet of muscle and bone. But with his mother's blond hair and more delicate features. They must be worried, Fallon thought. It was a long drive from Middlebury to Bennington. And it was seven o'clock on a Sunday morning. Christ, he thought, inexplicably. Why the hell had he set the alarm the night before? He must have been drunker than he'd thought.

"Daddy, what happened?" It was Liz again, and Fallon sat for a moment, wondering what to say. Christ, just tell her the truth, he decided. What else can you do?

"Your mother found somebody else. And she's moving in with him." *Moved* in, he told himself. She's already moved in with him.

"Who is he?" Liz asked. "Mom didn't say a lot, mostly that she'd explain later."

Fallon hesitated, wondering if he should leave that explanation for Trish. The hell with Trish, he decided. If the kids wanted to know, he'd tell them what little he could. He wasn't going to be dragged into Trish's game.

"His name is Howard," Fallon said. "Howard . . . Nowicki." Now the name comes, he thought. "He's a dentist. Somebody we played tennis with."

"Jesus." It was Mike this time, and there was a hint of disbelief in his voice. Fallon was grateful for it. Yeah, but he's also repositioned himself, Fallon thought.

"Look, kids, there's not much more I can tell you, except that your mother and this Nowicki guy will be living in Manhattan." *Are* living in Manhattan, Fallon reminded himself. Why was he playing this game? "I don't even have the address. But I'm sure she'll tell you."

"She already did." It was Mike again, blurting it out. Then he was silent—they both were. Probably embarrassed, he thought. He wondered if Trisha had asked them not to give him the address.

"Yeah, well anyway, I can't tell you much more. I just found out about it yesterday."

There was a pause—long and very pregnant, Fallon thought. Then Liz got them rolling again.

"Mom said you're having some trouble at work, that you might be leaving."

Shit, Fallon thought. Why the hell did Trish have to get into that? He drew a breath, felt the cotton in his mouth again, and wished he had something to drink. Anything but bourbon. "Yeah, there's some talk about downsizing, and things are tough right now. But your old man's not out the door yet." Yet. The operative word.

"Mom said the tuition and stuff would still be okay." It was Mike again, blurting out the real issue—the real reason for the joint call—in his inimitable, bumbling, honest way. It made Fallon feel slightly sick. Somewhere deep down in his gut.

"Yeah, well, let's not worry about that now," he said. His voice was sharper than he had intended, and he immediately softened it. "Look, if worse comes to worst, you might have to earn some of your spending money."

"Jeez, with my course load that would be hard, Dad." Mike again, and Fallon felt his gut tighten.

Yeah, well, life's hard, kid, he thought. He took another breath. "Let's not worry about it now," he said. "We'll work things out."

"It's just that we should know, Dad." Liz this time. Her voice slightly fearful.

"Hang on a second," Fallon said. He placed the receiver on the nightstand, went into the darkened bathroom, grabbed a glass of water, drank it down, then filled the glass again. His barely visible reflection jumped out from the mirror, the anger in his eyes shocking him. When he returned to the phone the anger, and the cotton in his mouth, were under control.

"Look, maybe it wouldn't hurt if you checked around for some part-time jobs, just in case. Just to cover your living expenses."

Silence again. Liz's voice sounded cool when she

finally spoke. "I don't know if I could manage that with *my* course load." Another pause. "Maybe I could apply for a student loan for next semester."

"Yeah," Mike chimed in.

"For spending money?" Incredulity hung heavy in Fallon's voice. When he had returned from Vietnam, and had enrolled at NYU, he had worked thirty hours a week in a Varick Street warehouse to cover everything the GI Bill had not. The thought of borrowing money to cover the time he had spent in gin mills and pizza parlors had never occurred to him. But he had created these ideas in his own children, he realized now. He had been a successful, doting father, who had never forced much reality into their lives. Now the situation demanded that he do so, and he wondered if it was too late.

"Why don't we just let everything ride for now?" he suggested, buying time.

"Are you sure?" Liz asked. There was a note of disbelief in her voice.

"Yeah, I'm sure. Look, the summer courses you're both taking will be over in a few weeks. I'll have a better picture of what's going on at work then, and we'll sit down and talk it all over. Okay?"

"Yeah, sure, Dad." It was Mike, suddenly uplifted, or at least sounding so. Putting problems off to a later date was Mike's forte.

"Maybe I should put in a student-loan application just in case," Liz said.

Fallon let out a long breath. He was starting to feel like a beaten prizefighter, fists slamming at every vulnerable spot. He fought to keep anger from his voice. "If that's what you want. You're twenty. I'm not about to tell you what to do." He hesitated a moment, carefully choosing his words. "Just give some thought about how you're going to pay it back. After you graduate, a student loan can take a heavy bite out of a paycheck."

He was greeted by momentary silence again, and he let it play out. "I thought you and Mom would handle that," his daughter said at length. Her voice held a slight tremor, and he wasn't certain whether it was from anger or renewed fear.

"Honey, I can't tell you what I *can* do or *can't* do right now. And I sure as hell can't speak for your mother." He fumbled with a pack of cigarettes he had gone out and bought the previous night, lit one, and blew a stream of smoke into the phone. He realized his voice had become harsh, and he tried to soften it. "Honey, listen to me. You do what you think best about a loan, but keep in mind that between my job situation and an upcoming divorce, I don't know what I'll be able to do for you and your brother. And that includes paying back loans."

He was met with silence again and hurried on, another accusation of failure suddenly draping his shoulders. "Look, why don't you wait it out a couple of months and see what happens?"

"Do you think you and Mom might work things out?" It was his son this time—naive to the core.

"Your mom's moved in with someone else, Mike. Reconciliation doesn't seem realistic."

Momentary silence again.

"But if you did, would that change things?" Mike finally asked.

Fallon smiled, shook his head. "I don't think it's a real option, Mike. So don't hang your hat on it."

"Oh."

"Are you sad?" It was his daughter, now. The romantic.

"Sure I'm sad, Liz." Maybe numb is a better word, he thought. Perhaps there's even a harsher word. But how do you explain that? How do you tell your daughter you haven't made love to her mother in a long time? That her mother hadn't wanted to? Probably because she was too busy repositioning herself under Howard. And doing it with her wedding ring still on her goddamned finger.

"Maybe if you let her know you still loved her, still wanted her, she'd come back," Liz added.

She doesn't know that? Fallon thought. After twenty-four years, after all the things they'd been through together raising two kids, she doesn't know?

"Sometimes you just have to respect people's decisions, honey. Have to know when to let go," he finally said.

Silence. Then: "I'm just saying maybe you should try."

"Yeah. Well, I'll think about it."

"Okay, Dad." It was Mike, now eager to get off the phone, Fallon thought.

"Dad, it's just that we're worried," Liz added, still hanging on to it. "We're worried about you, and we're worried about us too."

Fallon stared at his feet, naked against the carpet, then squeezed his eyes shut. There was something terribly vulnerable about a man without shoes, he decided. "There's nothing more I can tell you about either situation. We're all just going to have to hang tough for a while," he said.

There was a hesitation, then his daughter said, "Okay, Dad, we'll do what you want. And please take care of yourself."

"I will. And you guys, too. I love you both, and I'll talk to you both soon."

Fallon replaced the phone, stubbed out his cigarette, then immediately lit another. Shit, he thought. Shit, shit, shit.

He considered falling back into bed, then gave up on the idea. He'd only lie there and stew, rerun the conversation with his children; belatedly come up with the wise, fatherly comments he should have made. He stared across the room. The bedroom draperies were drawn, only the faintest light seeping in; the room attended by countless shadows. He pushed up from the

bed and shuffled back to the adjoining bath, switched on
the light, then closed his eyes against the sudden glare.

When he opened them again, he was standing before
the large mirror that covered most of the wall behind the
sink. He stared at the ruin that looked back, the face
puffy from the previous night's pity party of bourbon and
photo albums. Still, it wasn't that bad, at least from the
shoulders up. The hair was still thick and dark brown
and wavy, with only a touch of gray at the temples. The
face, sporting some lines now, was still a good one—
handsome even, according to some. It was craggy, with a
strong jaw and a hint of world weariness, not the smooth
innocence it had carried for so many years. So, too, with
the green eyes—bedroom eyes, Trisha had once called
them—only a bit bloodshot now. And the shoulders
were still wide, matching the broad chest. But each had
lost the definition they had once held. And from there
down, the ruin took over—the small, soft protruding gut,
complete with love handles. Christ, how had it happened? he wondered. He wasn't a couch potato. He
skied in winter; swam and hiked in summer. He shook
his head. Sure you do. Maybe a half dozen times each,
each year. Then you sit on your ass, even have a riding
mower to cut the goddamned grass. But you did play *tennis*, he added to himself.

Fallon drew a long breath, then turned sideways,
sucked in his gut, and let it out. The view was depressing. And the company even has a gym available to
employees, a room filled with exercise machines on
which you've never laid hand or foot. But Tuesday,
when you go back to work, you'll start working some of it
off. No, you'll work *all* of it off, damn it. Get the most
out of the place before they boot your ass out the door.
And you'll throw away the damned cigarettes, too.

Fallon turned back to the mirror and opened the cabinet that held his shaving kit, hesitated a moment, then
opened the adjacent one that had always held Trisha's

endless supply of creams and oils and other mystifying paraphernalia. The cabinet was bare. Even the dust motes had been carefully removed. He stared at the barren space. Not even a hint she'd be coming back. But you knew that already. And you don't want her back. Not after all the sneaking around with Howard. Not after moving in with him and turning you into the village cuckold. He drew a long breath, felt his oversized gut rise and fall. Except maybe you do. Maybe, deep down, you're that big a fool.

Fallon closed Trisha's cabinet. Shut it away. Just shut the door and don't open it again. He reached for his toothbrush, squeezed toothpaste on it, and began brushing his teeth so hard that it hurt.

Screw her, and screw Howard, too. Life doesn't end at forty-nine, just because one woman says you're a schmuck. Even if it's a woman you've listened to for twenty-four goddamned years.

He stared at the mirror and his foam-draped lips, closed his eyes again, and wondered if he was still lying to himself.

When he reentered the bedroom, the photo album he had taken to bed stared up at him from the floor and he kicked it out of the way. It slid several feet and miraculously closed itself. He stood momentarily transfixed by the posture it now presented, the smooth leather cover shutting out all the images of his earlier life. A small, sour grin formed on his lips, then faded, and he felt a small shiver in the center of his back.

Fallon turned away, averting his eyes from the album, and pulled open the large armoire that held his clothes. He hesitated; tried to decide what he'd do that day. He certainly didn't want to remain at home. The commuter towns of Westchester County were endless gossip mills, and his own quiet little town of Bedford would soon turn the marital triangle of Jack and Trish and Howard into a central topic of conversation. He could go to a ball game, he thought. Sure. Why not? The Yankees were playing a doubleheader against the Red Sox, and he knew the company's box seats weren't being used this holiday weekend.

"Yeah," he said aloud. Call Wally and team up with him for the day. Wally's been divorced for almost a year now, and he's probably sitting in his small Manhattan apartment trying to decide which bartender he'll favor with an afternoon's tale of woe. Fallon forced determination onto his face; shook his head. The hell with that, Wally. Not for you, and not for me, either. No, indeed. Call Wally, persuade him to swing by the office and pick up the tickets, then meet him at the stadium. Hell, maybe he can even recommend a good divorce lawyer. Fallon nodded to himself. The idea suddenly seemed to possess great merit. But first coffee. Some java to clear away the cobwebs, then get on the phone and start making plans.

Fallon slipped into the brightly patterned, Bill Blass terry-cloth robe that Trisha had given him the previous Christmas. The thought crossed his mind that it might be one of the things on her list—might be one of the items the packers would toss into a box for delivery to Howard the dentist. The thought continued to gnaw at him as he moved down the curving staircase that Trisha had always loved, and that had always reminded him of some outlandish scene from *Gone With the Wind*.

Maybe she'll want the staircase, too, he thought, as he reached the foyer and turned into the living room. An image of packers cleaning out the entire house flashed through his mind as he passed into the adjoining dining room, and he wondered which items he'd find missing when he came home one day to a half-empty house. Suddenly, everything seemed of value to him; each item some part of the stability he had built into his life. He stared at the dining-room furniture that now surrounded him. His mother's—something that went all the way back to his childhood—which they had brought to this house when his mother had entered the nursing home where she now lived. There was his father's mahogany desk. The ancient grandfather's clock that stood in the hall—the one he had battled for at an estate auction, finally outbidding a well-heeled banker. He paused just inside the kitchen and thought about having the locks changed; of letting Trisha's packers arrive, keys in hand, only to find the house locked and barred against them. It was a pleasantly vindictive thought. No, the hell with it, he told himself. Let her take any damned thing she wanted. She'd already taken what mattered. Taken it and trashed it. Let her have the rest, too, if it was so damned important to her. He hesitated again. Except my fish. He thought about the ancient sailfish that hung in his study, the one he had caught as a boy on one of the many fishing trips he had taken with his long-dead father. No, not the fish, he told himself. Everything but that.

Fallon marched across the kitchen and began to pull the coffeemaker from the dishwasher. Suddenly he had second thoughts. Somehow, the image of Howard sitting in one of his chairs was truly irritating. It was blatantly irrational, and he knew it. Hell, maybe Howard needed the chair. He sure as hell was headed for some pretty heavy alimony. But so are you, Fallon thought. You'll probably end up paying a good chunk of his, through Trish. Then what do you do? Go out and snatch somebody else's wife, so he can pay yours? Is that the end of the mating ritual? Monthly musical checks, going on and on in endless circles? He laughed out loud. The hell with it. Let Howard have the chairs. Let him screw Trisha in one of the chairs. In all of them, for chrissake. Howard wasn't the enemy. He suddenly realized he had been denigrating Howard—*the dentist*—to soothe his own bruised ego; that he'd have equal contempt for the man if he was a bloody astronaut. Howard was just a smarmy little prick who had chased after another man's wife, but he hadn't taken anything that wasn't offered. It was Trisha who had promised and professed faithfulness, not Howard. Howard was just another libidinous asshole, who had wanted to bed a married woman. And he had, and would continue to. Fallon offered the absent Howard a slight nod of his head. Good luck, Howard, he thought. Now you sit and wonder whose bed she'll climb into next.

Feeling satisfyingly smug, Fallon opened the cabinet that held the coffee. As he started to reach for the canister, his hand froze. "Shit," he muttered, as he stared at the inside of the cabinet door. There, facing him like some evil specter, was the monthly calendar Trisha always put up to remind him of things he was supposed to do. The box for Sunday, July 6, carried the note *Visit mother*, just as it had for the first and third Sunday of every month for the past five years. Trisha had even circled and underlined the entry, and he immediately remembered why. They had agreed he would talk to his mother, tell her about his problems at work; explain that he might soon be unable to pay her nursing home bills—that she might be forced to dip into her own resources to cover them.

Fallon lowered his head, shook it wearily. He had forgotten the regular semimonthly visit and especially the importance of this particular one. But he also knew if he called, said he couldn't make it, he'd spend an hour on the phone playing out a guilt trip he didn't need. He let out a long breath. He could stop on the way to the stadium and get it over with. Just suck it up and do it. "Shit," he muttered. "Shit, shit, shit."

2

"THE RESIDENCE AT WILLOW RUN" WAS SITUATED ON A
gentle hillside in the Westchester town of Rye, a ram-
bling, single-story structure composed of numerous
wings, each surrounded by ancient weeping willow trees
that Fallon had always thought appropriate. Most of the
rooms faced the distant water, providing the aging
inhabitants with a slightly obscured, yet supposedly
uplifting, view of the oil tankers that steadily plied and
polluted Long Island Sound. It wasn't a nursing home in
the true sense. Rather, it was an Assisted Care Facility—
to Fallon a mind-boggling term for a building that
housed those who had been abandoned to someone
else's care. But at least the majority of the elderly men
and women who lived here were still capable of providing somewhat for themselves, and each had a small stu-
dio apartment complete with a tiny kitchen, although
most ate their meals in a bright, sunny common dining
room.

Fallon parked his car in the visitors' area, also
encased in drooping willow boughs, and reluctantly
made his way toward the grandly columned front
entrance. Above, the sky was a cloudless, electric blue
and the sun beat relentlessly on the macadam walkway,

yet Fallon put on the blue blazer he had instinctively grabbed from his closet, even though it didn't quite work with his peach polo shirt and khaki trousers. Several years ago he had visited his mother sans jacket and had been told he had embarrassed her by his casual attire.

As he approached the entrance, his eyes fell on three elderly men seated nearby. Two were perched on a bench, identical aluminum walkers standing before them. The third sat beside them in a wheelchair—his frail lower body covered by a blanket, despite the July heat. The men weren't speaking. They just stared out at arriving guests, and Fallon wondered if they were waiting for relatives or just sitting there, envious of those who were.

A helluva way to finish out your life, Fallon thought, suddenly hit with a consuming sense of his own mortality, and he wondered if that was what lay in store for him as well—sitting outside some goddamned nursing home, waiting for death to pay a call. His situation at work rushed at him—the possibility of a forced retirement. Then the old cliché: Retire and die. He had never thought of ending his life this way, but now he did, and he quickly shook the image away and hurried toward the entrance.

Just beyond the front door was a large, sprawling area with a massive fireplace and an abundance of well-appointed chairs and sofas, available to the inmates—Fallon's word—and their guests, should they wish to escape the cramped confines of individual rooms. Fallon made his way across the carpeted floor toward a reception desk at the far end. Ten feet from his destination he skidded to a halt, as an elderly man in a motorized wheelchair flew by with the blast of a bicycle horn. Fallon watched the old man turn into a long hall, wisps of white hair flowing out behind him. He had never seen an eighty-year-old man, with or without a wheelchair, move at such speed, and when he turned back to the reception desk a look of utter amazement must have marked his face.

The young woman behind the desk—one he had not seen before—broke into a grin. She was slender and blond, and she reminded Fallon of his daughter—yet another younger version of what his wife, Trisha, had once been. He pushed the thought away as he reached the desk.

"Sorry," the young woman said, fighting off a laugh. "I think Mr. Rabinowitz is running the Indianapolis Five Hundred today. He used to be an automobile dealer, and he keeps souping up his wheelchair when nobody's looking." She covered her pouty lips to conceal a giggle.

"Who's he racing?" Fallon asked.

The woman, who wore a name tag identifying her as Rita, glanced to her left and raised her chin. Moving toward them with the aid of an aluminum walker—a look of grim determination set in a well-lined face—was another old man.

"*That's* the other half of the Indianapolis Five Hundred?" Fallon asked.

Rita giggled openly now. "That's what *they* call it," she said. She lowered her voice to a near whisper. "We call it the Tortoise and the Hare."

The second old man, also an octogenarian by his looks, had reached the desk huffing and wheezing. He appeared close to collapse.

"Rabinowitz cheated again," he gasped. "Sonofabitch."

"Don't worry, Mr. Marino, you'll catch him," Rita said.

Fallon stared after the second old man, listening to the plop, shuffle, plop of his walker as it picked up speed. He turned back to the young woman, stunned by her encouragement. The Residence must be suffering a bed shortage, he decided.

Fallon blew out a long breath. "I'm here to see my mother, Kitty Fallon," he said.

Rita flashed a wide, friendly smile, consulted a list, then smiled again. "She's in physical therapy right now, Mr. Fallon," she said.

Probably pulled a hamstring doing the pole vault, Fallon thought. "Do you know when she'll be finished?" he asked.

"Oh, fifteen, twenty minutes. If you'll wait in the sitting room we'll tell her you're here. Someone will bring her out as soon as she's finished."

Fallon thanked the young woman, checked in both directions for traffic, then headed back across the room.

The sitting room had become suddenly crowded and the only available seat was a small sofa directly across from three elderly women—each somewhere in her seventies—who sat together in a tight cluster of chairs. The first woman, who seemed prim and proper in a lace-laden blouse, and who sat rigidly straight in her chair, had the most strikingly blue-tinted hair Fallon had ever seen. The second was traditionally gray. She was plump and jolly-looking, her face so round she seemed to view the world through a permanent squint. The third, who was staring blankly into space, apparently oblivious to the conversation of the others, had dyed her hair honey blond and had it cut into sharp, girlish bangs.

"It's just terrible," the blue-haired woman said as Fallon seated himself. "I don't feel safe when I go there anymore." She glanced at Fallon to see if he was eavesdropping, then, satisfied he was not, continued.

Fallon picked up a magazine, partially hid his face, and listened intently.

"Where, dear?" the chubby woman asked. "Where don't you feel safe?"

The blue-haired woman stared at her, as if suddenly offended. "The A & P," she said. "I just *told* you." She rolled her eyes to show her irritation, then continued.

"Every time I go there all these hoodlums are lurking on every corner." She gave her body a small twist, adjusting herself to a more comfortable position. "You'd think a woman could go to the A & P without feeling threatened."

The chubby woman nodded sad agreement. The words also seemed to jolt the third member of the trio out of her catatonic stare. She patted her honey-colored bangs and gave the blue-haired woman a cold stare.

"If you don't feel safe, you shouldn't go." She offered up a cold grin. "Either that, or give those punks a good kick in their you-know-whats."

She watched the other women gasp in horror, and let out an exasperated sigh. "Don't be such sissies," she snapped. "Anyway, this conversation is ridiculous. I'm going to see what we're having for lunch."

The blue-haired woman's back stiffened and she momentarily glared at the other's retreating back. Then she turned back to the chubby woman with a knowing smile. "You know she drinks, don't you?" she asked sotto voce. She watched the chubby woman's mouth form a large circle.

"*Really?*"

"It's why she's here," the blue-haired woman said. She emphasized the point with a confirming nod. "I thought everyone knew about that." She raised a closed fist, extended the thumb toward her mouth, and made a drinking gesture. "Every day. All day," she said.

"Goodness," the chubby woman said. "I never even suspected."

"Vodka. You can't smell it." The blue-haired woman nodded again, then glanced past her friend's shoulder. "Shh, she's coming back," she said.

The chubby woman turned, as did Fallon, and they all watched the third member of the trio make her way back across the room, each trying to detect any noticeable sway in her gait.

"We're having Chicken Cordon Bleu for lunch," the woman announced, patting her honey-colored bangs again as she reclaimed her chair.

The chubby woman's face brightened, all talk of drinking suddenly forgotten. "That sounds delicious." She hesitated. "What exactly *is* Chicken Cordon Bleu, anyway?" she asked.

"It's Hawaiian," the blue-haired woman said. "My husband and I always had it when we went there." She straightened in her chair and offered up a superior smile. "The first time I had it was when we went to see Don Ho." She threw another withering look at the woman with the honey-colored bangs, defying her to challenge the statement. But it was wasted. The woman was staring off into space again.

Satisfied, the blue-haired woman prattled on. "He's *won-der-ful*. Just a *mar-velous* entertainer." She paused, poignantly. "Except he's just a bit . . . Well, *you* know."

"No, I don't," the chubby woman said. She twisted in her chair, excited now; wanting more. "Tell me."

The blue-haired woman leaned forward, prepared to offer a strict confidence, and Fallon found he had to resist doing so himself.

"Well," the blue-haired woman said, pausing to draw the moment out. She lowered her voice close to a whisper. The lessening of sound brought the third member of the trio back from outer space. "His singing is just *won-der-ful*, as I said. But after he sings, he just goes through the audience, kissing all the women." The blue-haired woman sat up; straightened her back again. "And on the *mouth*," she added.

The chubby woman put a hand over her plump lips and giggled. The third woman blinked.

Blue-hair's hands fluttered about the lace of her collar; her back became even straighter. Fully preened now, she continued. "Well, I certainly didn't let him kiss *me* like that."

"Lord, no!" the chubby woman said. She was nodding "yes," as she spoke the words. "Not with your *husband* sitting right there." She giggled again.

The blue-haired woman's chin shot up. "*That* wasn't the reason," she snapped. Her birdlike eyes bored into her friend's plump face. "I'm just *not* that kind of woman," she added fiercely.

"Oh, of course not," the chubby woman said. "I didn't mean . . ." Her words were cut short as the blue-haired woman leaned forward again.

"And *I*, for one, don't think he should do that sort of thing. Not with all this AIDS going around the way it is."

The third woman's head shot up as though someone had goosed her. "Don Ho has AIDS?" she barked.

"I didn't *say* that," the blue-haired woman snapped.

But her two friends were ignoring her now. They stared at each other, eyes wide; mouths open in horror. "I didn't know *that!*" the chubby woman said. "I didn't know Don Ho has *AIDS!*"

"I never *said* that!" The blue-haired woman was at the edge of her chair now, fighting to regain their attention. Her face was reddening quickly and Fallon feared a stroke was imminent.

"He shouldn't kiss people if he has AIDS," the third woman said. She patted her bangs again. "That's disgusting."

"I never *said* he has AIDS!"

The two women were still oblivious to their friend. They continued to stare at each other, mouths still agape in the horror of the moment.

"You should *never* kiss people on the mouth if you have AIDS," the chubby woman said.

"I think it's disgusting." The third woman patted her hair furiously. "Somebody should do something about it."

"I didn't *say* Don Ho has AIDS," the blue-haired

woman said. Her voice was close to a shout, and her face was twisted with frustration.

The chubby woman finally turned back to her. "You didn't *know* he had AIDS, dear? Well, thank God you didn't kiss him."

The blue-haired woman fell back into her chair and groaned. Fallon stared at her; wondered if she was dying; wondered if he'd be able to remember the CPR he had learned in the army. But she'll never let you give her mouth-to-mouth, he thought.

"John? Why are you here today?"

Fallon's head snapped around to the sound of his mother's voice. She was the only person who called him John. The sound always sent a chill through him, although he had never understood why. He stood quickly and stepped toward her.

"It's the first Sunday of the month, Mom," he said. "I always come on the first and third Sundays."

Kitty Fallon raised her chin. She was tall and thin and frail, with a hawklike face that seemed capable of looking inside you to ferret out any lies. Years ago she had been a second-grade school teacher, and Fallon — even as a child — had envisioned a classroom of seven-year-olds living in daily dread.

"Is it the first Sunday?" Kitty Fallon asked. "I didn't realize." She leaned forward, extending a powdered cheek, which Fallon dutifully kissed.

She knew, Fallon told himself. She knew he was due to visit today. She knew to the day and the hour. And if he hadn't come she would have called him at home and asked why, the guilt-inducing sound of abandonment heavy in her voice.

"Do you want to sit here, or go to your room?" Fallon asked.

Kitty stared down at the three women, who had stopped discussing Don Ho's imagined medical problems and were now listening intently. She glared at each, then turned back to her son. "Let's sit out here. But somewhere else." She turned abruptly and moved slowly away.

"But, Mom, there's no other . . ." Fallon stopped as he followed her progress. There were two empty chairs by the fireplace. They had miraculously appeared as if his mother had willed it. But then, they would, he thought. They wouldn't dare not.

When they had settled in Kitty stared at him, as if she could see into his soul. "Where's Trisha?" she asked.

Throughout the tedious drive, Fallon had debated telling his mother about the demise of his marriage. Now it seemed pointless not to. "Trisha and I have separated," he said.

Kitty nodded as if it were no surprise. "Has she run off with someone else?"

Fallon was jolted by the question, then wondered why he should be. It was a logical assumption. People didn't suddenly bolt from a marriage of twenty-four years unless their lives were a living hell, or unless they were running to someone else.

"Yeah, that's about the size of it," he said.

Kitty nodded. "I can't say I didn't expect it."

Fallon was stunned again, uncertain exactly what his mother meant. Was she implying that Trisha was a tramp, from whom it should have been expected? Or did she mean that her daughter-in-law had simply come to her senses and abandoned her dolt of a son? He decided not to pursue it. And he definitely would not tell her about Howard.

"So, what are you doing about it?" Kitty asked when her son failed to respond. There was no sympathy in her voice or eyes. She simply stared at him, the schoolmistress checking to see if he'd done his homework.

"Nothing yet," Fallon said. "It only happened yesterday." He felt sudden, irrational guilt over his inaction, and he wondered why this woman had that effect on him. He was forty-nine years old, the veteran of two terrifying years in a misbegotten war. He was the father of two grown children, an executive in a cutthroat business, who ran a division of more than a hundred men and women. Why in hell could this old woman still intimidate him?

"Get a good lawyer," Kitty snapped. "Or she'll pluck you like a chicken."

If there's anything to pluck, Fallon thought. The idea brought him back to the original reason for his visit. Another trip to the guilt factory. He leaned forward. "Look, Mom, there's something else I have to talk to you about."

Kitty stared at him suspiciously, but said nothing. The suspicion was enough to make Fallon's stomach turn.

"It's about my job. I may be losing that, too. And fairly soon." He paused, then pushed on. "That may mean . . ."

Kitty cut him off. "I told you not to go to work for that company. I told you to use your GI benefits to go to medical school, or law school. But you wouldn't listen."

Oh, God, Fallon thought. Why not throw in dental school? He drew a long breath and wondered if his mother knew what was coming, was simply avoiding it with a good offense. "Look, Mom, that's kind of a moot point. . . ."

"And I never wanted you to marry Trisha. But, as always, you did what you wanted."

Again, Fallon was shocked. "When the hell did you ever say anything against Trisha?" he asked. He was flabbergasted by her blatant lie. His mother had always adored Trisha.

"Don't curse," Kitty ordered. She waited until her son sat back, resigned to her tirade. "You never listened to me, John. Never. When you graduated from high school, I told you *not* to join the Army. But, of course, you did. Then I told you *not* to volunteer for Vietnam. But off you went. In each case, you did exactly what you wanted. Trisha was just another example." She raised a hand, warding off an objection that was not forthcoming. "Oh, I know. You came back from that stupid war with all those medals." She stared at him, preparing the coup de grâce. "*And* with a bullet hole in your belly." Another short pause. "But had you listened, you could have avoided that, and gotten on with your schooling, and then you could have done much more with your life." She paused a beat, then waved a dismissive hand. "Trisha was just one more mistake, John." She closed her eyes momentarily. "You're so much like your father."

Fallon's anger flashed. His father had lived with this woman for thirty-nine years and had endured her endless criticisms. James Fallon had been a dreamer, very much a romantic, who had loved life and the people who inhabited it, and who had spent every idle hour working in the basement of their small suburban New Jersey home, struggling to invent the "better mousetrap," as he had put it. In his real life, he had been a salesman for a paper company—a very modest success who had needed his wife's income to survive. It was something his mother had never let him forget.

"I'm what I wanted to be, Mom. And, right or wrong, I married the woman I wanted to marry." He fought for control; found it; drew another long breath. "Look, talking about all this is pointless. What I'm trying to tell you is that I'm about to hit a financial rough spot, and it may mean I can't keep up my end of your expenses here. At least not for a bit."

Kitty's hands fisted in her lap; her mouth tightened slightly. It was as if she were warding off a tremor, willing it away. Fallon suddenly realized she was frightened—something he had never seen before—and that unexpected vision sent his guilt soaring.

"Look, it will work out. It will only be temporary. And it probably won't happen for a time yet."

"Oh, I know, John. You've always been lucky. Things always work out for you."

His mother was looking away from him now, as though she couldn't bear to make eye contact. It made him feel desolate, miserable.

"Tell me about the children," his mother said. "They never come to visit me, you know."

Fallon stared at his well-polished loafers. Guilt washed over him; he was drowning in it. He had beaten his mother down, frightened her with his own failure. Now she could awaken each morning fearful that it might be her last day in this place he helped pay for each month. Maybe he should just finish her off. Do it now while he had the chance. Tell her everything. Even tell her that Don Ho has AIDS. He almost laughed at the madness of it all.

Fallon looked up at his mother and smiled. "The kids are fine," he said. "I just talked to them this morning. They're taking some classes this summer. That's why they haven't come to visit."

"So, when do you think they'll boot our asses out?" Wally ended the question with a huge bite of hot dog and began chewing furiously.

It was the seventh time Wally had brought it up. Seven times in seven innings, and Fallon still didn't have an answer; was sick of hearing the question, and now wished he had stayed home and mowed the goddamned lawn. And the Yankees were losing 10–2.

"Wally, if you ask me that again, I'll strangle you." A collective groan went up from the crowd. The Yankee first baseman had just made an error. Fallon wished he could strangle him as well.

"Oh great," Wally said. "So whadda you wanna talk about? Maybe we should talk about Trisha running off with her dentist. Or maybe I should tell you how *my* ex is running around with a Rolls-Royce salesman. Yeah, that'd be good."

Fallon turned to face him. Wally Green's fat face was red, and Fallon wasn't sure if it was from seven innings in the sun or the idea of his wife's new boyfriend.

Wally pulled a handkerchief from his pocket and mopped his balding head. He was Fallon's age, maybe a year or two older, and was in far worse shape. The man seemed short of breath even when he sat.

"Yeah, that's right," Wally continued. His soft brown eyes took on a glare. "A Rolls-Royce salesman. And where the hell did she meet a Rolls-Royce salesman? I'm asking myself this." He jabbed the remains of his hot dog at Fallon. A dab of mustard at its end barely missed his peach polo shirt. "Did *you* ever meet a Rolls-Royce salesman? I never met one." He waved the hot dog in a wide arc, taking in the sea of fifty thousand plus who had jammed into Yankee Stadium. "I bet none of these people ever met one, except maybe George Steinbrenner, sitting up in his goddamned sky box. Shit, I don't know anybody who's ever met one. So how does this happen? How does Janice meet one? She goes to her Hadassah meeting, and one of her friends says, 'Oh, by the way, I want you to meet my cousin? He sells Rolls-Royce luxury cars'?"

"What difference does it make?" Fallon asked. "What he does, I mean. You said you were glad to be rid of her. Hell, maybe she'll marry the guy, and the alimony will stop."

"No. She'll never let me off the hook. I think she met him at the showroom—that she was out looking at goddamned cars."

"That's crazy," Fallon said.

Wally was no longer listening. The Yankee pitcher had just walked a batter, and the bases were now loaded.

"Asshole!" Wally shouted. He was on his feet, pointing his hot dog toward the pitching mound. "How much are they paying you, you creep?" he roared.

Throughout the stadium angry jeers rained on the pitcher's mound. Fallon stared across the infield toward the third-base side. The crowd resembled a patchwork quilt of color, each topped with a white or brown face flushed in frustration. He pulled Wally back to his seat.

"Where would Janice get the money to buy a Rolls-Royce?" he asked.

"Where? Where? When the company throws my sorry ass out on the street, how much is my buyout gonna be?"

"Wally, she's not gonna get that."

"Hah! That's what you think. You don't know her cousin. Her fucking lawyer cousin. I know that bloodsucker. We went to the same synagogue for years." Wally's face had turned scarlet and his fist was squeezing the hot dog, turning it to mush in his hand. He got hold of himself, stared at the mangled frankfurter, then threw it down at his feet. "You should have heard that prick at the divorce hearing." His voice turned to a whining singsong. "How poor Janice had to pack up like a gypsy every time the company decided to move my ass to another city. How she had to leave all her friends, leave the home she had worked so hard to make for me and the kids. How she had to put the kids into new schools. Deal with all the trauma it caused. Start all over again and again and again." He began pounding his chest with the palm of one hand. "And what about me? For me it was party, party? I didn't have to deal with all the same shit? The house, the kids, the new schools, the friends? Plus take on a new sales territory I didn't know fuck-all about?"

"Wally, a judge is going to know all that," Fallon said.

"Oh, yeah? Yeah?" He jabbed a finger toward

Fallon's chest. There were remnants of mustard on it, and Fallon shrank back. "You go to Family Court today, all the judges are women. You haven't been there yet. Wait. They sit there and look down at your wife, who's sitting there in her oldest dress because her snake of a lawyer told her to come that way. She's not wearing any makeup, and she looks like shit—one step away from a cancer ward." He waved his hand in a broad arc. "All her goddamned jewelry is back at the house. All she's got on is her wedding band. One lonely little piece of gold on one finger. And it sits there like an accusation. There's no engagement ring. No goddamned tennis bracelet. No nothing. And already you can see it in the judge's eyes. She thinks the woman is a candidate for welfare."

Wally threw up his hands, gesturing toward the heavens now. "So some bitch in a black robe sits there and looks from you in your nice suit to your soon-to-be-ex wife in her old dress, and she figures: No way is this prick gonna move into a nice bachelor pad and start traipsing around with a bevy of bimbos. And bam. Right there go all the bucks you worked your ass off for. Bam. Shazam. Gone." He snapped his fingers. "Just like that. And now you end up living in some goddamned walk-up without a pot to piss in. And now you're out of work, too—a fifty-year-old hump out looking for a job, when the only guys who wanna talk to you are McDonald's and the asshole who runs the checkout aisles at Kmart. And your ex-wife, she's driving a Rolls-Royce."

They were seated at the bar of Café des Artistes, which seemed sadly empty that holiday weekend. The normally crowded restaurant, a popular after-theater haunt on West Sixty-seventh Street, was situated just off Central Park West, not far from Lincoln Center and about four blocks from Wally's three-room apartment on

Amsterdam Avenue. Wally had taken the subway to Yankee Stadium, and Fallon had decided to drive him home and buy him a drink on the way.

So there they sat, surrounded by the warmth of dark green walls and Howard Chandler Christy murals, as Wally—well into his second scotch, following four beers at the stadium—waxed poetic about the joys of divorce, the pleasures of rediscovered bachelorhood, and the hedonistic raptures of single life in Manhattan. Fallon, who had avoided the stadium's tepid beer, and who was still nursing his first very light highball, wasn't buying any of it.

"You should stay at my place tonight," Wally insisted. "We could do a little bouncing, check out the action, and I could put you up on the sofa." He picked up a dove's egg—the Café's exotic bar food offering—popped it into his mouth, and awaited Fallon's reaction. When none came he nudged his elbow and inclined his head toward a woman seated several stools away at the otherwise empty bar. "We could even have her, you know. Either one of us." Wally had lowered his voice and was leaning in close. "She could probably even dig up a friend if we wanted."

Fallon glanced at the woman who had become the object of Wally's sudden lust. She was dressed in matching white blouse and slacks, set off by a gold belt made up of repeated links forged into the Gucci logo. There were white sandals on her feet, and Fallon noticed she had painted her toenails the same color Trisha often favored—Watermelon. The woman was attractive— probably just over forty, he guessed—with well-coiffed dark hair and a slender, appealing body. There were no rings on her fingers, and unlike other fashionable New York nightspots, the Café was not frequented by hookers. Fallon couldn't help wondering why this woman was sitting here alone on a holiday weekend.

He turned back to Wally. "We could have her,

huh?" His tone was a mix of sarcasm and a clear lack of interest.

"Sure," Wally insisted, still leaning in. "She's probably a divorcée, looking for the same thing we are."

"I'm still too fragile," Fallon said wryly. "I'm afraid of being hurt again."

"Hey, it takes time," Wally said, missing the irony. He looked past Fallon and studied the woman. "You're probably right. She looks like your typical Manhattan barracuda. Chew you up and spit out the pieces."

"So, when do you think they'll toss us out on our ass?" Fallon asked. One more attempt at wry wit.

Still oblivious, Wally bit again. "Me? Probably tomorrow. You? I don't think you're on their goddamned list."

Fallon laughed softly. "Why the hell not?"

Wally turned suddenly serious. "Lots of reasons, Jack. First, you're the national sales manager of one of the biggest wire and cable companies in the U.S. A vice president, for chrissake. Me, I only head up the New York district." He shrugged, indicating some imagined logic in his words. "Let's face it—you're too close to the top, and the boys at the top don't screw with each other." Another shrug. "Also, you've been with the company since it started. You're one of the guys who bought in when everybody was being paid peanuts, when everybody worked out of that first half-assed factory in Jersey. Hell, you helped make the company what it is today—four manufacturing plants and a corporate headquarters in the goddamned Chrysler Building. And even that prick, our beloved founder and CEO Charlie Waters, can't forget you hung with him during the lean times."

Fallon took a small sip of his drink and smiled. "I like your theory, except for all the holes." He raised one of his own fingers. "First, I'm not at the top. Close, but no cigar. And, in case you haven't noticed, a lot of the guys who were up there with me—the guys I started out with—saw what was coming and folded their tents a long time ago." He picked up his glass, held it out, and stared at the amber liquid. "And, my observant friend, if you take a long look at the clowns who are sitting behind those desks now, you aren't gonna find any who want to be Jack Fallon's rabbi." Fallon put his glass on the bar and gave it a half turn. "Now let's take that beloved prick, Charlie Waters, who I sweated my balls off with all those years ago, and who now only talks to me through his high-priced lackeys. Hell, I could be gone three years before good old Charlie even noticed."

Fallon's mind went back twenty-three years to when he had first met Charlie Waters. He had been a kid—at least as much of a kid as you could be after two tours in Vietnam. Two years of being scared out of your wits, until you just wanted to crawl up in a ball and hide. And, yes, as his mother had so brutally pointed out, he had been awarded medals, although even then he hadn't been sure if they meant anything, had seen them as little more than yet another accident of fate.

His thoughts flashed to the day he had gotten the most impressive of those medals, just as it did, even to this day, during the occasional haunting nightmares. His company had hit a small village northwest of Bong Son, and had walked into a killing ground. The V.C. had been lying in wait and had chopped them up with heavy machine-gun fire, the rounds coming in from three sides. He had taken cover behind a battle-torn hootch, shaking like a leaf, the men on either side of him already dead. In the center of the village, only yards away, three more men lay wounded and screaming for help. He had waited, silently praying that someone else would go out and get them. Then his company had begun to withdraw, and there had been no one else left. He had lain there shaking, his bowels feeling as though they might burst. And then he had started to crawl toward the men—had been halfway there before he even realized he had begun to move. He had crawled through a drainage ditch filled with fetid water, incoming rounds churning up the stench. Then covering fire had come from the trees, and he had reached the first man and had dragged him back behind the hootch. Then the second. When he had returned with the third, other members of his company had gotten there to drag the first two into the surrounding forest.

He was covered in blood, uncertain if it was his own or from the men he had brought in. His fatigue pants were drenched, and he didn't know if it was from the putrid water he had crawled through or the result of his own terror. Overhead he could hear the choppers coming in to pull them out. Someone was shouting at him to leave the third man behind, and he had looked back and had seen the man's intestines spilled out onto the heat-packed dirt of the village. The man was dead, and Fallon realized it was the first time he had looked at his face. He was one of the replacements who had just joined the company, and Fallon didn't even know his name. That was when he had begun to cry, the tears streaming down his cheeks. But he had dragged the man out anyway, crouched low to the ground, back into the safety of the trees. Only five of them had made it back that day, including two of the men he had pulled to safety—only five out of thirty.

They had given him the DSC, and the medal, like his dreams, had haunted him. But it had seemed to mean a lot to Charlie when he learned of it. Charlie was six years older than Fallon—in his early thirties when they had met—and he had seemed slick and sophisticated, a brilliant young engineer out of RPI with a brilliant idea, and he was looking for people to help him sell it, to help launch a business that could revolutionize a small but vital segment of the aeronautics industry. They had met at a party, introduced by a mutual acquaintance, and immediately Waters had started selling Fallon on the idea of joining him. Fallon, he had argued, was just the man he needed, somebody who could go to government and military officials—a war hero who could get their backing to pressure government aircraft contractors into giving his idea a chance. Fallon had been reluctant. Not about the company, which excited him, but about his so-called hero status. But Waters had been a helluva salesman. It was something Fallon still believed, even now. So he had signed on, had worked his butt off, along with a handful of others. Later, when the war in Vietnam had turned into a fully accepted national disgrace, they had downplayed his war-hero image, but by then they were in the door, had their start, and could fight and scrape their way from there. And then the company had started to grow, to diversify, to become bigger than any of them had ever dreamed. He wondered now if it had simply become too big.

Wally had been staring at his drink for several minutes, digesting the information Fallon had given him; skepticism etched across his face. "You really believe that?" he said at length. "You think you're in the same boat as the rest of us—the dinosaurs?"

"Absolutely," Fallon said. "Hell, they may even toss me out first. Offer me a buyout, or whatever it takes to get rid of me without a lot of fuss. It would make sense. It would allow the guy who takes my place to get a feel for the organization, then pick his own team; hire the young Turks *he* wants before they start dumping everyone else."

"Unless it's that little shit Gavin." Wally was nodding now, then fell silent.

Fallon thought of his assistant vice president, Les Gavin, who wore his ambition like a big neon sign. "Hell, if that happens—if Gavin gets my job—then they'll probably dump us all at once," Fallon said. "Shit, Lester may already be interviewing replacements."

Fallon turned to face Wally. "So don't doubt for a minute that I'm on their list," he added.

Suddenly Wally's face burst into a broad grin. "Well, I'll be damned," he said. "I never thought of you as really being part of all this crap. I always thought you'd escape it. You know? I wasn't sure how. I just thought you would." His grin had broadened, and Fallon was both disturbed and amused by the pleasure it seemed to give him.

"I'm glad it's brought a little sunshine into your life," he said.

Wally tried to remove the grin, but couldn't. "Hell, I don't mean I want it for you, you know? It's just kind of good seeing somebody as competent as you being part of it all. It makes me feel like less of an asshole failure." He shook his head. "Shit, I don't know what I mean."

The smile suddenly faded. Wally stared at his drink, then turned back to Fallon. All the humor had fled his face. "I gotta tell you, Jack, I'm scared shitless. I don't know what the hell I'll do if I lose this job." He shook his head. "Hell, all this crap about Janice, it's just a smoke screen to keep me from thinking about all the stuff that makes me wanna wet my pants."

Fallon stared at his drink, embarrassed by the man's sudden burst of honesty; by the mirror image it presented. "I hear you, Wally," he said. "Believe me, I hear you."

Wally offered a weak smile, then shook his head again. "I know this guy—he used to live next door to me before my divorce, and I still see him from time to time. Anyway, this poor bugger lost his job a little over two years ago. Fifty-one years old and he gets downsized right to the goddamned street—a hundred thirty thou a year gone in a flash." Wally took a long pull on his drink. "Since that time this poor slob has sent out two thousand two hundred and five résumés." He laughed. "He's that kind of guy; keeps track of those things. Just a *little* anal retentive." The laughter faded. "And from all that—all two thousand plus of those goddamned résumés—he's gotten ten interviews and not one job offer." Wally let out a long breath. "But you know what scares me the most? Other than the fact that if it happens to me I'll never get another job like the one I have?" He waited, forcing Fallon to look at him. "It's the lack of control, Jack. The total inability to do anything about it." He shook his head. "Christ, all this shit, *all* of it, it all goes back to manufacturing. All these insane problems we're having with this fiber-optic cable. Jesus, I've been there. Right at the plant. We run in-house tests, and everything's perfect. Then we run the same tests for a potential buyer and everything falls apart. All the tolerances are suddenly off. It's crazy, and there's not a goddamned thing anybody in sales can do about it. We're screwed before we even begin."

"Tell me about it," Fallon said. "Christ, my background is engineering, and I've looked at it from every angle, and I can't figure it out."

"Yeah, but they expect us to—all the geniuses upstairs—that's what they expect. They say we're too old, just don't understand the technology well enough to get past the problem. They insist the problem's on the customer's end; that we can't identify what's wrong, work it out, and get the orders anyway. Like we're supposed to be magicians or something."

"They're looking for scapegoats," Fallon said. "We're convenient. We're also the people they don't want anymore."

Wally stared at his drink again; shook his head and laughed softly. "Shit. So you figure you're a scapegoat, too, huh? A goddamned dinosaur. Hell, we oughta form a club. You know? All the dinosaurs. Get together and find a way to screw them back."

Fallon smiled; shook his head, then thought about what Wally had said. "That's not a bad idea," he said.

"All of us getting together, I mean. It might give us a small edge if they start going after us one at a time. Kind of tip us off about how they're going about it. Maybe even give us time to force them into a better deal."

It was as though a lightbulb had gone off over Wally's head. He started nodding rapidly. "Hell, if it came down to the nitty-gritty, maybe we could even hire a lawyer to help us." He was already infatuated with the newly born idea. "We might even have a shot at some kind of class-action lawsuit. Or at least the threat of one." He was getting excited now. Ready to run with the idea before he'd even worked it through. But that was Wally, and Fallon saw no reason to throw water on his fantasies.

Fallon thought about it some more; inclined his head to one side. "Why don't you contact some of the guys, sort of feel them out," he suggested. "It wouldn't hurt to meet and talk to each other."

"Hey, I'll do it," Wally said. "I'll start first thing tomorrow. We can even meet at my place. And I'll even contact some of the guys in the other district offices. I know they're all shitting bricks out there."

"Just do it quietly, and make sure everybody keeps their mouths shut." Fallon lowered his voice to emphasize the point. "If the geniuses behind this downsizing crap think there's any organized resistance, they might decide to push the timing up a bit."

"Yeah, you're right," Wally said. "Mum's the goddamned word." He was grinning again, and again gave Fallon a light punch on the arm. "Now let's do some bouncing," he said. "Just to celebrate the formation of The Dinosaur Club."

Fallon smiled at the term, and the idea. "No. Not me, Tiger. Tonight I'll leave the ladies to you." He glanced to his right, where the woman who had inspired Wally's lust was still dusting a bar stool with her well-tailored slacks. He envisioned Wally sliding up to her using his best salesman's lines. He had seen the man charm women before—this fat, balding, red-faced man, whose self-deprecating wit seemed to exude an irresistible charm. It was probably what made him such a successful salesman. He turned back to his friend and lowered his voice to a whisper. "Just play it safe if it gets that far. I want you to live to be a big, grown-up dinosaur."

3

SAMANTHA MOORE STARED ACROSS THE ROOM, WATCH-
ing him as he spoke on the phone. Everything about
the man exuded confidence; a sense of power still
untapped. She studied his body language. Each gesture,
each inclination of his head, each smile was offered with
deliberate charm, even when he was speaking to someone miles away. She crossed one leg, rearranged the
legal pad on her lap, and continued to consider the
man. Carter Bennett had all the moves, derived from
breeding, education, and family conditioning. He was
the son of a successful investment banker and a socially
prominent mother. Doors were open to him on Wall
Street and in all the city's better clubs thanks to his family's reputation. And it was a family known to back its
progeny to the hilt, although Carter insisted that was not
true in his case. Added to that were Princeton, class of
1980, The Wharton School of Finance, 1982, and his
own considerable talents.

Now, with all paths properly paved, and at the tender
age of thirty-five, he was already near the top. In short,
he had every opportunity she wanted for herself and in
most cases would never have. In five years, perhaps less,
he'd be CEO of this company, or some other. And

Samantha had no doubt he'd run it competently. She tapped her Mont Blanc pen against the pad. And ruthlessly, she added to herself. She wondered which of Bennett's attributes had made her climb so willingly into his bed during a brief and ultimately unsatisfying affair. Or was it curiosity, the need to find some cracks in that all too perfect veneer? She, too, wanted to ride her career as high as it would go, though she was fully aware she could never reach as high as he. Her lack of suitable contacts, not to mention a penis, would keep her from being taken seriously enough for that. The best she could hope for was to become general counsel for this or some other corporation. But if that was the best she could do, she wanted it.

During their brief relationship she also had discovered she really didn't like Carter all that much. She couldn't quite put her finger on it, but there was something . . . hollow about him. She smiled at the idea, recognizing that whatever that something was, it was definitely not visible on the surface. The man appeared oh, so solid. He even smelled like success. Carter had definitely intrigued her at first. She also recognized she had never thought of him as a marriageable man. More as a handsome and interesting dalliance, who, if willing, could teach her some things that would help her career. And she fully understood that she, too, had been little more than a flirtation to Bennett—albeit a useful and usable one. His highly affluent, WASP background would never permit anything more. Like the rest of his ilk, Carter had been taught from birth that like people— read superior—should marry and mate. The idea disgusted her intellectually, but she couldn't dismiss it. It was simply there—very much a part of the real world— and the people of Carter's class, together with their money, set the rules for admission. And Samantha Moore, daughter of a Pennsylvania grocer, did not qualify, and never would. Law degree or no law degree.

Carter placed the phone back in its cradle, seemed to think something over, then turned his smile on her. It was quite a smile—beautiful really—but it also had a recognizable touch of self-regard to it, and she wondered if he knew that it did. No, she thought. That would be something he'd view as a liability, and he'd correct it. He'd stand in front of a mirror and practice until it was just right. She had seen him do it, sculpting and refining the Carter Bennett that the world was allowed to see. It was one reason their affair had ended almost before it began. Carter had let her catch a glimpse of the man behind the facade. It disturbed him that he had. And what she had seen had disturbed Samantha as well.

Bennett stood, stretching his tall, well-toned body to full height, back as straight as a tombstone. He was jacketless, projecting the image of a man who preferred to work in shirtsleeves. But the shirt he wore was custom-made and fit perfectly. It was all part of his performance: Here I am, bringing myself down to your level, even though I'll never truly be there. She smiled at the thought. Yes, she decided, that would be the image Carter would seek.

"The pension boys have finally crunched all the numbers," he said. His smile had widened.

"And?" Samantha asked.

"What can I say?" He spread his arms as if accepting warranted adulation; the candlepower of his smile intensified. "They fit my projections perfectly."

Samantha uncrossed, then recrossed, her legs, and Bennett admired *their* perfection. She was a beautiful woman with short, dark hair that seemed to flow along the finely etched lines of her face, accenting her delicate nose, the slight swell of her lips, the high cheekbones and almond-shaped brown eyes. Even in a severely cut business suit she couldn't mask the beauty, or the enticing body she carried on a moderately tall

frame. Carter recalled the pleasure he had taken from
that body. It had been almost three months now since
their affair had ended, but he still marveled at the blatant sensuality of the woman. He had never anticipated
such passion from so competent a lawyer.

"Have you factored in the possible costs of a class-
action suit?" Samantha asked, almost as though she had
read his final thought.

"If it ultimately comes to litigation, you mean."
Bennett smiled down at her. There was nothing patron-
izing about the smile, it was friendly enough, but somehow she instantly hated it. "Why don't you throw those
figures at me?" he said.

Her jaw tightened imperceptibly. She was annoyed
but really didn't understand why. After all, it was a legit-
imate business question. "If we're faced with a class-
action suit charging age discrimination—and if we lose
that suit—we could be talking about an award of several
hundred thousand dollars. Per individual, on average,"
she said.

"Define several." There was a hint of challenge in his
voice, but his eyes were still friendly.

Samantha let out a breath. "All right, Carter, let's say
two, maybe two hundred and fifty thousand for each
person we force out the door."

"Would that include punitive damages, if any?"

"No. But I see nothing right now that would warrant
punitive damages. Not if we offer a reasonable buyout
package with the appropriate counseling and other
perks. And providing we mask any flagrant age discrimination built into the plan. That figure, of course, would
be over and above the original buyout and pension benefits. It would be an add-on. However, if we are hit with
a credible class-action suit—one that could sustain a
charge of blatant discrimination, we'd probably be wise
to settle. Being found in flagrant violation of the federal
Age Discrimination in Employment Act, as well as the

New York City statute, which in some respects is even tougher than the federal law, could prove *very* expensive. So, either way, I think that two-fifty figure is a very real possibility." She saw the skepticism on his face and added, "Let's not forget what happened to the American Can Company a few years back."

Carter regained his chair, eased back, and steepled his fingers. He knew the American Can case, as anyone in his position would. The executives there had lacked any subtlety at all. They had literally flagged employees whose pensions were about to vest, then laid them off prior to that date. And they had left the evidence sitting in their records.

"They were careless," Bennett offered.

"Careless *and* arrogant," Samantha countered. "It happens. Even in companies that are well run." She decided to soften the rebuke. "I'm not being critical, Carter. It's my job to warn you about the pitfalls you face when you're considering an action that might be ruled illegal. And to advise you how to avoid the penalties if you choose to go ahead."

Bennett offered her another killer smile that spoke volumes. "So two-fifty per would be the max—if, of course, they have the resources and the inclination to fight us in court."

He had dismissed what she had said. She wasn't surprised. "Yes, that's my best guess, based on the facts I have at hand." She watched him mentally calculate the figures.

Bennett brought his chair forward and spread his hands. "Then we'd still come out well ahead. By nearly ten million the first year, and over a hundred million after that." He leaned back, steepled his fingers again, and seemed to think about what he had just said. "This is a young company—twenty-three years old. And its major growth has been over the last ten years—so many of our people don't have vested pension rights. That cuts long-term costs considerably. When you add the salaries that will be eliminated into that." He raised his hands, then let them drop.

Samantha tapped her pen against the legal pad and decided to inject one final point. "We'll still have to offer them buyout money—much less than the older employees, of course, but something. You have to remember that none of this is going to be pleasant. Not for anyone in the company."

"Yes, I know." He let out a heavy breath. "And I feel for those people. But I can't allow that to be a consideration. What I have to do is factor in the effect this type of downsizing will have on the market. That's my job. And for starters, the company will see an immediate jump on the big board." He rocked back in his chair, another small, almost imperceptible smile playing on his lips. "Layoffs have become a corporate asset." Another heavy breath. "And rightly or wrongly, investors love downsizing, especially when they see a company unloading enough senior people to get out from under the benefit packages they're tied into. They're quite astute about those things today. They know our pension costs go up one and a half percent a year—every year—for employees between ages fifty and sixty-two. When you add what we'll save in life, disability, and health insurance costs, then factor in the lower salaries we'll pay replacement personnel, you are talking about some serious money." He offered up both hands in a fait accompli gesture. "Throw in enough younger employees and it convinces everyone you're getting rid of deadwood as well, and investors love to see deadwood jettisoned. They know it leads to increased profitability."

"Are you sure we're talking deadwood? In every instance?"

Bennett shook his head, as though saddened by her naïveté. "Whether we are or not, it doesn't matter. That will be the perception. And perception is what counts.

That, and saving money. It's sad but true." He waved a hand before his face. It was the gesture of someone trying to brush aside irrelevancies, and Samantha wondered if it was defensive, if he was trying to avoid thinking about the lives he would devastate.

"You certainly can't argue that some of these people aren't excess baggage," he continued. "Any company, no matter how well run, has its share of corporate fat. It's why they need people like me." He allowed a hint of solemnity to enter his eyes—placed it there. He's missed his calling, she thought. He should have been an actor on a TV soap.

"Hell, Samantha, I'm just a reluctant surgeon, cutting away an economic cancer that's devouring an otherwise sound company." Solemnity faded into a faint smile. He apparently liked the metaphor, she decided. "It's just not called surgery." The smile grew. "The people we *disemploy* might take offense at that. So, instead, we call it 'a workforce imbalance correction.'" He chuckled over the terminology.

Samantha looked down at her pad, tapped her pen against it, then raised her eyes to Bennett's still smiling face. She momentarily thought of raising the question of corporate responsibility, but immediately knew it was pointless. "One could argue about the effect it will have on the younger employees who remain, and those we bring in," she said. "If we act too harshly there won't be much question of trust or company loyalty when they see long-tenured people jettisoned simply to increase profits." She paused. He was staring at her with disapproval now. "There's also the matter of the company's public image," she added. "The chief economist at Morgan Stanley has been predicting for years that corporate America will face a serious public backlash over this downsizing trend. I'm just suggesting caution."

Bennett held her gaze. "And I can name another economist who refers to downsizing as a *gale of creative destruction*. Creative being the operative word." He paused, readjusted some papers on his desk. "Besides, people worry too much about public image." He inclined his head as if indicating the obvious. "No one wants to stir things up unnecessarily, but we all know the public's memory span is quite short. What they really want—what they want to see each morning when they read their newspapers—is U.S. companies beating the hell out of the Germans and the Japanese. That's what gives them confidence in their future. Because deep down they recognize that what we're doing is right, that only in-your-face capitalism will keep this country great." He offered up another regretful smile. "And as far as employee loyalty goes, I'm afraid that simply doesn't exist anymore. People don't come to work these days with the idea of tying their tails down for thirty years. They come with the idea of moving with the currents. Moving *up*. From one company to the next. They're not fools. They understand the new corporate thinking. Nothing is forever. And when change is needed, more often than not, companies look to the outside." Bennett smiled faintly as he prepared another metaphor. "It's like the wife and the mistress," he said. "To the corporate mind, the guy on the outside *always* looks better than the drone you have working for you in-house. Especially when top positions need to be filled."

Samantha looked away. His argument repulsed her, but she knew Carter was simply acknowledging today's reality. Still, she could feel a tightness in her lips as she spoke. "It could be argued that the absence of loyalty is directly related to management's attitude," she said.

Bennett laughed. "So what? Why waste time with moot arguments?" He dropped his palms to the desktop and stood. "What I need right now is for you to draw up a draft buyout offer that will cover our backsides if it comes to litigation." He made a generous wave with one hand. "Offer psychological counseling, outplacement, whatever it takes. If we can avoid litigation, all the better. If we can't . . ." He shrugged. "Then we just want to minimize costs and their impact on the bottom line." He smiled at her again. "There are other bottom-line steps we can take as well, but I won't burden you with those now."

It was a dismissal. She was deputy general counsel and she was being told to do her job. And since the company's general counsel, her boss, was rumored to be on Bennett's hit list, the behind-the-scenes dirty work had been left to her. But that, after all, was what lawyers did.

"It will take me a week or so to work up a rough draft," she said. "Will that be satisfactory?"

Bennett caught the edge in her voice, and forced back another smile. The woman was beautiful and competent, but she had a great deal of bleeding-heart naïveté to overcome. "No problem," he said. "It will be a couple of months before we're ready to move, and when we do we want every *i* dotted."

He walked around his desk and came up beside her. His movements were quite graceful, she thought. There was a wisp of sandy hair on his forehead, and it made him seem boyish. She had caught a glimpse of the little boy during their brief affair and initially had been attracted to it. It had been something he had not wanted her to see and she soon realized that it was born of desperation. He desperately needed the love of a woman—any woman—but was determined never to show that vulnerability. He simply didn't know how to love; yet he wanted to *be* loved, to take. And that need was infinite, and his accompanying narcissism, and inability to have real feelings for others, had soon killed any attraction she had felt. But here, in his realm of power, there was nothing boyish about him. Here the contrived public personality was king. The blue eyes were hard—even cold, at times—and his handsome, patrician face always reflected the self-satisfaction of someone who knew the answers and harbored no doubts. Here, Samantha thought, Carter Bennett was dangerous.

She decided to take one parting shot. "Have you looked at the personnel records of the people you're considering for termination?"

"What for? Why would that factor in?" He seemed honestly taken aback, she realized.

"I thought it might help if you knew time of service; the number of instances an individual had relocated at the company's request; whether there were children in college; things of that sort."

"Help in what way?" Bennett had folded his arms across his chest and was staring at her, genuinely nonplussed.

"They're issues that could be raised in litigation," she said.

He let out a soft laugh. "Somewhat specious arguments, don't you think?"

"Perhaps. Perhaps not. It would depend on the judge."

He shook his head. "Look, as I said, I truly feel for these people. These are hard decisions, but I'm not a social worker. Nor am I paid to worry about personnel matters. This is a purely business consideration. A financial one. And I'm the chief financial officer of this company. I'm not about to get involved in any hand-wringing." Bennett unfolded his arms and placed a hand on each hip. "Look, you're the lawyer. If you think it could be a problem, you look into it. But only as a way of deciding how to combat it." He thought a moment, then added, "Although, as long as you're doing that, you might as well take on one other assignment." He hesitated, as if trying to decide how to say it. He began with a slight shrug. "Ideally, we'd like to get rid of everyone near or past fifty. Of course we realize that's not possible. But assuming we'll be getting rid of most of them, I'd like you to give me a figure on how much *destaffing* we'll have to do among our twenty-, thirty-, and forty-year-olds, so we can avoid the appearance of age discrimination." He considered that for a moment, then added, "And give me a separate memo on it. But mark it attorney-client privileged. I don't want some opposition lawyer to stumble across it six months from now and be able to use it to embarrass us."

Samantha nodded. "I'll look into it." Now it was her turn to pause. "Just how many people are we talking about, overall?"

Bennett looked at her coldly, as if deciding on her need to know. "We intend to downsize the company by one-third," he finally said. "That's highly confidential, of course."

Samantha held back a gasp. It was the first time she had heard the actual figure. Company rumors had gone as high as a thousand. But one-third of the workforce? That was nearly three thousand people. "I'll get on it right away," she said.

Bennett's smile returned. "Are you stopping off at the gym tonight?" he asked.

"Probably," she said.

"I'll see you there, then. Perhaps we can have a drink afterward." He grinned at her, but his eyes were cold. "It's been a long time since we socialized."

Samantha nodded. A bit tightly, he thought. "All right, but it will have to be a quick drink," she said. "You've given me a lot to do."

When she had gone, Bennett returned to his desk and stared at the pension figures he had just been given. It was coming together perfectly, he told himself. It was going to work just as he had planned it.

His intercom buzzed and he picked up the phone.

"I have your cousin Eunice on line one," his assistant said.

Bennett squeezed his eyes shut. Christ, the woman is

like a pit bull. She never lets go, he thought. His cousin flashed through his mind. Tall and angular, and until recently—until they had gone into this very private business arrangement—content with being a charter member of the horsey set. He let out a breath. "I'll take it. Thank you," he said.

Bennett punched line one and leaned back in his chair. "Hello, Eunice. What can I do for you?"

He listened to his cousin's plaintive query; his lips tightened; a silent, inner groan emerged. "There's nothing to worry about," he said softly. "Everything's going just as planned." He let out a breath. "In fact, by next week I should be ready to make a final presentation to Charlie Waters himself. Then it will just be a question of selling the board."

He listened again, squeezed his eyes shut a second time. "No. No. Not to worry. I don't anticipate any problems. None at all. The figures are all there, and they speak for themselves. Waters Cable stock will take an immediate jump when we announce it, and I can't imagine any opposition. It's what they've all wanted. Every board member. They've been pleading for it for a year and a half. It's why they *put* me in this job."

He listened to his cousin prattle on, heard the nervousness in her voice. "Listen, why don't we get together for a drink tonight? I can show you the figures, and then I'm sure you'll see it more clearly. There's just no need for concern."

Cousin Eunice babbled again. "That would be great. I'll see you at the club at eight." He lowered his voice and added an intimate tone, "It's been far too long, anyway."

Bennett leaned forward and replaced the phone. Christ, he thought. The woman would drive him insane before it was over. He shook his head, cautioning himself to look to the future. Just hang in there, he told himself. Keep her happy. The payoff will be worth it. Worth every maddening minute.

He spun his chair around and stared at a framed photograph on his credenza. It was a family portrait, taken at his parents' home in Glen Cove. His brother, Edwin, stared back with his perennially smug smile. His father stood next to Edwin, one arm draped about his shoulder. The favorite son, the eldest, who even bore his father's name—the son who had been brought into his father's bank, and who now had an earned income five times Bennett's own.

And what did your loving father do for you? he asked himself. Nothing. Even less than nothing. An almost insignificant trust fund that actually came from your mother. He drew a breath. *Insignificant.* In the photograph even his mother appeared to dismiss him. He sat there at her feet; her eyes were staring at something beyond him. She seemed unaware even of his presence. He fought off pain he had learned to hide many years earlier. You'll show them, he thought. Very soon you'll show them all.

Jack Fallon jogged in place as the treadmill rumbled slowly beneath him. He had been at it for five minutes and his gray T-shirt was stained with sweat, the matching gym shorts riding up into his crotch. He hit the stop button on the machine, lowered his head, and leaned against its handhold as he struggled to catch his breath. He felt as though his lungs might burst through his chest.

When he raised his eyes, he saw the woman enter the gym, and instinctively righted himself and sucked in his stomach. She was striking, about thirty-five, he guessed, and she made what little breath he had catch in his throat. He stared at her clothing. The fitness craze, he decided, had spawned an entire subdivision in the fashion industry, and he mentally compared this ensemble to others he had seen advertised in magazines. The woman was dressed in a one-piece Lycra that went to mid-thigh; solid black—something he thought they now called a unitard. It fit her like a second skin, something she had been poured into; accented by an overfitting pink thong that served no other purpose than to set off an incredibly well-shaped bottom. The clothing was similar to that worn by the other women scattered about the gym. Only on this woman it was far more effective. Had she walked into the room naked, she could not have appeared more erotic, and Fallon found himself gawking like a schoolboy.

He turned away and moved to an elevated incline board where he began a set of sit-ups. By the tenth repetition his underused stomach muscles screamed in protest, but he forced himself to complete five more before pulling himself upright, again gasping for breath.

Again his eyes were drawn to the woman. She was positioned over a narrow, padded bench, one knee on the bench itself, the other resting on the floor. She was wearing slouch socks that seemed to flaunt the perfect shape of her leg, but Fallon found his eyes drawn elsewhere. Her body was hunched forward, and with one hand she repeatedly pumped a ten-pound weight from floor to shoulder. Fallon found he also had no interest in the exercise itself—some foolishness for the upper arm, he decided. It was the woman's position that intrigued him. Her back was to him, and bent forward as she was, her well-shaped, pink-and-black-clad bottom was the most beautiful and arousing sight he had glimpsed in a long time.

He suddenly felt ridiculous. He was on the verge of making a middle-aged spectacle of himself. He shook his head; tried to excuse himself; tried to recall how long it had been since he had last slept with Trisha. Not long enough to be walking around like a teenager in perpetual heat.

Fallon agonized through two more sets of sit-ups, rested to regain his wind, then moved to the area that held the free weights—the same area where the woman was still exercising. He told himself he had planned to go there next anyway—which was true. At least he thought it was. Anyway, it was somewhere in his plan for a first workout.

He selected a pair of twenty-five-pound dumbbells and began a set of standing arm curls. By the tenth repetition his biceps had started to burn, and he found himself gritting his teeth by the time he reached twenty. He lowered the weights and sat on an exercise bench to rest his arms before the next set. The woman was a mere six feet away, having moved to a machine for lateral arm raises.

There was a sudden crash as the weights she was lifting fell back into place. A bolt from the machine rolled across the floor, coming to rest at his feet.

"Damn it," she said.

Fallon picked up the bolt and approached her. "Problem?"

"The machine broke," she said. She smiled. "And I forgot my tool kit."

Fallon looked at the machine, inclined his head to one side. "I have mine," he said. "Be right back."

Fallon returned from the locker room with the oversized Swiss Army knife he always carried in his briefcase. He studied the damage, refitted the bolt, and tightened it with a small pair of pliers. "That should hold long enough for you to finish," he said.

She gave him another smile, a dazzling one, mixed with open curiosity. "Do you always carry a miniature set of tools?" she asked.

"Always," Fallon said. "In this company, you never know when something's going to fall apart."

She laughed, and Fallon felt a rush of pleasure and awkwardness. "I've noticed that," she said. "You're Jack Fallon, aren't you? Vice president for sales?"

Fallon was momentarily surprised; struggled to identify the woman, but failed. He nodded. "I'm sorry. I can't place you. Have we met?"

The woman shook her head. "Someone pointed you out to me at that company golf outing last month. I met your wife, though. She's lovely. I'm Samantha Moore. I'm one of the lawyers up in legal. I do contracts, mostly."

Fallon extended his hand. "Then I'm surprised we haven't met."

"I've only been with the company a little over a year."

Fallon studied her more closely. She was probably one of Bennett's people, he thought. The man had brought in a small boatload since coming on board almost two years ago. He looked at her again and dismissed the idea. Paranoia seemed to surround him these days.

"Then I'm not surprised. We haven't had a lot of new contracts lately." He raised his eyebrows regretfully. "But maybe I should hire you outside the company. My wife's about to file for divorce."

"Oh, I'm sorry," Samantha said. Her words sounded genuine.

"It only happened this past weekend," he said. "I haven't figured out yet whether I am or not." He immediately wondered why he was even talking about it. If this woman asked why Trish had left, how could he ever admit she had abandoned him for another man? Especially Howard Nowicki.

"Well, you *should* get a lawyer," Samantha said. "The sooner the better."

"Why does he need a lawyer?"

Fallon turned to the sound of the voice, and found Carter Bennett grinning at him. Bennett turned to Samantha and the grin faded, and Fallon realized that his apparent amusement had never carried to his eyes.

Samantha seemed embarrassed. "Mr. Fallon has a

personal problem we were just discussing," she said. She seemed to be warning Carter off, telling him to mind his own business in as gentle a way as she could.

"My wife's filing for divorce," Fallon said. For some reason he felt he had to get the woman off the hook. He didn't quite understand why.

Bennett pursed his lips, and his eyebrows rose with fraudulent concern. "Sorry to hear it, Fallon," he said. But there was no regret in his words or tone, and Fallon felt like a fool. He should never have opened this can of worms in this of all places.

He pulled himself together and stared at Bennett. He was dressed in a blue Princeton T-shirt over matching shorts with a small tiger emblazoned on one leg. The man was handsome and even charming, when he chose to be—but he was really a killer. A professional WASP with all the right corporate moves, nurtured from birth to become exactly what he was. And right now, what he was, was the suspected mastermind behind a rumored downsizing plan, which, Fallon thought, also gave him the moral sentiments of a pit viper.

"Thanks for the condolence, Carter," Fallon said. He had layered the words with mild sarcasm, then had turned abruptly and gone back to his weights. But as he did, he caught a slight look of pain in Samantha Moore's eyes. She, too, had picked up an undertone of indifference and contempt in Bennett's voice, Fallon thought. And she hadn't liked it.

"I'm afraid our drink is off," Carter said. He was smiling again, and had placed a hand on Samantha's arm. "Something's come up that's unavoidable. Perhaps we could meet later?"

Fallon, back at his bench now, glanced toward them. Bennett's words had a touch of the proprietorial about them, and Fallon wondered if they were for his benefit.

Samantha stared at him and Fallon suspected that she resented Bennett's proprietary tone. "I don't think so, Carter," she said. "It's just as well. I have a full brief-case, and I'm tired."

Bennett offered the same pursed lips; the same raised eyebrows. Then another smile. "Another time," he said. He stepped to the weight rack, selected two forty-pound dumbbells, and began a set of the same exercise Fallon had just struggled through—only with weights fifteen pounds lighter. Screw him, Fallon thought. He instinctively noted the trim line of the man's waist, the perfect definition of his arms and shoulders, and immediately despised him for each. But it was pointless. The man was also fifteen years younger, and fifteen years fitter. And, if he wants to, he'll be running this company fifteen years from now. You'll be lucky if you're still here in fifteen months.

Fallon's eyes went back to the woman, and he realized she had been watching him watch Bennett. She smiled at him, and he wondered if it was by way of apology for Bennett, or something else. He decided it didn't matter, and he smiled back.

An hour later, Fallon was finishing off the evening's exercise on the stationary bicycle, huffing and sweating and determined to complete five miles according to the machine's calculator, which seemed to crawl along at a torturously slow pace. At three miles he saw Carter Bennett enter the men's locker room, and he was momentarily pleased that he had outlasted him in the company's gym. Whether he would outlast him in the company, he thought, was another matter.

At four and a half miles, Samantha Moore stopped beside him. There was a towel draped around her neck, and her face and arms glistened with sweat. He immediately thought about lying in bed with her on a hot summer's night, that sweat—and his own—having come from a different type of exercise. He pushed the thought away. He was starting to feel like an oversexed, middle-aged fool.

"If you're almost finished, I'd like to buy you a drink," she said.

Fallon felt his throat constrict—the invitation momentarily stunned him. "I'd love to," he said through labored breath. "But what about being tired, and having a full briefcase?"

A smile played across her mouth. "That was for Carter's benefit," she said. "I'll wait for you in the lobby."

With that she turned and walked briskly away, and Fallon found his eyes again following the pink and black sway of her walk. He glanced at the bicycle's calculator. Another half mile, he told himself, as he increased his speed on the pedals.

They sat at a diminutive table—the type universally used in cocktail lounges to create a false sense of intimacy and to crowd as many customers as possible into expensive space. The table was in the bar area of the Pen and Pencil, a small, upscale restaurant on East Forty-fifth Street, only a few blocks from their offices in the Chrysler Building. The restaurant was dimly lighted, with an abundance of highly polished dark wood and a decidedly British air, and it seemed light-years away from the cold decor of the company gym they had just left. It was also only moderately crowded, as Fallon had expected, being too pricey for the after-work-drinks crowd, serving instead a smattering of well turned out couples scattered through the dining room. Samantha fit in perfectly, now dressed in a severely tailored business suit that offered only a hint of the sensuality that had awakened and excited him. She had reapplied makeup, but so lightly it was barely noticeable in the dim lighting, and Fallon decided she really didn't need very much at all.

He felt strange, slightly ill at ease, and a bit guilty at even being there. He hadn't been alone with another woman under these circumstances in a very long time.

He wondered about that, wondered exactly what the circumstances were. Samantha's barren ring finger made it clear she was available, whatever the hell that meant. And so was he, he supposed. Perhaps that was it—that he hadn't thought of himself in that way for so many, many years.

Samantha took a sip of the white wine they had ordered and smiled across at him. Fallon decided it was a smile that could light up a room.

"Tell me about our sales operation," she said. "I know next to nothing about it, outside the contracts I hammer together. I always feel trapped in the arcane minutiae, never the realities of the company's business."

Fallon felt a momentary rush of relief. They were just two business colleagues having a drink, talking about work. The relief was followed by momentary disappointment. He forced a smile. "Lately there hasn't been a great deal to cheer about in our department," he said.

"That bad?"

"We're okay in some areas—like the modern aeronautical cable we pioneered." He ran a finger along the rim of his glass. "Do you know much about the product line?" he asked.

She shook her head. "On the technical side very little."

"Well, we're basically talking about wire, the electrical wires that carry the impulses throughout an aircraft, activating the hydraulics, the radar, computers, everything that puts those birds up, keeps them there, then brings them down. A large bomber or commercial airliner has miles of it threaded through its fuselage, and years ago, Charlie Waters figured out a way to make it thinner and lighter without losing effectiveness." He smiled, remembering the early years. "It was a tough sell at first. But once we got some backing from the military, things started to take off." He raised both hands in a sweeping gesture. "And, suddenly, *Shazam!* Waters

Cable went big time. And the growth has been extraordinary. Especially over the last ten years."

"And now?"

"Now we're diversifying, out of necessity, and it's killing us. The new line of fiber optics is just doing us in." He hesitated. "Actually it makes sense. On paper anyway. And we don't really have a choice. Fiber optics are nothing but wire—exactly our field. But it involves woven glass fibers, instead of metal, and the changeover, the technical problems involved, are enormous." He leaned forward, warming to the subject. "Basically fiber optics will do the same job as regular cable, only more of it, and a helluva lot faster. It involves the transmission of messages or information by light pulses along hair-thin glass fibers. They're smaller and lighter than conventional cables that use copper wire or coaxial tubes, but they can carry a near limitless amount of information.

"It's the coming thing; there's no escaping it," Fallon added. "Fiber-optic cable can transmit vast amounts of data between computers, or data-intensive television pictures, or thousands of simultaneous telephone conversations. And it's immune to electromagnetic interference from lightning, nearby motors, or other computers. It also requires fewer repeaters over distance than copper wire to keep signals from deteriorating."

He swirled the wine in his glass, recalling how hard it had been to play catch-up with this new technology—one that had been in its infancy when he had studied engineering.

"Eventually it's going to replace everything, not only for communications but in automobiles, conventional aircraft, and every vehicle sent into space, and we have to get into it if we're going to survive. That's our market."

"So why has it become a problem for us?" Samantha asked.

Fallon sipped his wine; shook his head and smiled. "We rushed into it. Too much, too soon. And without the technical expertise we needed." He raised his eyebrows slightly; indicated there was little that could be done about that now. "It was a management decision," he added. "Not sales management. Real management. We were just told, Here it is, sell it." The wistful smile returned. "But it's not quite that easy. It's a rough market, with strong competition, especially from the Germans and the Japanese. We're the premier company in the states as far as aeronautical cable goes, but we're the new kid on the block in fiber optics, and we jumped into it without the kind of preparation we needed." He looked down at his glass. "Now we're paying a price for it."

He began toying with the drink again. "Right now we've got our first, direct government contract. Up until now we've been primarily subcontractors, working with aircraft manufacturers. But now we have a research and development contract for an inertial guidance system that will be used in rockets and spacecraft." He smiled. "That means gyroscopes and accelerometers that calculate speed and direction using fiber optics." The smile faded. "It's been a disaster, and we could lose the actual production contract. Over the past couple of years we've hired several hundred computer wizards and engineers whose specialty is fiber optics." He grinned at her. "They're a strange breed, complete with the inevitable pocket protectors and nerdy haircuts, and they're spread out in our four manufacturing plants. Hopefully, they'll solve the problems and we'll come out of our tailspin and, eventually, get a fair share of that market. But some people think we should dominate the market—just as we have with aeronautical cable—and that's just not in the cards. At least not for some time. Perhaps never."

"And the powers that be don't like that," she said.

Fallon laughed. "They never like being told they were wrong. It's always easier to point the fickle finger of failure at someone else. And there's no question our department hasn't done the job they expected. Even though that failure had more than a little help from above."

"So you're taking the heat for it."

"Indeed we are." He shrugged, as though it didn't matter. "Among others. The guys upstairs also haven't been thrilled with some of the manufacturing disasters they've encountered." He sipped his wine and grinned. "Our leaders want results, not excuses." Again he smiled, accompanied it with an almost inaudible sigh. "And those results were supposed to come from my division, and they didn't. Unfortunately, it's a division that doesn't have the internal power to fight off that criticism."

"What do you mean? You're top management."

"There's top, and then there's *the* top." He smiled at the simple truth he was about to impart. "What I mean is that the corporate culture has changed in recent years. Especially at the top. Years ago, sales was a controlling force. Primarily because we were a young company and we needed to carve out a share of the market. But we succeeded and other areas became more dominant. Manufacturing, research and development, and especially the financial side of the business. They made the decisions; set the policies, and we weren't asked for input; we were just expected to carry them out. If we failed to meet expectations, it was never because the decisions and policies were wrong." He grinned. "It was simply our failure."

Samantha decided she liked his smile, liked the slightly self-deprecating way he spoke about himself. "It doesn't sound like you had much of a chance," she said. "At least in this instance."

"That's an excuse," he said. "Maybe it's a good one, but it's still an excuse. And as your friend Carter will happily explain, guys like me are paid to carry the ball, not make excuses."

Samantha could see Carter doing just that, defending

a poorly conceived corporate decision—whether he believed in it or not—by insisting others had simply *dropped the ball*. And he would probably use exactly those words, she decided. Clichés involving ball games seemed to obsess men. Even men like Fallon. She had always thought it had something to do with a fixation on their genitals.

"So the entire sales division is under fire," she said. She was probing now, trying to get information that might help her carry out her assignment for Bennett. It was why she had invited Fallon for a drink. She had her hatchet work to do, and stumbling across Fallon as she had had seemed almost serendipitous.

"Not the whole division," Fallon corrected. "Just the older hands, the ones who have been around forever. The corporate wisdom seems to be that my guys are up to speed on aeronautical cable, but we can't cut it with the newer technology."

"And you don't agree?"

Fallon thought about the question. He ran his finger around the glass again, forcing his mind back to his own sales team. "In a few cases that might be true. There are always some people who have trouble changing tack."

"And what do you do in those instances?" she asked.

He grinned, a bit boyishly, she thought. "You boot them in the backsides, and get them on track."

"And if you can't?"

The grin faded. "Then you tell them to start looking for work elsewhere. It's a part of the job nobody likes, but it happens," he said.

Samantha wondered how the man would feel when he was handed Carter's hit list. Presuming he wasn't on it himself. Her interest, she thought, bordered on voyeurism, given her own involvement, and she began to feel like some kind of spy, or worse. But that was why she was here—to get to know someone who might be at the heart of Carter's downsizing plan, to get a feel for

the people it would affect. Now the idea made her somewhat uneasy, and she wondered why. Perhaps she was
simply beginning to like the man, and that was something she couldn't afford to do. She decided to drop the
subject. But still, she knew that when the time came—
when she finally got a copy of Carter's hit list—she
would look and see if his name was there. She also
thought she might review his personnel records, just to
satisfy her own curiosity. She was momentarily puzzled
by what it meant—that she was taking such an interest
in this one man. Or if it meant anything at all.

"You seem to be having more than your share of pressure," she said. She paused, offered him a smile, used it
to ease her way into the new probing she wanted to do.
"Given all the headaches at work . . ." She paused again.
"And the unpleasant news your wife handed you last
week."

"It was only this weekend, actually. I suppose I'm still
numb." He thought about that. "Or maybe I cared a lot
less than I thought I did. The last few years haven't been
all wine and roses." He wondered why he had told the
woman that, wondered if he was trying to sound more
available than he felt.

"How long have you been married?" she asked.

"Twenty-four years." He thought about that. "Almost
half my life." He laughed softly, but the sound was hollow and mirthless. "When I think about the early years it
seems as if they happened only yesterday. And the other
stuff—the stuff that happened before we were
together—that's like something that happened in real
time." He offered up a somewhat pained smile. "Does
that make sense? Or is it just part of getting older? I
know I think about that a lot—the getting older part, I
mean."

"I don't know, Jack. I'm thirty-five, and I sure think
about getting older. But I've never had that kind of relationship. All mine—especially the more recent ones—

started to feel old fast, even when they were new." Samantha returned his smile, as if acknowledging her own bit of self-deprecation.

Fallon considered what she had said. He wondered if he was still clinging to his relationship with Trisha, even secretly hoping for some reconciliation. If he was, he was a bigger fool than even he suspected. But perhaps it was simply that no one had yet come along to replace Trisha in his thoughts—or his life. Suddenly he wanted to escape that whole area of conversation.

He rearranged himself in his chair. "Anyway, that's all too maudlin to talk about. The status of my marriage, I mean." He picked up his glass of wine, more to have something to do with his hands than because he wanted it. "You said you've been with the company for a little over a year. What brought you to us?"

"I think the company finally woke up and found itself in the nineties," Samantha said. "It suddenly realized its legal department was almost devoid of women—at least as far as lawyers went—and I was part of the remediation process." She laughed at the absurdity of it. "Odd place to discriminate, isn't it? Try to answer that one in court. Now there are three of us. I think our general counsel, Walter Morrisey, is still in shock. But what can you expect from a man who continues to smoke cigars in his office, even though the entire company is supposed to be smoke free? But at least he opens his window. Sometimes I think he wants to jump out that window whenever he has to deal with one of us." She laughed again, then raised her glass in a self-congratulatory toast. "Anyway, here I am, one year and four months later."

"Where'd you go to law school?" he asked; realized he was interested, not just making safe conversation.

"Columbia. It was my first time in New York. I always thought I'd hate it. I was raised outside Philadelphia near New Hope—just a little country bumpkin—and the idea of the city didn't really appeal to me at all. But that's where the law school I wanted was. So . . ."

"I've been to New Hope," Fallon said. "It isn't exactly East Jesus."

"It isn't Fifth Avenue, either."

He inclined his head in surrender. "And did the country bumpkin like New York?"

She laughed. "I loved it. Right from the beginning, and still do. Now I'm big city through and through. You'd have to drag me kicking and screaming away from here." She laughed again. "Although I don't think I'd like to practice *real* law here. Have you ever seen the courts in this city?"

"No. Bad?"

"We used to go there as students, just to observe. They should move them all up to the Bronx Zoo."

They were both laughing now, and Fallon realized he was truly enjoying himself.

"You just said that would be practicing *real* law, like what you do *isn't* real law."

"I know." She smiled at him again, but this time there was a touch of impishness in it. "I shouldn't say it, but it's how I feel most of the time." She brushed a strand of hair behind her ear, and Fallon thought the gesture made her look suddenly younger than she was. "In law school, the students who really cared about it all—and there weren't many of us—most of them were there because they thought they could make big bucks, or use it as a stepping-stone into politics. Anyway, the *real* students—well, I think they envisioned themselves standing in court and fighting for some principle, maybe once in a while even defending someone who was actually innocent. . . ." She stopped, as if her own words had shocked her. "Sometimes I'm not sure there *is* such a thing as an innocent person. But that's just from living in New York. It's not the mental picture I had back in law school, and I suppose, to some degree—way back in my head—that picture is still there. And that's why I refer to it as *real* law, as opposed to what I'm doing, which most of the time seems like furthering executive fantasies, or covering up their blunders."

Fallon inclined his head, indicating agreement. "Somebody's got to do it," he said. "And it pays well. Besides, I thought *all* lawyers wanted to make big bucks."

Samantha laughed again. "They do. Well, almost all. I sure did. I grew up without any. Then a maiden aunt died and left me some. Enough for law school, and a bit left over. What you guys call fuck-you money. So, maybe, back in law school, I could just afford to be altruistic."

Fallon raised his glass to that. "To altruism," he said. "And the ability to afford it."

Samantha felt mildly cheapened by the remark. It had sounded, to her, as though true altruism shouldn't be based merely on the ability to do something without risk. But she didn't think he had intended it that way—as an insult. Perhaps it was only her own sense of professional loss shining through.

Still, she felt defensive. She stared at him for a moment. "Don't get me wrong, Jack. I graduated from law school full of ambition. And it's still very much there."

Fallon recognized he had somehow blundered. He raised his glass again. "To ambition," he said. "An affliction we all suffer from."

Samantha felt only partly mollified. "So tell me how *you* came to the company," she said, pushing past it.

"Me? That's a simple story. Charlie Waters talked me into it at a party we were both at. About a hundred years ago."

"Waters himself?" she said, raising an eyebrow. "Impressive."

Fallon smiled, as if the idea of being impressive was comical. "Not really. Not back then, anyway," he said. "Certainly not to me. And, I'm sure, not to Charlie, either." He leaned forward, still smiling at the memory of it. "Charlie was just starting out in those days; trying to peddle the concept for his new aeronautical cable, and he didn't have the proverbial pot. He was really scratching, and he was looking for someone—anyone—to scratch with him. But he was a helluva salesman back then. It was 1974, and I'd just gotten my engineering degree and been offered a pretty good job with Eastman Kodak. Charlie couldn't come close to the salary I'd been offered, but he promised me a small chunk of stock when the company went public and convinced me I'd be part of building something from the ground up; that I'd work at a level I wouldn't reach for years with anyone else. That, together with Charlie's unbridled enthusiasm, sold me on the idea of throwing in with him."

Fallon stared at his drink. "A few years back Kodak went through a brutal downsizing. It was a bloodbath, and I remember feeling lucky I had made that decision. Now, if the rumors I keep hearing are true, it looks like the downsizing mania is following me anyway."

Samantha twisted nervously in her chair, then forced a smile, as though what he had said had gone past her. "So you've been with him from the start. You're friends."

"I've been there from the start," Fallon said. "I wouldn't say we're friends." He paused and considered it. "We were, I guess. Back then. There were a lot of evenings spent plotting company strategy over a few beers. A lot of time spent talking about our personal problems, our private hopes. But the company has grown so much, gone in so many different directions." He offered a wistful smile. "And Charlie has gone with it. I don't think we've spoken more than a dozen private, personal words in the last eight or nine years."

Samantha stared at him, tried to gauge his reaction to what he had just said. "You sound sad about that," she said at length.

Fallon thought about that, wondered if it was true. "I don't know," he said. "I guess I'm sad for him."

"Why?" she asked, surprised again. "I mean he's certainly prospered."

"He sure as hell has. And he's deserved to. He worked his tail off in those early years."

"Then why feel sad for him?"

"I guess because he's lost touch with things that used to matter. Especially the people who work here, and who really care about this company." He considered what he was about to say. "I never put it in words before. But it's very different now. . . ." He hesitated, looked past her, as if trying to see his own thoughts. "Now it's just about the money that's there to be made, not at all about the people who make it happen." He shook his head, as if dismissing what he had just said. "But I guess we did it—did what we started out to do, built a new company, and now the people are irrelevant and making money is the only thing that's left. For Charlie, anyway." He stared at her, all the smiles gone now. "But back when we started, it was fun, too. It was *our* company, not something that just belonged to the board and the stockholders and the people who managed it for them. Everyone mattered and everyone cared. When we succeeded we were excited and proud of ourselves, proud of *our* company. When we hit a rough spot it hurt us—as if something bad had happened to a member of our family." He stared at her, hoping she could understand. "It's what the company felt like to us, and we fought and scratched to overcome anything adverse that was thrown in its path." He forced another small laugh. It was weak and ineffective this time, and directed more at himself, Samantha thought. "Now, I guess it's not a *real* job anymore," he said, using her own words. "Now it's just something we all do to make a living."

"Perhaps the company's just gotten too big to be what it was," she offered.

"Maybe. But I'll tell you a secret. The people who work for it haven't changed. They still want to feel the same way . . . if we'll let them."

She was watching him. There seemed a touch of sadness in her eyes, and he felt a sudden need to explain himself further.

"You see, it's the company who's telling them they're not important, at least not as far as the future is concerned. Everyone is being told they're only temporarily relevant, that they're really only part of the short term. Now only money is part of the long term. As much money as the company can get its hands on." He watched her watching him and smiled. "You think I'm naive, don't you?"

"Maybe a bit. It's the way things are, Jack. It's the nineties, and you can't change it, and neither can anyone else."

He smiled at her. "You never know unless you try," he said. He drew a long breath. He realized the thought he had just expressed was one his father had uttered many years ago. He'd been a teenager, thoughtlessly accepting the values of his peers. His father had urged him to set his own, and to set them higher than those of the herd, or he'd be doomed to be nothing more than a part of that herd. The idea had impressed him, perhaps more than even he knew. He also realized he liked the comparison of himself to his dad. Whether he was worthy of it was another question.

"Anyway," he continued. "I guess I'm sad Charlie hasn't taken the chance and stuck to the values he started out with." He smiled at himself again. "Except, maybe he has. Maybe money was what he was always about. I'm just not certain anymore."

Samantha continued to stare at him. "You're a romantic, Jack Fallon." But it's a very old-fashioned romanticism, she thought. She covered the observation with a warm smile. She wondered if, deep down, she admired what he had said, or thought him a fool. She hoped not, but she wasn't sure. She knew she found him attractive. She reached across the table, took his hand, and squeezed it lightly. "I'm glad we had a chance to talk," she said.

"Me, too," Fallon said. He forced another smile, as if trying to dismiss all the melancholy he had dropped on her. "Who knows?" he said. "Maybe if you start practicing *real* law, I'll hire you to handle my divorce."

"You're on," Samantha said.

4

FALLON TURNED INTO THE LONG, WIDE HALLWAY THAT
held the executive offices. Here, and only here, the corporate headquarters of Waters Cable still retained the
gracious splendor the Chrysler Building had offered
when it first opened its doors in 1930. He recalled his
conversation with Samantha the previous evening;
thought about the day he and Charlie Waters had first
walked into this cathedral of American business where
they had set up their offices; how in awe they'd been
with the art deco wall sconces, the thick carpeting, and
spacious office suites; the step they were taking away
from that first run-down plant in New Jersey; the feeling
they both had that their company had finally arrived.

Some of that graciousness had been lost, of course,
if not on this floor, then on others. Fallon had just
come from the floor below, where most of the sales
force was located. There, as in most other parts of their
offices, work areas had been chopped up with movable
partitions that could be easily altered as the need arose.
And over the past ten years those needs had arisen con-
stantly as the company had grown. Now none of it, not
even that sense of graciousness he and Charlie had
been so taken with, seemed to remain. And not here,

either, he told himself. *This* floor has changed, too. It's just harder to see.

Les Gavin entered Fallon's office at nine-fifteen and dropped into one of the two leather chairs that sat in front of Fallon's oversized mahogany desk. Fallon studied him, realized again how much he despised the comfortable attitude the man showed toward his office. Normally he liked to be informal with a member of his staff, but with Gavin it was always as though the man was sizing up his chair, deciding what color he'd like the office repainted. He found it a disturbing image, as he watched Gavin open a folder in his lap, shake his head, and begin.

"I'm afraid the updated sales figures you asked for aren't any better than the preliminaries you took home over the weekend." Gavin's tone was laced with regret, but Fallon thought he could detect an undertone of pleasure.

Fallon remained seated, extended his hand, then waited as Gavin rose from the chair and handed the folder across the desk. He was tall and slight, thirty-three years old, and had been foisted on Fallon by more senior managers a year earlier. He had been brought in from another company to fill a previously nonexistent position; one created ostensibly to help ease Fallon's workload. Fallon had disliked the man from the outset—from the top of his blond head right down to his very hip tasseled loafers. He knew Gavin had no loyalty to him as his boss, regularly went behind his back, and fully intended—perhaps with assurances from above—to fill Fallon's chair in the not too distant future. So, making him stand to hand over the folder gave Fallon undiluted, if petty, pleasure.

Fallon quickly studied the figures, inclined his head grudgingly, and stared across the desk. "You sure of these figures, Lester?" he asked. Gavin hated to be called

Lester—his proper given name—preferring the more upbeat Les. Calling him Lester was another small satisfaction in which Fallon indulged himself.

"They're fresh out of the computer. It's as accurate an update as we can get right now," Gavin said. He rearranged his angular body in his chair—but Fallon wondered if it was a sign of discomfort, or if he was squirming with delight.

"I think there are several scenarios we can play to explain it away," Gavin continued. "I mean if we have to . . . if the boys down the hall get hard-assed about it."

This should be good, Fallon thought. Gavin's ideas on how Fallon should explain the recent failures of his division. It was almost worth listening to, just for the pathetic comedy of it. He continued to stare across the desk. The thing he despised most about Gavin, Fallon decided, was his phony show of personal loyalty.

"How about we just tell them the truth?" Fallon suggested. "That we're getting our asses kicked in a market we're not ready to go after?"

Gavin seemed momentarily shocked, then recovered and shook his head. "Jesus, I'd love to, Jack. I'd love to personally deliver that message. But it would be like begging them to boot our butts right out the door, don't you think?"

"You afraid they're going to fire you, Lester?" Fallon smiled across the desk, his face empty of any emotion. He, too, shook his head, in imitation of Gavin. "Don't you think they'd just fire me?"

"Well, I'd go with you, then," Gavin said. "I'd have to."

Fallon grinned at him. Gavin's demeanor was so serious, the words so sincere. He wanted to laugh in the man's face, but there really wasn't anything funny about it. "Don't fall on your sword too quickly, Lester," he said instead. "Hell, they might even ask you to replace me. You never know."

Gavin shook his head again, vehemently this time. Again, he seemed shocked, incapable of considering the notion that he could fill Fallon's shoes. It was enough to make you puke, Fallon thought.

"I could never do that, Jack." Gavin paused, drawing himself up. "I mean, even if they offered it—which, of course, they wouldn't. I mean, after all, Jack, I've backed all of your decisions." He hesitated, just an instant. "Well, almost all of them, anyway."

"Which one didn't you back, Lester?" Fallon suddenly decided he should enjoy this little game—deviousness played as comedy.

Gavin twisted in his chair again. His thin features fought to mask momentary confusion, but recovered quickly. Fallon decided the man was good at what he was—a born, backstabbing little shit.

Gavin rushed into an explanation. "It's not that I didn't back a decision, Jack." He paused just a beat. "It's just that maybe I didn't always fully agree." He tried to smile the words away. "But perhaps I just didn't have enough information." A small shrug. "But, Wally Green, for example. I didn't fully agree when you had a chance to replace him last year, and chose not to. But, hell, I was the new kid on the block, and I decided you knew what you were doing and backed you completely. Once the decision was made, that is."

Fallon had been reading the updated sales reports as he listened to Lester's little tap dance. He glanced up now. He wanted to catch the look of angelic sincerity he expected to find on the man's smooth, preppy face. It was there. He smiled across the desk again and thought back to the little corporate game to which Lester alluded. Fallon had fought that plan, and Wally had remained in his job, had never even known about the demotion they had wanted to force down his throat. And the Gavin clone they had chosen to replace him as New York district sales manager had, instead, been shifted to a job in marketing. Unfortunately, Fallon hadn't had the sense to resist having Gavin imposed on him. Now he had an assistant VP who undoubtedly carried tales back to his mentor, Carter Bennett, as they both patiently plotted his extinction.

"Your support has always been a strength to me, Lester," Fallon said. He watched Gavin blink, wondered if his sarcasm ever made it through the icy shell that surrounded the man. He went back to the sales reports convinced it never did. They must have a special course in obtuseness at Princeton, he decided. He tapped a finger against the reports. "I'll go over these and get back to you if I need anything else," he said. He heard Gavin rise and start for the door, listened to him mumble some acknowledgment that he really didn't hear, and wondered how many minutes would pass before Gavin reported in to Carter Bennett's office.

Fallon leaned back in his chair and decided it really didn't matter. He had more pleasurable things to contemplate. On the train, coming to work that morning, he had decided to ask Samantha Moore to have dinner with him. That he had the courage to even consider it amazed him. That she had accepted, when he had telephoned her office, amazed him even more. She had even seemed pleased—truly pleased that he had asked her. He shook his head. Amazing. A small, satisfied grin edged the corners of his mouth. The idea of it all made him feel ten years younger, and he decided he very much liked the feeling.

The Dinosaur Club held its first meeting that afternoon in a private tatami room at a Japanese restaurant four blocks from the office.

It wasn't an authentic Japanese room—not like the ones Fallon had visited on R&R during his two tours in Vietnam. In those rooms diners had been seated on the floor, their legs folded beneath them. Here the floor had been elevated to create a well beneath the low table, a design that accommodated long Western legs ill-suited to the yogalike sitting posture of Japanese custom. Fallon was grateful for it. He doubted his fellow dinosaurs could handle extended contortions.

Still, Wally Green groused. As the others were being seated, he pulled Fallon back, leaned in close, and hissed in his ear, "Hey, Jack, nice place. I guess nobody told you sushi is passé. Or is this part of the downsizing plan? We all die of terminal leg cramp and fish-borne parasites?"

Fallon cupped a hand over Wally's ear and whispered back. "Janice recommended the place. She told me all the Rolls-Royce guys hang out here."

Wally had contacted the other likely targets in their department, had arranged for them all to meet, then had left it to Fallon to choose the time and place. Fallon had selected this restaurant because it had a private room in which they could talk, and had chosen lunch to make it appear like an impromptu sales meeting. He also intended to pick up the check and then put it on his expense account. The idea of making the company pay for their plotting pleased him.

Fallon glanced around the room, and thought of similar rooms he had visited after deadly weeks in the Vietnamese jungles. The army had used Japan as a rest and recuperation area, a place to bring people back; briefly restore some sanity to their lives. Then, of course, it sent them out for another dose of madness. This room offered the same simplicity as those others he had known, the same clean lines, the same sense of heart-easing quiet; even the decorative fans placed along the walls brought back memories. Now he wondered if he had somehow chosen the restaurant for that reason—and if he, too, was offering some temporary respite before sending everyone back to fears they couldn't escape.

As they sat across from each other now, Fallon realized what a curious group they were—a mix of sales and sales management—all approximately the same age, all hovering around or just past fifty; each with a similar lifestyle, similar problems: kids in school, large mortgages, too many bills to pay, all the time-honored trappings of middle-class success. And, now, each one terrified it was going to end; all of them looking to him for salvation.

"So what's the picture as you see it, Jack?" It was Ben Constantini, a short, squarely built man, who had joined the company after putting in twenty years in the army. Constantini, Fallon knew, had once flown helicopters, had risen to the rank of chief warrant officer, then had spent his last five years at the Pentagon working in military procurement until Waters Cable had lured him away. At fifty-five, he was the oldest of the group but had the least seniority. With sixteen years in, he was four years away from a full company pension, and Fallon knew he was terrified.

Fallon momentarily lowered his eyes. "I'm not going to dance around it," he began. "I think they want us all gone—all of you, and me—everyone in our age group, no matter how well or how poorly we've performed recently." Fallon allowed the shock of his words to settle in. He realized he had to soften them to some degree; make them less personal. "But it's not just us. I'm sure they'll hit other departments, not only sales." He raised his hands, let them drop back to the table. "What I don't know is who'll be first, or if they'll hit everyone at once."

"Wait a minute. Wait a minute." It was Jim Malloy, who headed up the Washington sales group for which Constantini worked. He was a tall, rawboned Irishman, with a shock of red hair, and a florid face that always made him seem on the verge of a stroke. Six years ago Fallon had recognized him as a chronic alcoholic and,

despite the man's abilities, had given him a choice:
clean up your act, or hit the bricks. Malloy had heeded
the warning and had joined Alcoholics Anonymous. To
Fallon's knowledge he hadn't touched a drink since.

"Look, I know that everybody's into this downsizing
crap," Malloy continued. "But what you're talking about
would be suicidal for this company. Especially now.
Without experienced people sales would take a nose-
dive. Everything would. They have to know that."

Malloy's color had deepened, the clusters of burst
capillaries that filled his cheeks turning a rosy red.
Fallon eyed the glass of sparkling water that sat before
the man and wondered if Carter Bennett's little plan
would soon drive him back to bourbon instead.

"I don't think that matters, Jim. We're not talking
about productivity. It's not a question of whether our
sales are up or down."

Fallon was greeted with stony silence, which was
what he wanted. It was time for sobering reality.

"Then what the hell *are* we talking about?" Malloy
finally asked.

Fallon offered a wry smile; wondered if he really
knew the answer. "I can only tell you what I think, Jim.
Look, the people who are making this decision know
sales will drop even further if they bounce their most
experienced people. And they know it will take time to
build it back up again. But it will go back up. And in
the meantime, they'll have cut some large salaries. In
the long term they'll be way ahead. And that's what matters to them. It's pure bottom line, simple profitability
that we're talking about."

"You almost sound as if you agree with them." It was
Annie Schwartz this time, and she was eyeing Fallon
with a mix of confusion and suspicion. Annie covered
New England for Wally Green, part of what Wally
called his *Jewish army*. Born with an acid tongue, Annie
fought a constant but successful battle with her weight.

She was an attractive midde-aged woman, with soft features and bright red hair, and there was a definite aura of sex appeal about her, which she used unabashedly when wining and dining corporate clients.

"Look, I just came back from a vacation. So now you're telling me I spent a fortune this past week on body slimmers, hair dye, body waxing, and every cosmetic treatment known to man, and these schmucks are gonna dump me because I'm *too old?*"

"You should invest in Valium, instead," Wally suggested.

Annie glared at him. Then she spread her arms so everyone could take in the new her. "They fire these gorgeous, middle-aged buns, I'll need something a lot stronger than Valium," she snapped.

Fallon smiled across the table. He knew the life Annie faced at home. She had a husband who had suffered a serious coronary and was no longer able to work. She had two daughters in their mid-twenties, still living in the family nest. She had once told Fallon that going on the road was the only thing that maintained her sanity. "Understanding their argument, and agreeing with it, are two different things, Annie. And, for us, it's also moot." He paused a beat; forced the smile again. "Me? I think Carter Bennett's downsizing plan stinks. But that doesn't change the fact that he's pushing it." He paused again for effect. "Or that Charlie Waters seems to have bought into it." Fallon drummed his fingers on the table. "How they're going to do it is the question. Whether we can fight them off, or just make them pay for the privilege of canning us, is another."

"So you think it's a done deal?"

Fallon turned to Joe Hartman, another of Wally's men. Did he think that? He had denied even the idea of it for so long now. Rumors of Bennett's plan had begun circulating at his level of management almost a year ago, and Fallon had dismissed them as the plottings of a young Turk who had been named chief financial officer and was flexing his newly acquired muscle. Then, only two months ago, Charlie Waters had dropped the other shoe. It had happened at the company's annual golf outing, or rather at the dinner that had followed it. They had all gathered in the country club dining room and Waters had given his little speech. He had talked about the company's past, and the new directions it must now take if it was to continue to prosper and grow, and he had taken time to praise the old hands, as he had called them, for bringing the company so far. Then the tone had changed, as Waters singled out the new "young fighter pilots on our team," as he pointedly proclaimed them the future of the company to whom the baton would soon be passed. The message had been clear and cutting, and Fallon could still remember the look on Carter Bennett's face. He had sat there at Waters's right hand, looking like a puffed-up bantam rooster that had just killed off a rival and now had the chicken coop all to itself.

"Yeah, I think it's a fait accompli," Fallon said. He stared at Joe Hartman, raised his hands, then let them fall back to the table. "There's no sense kidding ourselves, Joe. It's probably six months off, but it's going to happen." He watched Hartman's eyes flicker with fear, then harden. He was, perhaps, in the worst predicament of them all. Having already raised three daughters, he had divorced, remarried, and now had two young sons who had just started school, together with an older stepson who in a few short years would have his eyes on college. He was also faced with the first major financial insecurity of his adult life, and Fallon could see him beginning to wilt with the pressure. Now his square face sagged just a bit, and his blocky body seemed somewhat smaller in his pin-striped suit. Hartman had switched companies ten years ago when he had switched wives, and like Constantini, he was short on time and would lose the bulk of the pension money he had counted on if pushed out early. What he wasn't short of—like all the others—was the debts and obligations accumulated by men who had expected their livelihoods to continue, and who had based their retirements and their savings on the assumption that their jobs would remain secure until they hit their sixties.

"It's all Bennett's doing. The little Princeton prick is trying to make his bones by tossing us on the god-damned trash heap. I'd like to walk into his office and blow his goddamned brains out."

The anger seemed to erupt, to come out of nowhere. The vehemence, the pure, undiluted hatred made Fallon's head snap around. George Valasquez glared back at him, still seething with the words he had just spoken. "And why haven't you gone to Waters person-ally, Jack?" he snapped. "You're one of the few people he'd listen to. Christ, you've been with him right from the start."

Wally Green leaned forward and jabbed a finger at Valasquez. "Cool it, George," he ordered. "Jack's in the same boat as the rest of us. We start fighting among our-selves, we're not going to accomplish one damned thing."

Fallon raised his hands, asking both men for quiet. He thought, Maybe George was right. Maybe he *should* see Charlie. Lay it out for him. If nothing else, force him to acknowledge what he was doing to these peo-ple—people who had worked their tails off for a lot of years. He stared at George Valasquez. He was a short, thin, normally docile man, with prematurely white hair, who at fifty-two looked ten years older. Fallon studied his slender, hawk-nosed face. The usually soft brown eyes were blazing, and he suddenly had no doubt that George could do exactly what he had said. He wondered what else was going on in George's life. He had seen that look years ago in Vietnam, men who had been terrified to the point of irrationality, and who wanted to strike out wildly at the source of their fear.

"I'll go and see him, George. Actually, it's a good idea. And who knows?" He watched a glimmer of hope come to the man's eyes, and decided not to say anything that would drive it away. How could he explain that his old friend Charlie had all but ignored him for the better part of a decade? No, he'd see the man; talk to him, even if he had to grab him in the lobby. He owed these people that much effort.

Fallon leaned forward, resting his forearms on the table. "But let's also look at some contingencies," he said. Fallon noticed that George Valasquez wasn't listening. He was still hanging on to the proffered hope, allowing it to ease his personal terrors.

"Exactly what contingencies are you talking about?" Jim Malloy's red face stared across the table like a beacon.

"Bennett's contingencies," Fallon said. He watched confusion spread across their faces; satisfied himself they were all hooked, then continued, "I'm talking about the chances *we* might give him; make it easier for him to pull this off."

Wally Green turned to him. His face was fixed in a wide, confused grin. "Jack, what the hell are you talking about? You're starting to sound like my ex-wife's lawyer."

Annie grinned at him. "Pay the alimony, Wally. Janice put up with you for God knows how many years. She deserves every penny."

Wally threw her a mock glare and jabbed his thumb into his chest. "Hey, don't forget I'm your boss."

"*This* week," Annie said. "If you're still here next week, I'll bow down."

Fallon grinned at the banter, the sense of camaraderie that just might hold them together. "Look, I've been thinking about it," he said. "Or rather, trying to think about it the way I think Bennett would." He picked up a chopstick and began lightly tapping it against the table. "First, Bennett knows he's targeting one specific group—a specific age bracket—and he's doing it for one reason, and only one reason: to cut out some heavy salaries and benefit packages that he considers burdensome." Fallon waved the chopstick; he had everyone's attention. "But he knows this isn't completely kosher; he knows it could end up as a very messy fight, even as a class-action lawsuit that could cost the company some big bucks."

"Not to mention that it will make them look like a bunch of scumbags when it hits the newspapers." Wally added the observation with a self-satisfied smirk.

Fallon laughed at the joy it seemed to give him. He gestured at Wally with the chopstick. "You're right, Wally. But I don't think they care about that. I don't think the board of directors, who'll eventually have to okay Bennett's plan, will give a rat's ass about the public. They'll look at it and see that it's the same game a lot of other companies have played. Hell, AT&T laid off forty thousand, and the public didn't rush off to sign up with Sprint. And our guys will expect the public to look at this the same way and be damned happy it isn't happening where *they* work." He paused. "And you know what? They'll probably be right."

He watched Wally slowly deflate and immediately wished he had allowed him to enjoy his media fantasy for a while. "But I do think they'd like to avoid both a fight or a lawsuit," he added. "Not just because of the money. I think Bennett's factored that in; made it part of the overall equation and convinced everyone it still makes financial sense." Fallon looked at each of them. "But why risk it if you don't have to?" he continued. "Or, at least, why not limit the number of people involved?"

"I still don't understand, Jack." It was Ben

Constantini this time. He was leaning across the table, his whole body seeming to ask the question.

"What I mean, Ben, is that if I were Bennett, the first thing I'd try to do is force as many of us out as possible. Just make life so miserable that some of us— maybe even a lot of us—would just pack up and leave." He held up his hands, holding off any comments. "Now this can do a lot of things for Bennett. First, if they go to court and lose, it can cut down the cost of any judgment. Just by cutting down the number of people. It might even avoid a lawsuit altogether if enough people pack up and quit." Fallon waited again, allowing his initial points to sink in. "And it can also save them money in other ways."

"How?" George Valasquez asked. He was back with them now, and the anger had returned to his eyes.

Fallon turned to him. "When companies do this type of thing, George, they like to mask it as voluntary retirements, right?" He smiled at the phrase, watched George nod in agreement. "In corporate terms, that means you put a financial gun to someone's head, then show them a fistful of money and ask them which they'd rather have. It's called a buyout. Sort of a corporate term for extortion." He smiled again; waited again. "It's usually a nice-sized fistful that's based on the number of years of individual service. But you have to offer it only to the people you haven't driven off first. Anybody who's left voluntarily, well, they're just screwed."

"And you think Bennett plans to screw as many of us as possible," Wally said.

Fallon turned to him; raised his eyebrows. "You know Carter, Wally. And you've seen him operate. What do you think he'll do?"

Wally shook his head, the heavy jowls waving under his chin. Then he spread his arms, clearing an imaginary spot on the table. "I'd like to lay the bastard out right here. Do a goddamned sex change on him."

"You'd have to find his little wee-wee first," Annie snapped.

"You get him and I'll hold him down," Fallon said. "Then the two of you can look for it." He laughed as Annie wrinkled her nose in disgust. He shook his head, then waved his hand, as if driving off their combined insanity. "But the point is, we *don't* let that happen. No matter who they single out, no matter what they pull, we recognize it for what it is, and we sit tight." He looked at each of them again. "Can we agree on that?" He waited; watched everyone nod; could almost hear the gulps in each of their throats.

Fallon leaned into the table, as if trying to weld them together. "There're some other things we can do, too. First, we can really start watching our backs. You all know what a snakepit an office can be, especially when someone is considered vulnerable. People start taking credit for other people's work, or they come in on Saturdays so they can read someone's mail, or maybe steal a crucial memo or two. They even start rumors to denigrate someone's job performance. It's a whole bag of tricks, and at some point we've all seen them used. But when people in upper management start doing it, it can be done a lot more effectively, and with a lot more power."

"So how do you stop it?" It was Joe Hartman, looking even more frightened now.

"You don't stop it," Fallon said. "You expect it to happen, you protect yourself against it, and you use it."

"How?" Jim Malloy asked.

"We've got to turn it back on them. First, we've got to make them think there's more organized resistance to their plan than there is. And that it's broad-based. We've got to make them believe the price is going to be very high if they try to pull this off. Maybe even too high.

"Look, we can start our own little false-rumor department. We can even start sending out phony memos, maybe even a one- or two-page newsletter. We can start leaving things around that we know Carter and his minions will pick up on. But not just in our own offices. In other people's offices, too. Especially people Carter would expect to be on his side. In the military they call this kind of thing psyops."

Fallon placed on the table a small bag he had brought with him. Early that morning he had gone into his basement and rummaged through some old boxes of childhood toys. Back when his son, Mike, had been four or five, he had become dinosaur crazy, and had begun collecting plastic models. For almost a year he and his son had spent countless hours playing with them; even bringing books home from the library so they could identify the various types.

Fallon dumped the plastic toys out. "Pick one," he said. "Keep them on your desks for Carter's spies to find. Hell, put some on other people's desks."

Joe Hartman snorted. "Maybe I'll mail one to Charlie Waters. One with a noose around its neck."

Ben Constantini nodded. "Couldn't hurt."

"Hell, forget the dinosaur. Put the noose around Charlie's neck," Jim Malloy added.

"And Bennett's," George Valasquez chimed in.

"The important thing is that we keep them off-balance," Fallon said. "Keep them wondering what's really going on. And that we keep track of what they're up to."

Annie let out a low chuckle. "I know one way to do that." She glanced at each of them. "Did you guys know that early in the mornings—before everything gets too chaotic—if you put your ear *real* close to certain heating ducts you can hear conversations in some of the executive offices?" Now she grinned at each of them in turn. "The women's john on the twenty-ninth floor has especially good reception."

Fallon stared at her, then at Wally. "Remind me to block off my heating duct the next time we do personnel evaluations," he said.

"Speaking of personnel, I heard something interesting today," Annie added. She gave Fallon another grin. "But I heard it through the all-girl grapevine, not the heating duct. According to my information, our legal department asked human resources for a breakdown of employees based on their ages."

"What are you talking about?" Fallon asked.

"There's this woman who works there—Miriam Silver. A few years back she was running that intern program we were involved in, and she and I became friendly. This morning I ran into her in the hall, and she told me that legal was asking for a breakdown of employees by age groups. She overheard her boss talking about it, and when she asked him later, he claimed it was for some demographic study, but Miriam thinks that's a lot of B.S. She's fifty, and she's scared witless about losing her job. But what really ticked her off was that it was another woman asking for it."

Fallon stiffened slightly. "Which one? Did she say?"

"Samantha somebody. Miriam didn't know her last name. She only said she was 'some cutsie-putsie named Samantha.'"

Fallon felt stunned, then angry. He realized Annie was still talking to him, and he hadn't heard what she had said.

"I'm sorry," he said. "I didn't hear you."

Annie was grinning at him. "I said, so what about other departments? Manufacturing, whatever? Do we try to bring them in on this plan of ours?"

Fallon pushed away what he had just heard and struggled to refocus. "That'll be harder," he said. "We may not even hear what's going on there. That's where the company has an edge. They've already got us divided, and most of us don't even know people in other departments that well. But we can try. Get the word out as best we can. If we start putting out a phony newsletter we can send it by E-mail; send it to the plants and the other offices. The important thing is that *we* stick together. Our division. Sales. If we can add anyone else, great." He looked around the table. "But we can't trust anyone else. Maybe it will snowball all by itself if people in other divisions see what we're doing. But the important thing"—he waved his hand again, taking in the group—"is that the seven of us stick together and run our own tight little show; watch Carter Bennett's little maneuvers and fight the sonofabitch in whatever way we can."

"Maybe we should skip all the bullshit and just shoot the sonofabitch right between the eyes."

It was George Valasquez again. Fallon stared at the man, saw the uncontrolled rage that had reasserted itself, and again realized just how close to the edge George really stood. He felt his stomach tighten, and he suddenly wished Carter Bennett could see George's face, and understand what it meant. He wished his old friend Charlie Waters could see it, too. And Samantha Moore. See just what their little plan had wrought.

Wally Green slumped into the chair that Les Gavin had occupied earlier that day. He had closed the door to Fallon's office.

"So tell me, Jack. You think we have a shot at beating this little prick Bennett?"

Fallon leaned back in his leather executive chair. "Depends on what you mean, Wally. You mean stop his plan, keep him from getting rid of us? No, I don't think we can beat him that way." He saw an almost imperceptible sag come over Wally's face, and hurried on. "But if you mean we get everything out of it we possibly can, then, yeah, I think we can do that. And I think we will."

The answer didn't seem to hit the way Fallon had hoped it would. He leaned forward, intertwined his fingers. "Look, Wally, have you ever seen a prizefight where one of the fighters was really outclassed, just didn't have the tools to win, but still wouldn't go down? Just wouldn't quit?" He watched Wally nod his head. "Okay. So in the end, what happened? The stronger fighter, he got to raise his hand and hear all his fans cheering for him. But when he did, he also felt all the hurt the other guy had laid on him." He smiled across the desk. "Well, that's us, Wally. You have to face reality. We're outclassed in this fight. But if we stick together and fight back, then we're going to lay a lot of hurt on Carter Bennett. And then we're going to walk away with our prize money."

"Yeah, but it's gonna be the loser's share of the gate, isn't it?"

Fallon inclined his head in a modified shrug. "Sometimes you have to take what you can get, Wally." He smiled again. "Then walk away. How do they say it? Bloody but unbowed?"

Wally imitated Fallon's gesture, inclined his own head as if saying: Yeah, okay. Then his face broke into a grin. "Hey, maybe it won't come to that," he said. "Maybe Georgie Valasquez will shoot the sonofabitch first."

Fallon blew out a breath. "You know, he scares me a little bit. He reminds me of guys I saw in Nam. What's going on with him? I know he doesn't have any kids, but he seems even more shook up than the rest of us."

Wally wrinkled up his nose. "The poor bastard just found out his wife has cancer. He's probably scared shitless that he'll lose his medical benefits along with his job."

"Jesus, I didn't know. And damn it, I should have."

Wally shook his head. "He just found out, Jack. Look, don't worry about Georgie doing anything crazy. It's just Spanish machismo. All that hot blood, that's all. That, and all the other crap he's got coming down right now."

"You may think it's machismo," Fallon said. "But I've

seen that look before. I'm about ready to refer George to a shrink who wrote me today."

Wally raised his eyebrows. "How come you're getting letters from shrinks?"

Fallon glanced at the letter that lay on his desk. It had arrived that morning, written by the therapist Trisha had been seeing. It was solicitous and—he was sure—well meaning. But it had angered him on first reading. Then it had made him laugh out loud.

"It seems to have been Trish's idea. The shrink is her therapist. Apparently my soon-to-be ex-wife expressed concern about my mental health. She seems to think the breakup of our marriage will leave me at loose ends and feeling unfulfilled. Her therapist is offering to recommend someone I can go to for counseling."

"Jesus Christ," Wally said. "Janice never offered to send me to a shrink. And she thought I was as crazy as a bedbug."

Fallon grinned. "Are you feeling unfulfilled?"

"The last time I felt unfulfilled was when I was *married* to Janice." Wally's face suddenly brightened. "Hey, speaking of unfulfilled, you remember that woman from the other night? The one sitting down the bar from us at Café des Artistes?"

"Yeah, I remember," Fallon said. He sat back in his chair, awaiting Wally's story, George Valasquez and Samantha Moore almost forgotten.

Wally rolled his eyes. "What a fiasco. You sure made the right move when you left."

Fallon started to laugh. "Tell me," he said.

Wally glanced over his shoulder, as if someone might be listening, then leaned farther forward, lowered his voice another notch. "Well, after you leave, I figure: What the hell, and I go up to her, okay? And, right away, I put on my best moves."

Fallon imagined Wally's best moves and fought off a smile.

Wally began rolling his hands and shoulders in a circular motion. "Well, we're getting along great. I tell her all about myself; the divorce, everything. She tells me all about herself. Same goddamned story, you know? Then I'm schmoozing, she's laughing, so I decide it's time to turn this conversation to the *real* subject. So I tell her about this special set of exercises I do every morning: how I do pushups with my goddamned *tongue*. And I think I see this little light come into her eyes, and I figure, right then and there, that old Wally is about to get his dicky dipped. I figure, screw my ex-wife; screw her car salesman boyfriend; screw the Rolls-Royce I keep telling myself she wants to buy—old Wally is about to get laid."

Fallon leaned his head back and started to laugh. "So what happened?" he finally asked.

"What happened? What happened? I'll tell you what happened. The woman turns out to be the queen of barracudas, that's what happened." He shook his head, pushed himself forward even more, his protruding paunch almost touching his thighs. "This lunatic, she reaches over and pinches my cheek, then gives me that quote from *Macbeth*—the one about booze lighting the fire of lust but not fueling performance. Then she picks up her drink and pours it over my head."

5

THE REALITY OF WHAT SHE WAS READING HIT HOME, AND
Samantha Moore looked at her notes with a sinking feeling she could not seem to shake. Carter had used the
Chase/Chemical Bank buyout as the model for his own
proposal. It called for a flat payment of three weeks'
salary for each year of service, an additional twenty-six
weeks for those employed twenty years or more, and a
twenty-five-hundred-dollar flat grant toward retraining
for a new job. She punched up the personnel records
she had been given access to on her computer screen,
then typed in the code for the sales division. She had
chosen it, in part, because of her interest in Jack Fallon,
but also because its employees carried some of the
higher salaries within the company. She scanned down
the list, stopping at Wally Green.

As New York district manager, Green earned a base
salary of seventy-eight thousand dollars, plus a yearly
bonus based on his district's overall sales performance.
In recent years that had put him in a low six-figure
range. But bonuses were not factored into Carter's plan,
and Green—like most employees in this twenty-three-
year-old company—did not qualify for the additional
buyout for twenty or more years of service. Employees

who fell into the forty-five-to-sixty-year-old hit-list spectrum, she had found, had on average eighteen years with the company.

Samantha pulled a small calculator from her desk and punched in the numbers. That would mean the company could rid itself of Wally Green with a flat payment of sixty-seven thousand five hundred dollars. Even with the twenty-five-hundred-dollar retraining grant thrown in, that would still be eight thousand dollars short of his annual base income. She closed her eyes, tapped her fingers on the desk. Green, should he make Carter's list, also wouldn't be able to touch his vested pension until he reached age fifty-nine. The defined benefit package the company operated under limited the portability of those funds. It was a system most major corporations had opted to use, for the simple reason that it kept the maximum amount of money in their pension plans, which, if the plans performed well, lowered the amount those companies had to contribute. In short, Mr. Green would have his vested pension; he simply would not have access to it until it had served its maximum use for the company that had just put him out of work. And he would also have to start paying for his own health insurance unless he was lucky enough to find another job where it was offered.

She went back to the computer screen and pulled up Jack Fallon's file, then began punching numbers into her calculator. Fallon's base salary was one hundred and fifty thousand, with annual bonuses that had pushed it to around two and a quarter a year. He was also eligible for the additional twenty-year-service payment. Using Carter's buyout figures, Fallon would walk away with slightly less than three hundred thousand dollars—certainly much better than Wally Green, but a far cry from real retirement money. And, like Green, he would be unable to touch his pension for another ten years. She closed her eyes; thought of Fallon's upcoming divorce, which would probably cost him half of that settlement package. Then there was the continued expense of educating his children. No, she decided. He wouldn't be much better off than Wally Green. She kept her eyes closed and silently hoped the higher cost of pushing Fallon out the door might give Carter pause. She did some quick mental calculations. Assume they replaced Fallon with a younger man, whom they could probably hire at a base salary of one hundred thousand dollars. Then factor in lower benefit costs at about 30 percent, and it would mean they could supplant Jack Fallon at an annual savings of about sixty-five thousand dollars. She knew it would be the only figure Carter Bennett would consider.

She looked back to her own notes. Carter had asked her to calculate how many younger employees the company would have to *destaff*—his word—to avoid the perception of age discrimination. She had done that and had found a simple formula that would work. He had also asked her to itemize some added perks that would make the company appear generous to the courts. She had come up with psychological counseling, temporary off-site office space and secretarial assistance to help with letters and résumés, and a six-month extension of health benefits. It would be expensive, but not prohibitively so when compared to the cost of a losing court battle. And it might even serve to avoid litigation. But it was also a hoax, a blatant placebo, designed to obscure the human wreckage the plan would leave scattered in its wake. Wreckage like Jack Fallon.

Samantha sat back in her chair. Why was she fixating on this one man? They had had a drink together, nothing more. Had she been that attracted to him? And why, knowing what she knew, had she agreed to have dinner with him?

She shook her head. Face the facts. There is nothing you can do.

You could warn him. Give him a running start to

either fight it or find another job. The sound of that inner voice shocked her. The *company* was her client. And its stockholders. So how did professional ethics square with that misguided scenario?

The word seemed to stick in her throat as she repeated it aloud. "Ethics." And how do you apply that lofty word to what you're doing now—helping your client subvert the laws governing age discrimination?

She stiffened slightly and pushed the thought away, relegated it to its place of origin: law school debates among temporarily ardent students, who—diplomas in hand—would sacrifice both scruples and sense of culpability and move on to more important matters. She looked back at the computer screen and stared at Jack Fallon's name and tried not to think of the man. Just do your job, she told herself, and forget this byzantine twist you're trying to inject into your life.

Her intercom buzzed, and she pressed a button; listened to her assistant explain that a Mr. Fallon had just called to cancel their dinner engagement.

What was this? Telepathy? She felt a sudden rush of something she couldn't quite identify. Was it guilt? "Did he suggest another time?"

"I asked him about that," her assistant answered. "He just said, 'No, no other time.'"

She felt inexplicably hurt, and immediately dismissed it. "Very well. Thank you." She sat back in her chair. She had a sudden urge to go to Fallon's office. "What are you thinking?" she whispered to herself. She shook her head, surrendered hope of understanding her decision, then stood and walked out her door.

The door to Fallon's inner office was open, and Samantha could see him standing behind his desk, talking on the phone. His face seemed dark and angry, and she felt a momentary urge to turn and leave.

He put the phone down, looked up, and saw her

standing there. His features softened slightly; the anger replaced by what seemed to her curiosity tinged with suspicion. She stepped through the door.

"My assistant tells me you're standing me up," she said. She forced a smile as she stopped in front of his desk.

"I can't talk about it right now." He glanced back at his phone as if that somehow explained his words. "I just got a call from a neighbor. A half dozen movers are cleaning out my house. I have to get up there and toss their butts into the street."

"Oh, I'm sorry, Jack." She felt a sudden impulse and decided to follow it. Blindly? She pushed the thought away. "Look, why don't I go with you? I *am* a lawyer. Maybe I could help."

She was stunned by her own words and could see they had had the same effect on him. He hesitated, seemed to come to a decision. "Sure. But I have to leave now."

"Just let me call my assistant. She'll have to reschedule a meeting." She decided not to tell him the meeting was with Carter Bennett.

They rode the Metro North train, enduring great gaps of silence, as each tried to understand why they were making this trip together.

Fallon knew he was attracted to the woman; even strongly attracted would not have been an inaccurate description. But he also knew he couldn't trust her. Not after the bit of information he had picked up from Annie Schwartz. Her offer had taken him by surprise, but he had told himself that he could use the opportunity to pump her; to find out exactly what she was doing for Carter Bennett. It had been an impulsive decision, and he wondered about it now. But, what the hell. She *was* a lawyer, and maybe he could use her in any battle with the movers.

Throughout the train ride, whenever they did speak, he tried to keep the conversation light; to keep his suspicions hidden. He made small talk, pointed out various towns along the way, and explained what they did and did not offer to the commuter class who lived there.

Samantha, for her part, avoided any legal advice about the movers, explaining that it would be better to wait and see exactly what the situation was. To herself, she simply rationalized that she was helping someone she liked. She intentionally ignored the small voice in the back of her mind that also told her it would be a perfect opportunity to warn Jack Fallon about the dangers that lay ahead.

They left the train and made their way to Fallon's car in the Bedford Station parking lot. It was a year-old Mercury Marquis, the company's car of choice for executives whose jobs warranted one. Fallon continued to make small talk, but she thought it seemed strained, halfhearted. She told herself his mind was elsewhere—at his house, his home, where unknown men were carting his possessions away.

They drove through the center of the town. It was clean and ordered and suburban, not unlike New Hope where she had grown up; a bit less rural perhaps, but still very much a bedroom community—only one that served New York instead of Philadelphia. Her father had run a grocery store in New Hope, and he had known practically everyone. She had too. She had worked the cash register in the store after school and during the summers, although she had paid far less attention to their customers than he. She had not planned to remain. Even then she had a bigger future in mind.

They drove past a sizable town green with its obligatory Civil War cannon and bandstand. Surrounding it on all sides were a mix of churches—two Protestant and one Catholic, she noticed—a small shopping strip of apparently upscale shops, and some stately older homes, most of which had been converted into offices.

They turned off into a side road that took them into a strictly residential sprawl, most of the homes set on lots of a half acre or less, then gradually increasing in size as they moved farther out.

"Have you lived here long?" she asked.

"About twenty years," he said. "When I started at the company, Trish and I—that's my wife, Trish—we lived in a hole-in-the-wall apartment in the East Village." A small smile played across his lips. "Two rooms, each the size of a closet. With the bathtub in the kitchen. A big old monster with claw feet, that you could lie down in. We covered it with a piece of plywood and draped a cloth over it so nobody could tell it was there." He shook his head. "God, I loved that old tub. You could reach out, open the door to the fridge, and grab a beer while you were taking a bath." The smile remained, and he realized he still had fond memories of that apartment— East Fourth Street, only two blocks from the old Fillmore East Theater and its weekly rock concerts with the likes of Janis Joplin and Joe Cocker, and a few blocks more from NYU where he and Trish had gone to college.

The smile faded, and he glanced out the driver's window, as if looking away from the past, Samantha thought.

"Anyway, we moved up here in seventy-six after our first child was born. We got a small house in a development; told ourselves we had to have good schools, a safer place to live, a backyard, all the usual reasons. Then, about twelve years ago, when the company really took off and I started making decent money, we decided we needed a bigger house." He shrugged. "We did, I guess. So we started looking around—but still here. The kids were in school here; all their friends were here; all of that. So we bought the place we're in now, mortgaged ourselves to our ears." He glanced across at her, gave her a look that said: So what else is new? Then he went on. "I call it Toad Hall," he said. "It's just a lot more house than I ever wanted. Four bedrooms, three and a half baths, a family room, a study, a finished rec room in the basement. And all of it plunked down on three-quarters of an acre of very expensive, sickly lawn." He rolled his eyes. "Jack Fallon's baronial crabgrass emporium. The Lawn Doctor guy smiles every time he sees me coming."

"Still, it was a good investment. It must be worth a pretty penny today." She immediately regretted the remark—suddenly felt as though she was calculating the value of his home into his buyout agreement.

Fallon stared at her, almost as though the same thought had crossed his mind. His eyes seemed to have hardened imperceptibly before he turned back to watch the road. She told herself not to be ridiculous, then tried to cover her faux pas. "It sounds like everybody's dream," she said.

Fallon nodded, glanced out the side window again. "Yeah, I suppose it does. But for the last ten years I've wondered if that's all my life has been, just an accumulation of possessions." A small shake of his head. "Yeah, I know. I'm forty-nine years old. I hit the big five-oh next year, and maybe I'm just getting a sense of my own mortality." He smiled at himself. "But I can't help wondering what I'll see when I stop working in fifteen, sixteen years. Will I sit there and look back at some mountain of widgets I've sold, and say: That's it, that's what Jack Fallon did with his life?" Another smile. "It's not like I've composed music that people will still listen to. Oh, sure, I'll have helped raise two great kids, who I'm crazy about. But rightly or wrongly, they'll be off finding their own widgets to sell; getting all wrapped up in their own lives." He let out a breath that was almost a laugh. "Hell, they're already there, I guess. But what I mean is, what have I done for me? Over all that time? When I think about it the answer just flies past."

"Sounds like a baby boomer's midlife crisis," Samantha said.

Fallon laughed, genuinely this time. "Yeah," he said. "Classic. I suppose after the divorce I'll start dating cheerleaders."

They pulled into a winding road dominated by mature trees, each house a living advertisement for upscale garden centers, replete with a smattering of obligatory dogwoods and Japanese maples, an occasional magnolia, a weeping pine, clump birches, and enough azaleas to turn the road into a highway of shimmering pink each spring.

"Here we are in Executive Heaven," Fallon said. "Where lawn tractors duel weekly in the sun."

Halfway down the road, Fallon pulled into a blacktop drive that led to a Colonial house set back thirty yards from the road—traditional painted white brick, flaking prestigiously with hints of red showing through; dark gray shutters and gleaming brass carriage lamps on each side of the front entryway. There were flower beds and strategically placed shrubbery that spoke of professional landscaping, an attached two-car garage, and an arbor in the sideyard, covered with wisteria.

"Toad Hall," he said, as they pulled to a stop.

"It's lovely, Jack. And you've earned it," Samantha said.

"Yeah, I sure have," he replied. Samantha heard the sarcasm in his voice. "And where the hell are these movers?"

A neighbor strode across an adjacent lawn, an overweight woman, about forty-five, Samantha guessed, dressed in too-tight fawn slacks and a beige silk blouse. She had blond hair, obviously out of a bottle, and wore a full face of makeup thick enough to form a second skin.

"The truck left about half an hour after I spoke to you," she said, almost as though she had heard Fallon's question. She was still a full ten yards away from them when she spoke. She eyed Samantha with knowing suspicion, then prattled on. "I didn't know whether to call the police or not. When I asked them what they were doing, they said Trisha had sent them. That's when I called you. It just didn't make sense."

The woman looked at Samantha again, her eyes saying it made great sense to her now. Fallon seemed to catch the intent of her eyes, and made quick introductions. "Margot, this is Samantha Moore—from my office." He seemed to hesitate, as if more needed to be said, then gave up. "Samantha, this is my neighbor, Margot Reed." He turned back to the woman. "Margot, Trish and I are getting a divorce—at least I think we are." He shook his head. "No, we are. She's moved to Manhattan, and she told me she was sending some people out to pack a few things she wanted. I just didn't expect them this soon. And I certainly didn't expect the full-sized moving van you told me about."

Margot pursed her lips, threw another quick glance at Samantha. "Well, I think a few things turned into quite a bit, Jack. I was out on an appointment." She looked at Samantha—directly this time, and smiled. "I'm a Realtor," she said. Then back to Fallon. "Well, anyway, when I got home I saw the truck and came over. They'd obviously been here a while, Jack. The truck was almost full."

"What?" Fallon stared at her, incredulous.

"I don't think you're going to find a lot left in there, Jack," she said.

"Jesus Christ." Fallon let out a breath.

Margot eyed Samantha again, and the edges of her mouth inched upward. The words Wages of Sin seemed etched in her expression.

Fallon either didn't notice or chose to ignore it, and

Samantha offered a slightly ironic smile. Suburban bitch, she thought.

Fallon shook his head; stared around the yard, as if checking to be sure the lawn was still there. "Thanks, Margot," he said. "I'd better go inside and see what's left." He turned and started for the front door, but Margot's voice stopped him.

"Will the house be going on the market, Jack?" she asked.

He turned, looked at her, seemed confused, then shook his head again. "I don't know. I haven't gotten that far yet. If it does, I'll let you know."

"I'd appreciate it, Jack."

So much for heartfelt loss of a neighbor, Samantha thought. She upgraded her appraisal to bitch and a half.

Fallon led Samantha to the front door, took out a key, then stopped.

"You know, I thought about calling the cops when Margot called. Before that, I'd even thought about having the locks changed." He looked at her. "You think I should have done either?"

Samantha shrugged. "Six of one, half dozen of another," she said. "How's that for clichéd legal advice?" She tried a smile. "In the long run you'd have ended up in court, and equitable distribution is the rule in New York. But your wife probably would have gotten whatever furniture and things she wanted. Maybe she would have asked for the house, too. Her lawyer certainly would have advised it. And it would have cost you a chunk of money for your own lawyer." She arched her eyebrows. "I guess it depends on how much you want to fight."

"I don't want to fight at all," Fallon said. "I want . . ." He stopped, seemed to think about it. "I don't know what I want. I guess I just want it over. And I don't want to get screwed in the process." He looked at Samantha for a moment, as if deciding something. "And she wouldn't want the house," he finally said. "She moved into a condo in Manhattan. With her boyfriend, Howard."

Samantha fought a sense of surprise that Fallon's wife had left him for another man. She went on. "Her lawyer still would have told her to take the house, Jack. Even if she wasn't going to live here." Samantha raised her eyes, as if to say that's the way things were. "Your wife's lawyer is going to be a prick, Jack. Get used to that idea. You won't be disappointed."

Fallon stared at her, seemed to shudder inwardly. "Christ," he said. "I guess I better get a lawyer of my own," he said.

"Yes, you should," she said. "But also expect to walk away fifteen to twenty thousand dollars lighter if it turns into a fight. And that's for your lawyer. Double it for hers."

Fallon's eyes widened. "I have to pay for her lawyer, too?"

"Unless she's independently wealthy, or has a job earning big bucks, you probably will."

Fallon closed his eyes. "Christ," he said again.

When he opened the front door the vast emptiness hit Fallon like a hammer. To his right the large, rectangular living room was empty of everything but a single chair, a side table, and a lamp. He stepped into the room, stared through the wide arch that opened on to the dining room, and found himself with another barren view.

"Jesus," he said. "The dining room furniture was my mother's."

"Get a pad and pen and start making a list of everything that's missing," Samantha said. "Do it now, while it's fresh in your mind."

Fallon did as he was told. He felt an enormous sense of anger, mixed with bewilderment. He wasn't sure which was more disturbing; voted for the latter.

Pad and pen in hand, he stood in the center of the empty dining room, turned in a slow circle. "How the hell do you remember everything that was in a room, after it's been emptied?" he asked. "There were two sideboards, full of all kinds of stuff—china, silver, crystal—some of it ours, some of it stuff my mother gave me when she went into a nursing home."

"Forget the things that were yours jointly. Things like crystal and silver. You can get a list from the movers, but your wife probably would have gotten those anyway. Concentrate on what she had no right to move."

Fallon stared at her, blinked. "What is this? Some kangaroo court I'm going to?"

"The rule is equitable distribution, but that often means that the person who has the greatest need, or the least ability to replace things, gets them," Samantha said. "That usually means the wife." She arched her eyebrows again in a needless apology. "But the things that came to you from your mother *should* be returned. But you'll have to document that they were given to you, not *both* of you."

Christ, Fallon thought. Another joy-filled trip to The Residence. Another confessional scene with his mother. Then condemnation. "I knew you'd lose my dining-room table," she would say. "I knew it as soon as I gave it to you." Or, perhaps: "So you're letting Trisha pluck *me* like a chicken, too. I told you to get a lawyer, John. But you never listen to me. You never have. You're just like your father."

In the kitchen, Fallon found everything but a handful of older dishes, cups, glasses, and dinner utensils missing. Three old pots and a small black frying pan remained. The liquor, however, seemed intact, save for an unopened twelve-year-old bottle of single-malt scotch that was apparently en route to Manhattan. He decided Howard's palate was beginning to annoy him.

He pulled two glasses from a cabinet. "How about a drink?" he said.

Samantha noted the bitterly ironic grin on his face, lowered her eyes, and smiled. "Sure, Jack. Are we celebrating the survival of the booze?"

"As long as you don't want twelve-year-old scotch," he said. "If you do, you'll have to ferret out Howard. But watch out he doesn't sell you on some bridgework. Howard has to pay the rent on four offices. He's practically a one-man HMO. A true man of the nineties."

She reached out, squeezed his arm, and eyed the liquor. "A little wine would be great if you have it. I never cared much for scotch—new *or* old."

"Me either," Fallon said. "It just ticks me off, thinking about Howard, sitting in one of *my* chairs, drinking *my* booze, out of one of *my* glasses."

And sleeping with *your* wife, Samantha thought, repressing an urge to ask him how he felt about that.

Drinks in hand, they wandered into Fallon's study. He stopped just inside the door; stared at the desk. "The computer's gone," he said. "Christ, Trisha doesn't even know how to use it. She hates the thing." But now his hard drive would be filling up with dental records, he thought. He had a sudden urge to strap Howard into his dentist's chair and start experimenting with various drills. He spun around and checked the wall. His ancient sailfish—the one he had caught as a boy, out fishing with his father—was still there. One small blessing, he decided. Then Samantha's words brought him back to reality.

"Were your personal financial records on the computer?"

Fallon's eyes widened. "Yes, dammit."

"Do you have an up-to-date hard copy?"

"Yeah, I do. I was just going over everything the other day."

"Get it to a lawyer, Jack. Do it tomorrow if you can. In

the meantime, do you have a laptop at the office?" Samantha asked.

"Yeah," Fallon said. "The company's."

"Just bring it home when you need it," she said. "The financial records are important, but if you start getting hung up on everything that's missing, you're going to put yourself in a rubber room. Decide what you really want; what really matters to you, and be prepared to give up the rest."

Fallon struggled to accept her reasoned solutions; found the fact that they were reasoned had begun to annoy him. He stepped to the desk, stared at it, and picked up a yellow sheet of paper.

"Jesus, Mary, and Joseph," he hissed.

"What is it?" Samantha asked, coming up beside him.

"A bill from the goddamned movers. Like I'm supposed to pay for this."

Samantha took the bill from his hand, laid it back on the desk. "Call them tomorrow. Better yet, go and see them and get a copy of their bill of lading. Then tell them they entered your home without your permission, took things that did *not* belong to your wife, and that you're turning the matter over to your attorney. It should stop everything until the court sorts it out. And they'll probably send a new bill to Trisha."

The thought brought a sudden, rather evil grin to Fallon's lips. Suddenly, he couldn't wait for the call he'd soon receive from Trish, decrying his penurious attitude toward the movers. Perhaps Howard would even call. That would indeed be heaven, Fallon decided.

They moved out into the garage, and again Fallon stood dumbstruck. "They took the goddamned riding mower," he said. "Christ, they live in a condo in Manhattan. What the hell is Howard planning to do? Mow Central Park?"

Samantha bundled him out of the garage, back to the

foyer, and up the curving staircase. They found the children's bedrooms intact, and Fallon mumbled something about his wife not wanting the intrusion of college-aged kids into her love nest.

His own bedroom was another matter, however. There, all the furniture, save the bed, was missing— even the armoire that had held much of his clothing was gone, the clothing now piled unceremoniously on the bed. Fallon stared in disbelief, then walked into the adjoining bath. The Bill Blass terry-cloth bathrobe he had hung behind the bathroom door that morning was gone. Fallon moved back to the bedroom like a somnambulist, and sat on the edge of the bed.

"Howard is wearing my bathrobe," he said.

Samantha sat down next to him, placed a hand on his. "You can get another bathrobe," she said.

"I have another bathrobe," Fallon said. "It has a hole in it. I'm sure Howard didn't want it."

Samantha started to laugh, forced it back. "I'm sorry, Jack. I know it's not funny."

Fallon blinked, shook his head, then looked at her. "Yeah, it is," he said. "In a sick sort of way." He stared down into the drink he still held. "It's just stuff, you know? All of it." He turned toward her. "You remember, earlier, I was talking about that closet-sized apartment I had in the Village?"

"I remember."

"Well, I never really needed anything more than that. Not me, personally." He tried a smile; felt it fail. "Then, after the kids, we had that small first house. And that was great. Really as much as any family needed." He waved the hand that held the drink, taking in the twenty-by-twenty bedroom. "Who the hell needs a bedroom this big?" he asked. "I mean, what the hell do you do in a bedroom that requires something almost half the size of a tennis court?"

A small smile played across Samantha's lips, and she

had a sudden urge to show Fallon just what could be done in an oversized bedroom. Was it pity? She suddenly wasn't sure. It was certainly inappropriate, given the work she was now doing for Carter. She squeezed his hand again, wondering if she could bear to deliver the next telling blow the man would receive. "No one needs it, Jack," she said.

"No, they don't. It's all stuff. Every last bit of it. The house, every damned thing that's in it. Houses like this aren't because people need them. They're to show everybody else that they can *have* them." He shook his head. "And so I keep asking myself why I'm so pissed off. And I keep asking why Trisha needs all the stuff she took."

"Maybe Trisha feels that losing her didn't mean very much to you," Samantha offered. "Maybe by taking everything—all your joint possessions—she's trying to make you feel that you really did lose something."

Fallon stared at her, blinked again. Then his eyes took on a far-off look. "Maybe," he said. "And maybe she was right."

Fallon renewed his offer of dinner. He wanted to thank Samantha for her help, and he also wanted to find out just where she stood in Carter Bennett's downsizing scenario.

They dined in a small French restaurant in the center of town. It was gracious and subdued with candlelit tables covered in starched linen. It was also nearly empty, with only two other couples seated at the other end of the dining area. The day had taken on a funereal feel, and as they settled in over coffee, he was momentarily reluctant to place another dark subject between them. But he had to know.

"Look, there's something I want to ask you about," he began. He stared into his coffee, as though it might tell him how to proceed.

"I heard something on the corporate grapevine that involves you. It was about a request you supposedly made to human resources, asking for a breakdown of employees by age group."

Now Samantha looked into her coffee, but said nothing.

"It's no secret that the company is looking to downsize," he continued. "It's also no secret that employees in a certain age group are usually the hardest hit when that happens. I understand the financial thinking behind that. I don't agree with it, but I understand it."

Samantha looked up. "Is that why you broke our dinner date?"

He nodded, then added, "Yeah, that's the reason. I guess I felt . . ." He hesitated, looking for the right words. ". . . Insecure about seeing someone who might be involved in something that could end up cutting my financial throat. Or the throats of people I care about."

He saw her stiffen at the imagery, and immediately regretted it.

"Then why did you agree to me coming with you today?" she asked.

A small smile formed, then faded from his lips. "I decided I wanted to talk to you about it. I also thought I might need your help with the movers and all. Those moving guys can be pretty tough. I thought you could help me throw them out the door." He smiled again, hesitated again. "And I very much wanted to see you." The final words came hard, made him feel suddenly vulnerable.

"I wanted to see you again, too, Jack. It's why I came to your office. I tried to deny it, but that was the reason."

He felt a wash of relief. "Tell me what's going on."

"I can't, Jack. Other than what you already know." She shook her head. "They could fire me if I did, and they'd be justified. I'm a lawyer, and they're my client. I owe them confidentiality." She paused. "Believe me, I wish I could."

"Do you know if I'm on their hit list, or if any of my people are?"

"As far as I know, there is no final list yet—not one I've seen, anyway. I don't think the plan has even been approved by the board. But I think it's close to happening."

"Will you tell me if, and when, you find out?"

She shook her head again. "I don't know." She raised her eyes to meet his. "I'll want to, but I don't know if I will. That's as honest as I can be, Jack."

He nodded. "Can you tell me how many people they're talking about?"

Samantha closed her eyes, then looked at him again. "You're making this very hard for me."

"I know. But I can't help it. Having information is the only way I'll know what to do."

She looked away, then drew a deep breath. "They're talking about one-third of the workforce—about three thousand people."

"Jesus Christ."

"Please don't repeat where you heard that. Just talking to you could put me in front of the bar association's disciplinary committee."

He seemed not to have heard. "Those bastards."

"Jack?"

"Don't worry, I won't say anything." His face had darkened and his voice had a bitter edge. "Wouldn't it be ironic if you were accused of an ethics violation for telling me about something that was so morally repugnant?"

Samantha bristled. "That's not fair, Jack. I'm a lawyer. I'm doing what I'm paid to do. I'm giving legal advice."

His own anger flared. "That has the uncomfortable sound of someone who's just following orders."

"You're out of line," Samantha snapped. "The other day you told me about problems with the fiber-optics line we make. But you're still out there trying to sell it, even though you know it's technically flawed."

"We're trying to fix the flaws," he snapped back. "These bastards are setting out to disrupt people's lives—in some cases to destroy those lives. And their victims haven't done a damned thing to deserve it." He drew a breath, shook his head. "Look, okay, I know it's not your fault, that you're not behind it. And maybe I'd feel differently if I didn't feel the noose tightening around my own neck—or the necks of people I care about. But, God, I hope not."

"Damn it, Jack. I told you I was ambitious. I will not make excuses for the work I do." Samantha swallowed, still feeling the sting of rebuke. "And it could be worse. Understand that." She drew a breath, then continued. "A while back the U.S. Supreme Court handed down a decision against a company named Massey-Ferguson that pulled off an even crueler downsizing plan. Massey-Ferguson was saddled with several divisions that were losing money and long-term employee-benefit packages that they considered a financial burden. But they didn't want to terminate those benefits and face the fallout. So they developed a plan they called Project Sunshine. They set up a new company—Massey Combines—then sent fifteen hundred employees over to run it. They transferred all their benefits from the old company to the new one. They also transferred the benefits of four thousand employees who had already retired, along with the other debt of their unprofitable divisions. The new company was set up to fail. It never had a chance, and it went belly-up two years later, just as everyone knew it would." She snapped her fingers. "And all those employees were gone, and they got *nothing*. No buyout, no extension of health insurance. Nothing. And those who had already retired lost most of their benefits as well."

She paused again, allowing it to sink in. "At least Waters Cable is prepared to buy everyone out."

Fallon snorted. "Only because they know everybody has gotten wise to so-called downsizing. They know they'd be hammered if they didn't."

Samantha closed her eyes, then looked at him again. "That's true. And for other reasons." She hesitated, not certain how far she wanted to go. "I've run the figures, Jack. Just using an average salary of thirty thousand dollars, plus another thirty percent for the cost of benefits, a one-third reduction in the workforce will save the company one hundred and seventeen million dollars a year. In most cases they'll pay the cost of their buyout in less than the first year, and after that the savings will be pure profit. And that's all they're after. Increased profit. It's how they see their job. Their only job." She shook her head again. "Damn it, I find it just as morally repugnant as you do. But there's nothing I can do about it. I wish there were." She picked up her coffee, then put it down again, untouched. "I shouldn't be telling you any of this."

He reached across and took her hand. "I know you shouldn't." He smiled, trying to soften everything he had said. "Hell, I didn't mean to make you sound Machiavellian. Thanks for what you did tell me."

She looked down at his hand on hers. "I hope you're not hurt by this, Jack. I really mean that."

"I know you do. But I'm afraid that may be unavoidable."

Fallon offered to drive her back to the city, but Samantha insisted on the train. She wanted time alone to think, to sort out her thoughts and feelings.

At the station he seemed nervous. He shifted his feet, almost like a teenager struggling for words.

"Look," he said. "I'm sorry about today. All of it. My crazy marital situation, all the things going on in the company." He touched her arm lightly. "I don't know if it's possible, or if you even want to, but I'd like to put all of it aside and just see you."

"The day was fine, Jack. And the awkward parts weren't your fault."

"No, the day sucked," he said. "But I'd like another chance at it." He paused again, toed the station platform. "Look, I'd love it if you could come out this weekend. We could cook some steaks in the backyard, go for a drive, do whatever you'd like. Just spend some time together."

A small smile played at the corners of Samantha's mouth. "Are you talking about the day, or the weekend?" she asked.

Fallon seemed to gulp, widening her smile. "Well, the weekend would be terrific," he said, then rushed on. "I mean you could stay in one of the kids' rooms. I wouldn't expect you to . . ."

Samantha touched his arm, cutting him off. "I'd love to, Jack." She leaned up, kissed him softly. "I'll get a train schedule in New York and let you know which one I'll be on."

Fallon stared at her, a small smile playing on his own lips now. "I promise you it'll be different."

The train pulled into the station, and Samantha took his arm again. "Take tomorrow morning off," she said. "Go see a lawyer. Get a real killer—because that's the type your wife will hire. You can bet on it!"

6

THE LAW OFFICES OF ARTHUR C. GRISHAM, ESQ., WERE located just off the Village Green, a rectangular square of public grass where the inhabitants of Bedford gathered periodically to celebrate patriotic events and summer band concerts. Fallon, whose civic involvement began and ended at the train station, hadn't set foot on its well-manicured lawn in four years.

He also had never really noticed Grisham's office, lawyers being relegated in his mind to real estate closings and wills. But the office was far from hidden. Grisham's legal lair took up the entire first floor of a vintage Victorian house set behind an encircling white picket fence, with an oversized shingle hung from a post, intoning the attorney's presence.

After putting Samantha on the train, Fallon had contacted several local friends who had endured recent divorces. Grisham had represented the former wives of two, and each had told Fallon to hire the man, whom they alternately described as *a shark*, and *a backstabbing bloodsucker*. "Get to him before Trisha does, Jack," the more vehement friend had urged. "Otherwise you'll find yourself sitting in court while that cocksucker Grisham feasts on your flesh."

Fallon entered the office half expecting to find ghoulish cobwebs draped around well-used candles. Instead he found a sedate waiting room, dominated by a middle-aged woman seated behind a polished mahogany desk.

The woman, about forty, Fallon guessed, viewed him with open suspicion through rhinestone-studded glasses, shaped incredibly like the eyes of a voracious jungle cat.

"You're here for a deposition?" she asked. The woman spoke behind one arched eye, with the wary tone of a gatekeeper who had handled many a troublesome visitor in her time.

"No. At least I don't think so," Fallon said. He tried a smile. "My name's Fallon. I called for an appointment earlier this morning."

The woman's face suddenly changed—would have become benignly maternal had the cat's eyes not intruded. She offered a now consoling smile. "Oh, yes," she said. "I remember now. You're taking Attorney Grisham's cancellation. I thought you were here to see one of the associates. They do most of our defendant depositions." She took a clipboard from her otherwise uncluttered desk and handed it to Fallon. "Please have a seat, and fill out this financial questionnaire. Attorney Grisham will need the information when he consults with you."

Fallon smiled at her use of the formal title—attorney—then took a chair. The clipboard had a cheap ballpoint pen attached—held in place by a long, beaded chain. *Attorney* Grisham wasn't about to suffer any felonious theft of his Bics, Fallon decided. He placed the clipboard on his lap and glanced about the office. The reception area was also inexpensively, though comfortably, furnished, with an assortment of upholstered, institutional chairs, and an eclectic collection of frame-shop lithographs hung from the walls. There was only one other waiting client, a woman seated to Fallon's right, and she glared at him as though he were some recently revealed child molester. Fallon fixed his eyes on the clipboard, certain the woman would scream for the police if he so much as blinked.

Grisham's questionnaire didn't seek much—only every financial fact about Fallon's life: real estate, stocks, bonds, IRAs, 401-Ks, bank accounts, pension and medical benefits, credit-card limits, club memberships, and a detailed accounting of all indebtedness, including judgments, liens, mortgages, and assignments. Fallon suddenly wondered if he was getting a divorce or trying to buy a Rolls-Royce from the lover of Wally's ex-wife.

Ten minutes after he had finished detailing his innermost financial secrets, the door to Grisham's office opened, revealing a thirtyish woman, hankie in hand, with a tall, slender, hawk-nosed man firmly attached to one elbow. The man, attired in a gray three-piece suit, offered muttered final words, several consoling nods, and a look that said: Fear not, we shall impale your wayward husband in due course.

As the woman left, Grisham paused in the door, smiled confidently at the other who was still waiting, then turned his gaze on Fallon. It was a look a bird of prey might give a wounded rabbit, Fallon thought, and he struggled for a neutral expression. The receptionist saved him.

"This is Mr. Fallon, your ten o'clock."

Grisham's eyes immediately softened, and he smiled broadly. "Come in, Mr. Fallon, and tell me how I can help you."

Fallon followed his lanky form into a spacious office, furnished in rich walnut and leather and set off by a massive fireplace and a wall-sized bookcase filled with legal tomes.

Grisham slipped into his executive desk chair, quickly perused the clipboard the receptionist had handed him, then looked back at Fallon.

"Well, you seem financially sound," he began, his Adam's apple bobbing with each syllable. "That's bad."

"It is?" Fallon said.

"Well, it's good for me, because you'll be able to pay your bill." A small chuckle. "And it's good for your soon-to-be ex-wife because there will be plucking potential." A regretful shrug. "But for you, not so good, unless I can come to the rescue." Grisham rubbed his long-fingered hands together like a man preparing for a feast. "Tell me the particulars of this affair," he urged, Adam's apple bobbing expectantly. "Start at the beginning, and bring me up to the present."

Fallon began as instructed—starting with his and Trisha's marriage twenty-four years ago; their early years together; Trisha's decision to stop working when their first child was born; their typical middle-class struggle to buy a home, raise children, fight for some semblance of modest affluence. It all sounded trite and commonplace, and, he thought, more than a little boring, and he wondered how you told someone, how you explained the joyful times of it all, or if they ever really existed. When he reached the point about Howard, he discovered a surprising reluctance to discuss it. Wounded pride? An attack against his own sense of manhood? He forced himself through it, as openly and honestly as he could, on down to Trisha's move to the Manhattan condo, and the subsequent invasion of his home by the movers, even his own petty anger at finding his possessions—his *stuff*—suddenly gone. Now this stranger would be arbiter and potential savior in Fallon's parsimonious battle to save his stuff and his resources. It left Fallon feeling sick.

"So, she ran off with a mutual tennis friend." A small smile played on Grisham's lips. "And am I to be given to understand that you've been served no papers yet?"

"That's right," Fallon said. He could taste his meager breakfast in his mouth.

"Do you know if Dr. Nowicki's wife has filed against him, or if she's engaged counsel?"

There was a glitter in Grisham's soft brown eyes, and Fallon was certain that Arthur the bloodsucker was now considering Howard's plucking potential, and the possibility of playing a part in it.

"I have no idea," Fallon said.

Grisham drummed his fingers on the desk. "I shall contact her," he said. He gave Fallon a sly wink. "She may prove beneficial to us." He raised a knowing finger. "Especially if she's engaged a private investigator to document this adultery. It could save us the expense."

Bile rose to meet Fallon's breakfast. "I don't want to get involved in that," Fallon snapped. "We have kids. I don't want them sitting in court, listening to details about who their mother was screwing. Thinking their father sent some peep out to document all of it." He shook his head. "I mean she's done it. Quite openly. I can't see how all that other stuff matters."

Grisham offered a broad shrug. "But it could. Depending on circumstances." He leaned forward. "I noted that you made no mention of any adulterous affairs you engaged in. Were there any that your wife is privy to?"

"No." Fallon shook his head, as if clearing away cobwebs. "I mean I never had an affair."

"Not even a one-night stand? On a business trip, perhaps?"

Again, Fallon shook his head. "No." He paused, thought of Samantha, and his growing desire. "Until the last year or so, our sex life was never a problem." Another pause, coupled with embarrassed uncertainty. "At least not for me." A renewed testosterone attack—the exposed cuckold.

Grisham sat back in his chair, tilted it precariously. "Well, if you remain celibate throughout the divorce, it could be important."

Samantha again rushed to Fallon's mind, that slim—albeit foolish, he was sure—hope of a budding romance. "What difference does it make if *I* sleep with someone, now that she's run off with Howard?" Fallon demanded.

A small, knowing smile played on Grisham's lips. He sat forward again, patiently coaching Fallon in this new, horrific game. "In the eyes of the court it would be the same thing," he intoned. "The timing would be inconsequential. The whole question of adultery would become—shall we say—a wash." One finger shot upward. "*If*, however, you remain celibate while your wife enjoys her adulterous affair—*and* feathers her love nest with your hard-earned possessions—then *she* becomes the villainous party. Do you understand?"

Grisham waved one hand in a circular motion, stopping any response. "All of this, of course, depends on the judge we draw. Certain judges, especially some of the men, are more inclined to look favorably on a man who's been vilified. Some women on the bench, however . . ." He rocked his head from side to side. "But that, of course, is where I come in. I shall endeavor to get a judge favorable to our view." Pursed lips. "Your wife's counsel, of course, will attempt to do the same." A small chuckle. "That's why judges wear those billowing black robes," he added. "So opposing lawyers can climb up beneath and kiss their asses."

Fallon thought about the allusion, shook his head. "So, what do *I* do?" he asked.

"Several things," Grisham began. "First, try to keep your trousers zipped." Another chuckle. "If you can't . . ." A shrug. "More importantly, when you are served, contact me at once. I expect that will be relatively soon. If not, of course we can file. If you are approached by your wife's attorney, say nothing. Just refer him to me. Next, there are certain steps you must take. You must close out all joint bank accounts, investment accounts, whatever, and place the proceeds in new accounts in *your* name only." He watched Fallon wince, smiled at the reaction. "Mr. Fallon," he soothed. "You may well find that your wife has already done that, and that there is nothing left to safeguard."

Bile surged again, and Fallon stared at him in disbelief. Would Trisha do that? He thought of Howard wearing his Bill Blass robe.

"Next," Grisham went on, ignoring the reaction, "cancel all joint credit cards, and take out new cards in your name only." Another regretful smile. "Again, you may find that your wife has already run up some extraordinary purchases. We will fight them, of course, but in the end you'll probably be screwed." He said the last with a certain glee—thinking from the other side, no doubt, Fallon decided.

"Jesus Christ," Fallon hissed.

"Indeed," Grisham replied. "We are at war, Mr. Fallon. Have no doubt of it."

"How about we just split everything down the middle?" Fallon offered. Grisham gave him a smile—the kind one would give a particularly stupid child.

"As you may already know, the law in New York is equitable distribution. But what is equitable to the courts may not seem so to you."

"Yeah, I've heard that," Fallon said.

"That brings me to my final point," the lawyer said. "You must decide *what* you want to fight over. And you must be aware that the degree of fighting we do, both in and out of court, will directly affect how much this divorce will cost you." Another solitary finger shot into the air. "I, of course, will be pleased to fight for everything. But you must look at it from the viewpoint of what you actually need." He sat back again, stared at Fallon through steepled fingers. "For example. How are you going to live after the divorce? Do you plan to remarry, begin a new family, with a new partner? Or do you plan the less involved life of a bachelor?" He rocked his head from side to side. "Serious questions, and also important. If, let's say, your needs will be those of a small but comfortable apartment, then fighting over every stick of furniture becomes a foolish enterprise. And a needlessly expensive one."

Grisham sat forward, intent now. "You will get *some* furnishings. But a prolonged battle over unnecessary possessions could easily raise your costs by ten thousand dollars. So you must consider how much you would spend to furnish an apartment anew." A wise tilt of the head. "Do I make my point?"

Fallon let out a weary breath. "Yeah," he said. He decided that law offices, like airlines, should provide barf bags for their clients.

With Fallon beaten into submission—and dependence—Grisham eased back in his chair. "Now the question of *my* fee, and the retainer I shall ask you to give me."

Fallon closed his eyes; sighed. What the hell, he thought. Take it all. Every cent. Anything that Trisha hasn't already grabbed.

Samantha laid the proposal on Carter's desk and leaned over his shoulder ready to point out various items and the reasoning behind them. Carter felt her closeness, inhaled her scent, and momentarily thought about slipping his arm around her. Then he recalled how firm she had been when she had ended their brief relationship. The idea of another rejection was something he did not want to risk.

He studied the rough draft, listened to her explanations, and when she finished, blew out a slightly weary breath. "You were feeling very generous when you did this," he said. "I hadn't anticipated offering quite this much."

She straightened, her tone stiffening like her back.

"It's similar to what other companies have offered, and, more importantly, I think it will help us avoid litigation," she said.

"Yes, I can see that. But I don't want to avoid it to the point of giving away the store." He drummed his fingers on the desk. "I had hoped to have something I could show Charlie Waters today. But this isn't it."

Samantha walked around the desk, jaw tight, and took a seat opposite him. "You've really got me working at a disadvantage, Carter," she began.

"How so?" His eyes glittered with amusement. She was angry, and it gave her a combative look that he found quite appealing.

She leaned forward. "First, I have no idea who you have on your hit list." She immediately regretted the term, but hurried on. "So it's hard for me to anticipate what legal arguments might arise. I'm working strictly from generalities that deal with age and length of service. It would help if I could go through specific personnel records. It would help me isolate specific problems."

Carter pursed his lips. "Just assume everyone close to fifty and above will be going," he said.

"Even the executives?"

"Even the executives." He raised his eyebrows, as if questioning his own claim. "There may be some exceptions, but for your purposes assume there aren't."

She shook her head in frustration. "That's hard, Carter." She decided to push ahead with what she wanted to know. "It would be easier to anticipate problems if I had specific names. As you know, I reviewed random personnel records in order to put together this proposal, and even that haphazard search produced some potential problems."

Carter's face screwed up with doubt. "How so?" he asked.

Samantha twisted in her chair. "Well, for example,

one of the individuals I came across was a war hero. And years ago the company used that fact rather extensively to get military support for a number of its contracts. That's something to which the court might lend a sympathetic ear."

Bennett shook his head. "I'm not impressed."

Samantha bridled at the rebuke. "Well, be that as it may. But a judge *might* be. This individual was awarded the Distinguished Service Cross. I checked. It's second only to the Medal of Honor, and the only difference between the two is the number of witnesses you have to the act of heroism."

Bennett sat back, gave her a bored look. Then he flashed a wide smile. "Sounds like a great movie. But it still boils down to a second-rate medal. And I'm afraid that's what most of these people are. Second-rate." He shook his head, allowed his smile to become one of regret. "If you must know, very few—I repeat, *very* few—of the people in the age bracket I mentioned will survive this downsizing effort. And the few who do survive will be left on board only temporarily—essentially to avoid any claim of age discrimination. So, you see, I just can't concern myself with the fact that half a century ago one of them did something that some people might consider extraordinary."

"It wasn't half a century, Carter. And the important point is that the company *used* this war record to its advantage. A court might consider that."

Bennett's smile faded, his handsome face becoming more thoughtful. "Who is this person we're talking about?" he asked.

Samantha had dreaded the question but had prepared an answer she knew Bennett would accept. She shook her head. "I can't recall the specific name, Carter. I really wasn't concentrating on *who* these people were, just ages and particular situations that might prove difficult."

Bennett nodded. "Well, it's all specious as far as I'm concerned." There was a light snap in his voice now, as he added, "But if it's a problem, you'll have to deal with it."

Samantha sat back; let out a breath. She had what she wanted, though wished she didn't. "Well, it's a problem, but as you say, I'll deal with it."

"*You* think it's a problem," Bennett said. "*I* don't." He softened the words with another smile, a particularly handsome one. He was still hanging on to his argument, and his voice and eyes had grown momentarily hard. He made an effort to soften both; smiled again. "Besides, I don't think any of these people will be party to any litigation."

Samantha cocked her head. "Why?"

"Because I fully expect most of them will opt to leave before we make *any* offer. You might say I intend to see that most of them do."

Momentary silence. You son of a bitch, she thought, then forced herself to be a lawyer again. "Do it carefully, Carter," she finally said. "That could be a dangerous game. Legally dangerous."

Bennett's smile widened. It was false, but fully secure. "I do everything carefully, Samantha. Or haven't you noticed."

Charlie Waters's office was a sprawling suite almost triple the size of Bennett's; with the added luxury of a private bath. Waters liked space spread out before him, an illusion of something vast under his sole command. As usual, Waters was seated behind his desk in shirtsleeves. He stared at the younger man over half glasses and gestured toward a plush leather sofa.

"You have that buyout proposal for me, I take it," Waters said. He came out from behind the desk, took a chair opposite, and propped crossed feet on the sofa table between them. He was a large man, three inches taller than Bennett's own six feet, and his ample middle bulged over his belt. He had a red face, and thinning silver hair, and had the look of a typical aging executive, blithely en route to his first coronary.

"I'm afraid not," Bennett said. "My legal beagle came up with a proposal I felt far too generous." He drew a long breath, shook his head, and gave Waters a disappointed smile. "I sent her back to do it again," he added.

Waters grunted dissatisfaction. "Goddamned lawyers," he snapped. "Shakespeare was right about 'em. Except if we killed the sonsabitches, we'd all end up in jail." A hearty laugh. "So when will we have something?"

"Early next week, hopefully. But I was presented with a problem I thought we should discuss."

"Go on."

Bennett sat forward and placed a thick manila folder on the table. Waters looked at it as though it were some venomous reptile that had crawled into his office—one he might have to kill with a stick. Thick folders filled with facts and figures were always potential trouble.

Bennett noted the look and hurried on. "The attorney—Samantha Moore, our deputy general counsel—claims we're making it difficult by not giving her a list of the people we plan to . . . *disemploy*." Bennett made a small gesture with his hands. "She feels she has to go through specific personnel records, just to be certain there aren't any unusual circumstances that could cause legal complications."

"Such as?"

"Nothing specific," Bennett said. "She raised a point about one chap—about his standing as some kind of war hero. Said the company used that status to get some government contracts."

"That would be Jack Fallon," Waters said.

Bennett tried to hide his surprise. He wondered if Samantha had really forgotten the man's name, or simply not paid attention to it, as she said. Regardless, he tucked that bit of information away.

"Fallon's on your list?" Waters asked.

"Definitely."

Waters stuck out his lower lip. Nodded. "So why not give Ms. Moore the list? No harm there. The names aren't final until I sign off on them. Just make that clear to her."

Bennett hesitated, uncertain if that meant some names might eventually be struck in some last-minute edict. The idea irritated him, but he could deal with it later. He opened the manila folder and withdrew a computer-generated list of names.

"I was thinking along those same lines," he said. "But I wanted you to have a look at this before I gave it to her." He handed the list to Waters and made a dismissive gesture. "Nothing's written in stone, of course. This is based solely on financial considerations. You'll see it includes a percentage of employees in varying lower age groups, whom we'll need to avoid the appearance of age discrimination. We haven't identified this additional destaffing by individual yet, just by work area. All of it, of course, right down to the specific saves we make, is contingent on any changes you may want to impose."

Waters chuckled. "I like your terminology. Saves, indeed. It makes you sound like a relief pitcher coming in for the final inning of play."

Carter smiled, then picked up a second computer printout that had been hidden beneath the first. "Each one who goes saves the company money. I think the terminology is more than supported by these financial projections I've worked up. They're accurate to within half a percent if we follow that first list exactly, and stay within certain parameters in our buyout offer."

Waters placed the second printout atop the first and began leafing through its pages. His lower lip came out again—this time in appreciation. "This is impressive,

Carter. Very impressive. You're certain of these figures?"

"Completely," Bennett said.

"And they include the cost of the buyout and any litigation we might face?"

"Yes."

Waters nodded absently, still immersed in the figures.

"In fact, I think I can even improve them slightly," Bennett added. He watched Waters's eyes shoot up. "By reducing the number of people *on* the list."

Waters shook his head. "Now you're confusing me."

Bennett sat back; laced his fingers over one knee. "I think a number of these people—a select number in the higher salary ranges—can be encouraged to leave the company before any buyout is offered," he said. "This would reduce our costs from the initial settlement side, but, more importantly, from the standpoint of any legal judgment eventually leveled against us."

"You anticipate us losing any class-action suit that's filed, then," Waters said.

"I think it's unavoidable," Bennett said. "But any judgment would be comparatively insignificant." A smile. "In the overall financial picture." He paused a beat. "*And*, if we're successful in encouraging a significant number of voluntary separations, the amount of any judgment would be reduced accordingly. In fact, legal action might easily become moot. There simply wouldn't be enough older employees left to make an adequate case for age discrimination." Bennett pointed to the list of names he had given Waters. "If you study that list, you'll find I've included nearly all the older employees, but also a significant number of younger staff. That's designed to further weaken any argument that our decisions were based on age and pension costs."

Waters jabbed an emphatic finger. "That's good thinking. All of it. Excellent." He let out a weary breath. "Frankly, I wasn't looking forward to being pilloried in the courts and the press as some money-grabbing bastard who threw his older employees to the dogs. Christ, did you read what they wrote about Al Dunlap, after he cut eleven thousand jobs over at Scott Paper. They called him 'Chain Saw Al,' for chrissake."

Bennett seized the opportunity. "I think we can easily avoid that with this approach," he said. "We'll present our plan as a *personnel surplus reduction*, or perhaps a *redundancy elimination*. But the real key to avoiding litigation—and any bad press—will be in forcing some voluntary separations. And I'd like to start encouraging those as soon as possible."

"Damn sharp thinking," Waters said. "Damn sharp."

Waters put the list of names aside, concentrating again on the financial projections. "This should significantly improve our picture on The Street," he said.

"Without question," Bennett said.

Waters dropped the printouts on the table, and served up a wry smile. "That brings me to something else, Carter. Seems a cousin of yours has made some significant purchases of company stock." He took in the expression on Bennett's face, and let out a small laugh. "Don't be surprised, Carter. I have people who keep a rather close watch on any sizable purchases of our stock." He paused. "Just to safeguard against any subtle attempts at a takeover."

Bennett remained silent. Waters offered up another smile.

"Not to be concerned, Carter. Not about me." Another pause. "But I might point out that if my people can spot this purchase, so can the SEC. I suggest you have your cousin sell off her stock, then repurchase it in—shall we say—a more *secure* manner."

Bennett nodded, tried to appear at ease. His body had coiled like a spring with Waters's little bombshell—due more to the exposure of his own stupidity than to any fear of the man seated across from him. No, Waters was no threat. Good old Charlie had his own skeleton to hide—quite different, but there all the same—and Bennett knew that alone would keep him safe. But the stupidity of his action still rankled. It had been born out of arrogance, and there was no excuse for it.

"I'll speak to my cousin today," he said.

"That's probably a very good idea," Waters said.

Fallon had spent the remainder of the day dealing with bankers, stockbrokers, and credit-card companies, just as Arthur C. Grisham had decreed. It had started badly at his bank, where he found that Trisha had already closed out their joint checking and money market accounts to the tune of nine thousand dollars, leaving only five thousand in CDs that would not mature for another month. She had also made application for a sixty-thousand-dollar loan against 80 percent of the equity in their home. But the application had required both their signatures and lay stalled on the loan officer's desk. Fallon subjected it to a quick and painless death. But the credit-card company was a different story. The one card in both their names—which he had paid off a month earlier—had been maxed out to the tune of ten thousand dollars in a combination of purchases and cash advances. Trisha had not yet made it to the stockbroker, however—although she had telephoned, asking about balances in those accounts—and Fallon immediately closed out each and reopened them solely in his own name. Out of eighty-six thousand dollars in savings, he had managed to safeguard seventy-five, along with the equity in his home. But only temporarily, he told himself, and only by the skin of your now grinding teeth. That, and the perverse but accurate wisdom of Arthur C. Grisham, professional bloodsucker. And even with those efforts, he still faced ten thousand dollars of unanticipated debt on his and Trisha's credit card.

Fallon sat in his car outside a local dry-cleaning establishment. It was four-thirty in the afternoon, and he had never made it to his office; had never found time to eat lunch; had never taken the time to think about the one bright prospect in his immediate future—the planned weekend visit by Samantha Moore. The day's experiences had played through a myriad of conflicting moods. Depression had ruled as he had entered the bank, still questioning the need to protect himself from a woman with whom he had raised two children. But those depressing doubts had quickly turned to blistering rage when he had found himself nearly bereft of funds. At the stockbroker's office he had enjoyed a certain vindictive glee, but that had quickly changed to visions of murder and mayhem when the credit-card company had informed him he was ten thousand dollars in hock.

Now he felt bruised, battered, and beaten, and still faced with one more stupid incident in the ever downward spiraling vicissitudes of his middle-aged life.

Fallon entered the dry-cleaning shop carrying the suit coat he had picked up three days earlier. Upon arriving home that day, he had found three of the four buttons on the left sleeve missing or mangled, and the fourth dangling by a thread. He handed the jacket to the rather dull-eyed young woman who stood behind the counter.

"It seems your pressing machine ate the buttons on my coat," he said. "I'd like them replaced."

The young woman took hold of the sleeve, studied it, then compared it to the other, as if to be certain that missing, mangled, and dangling buttons were not the intended style. Then she looked up and smiled uncertainly.

"That'll be two dollars per button," she said.

Fallon stared at her. "I don't think you understand," he said. "You people did this. And I would like you to correct it. Not *charge* me to repair a coat you damaged."

"You'll have to speak to the manager," the young woman said.

Fallon gritted his teeth, nodded, but the woman just stood there, rooted to the floor.

"Is he here?" Fallon asked.

"Yes."

"Can you get him?"

"Oh. Okay."

The woman returned a few minutes later with a short, sallow, equally dull-eyed man, wearing a white shirt that had one central button missing. He has his shirts done here, Fallon decided.

"Is there a problem?" the man asked.

Fallon looked from the man, to the woman, to the coat the man now held, and wondered if a home for the severely retarded had recently gone belly-up and spewed its patients into the world of dry cleaning.

"The problem is in your hand," he said, struggling to keep his voice even and controlled.

"Well, we can fix it, but we have to charge you," the man said.

He was about thirty, Fallon guessed, and he fought off a sudden urge to see that the man never saw another birthday. Instead, he blew out a long breath.

"I don't think you understand," Fallon said. He was close to speaking through his teeth now. "*You* mashed the buttons. I want *you* to fix them. And I don't think *I* should pay for it."

The manager let out a beleaguered sigh. "I guess you never noticed our sign," he said. He raised his chin, indicating something to the rear and above Fallon's head.

Fallon turned, found the sign high on the wall. He would have noticed it, without question—had he ever exited the store on stilts. It read: WE ARE NOT RESPONSIBLE FOR LOST OR DAMAGED BUTTONS.

Fallon turned back and offered the man an icy smile. "Never saw it," he said. "But I guess you never read the sign on my car. I've probably driven in and out of here too quickly." The smile became wider, slightly insane now. "My sign says, 'I throw rocks through store windows late at night.'" He leaned on the counter, bringing his face to within a foot of the manager. "Fix the goddamned coat," he snapped. "I'll be back for it tomorrow."

Two blocks away, stopped at a traffic light, Fallon leaned his head against the driver's headrest. You have lost your mind, he told himself. You are around the bend. Just one more step on the slippery slope to Shady Pines.

The stoplight changed, and a horn behind him immediately blasted. Fallon spun around and glared through the rear window, ready to kill. The driver was an old woman—eighty, if a day. She glared back, then defiantly raised the middle finger of one hand.

"Oh, my God," Fallon said. His mind began to shout at him. Go home, Fallon. Go home and lie down before you hurt yourself. He spun back to the steering wheel and drove off.

7

SAMANTHA ARRIVED ON THE NOON TRAIN, FALLON THERE to meet her. She was dressed in shorts and a T-shirt, a red headband across her forehead, and she stood out vividly among the arriving passengers. She smiled when she saw him, and his spirits—still battered by domestic woes—immediately soared. She looked bright and beautiful, and the small suitcase she carried left only a solitary doubt in his mind: Why in hell is she here . . . with you?

They ate brunch in a typical suburban restaurant—what Fallon referred to as a Fern Palace—lingering over Bloody Marys and laughing at Samantha's story about an elderly man who had attempted to pick her up on the train. Fallon wondered how much more elderly the man was than he, certain the entire restaurant was staring suspiciously at this unlikely pairing.

He fought it off, told himself their fourteen-year age difference was not extraordinary, then launched into his own stories about The Residence at Willow Run, the great Indianapolis 500 run there via walker and wheelchair, and about the three women and their dotty debate about Don Ho's imagined malady. Samantha laughed and urged him to tell more stories about the place.

"Does your mother like it there?" she asked.

Fallon let out an exaggerated sigh. "There is not a place on this earth that Kitty Fallon approves of," he said.

"Oh," Samantha said. "You have one of those, too."

They lingered further over lunch, telling stories about their families and parental struggles that continued into adulthood. It left them each with a warm sense of intimacy, and when they finally left, Samantha slipped her arm into his. "So, Jack Fallon, what do you have planned for me this weekend?" she asked.

Fallon felt his face color, bringing an immediate smile to Samantha's lips. "Do you know you're blushing?" she asked.

"Yes, damn it," he said. "Next I'll break out in pimples."

She squeezed his arm against hers. "Don't," she said. "I never date guys with pimples. Or tattoos."

"Thank God I don't have any tattoos," he said.

She looked at him impishly. "That's what they all say."

The implication was there, unspoken: A thorough inspection of his body might be required. Fallon thought about the first time he had seen her, dressed in a unitard, bending over the exercise bench in the company gym. It made his knees grow weak. He struggled for humor to ease the moment. "Maybe we could stop at the drugstore, and I could get some Clearasil," he said.

She bit her lip, fighting off laughter, thinking of what else he might buy there. Fallon caught the thought and blushed again.

"Jesus," he said. Then they both laughed.

When they arrived at Fallon's home another awkward moment emerged. Fallon stood in the foyer, Samantha's suitcase in hand, trying to decide what the hell he should do with it. He knew what he wanted to do: simply place it in his room. It was honest, it fulfilled his hopes for that evening, but it was definitely presumptuous, possibly insulting. He decided to surrender to caution.

He lifted the suitcase slightly. "Why don't I take this upstairs and show you where the bath and everything is. Then you can unpack if you want."

Inside the guest room, he laid the suitcase on the bed, then opened the door to the bath. A second opened door led from the bath to his own bedroom.

"The kids' rooms are across the hall," he said. "And they also have an adjoining bath. So, if you'd be more comfortable there . . ."

A small smile toyed at the corners of Samantha's mouth; then she turned to the suitcase. "No, this is fine, Jack. I'll just unpack, and be down in a minute."

Fallon descended the stairs. Jesus, he thought. You're like a kid, hoping to get laid for the first time. His mind flashed back to his first serious, lust-laden date. Sitting in a movie theater with Becky Ann Wallace—Becky Ann of the generous breasts and the pouting lower lip—his arm around her, feeling the silky smoothness of her angora sweater, imagining the hoped-for touch of the equally smooth skin cupped in her bra; his erection so hard and lasting and inconsolable that when they finally left the theater his testicles ached, making it difficult to walk.

Then, two weeks later, alone together in the family room of her home, he had finally allowed his hand to stray to those swelling breasts, and Becky's slender fingers had found their way to the bulge in his trousers, and he had ejaculated so quickly, only embarrassed terror had kept him rooted to the sofa. Even to this day, he would have sold his soul to escape the humiliation of that moment.

Fallon busied himself opening a bottle of white wine; then he retreated to the patio. Samantha came down ten minutes later. Her hair was brushed and she had changed into loose-fitting slacks of yellow crimped cotton with a sleeveless matching top. The outfit was simple, comfortable, and—to Fallon—stunning, a far cry from the cliché business suits she wore in the office as a way of projecting herself as a serious professional.

Fallon poured her a glass of wine and freshened his own. Samantha had taken to a chaise longue, legs crossed at the ankles.

"If you'd like to take a drive later, and see some of the area, we could do that, then come back here and cook some steaks, or chicken, or whatever," he said.

She laid her head back; closed her eyes. Sunlight flooded her face. "The chicken sounds great, but if you don't mind I'd just like a lazy, languorous weekend. It's so good just being away from the heat of the city."

"Lazy and languorous are my best tricks," he said. "I've raised it to a near art form."

Samantha opened one eye. "I doubt that, Jack Fallon. I've read up on you."

"You have? Where?"

"The personnel records in our beloved Human Resources Department. There are some advantages to being deputy general counsel." She felt a sudden rush of guilt at what she was not telling him, but put it aside for the moment.

Fallon felt momentarily tense. He wondered if reading up on him involved the work she was doing for Bennett. But he had promised to put all that aside. "That's not fair," he said. "Now I have no secrets."

Both eyes opened this time, looking at him through a haze of sunlight. "Our personnel records aren't *that* thorough," she said. She let the innuendo slide. "Tell me about the war," she said, changing tacks. "Even the brief summary I read made it sound pretty grim."

He inclined his head; thought about it. "It was indelible," he said. "I wish I could say forgettable, but lot of it still floats back every now and then."

"What do you remember most about it?" she asked.

He answered without hesitation. "The guys who didn't make it." He paused; remembering. "Each time something good happens in my life, I remember that it never had a chance to happen for someone else I once knew . . . intimately. And all because some overfed politicians wanted to play their little games." He seemed to sense the bitterness in his voice and paused to let it pass. "But essentially I remember the fear," he added. "Mine and everyone else's. But mostly mine."

"It didn't sound as though you were afraid," she said. "Not with all the citations you were given."

He laughed. "Only every waking minute."

"Why did you go?" she finally asked. "So many didn't." She was watching him now, intent on his answer.

"I haven't the faintest idea," he said. Another smile, weaker this time. "It seemed like a terrific idea when I was eighteen. Just like driving a car at ninety miles an hour seems like a great idea." He raised his hands in a futile gesture. "After I was there, then I knew it was crazy."

Samantha bit her lower lip; continued to stare at him, thinking about what he'd said. "But you stayed for two tours, a year longer than you had to."

"Yes, I did. And that's the scariest part." His eyes were soft now; filled with regret.

"But why?"

Fallon looked out at the tree-filled yard; the flower beds Trisha had cultivated so carefully. He gave a small shrug. "I think it's the war itself. It takes hold of you and won't let go. Because it wants to kill you, too." He shook his head. "You see, I just don't know. And I've asked myself those same questions over and over for all these years. Especially why I went in the first place. I've even wondered if it was like not being able to pass a bad accident without slowing down and looking. Except this time I stopped the car and got out, even though I knew it wouldn't help; that it was pointless."

Samantha continued to stare at him, wondered if he was avoiding the real answer. "Do you still have your medals?" she asked at length.

Fallon nodded. "Someplace," he said. "I thought about sending them back, but never did." He gave an uncertain shrug. "When I got back, had time to think about everything, I was really ashamed of what my country had done there—what I did there. But it seemed like a pointless gesture, somehow. So I never did. I guess I decided that would still be running away—from the truth of it."

"It sounds very sad."

"Yeah, I guess it does. But that's what wars are. Sad. With a heavy touch of unendurable stupidity." He smiled across the patio, more genuinely this time. "And that's why governments don't try to recruit thirty-year-olds. They need their fodder young and naive and certain of their immortality."

Samantha sighed. She looked across the lawn at the rich green trees and shrubs that encircled the patio, giving it the feel of a safe island. Fallon had just told her a sadly subtle story about why children were chosen to die, and she suddenly wondered if he had ever made a mental comparison between the military and the corporate world—if he understood the equally subtle similarity between one, which callously destroyed its children, and the other, which took them, used them up, then did the same when they were fifty.

She studied her hands for a moment. "I was just wondering why thirty-year-olds don't take the same attitude toward the companies they work for." She looked up at him. "Do you think they should?"

Fallon stared at her, wondered if there was a message

in the words. "Yes, I do," he said at length. "But we agreed not to talk about that."

"Yes, we did," she said.

They spent the rest of the afternoon lazing and talking, and discovering small things about each other. It was the playful banter that always seemed an early part of the pre-mating ritual, and the mere thought that this was what they were doing made Fallon slightly nervous. Yet, at the same time, he couldn't deny the depth of his attraction. With every smile, every small gesture of warmth from her, he found himself arguing against reason that the woman had come to his home for the weekend because the attraction was mutual—or perhaps just praying that it might be. Later, as they wandered about the yard, ostensibly looking at the beautifully maintained flower beds, Samantha slipped her arm in his and he felt a sudden rush of pleasure, and again, when she allowed a hand to rest on his a bit longer than necessary, he was seized by an impulse to draw her to him and kiss her. Only doubt stopped him. He wanted to believe each gesture was a signal, indicating a willingness for greater intimacy. He recalled those signals—or what they had been years ago when he was dating—but now there was doubt. So he demurred, awkwardly, and with regret, cursing himself for his lingering uncertainty and his unwillingness to risk rejection.

At six o'clock Fallon started dinner. He was at the grill, dealing with the ritual of the chicken. He tried to recall the last time he had done this. It would have been for Trish—perhaps Trish and the children. Now he was here with another woman; telling her about his life; even talking about a war he had refused to discuss for over twenty years. It suddenly hit him how much everything had changed.

Samantha watched him from across the patio. She

rose from her chair and moved quietly to his side, then leaned toward him and kissed his cheek.

"You look sad," she said.

He turned and placed his hands at her waist. "Not sad. Reflective, maybe." Her returning smile was soft, caring, and he was again seized by an impulse to kiss her. Slowly, he lowered his lips toward hers.

"Daaad!"

A chill went through Fallon's body, freezing him in place. He momentarily closed his eyes, then turned and looked into his daughter's horrified face. Two steps behind stood his son, Mike.

"Uh, hi, Dad." Mike was staring at Samantha, his face filled with uncomprehending awe. Slowly, a small smile began to threaten the corners of his mouth. Fallon felt sudden certitude that his son was about to say: "Wow."

Fallon removed his hands from Samantha's waist and stepped back. Uncertain what to do with his hands now, he placed them awkwardly on his hips.

"Jesus. I didn't know you were coming home," he said. He forced a smile, trying to fight his way through the moment. He looked back at his daughter. She had struggled for composure—found it—and was now staring at him coldly. Another vision appeared, as his own adolescence again flashed to mind. Instantly he was standing before Sister Urial, his high school principal, a Dominican nun who could render you hell-bound with one withering look.

Liz fought off a slight tremble in her lower lip. "Can I speak to you, Dad?" Ice-blue eyes went to Samantha, taking her in from head to toe. Mike continued to stare, uncertain what mischief he had discovered, but fascinated by it. Fallon suddenly wanted to grab his shoulders and shake the look from his face.

Instead, he straightened, sucked up all the internal organs that seemed to have fallen into his shoes, and began floundering for some semblance of normalcy.

"This is Samantha Moore, a friend from work," he said lamely, praying there was no guilt in his voice. He turned to Samantha, who seemed inexplicably calm. "These are my children: Liz and Mike."

"Hello," Samantha said.

"Dad, can I *please* speak to you?" Liz repeated, then spun on her heels and marched back into the house.

"Uh . . . Hi, I guess." Mike said. He glanced at his father as if asking what he should do next.

"Excuse me," Fallon said. He started after his daughter, grabbed his son's arm as he moved past, and pulled him along. "Close your mouth," he hissed, as they entered the kitchen.

Liz stood with her back to him, shoulders trembling as she stared out a side window.

"Look, honey," Fallon began. "Let's not overreact to this."

Liz spun on him, eyes glaring through a film of tears. "Is this the reason Mom left, Dad? Because of *her?*" The jaw quivered again.

Fallon's own jaw dropped. Then he caught hold of himself. "*What?*"

"That's certainly the way it looks," Liz snapped. Another quiver of jaw and lip.

Fallon stared at her, incredulous. "I never even *met* Samantha until your mother left. Until she ran off with Howard."

Liz's jaw began a foxtrot. "That . . . that was less than a . . . a week ago. And y- y- you're . . . already . . . making . . . l- l- love to her . . . in . . . the . . . back . . . yard."

Fallon stood thunderstruck. Words formed in his mind: I wasn't making love to *anybody*. Your mother's making love to somebody. She's moved to Manhattan with Howard. They're making love all the time—or at least whenever Howard isn't flossing someone's goddamned teeth, or driving my goddamn lawn mower through Central Park.

Instinctively he knew he could say none of it, that it would only inflame the situation, so he choked the words back before they made it past his lips. Instead, he said: "Look, Liz, you're acting like you walked in on something flagrant. All you walked in on was a display of affection between two friends. If I'd known you were coming home—if you had called first—you wouldn't even have walked in on that."

Liz straightened and glared at him. "Is that what we're supposed to do now? Call first before we come to our *home*?" She stared at his face, trying to see if he realized how unfair his comment had been. "And we did try to call," she said, hurrying on. "You forgot to turn on the answering machine."

"No, I didn't," Fallon said. "Your mother took it. Along with the rest of the furniture." He watched his daughter's lip begin to tremble again.

"Oh, *Dad*," Liz intoned. "How . . . how can you do this? And how can you say things like that about Mom? Her heart's probably broken."

Fallon's jaw dropped again. He stared at his still quaking daughter, shook his head, and drew a much needed breath. Again, he knew what he wanted to say: Her heart's not broken, Liz. She's too busy moving furniture to have a broken heart. She's too busy cleaning out bank accounts and maxing out credit cards. She doesn't have time for heartbreak. Right now, she's probably sitting in her Manhattan condo with a needle and thread, making alterations to my goddamn Bill Blass bathrobe so Howard can wear it.

His son saved him. "What happened to all the furniture, Dad?" he asked.

Fallon turned to his son, shook his head again. "Mike. Have you been listening to any of this?" he asked.

"Sure, Dad." Mike, tall and lean and handsome, blinked.

Fallon stared at the floor. "The furniture's gone,

Mike. Your mother took it. I came home from work one day, and it was gone." He raised his eyes to his son's still blank face. "The furniture was gone. The lawn mower was gone. Even my goddamn bathrobe was gone. You got all that now?"

"Did she take the Mustang?" Mike asked.

Fallon turned in a slow circle, then placed his hands over his face. He drew another breath, then dropped his hands to his side and stared at his son again. "Yeah, Mike. She took the Mustang, too," he said.

"Jesus," Mike said.

Fallon momentarily closed his eyes again, then turned back to his daughter—weary now. "Look, I'm sorry you guys walked in on something that upset you. But there was nothing wrong with what you saw. I'm just trying to get on with my life, and I had no idea you were coming home this weekend. . . ."

"We were *worried* about you," Liz moaned.

Fallon nodded. "And I appreciate that. I really do. And I certainly wouldn't have invited anyone for the weekend if I had known you were coming home."

Both mouths now went to half mast, both sets of eyes bored in on him. Fallon drew another guilty breath.

Liz recovered first. "The weekend! Oh, Dad! How could you do that to our mother?"

Before he could speak, Liz stormed past him. "I'm going to stay with Mom!" she snapped.

"Now, wait a minute, Liz. Liz?"

Mike watched his sister go, hesitated, then shrugged. "I guess I better go, too," he said. He shifted his weight awkwardly. "Liz is driving," he said, by way of explana-tion. "Gee, I'm sorry about this, Dad."

Fallon squeezed his son's shoulder. "Yeah, me too," he said. "Look, try and talk to your sister." He paused, then shook his head. "No, forget that. I'll talk to her myself. Later." He drew a long breath. "Look, this time, just make sure you call before you go to your mom's apartment, okay?"

Mike blinked. "Wow," he said. "This is getting really complicated."

Fallon returned to the patio, a slightly bewildered look on his face. Samantha had overheard much of the conversation in the kitchen, and the unfairness of it had angered her. She moved toward him, struggling to hide it.

"Jack, I'm sorry," she said.

"It's not your fault. It's not anybody's fault."

"Look, I couldn't help overhearing some of that. Maybe it would be better if I just left."

He stared at her, shook his head, then placed his hands back on her hips. "Like hell," he said. "I just hope you're willing to sit by while I deal with an outraged phone call in about an hour or two." He allowed her questioning look to settle in. "They went to my wife's apartment in Manhattan," he explained.

"Maybe she won't be home," Samantha offered. "Your children could turn around and come back. It might be better if I just leave."

"No. I don't want that. Please stay. Liz will wait for her mother. And Mike will do whatever his sister wants. He has since he was two." He forced a smile. "I only hope Trisha and Howard are dressed. Or at least have a doorman who'll give them time to get their clothes on."

Samantha laughed softly. "Oh, God. I shouldn't laugh. That would be awful if they weren't. For your children, I mean."

"Yeah," Fallon said. "It could be the end of civilized parenting as they know it. Noncelibate parents. Who would have thought it?"

Samantha slipped her arms around his neck and smiled. "I should tell you something," she said. "When I was a little girl, if someone accused me of something I hadn't done, I immediately had to go out and do it." She pressed against him, gave him a long, hard kiss.

When she pulled back, Fallon grinned at her. "I just thought of a few more wrongful accusations I'd like to make," he said.

She returned the grin. "Go slow, Mr. Fallon. And be careful what you wish for," she said.

The phone call came two hours later. Trisha's voice was cool and reproachful—the return of Sister Urial.

"I have to say that I'm really shocked, Jack. This time you've truly outdone yourself."

"Hello, Trisha," Fallon said. He and Samantha had just finished dinner, and were enjoying snifters of brandy on the patio. Fallon had placed a portable phone next to his chair in anticipation.

"The children were equally shocked, Jack. I mean, *really* shocked."

"Weren't you and Howard dressed?" Fallon asked.

There was momentary silence; then outrage reasserted itself.

"That's not funny, Jack. But I suppose I should expect that kind of callous remark."

"That's me, Trish. Callous to the core. By the way, how does Howard like the lawn mower? I bet he's tearing the hell out of Central Park."

Silence hit the line again.

"That brings me to something else, Jack," Trisha said at length. "Howard wants me to tell you that he's very disappointed in you."

This time the silence came from Fallon, broken finally by soft laughter. "Howard's disappointed? Oh, Jesus," Fallon said. "What happened? Did I forget to put gas in the lawn mower?" He glanced at Samantha. Her mouth was hidden behind her hand. She, too, was laughing.

"That's very funny, Jack," Trisha snapped. "But you

know exactly what I'm talking about. I got a bill from the movers yesterday."

"Hey, movers do that, Trish. They send bills to people who hire them."

"That's not what happened in this case, Jack. I spoke to a woman in their office. They left a bill for you. Just as they were supposed to. The woman said you came by and threatened them—claimed they had entered your house without your permission, and that they took things they had no right to take."

"They took my mother's furniture, Trish. I want it back. I don't want to have to tell her that it's being used to furnish your boyfriend's condo."

"Jack, you know very well that your mother always said the furniture would be mine."

"She's not dead, Trish. And I think she said that with the expectation that we'd still be living together when she finally did croak. You can't just take her stuff away from her—no matter how much Howard wants it."

Trisha ignored the final remark. Her voice became condescending. "Oh, Jack. What would you do with it?" She let out an exasperated breath.

"I might sit on it," Fallon snapped. "I might take her plates and put them on her goddamned table and eat dinner. I might even do what I promised to do, and keep them for her."

Trisha fell silent, then forced herself back to the issue. Her voice was softer now. "All right, Jack. Maybe I should have discussed it with you before the movers came. But it seemed like the right thing to do. After all, Howard's wife got all *his* furniture, and the lawyer Howard found for me said I should take ours."

"And, of course, Howard agreed with that." Fallon tried to keep the snarl out of his voice, but failed.

"Oh, Jack. Let's not turn this into a big macho thing. You know your mother would want me to have her things, because she knows I'd care for them. And that's why Howard suggested you pay for the movers. After all, we only needed them to carry out your mother's wishes."

Fallon turned red; his hand tightened on the receiver. "I'll tell you what. Why don't you have Howard stop by and discuss that with me? I'd really like to hear his views on my mother's furniture and the moving bill, and any other philosophical wisdom he'd like to impart. You see, I have some things I'd like to impart to Howard as well. I'd also like to give him a chance to go through the god-damned house, to see if there's anything your movers missed."

A longer silence came from her end now. "Why don't we just stick to the issues?" she finally said. "Why don't you tell me what you intend to do about the movers? And also what you intend to do about the children?"

"I've already dealt with the movers, Trish. And I don't intend to do anything about the kids, except explain that we each have our own lives now, and that they'll have to accept that."

"*Jack!* I can't believe you're saying that. I can't believe you expect your children to come home to a house where their father is shacked up with some woman they've never even seen before."

"Trish, their mother is shacked up with a goddamned dental philosopher. If they can handle that, I expect them to handle anything I might do."

"Oh, Jack. That is so callous. Their summer classes will be over in two weeks. What do you expect them to do? Stay with me?"

"I think that would be lovely, if that's what they want. Hell, they could get to know Howard better. And their grandmother's furniture would make them feel right at home."

"*Jack!*"

"Look, Trish, the kids are welcome to come here anytime they want. It's their goddamn home. As far as

I'm concerned they live here. But they're adults, and they'll have to accept there *is* a new life going on for each of us."

"Well, I certainly don't have room for them here, Jack."

A slightly evil smile came to Fallon's lips. "Sorry, Trish. I guess you'll just have to earn some points toward your mother-of-the-year award."

"Jack, you sonofabitch!"

"Bye, Trish."

Fallon placed the phone on a table next to his chair, looked across at Samantha, and shrugged.

She fought back a smile. "Did that make you feel better?" she asked. The smile broke through.

"Much better," he said.

Samantha took a small sip of brandy. "Perhaps you should consider what your lawyer would say about my spending the night here," she said.

Fallon thought about Arthur C. Grisham and his ominous warnings about mutual marital infidelity. "I know what he'd say. I'm just not going to worry about it."

Samantha studied his face. It was craggy and world weary and quite handsome, she thought. Still, despite the attraction, it surprised her how much she wanted this man, and she wondered just how much his daughter's accusations played into that. She smiled inwardly. Those accusations had angered her, still did to some degree. But it was far from an overwhelming consideration. She weighed the possibilities—considered the consequences and tradeoffs, just as she had been taught to do in law school. The hell with law school, she thought. Everyone seems to be screwing this man. Both at work and at home. Maybe *you* should screw him the right way.

Samantha put down her drink. "Well, apparently I've already been labeled a brazen hussy," she said. "And you've certainly been denounced as a libertine."

Fallon grinned. "Indeed."

"That being the case, I think we're entitled to live up to those expectations, don't you?"

"I think that's a wonderful idea."

Samantha returned his grin. "Then you'd better take me up to your bed, Jack Fallon. Otherwise, we're liable to scandalize the neighbors."

Samantha awoke first, slipped quietly out of bed, and went downstairs. She was wearing a short silk robe she had brought from home. It went to mid-thigh and there was nothing but panties beneath it. A cup of coffee in hand, she curled up on the chaise longue and took in the sultry July morning warmth that spoke of oppressive heat yet to come. She looked down into the oracle of her coffee. Her mind was filled with the man, with the previous night and his surprising gentleness. It hadn't been that way at first. Then, he had been eager, perhaps even anxious. But so had she, and they had devoured each other, as though both knew the chance might never come again. But later, when they had made love a second time, he had become the generous lover she had always wanted. Then the tenderness had come forth—soft and giving.

She stared into her coffee. Why did it always surprise women when men were tender and giving in bed? Samantha smiled as she answered her own question. Because so few ever were.

She stood and walked out into the garden—leaves, flowers, and grass still moist with dew—then turned and came back to the chaise. She wanted to think about the man, to make sure she wasn't building up an image that really wasn't there. Years of working in the upper levels of competitive business appeared to have spared him somehow—had failed to eradicate the romance of his soul, had not turned him into a self-absorbed narcissist for whom self-gratification and recognition were the ultimate goals. She had heard him speak about the men

who worked under him, had seen him—albeit briefly—
with his children, had watched him deal with the initial
brutalities of divorce, and even listened as he dealt with
a wife who had wounded him as badly as one could be
hurt. The thoughts became more personal. Yes, and she
had felt him, felt his hands and lips and tongue, seeking
to give her pleasure without a need to self-aggrandizingly
prove his abilities, or to simply take—selfishly—all there
was to be had.

She began to replay their lovemaking, began to feel
herself become aroused.

"Good morning."

She looked up and saw Fallon standing in the doorway. He was dressed in shorts, T-shirt, and boat shoes
without socks, and he was smiling at her. Suddenly she
had a vision of his son from the previous day, and
together with the casual clothes, there it was—an image
of Fallon twenty-five years ago.

Samantha stared at him for a long minute, then
returned the smile. "You should have stayed in bed," she
said. "I've been sitting here thinking about last night,
and in a few minutes I probably would have slipped
back upstairs for more."

Fallon stood still, as if flabbergasted by the words.
Then he smiled again, came to her, bent down, and
softly kissed her lips.

"You certainly know how to make a middle-aged ego
fly," he said. He slid onto the chaise next to her, his face
laughing. "And how to make my toes wiggle."

Samantha laughed at the phrase. "Is that what I did?"

"Without question," he said.

She leaned against him, kissed him again, then nuzzled his ear. "Next time I'll have to remember to look at
your toes," she whispered.

Fallon turned toward her and slipped his arm around
her waist. Samantha drew herself closer against him; felt
her passion matching his own.

"Oh, Jack, I'm glad I caught you."

Margot Reed came around the side of the house, dressed in a real-estate costume similar to the one she had worn a few days before—silk blouse and slacks, each full enough to hide the pudginess of her body.

She trudged forward, oblivious. The back of the chaise was to her, and Margot could only see Fallon's legs draped over the far edge. She continued to prattle as she moved across the rear lawn.

"I had some clients in the neighborhood yesterday," she said. "And when I told them your house might be going on the market, they said they just *had* to see it."

Fallon twisted in the chaise, stuck his head out from behind its back, and stared at her. "Margot, this is really not a good time."

His eyes were pleading, but still the woman moved on. Samantha's head slowly rose into view above the back of the chaise, and the woman suddenly saw her, staggered slightly to one side, then came to an immediate halt.

"Oh . . . Oh, Jack, I'm so sorry." Her neighborly, professional smile had evaporated, replaced now with shock and dismay, and a sudden, visible urge to turn and run.

Fallon stared into her wide-eyed face. Her blond hair seemed to have frozen into a sprayed, steel helmet, and the heavy makeup she wore looked as though it were about to crack and fissure. He forced a smile. "How about I call you later today, Margot?" he suggested.

The woman began to stutter, her head nodding repeatedly, as though disjointed from her spine.

"Of course, Jack. Of course." She glanced around, as if deciding where to run, then turned abruptly and retreated to the corner of the house.

Samantha began to laugh. The laughter became contagious, and Fallon began, too.

"Oh, Jesus. I'm sorry." He pushed himself up, and threw a mock glance at his watch. "The local high school band is due in half an hour. They practice in my backyard every weekend." He grinned at her. "So how would you like to pass the time until *they* get here?"

She reached out, took his hand, and let him help her out of the chaise. "I'm taking you up to your bed. And I'm locking the back door and putting a chair against the doorknob." She had begun to laugh again.

"When the band gets here we'll feel like we're being serenaded."

"You'll be too busy to listen," she said. Laughter boiled up again. "Oh, God, Jack. Did you see that poor woman's face?"

8

CARTER BENNETT CRAWLED THROUGH THE HIGH GRASS and peered out toward the old T-38 tank that stood ten feet away at the crest of the hill. Slowly he brought his weapon up, spread his legs for balance, and using his elbow as a brace, leveled it toward the field of fire. A fly threatened the tip of his nose, but he ignored it, determined not to give away his position. His patience was rewarded as a face, covered in daubs of camouflage like his own, emerged from the other side of the hill. Bennett drew a shallow breath and waited. Gradually, the figure began to rise, the green and black battle fatigues coming up into the cool morning air. Bennett drew another breath, let it out slowly, and squeezed the trigger. A dull splat filled his ears.

"Aw shit!" The enemy kicked at the dirt in front of him. "Sonofabitch!"

Carter rose and began to laugh. His opponent stared at the bloom of yellow paint that stained the center of his chest.

"Goddammit. You nailed my ass good," the enemy said.

Carter grinned with undiluted pleasure. "I heard you coming ten minutes ago, and just got in position and waited."

"Sonofabitch. Musta been that loose rock I stepped on."

"Perhaps you're just old and clumsy," Bennett said. He was still grinning at the man—so boyishly he could not possibly take offense.

"I'll get your ass this afternoon in the swamp," he snapped.

"Never happen," Bennett quipped. "I'm invincible."

"Yeah, we'll see about that, you cocky sonofabitch."

Bennett threw his arm around the man's shoulder, and they turned and started down the hill. The man was pushing fifty, or just past it. He was a local, a member of the VFW post that furnished almost a dozen of the tournament players, and a Marine Corps veteran of the Vietnam War. Or so he claimed. He was also fat and awkward and an easy mark, and Bennett had been delighted when he had drawn him for the day's war games.

They moved through a line of trees and across a small meadow, headed toward the judge's shack. The man had his jungle hat off now, and was mopping the sweat from his balding head. Bennett could hear his breath wheezing past his teeth.

"You're out of shape, George. You should spend a couple of evenings in a gym."

"Hey, you little smart-ass. I'll show you this afternoon who the hell needs a gym."

Bennett threw back his head and laughed. "I'm available for a side bet, George," he said.

"You got it," the man snapped. "Ten bucks says I nail your ass."

"You're on," Bennett said. He only wished the man had some serious money to bet with. Carter knew just where he'd ambush him that afternoon. The fat, sorry, old fool wouldn't have a chance.

They entered the judge's shed and walked up to a small desk, behind which sat another fat, balding, middle-aged man. Another woodsy Vermont yokel, Bennett thought. He flashed a smile. "Do you want to tell him, or should I, George?"

"Score one for the little shit from the big city," George snapped.

The judge turned to a scoreboard fixed to the wall behind him. Bennett's name sat at the top of the list, along with three others who also had scores of seventeen kills and no defeats.

"That gives you eighteen, and keeps you on top," the judge said.

"Just where I belong," Bennett said. He was smiling again, the warmth of it hiding the contempt he held for both men.

"Be a different story this afternoon," George said.

Bennett winked at the judge. "Just bring your wallet," he said. He grinned again. "I want to take it off your dead body."

Carter entered his cabin, laid his weapon on a small table, and stared across at the bed. His cousin, Eunice Whittaker, sat against a propped pillow, the sheet drawn up just below her small, round breasts.

"My hero, home from the war," she quipped.

"I'm astonished to see you awake," Bennett said.

"Astonished? I've been awake for nearly an hour," she said. "Actually, I've been lying here trying to decide if you'd been killed, and if so, whether I should just go ahead and masturbate."

Bennett grinned at her. "Why don't we say that I was, and I'll just sit here and watch."

Eunice gave him an imperious smile, her blue eyes taking on a lascivious glow. "Actually, I'd rather you did it for me," she said. "But first take that ridiculous paint off your face."

Later, over breakfast at a small roadside restaurant, Eunice seemed particularly content. Her thin, angular, slightly pinched face had a certain glow, he thought, and there was even a slight upturn to her normally tight lips. Looking at her, he could see now how she would change over the years: first into middle age, then as an old woman—her face always tanned, but with gradually deepening lines; always bearing that certain elegance of wealth, but always lacking any degree of warmth. Yes, he thought, wealthy women of his class always aged elegantly, but never beautifully.

But now she was content, and Bennett seized the moment to raise the question of their behind-the-scenes stock acquisitions. Eunice's eyes immediately widened, first at the realization they had been discovered, then at his solution.

"But the price of the stock has dropped. We will lose *thousands*."

The horror in her voice made Bennett cringe. She could be obstinate, and that was not the reaction he needed. He forced one of his better smiles.

"Only temporarily," he soothed. "And we must think of it as the cost of doing business—safely." Eunice began to object—a loss was a loss in her eyes, even if it would be more than recouped over time. Bennett raised a mollifying hand. "The exposure is too great—more than I expected. But we can sell and immediately repurchase through the shell corporations I'm setting up. Any loss will be insignificant in the long run."

Eunice's eyes and jaw tightened. "It's still a loss," she snapped. "No matter how you paint it." She leaned forward in an open challenge. "I thought you knew enough about Charlie Waters's own activities that we didn't have to concern ourselves with him."

"I'm not *worried* about Waters," Bennett snapped back. "But if that pompous old man has been able to stumble onto our little game, so can others who do worry me. The SEC, for one. I have no intention of ending up in some federal prison."

Eunice twisted her napkin. "You realize we are risking both our trust funds—and that mine is almost quadruple your own." She stared at him, hard. "Carter, I agreed to give you one-third of my profits, but only because the return was so enormous, and the risk—according to you—nonexistent. Now I'm seeing very real, and very terrifying, risks."

Bennett paused; forced another smile. "You're seeing nothing of the kind. What you are seeing is very deliberate caution. Not to mention our agreement that any loss to you—should the price of Waters stock *not* rise as expected—will be made up by *me*."

"And you're not concerned about the four million dollars I've invested—*half* of my trust fund?"

"Not in the least. The money will triple over the next year. Two and a half fold at the minimum if I'm overstating. That's a ten to twelve million return on investment."

"With a third going to you," she added coldly.

"*With* the guarantee that I'll make up any losses from my so much more anemic trust fund." He shook his head sadly, chastising her. "That leaves you with a profit of at least six million without risk of losing your investment. God, Eunice, for you it's a deal made in heaven. One solely available because of my knowledge about what is taking place."

Eunice turned and stared out the window at an empty Vermont highway. "Why am I suddenly not reassured?" she asked.

Bennett reached out and took her hand. "Be reassured," he said. "Eunice, you know how I feel about you—how I have felt since we were children."

The memory of their experimentations, which had begun years ago when each was an adolescent, finally brought a smile to her lips. Since they were only second cousins, the incestuous nature of their liaison was borderline at best, but the mere thought of it had always added a certain spice that each secretly relished.

She stared across at him and lowered her voice. "I definitely like your penis better than your plots," she said.

"But my plots will make us richer than we ever hoped," he said.

Samantha's kiss left Fallon breathless. He felt imbued with inflorescence; as though someone had erased all the mundanity of the last twenty years; left him suddenly less the middle-aged man stumbling through life but now surprisingly vital, virile, and yes—inexplicably—wanted.

They were standing on the platform awaiting Samantha's train. It was five o'clock and a handful of middle-aged denizens were headed into the city for Sunday evening dinner. Fallon was oblivious to them, could not have said if any were neighbors or a gathering of ambulant gypsies.

"Despite the unexpected guests, it was quite a weekend," she said. "I wish we could play hooky from work." She raised her lips and kissed him on the point of his chin.

"I know," Fallon said, recalling it all. "My toes are still wiggling."

"You and your toes," Samantha said. "It's a devious fetish."

She laid her head against his chest and hugged him. The man was a joy, she told herself—tender, self-deprecatingly funny, and uncommonly sensitive—yet all man, minus the annoying machismo she had encountered so often, and throughout the day she had felt an irrepressible need to warn him about the threats to his own survival that lay ahead. She felt it again now—again torn between professional ethics and a growing moral certitude that she should speak.

She eased back, hoping to find some commonality. "Jack, I learned something the other day you should know about." Samantha hesitated, searching out some phrasing that might play to the ethical balancing act she sought. His words stopped her.

"You found out we're all on Carter's hit list, right? Everyone over forty-five?"

"I haven't seen any final list yet," she said. "But, yes, I think you'll all be on it. And quite a few who are younger, too. Just to make it all appear kosher to the courts." Her eyes took on an imploring quality. "There's not much I can really tell you." Another pause. "I haven't been told the when or the how of it."

He placed a finger on her lips stopping her. "Some of us have figured out what Carter's up to. We've even formed a little club to deal with it. Or to try to." He noted the surprise on her face. "And I plan to see Charlie this week." He inclined his head to one side. "I don't know if it will do any good, but I plan to take a shot at it."

Her eyes blinked again. "Do they know about your . . . club?" The fact had registered in the legal corners of her mind, the synapses of which were now screaming class-action suit.

"Not yet," Fallon said. "But we intend to make our presence felt. Subtly, of course. If the company reacted badly it might prove painful to some of us."

Samantha nodded; thought: Yes, I think so, too.

The train conductor opened the doors and called for boarding. Samantha found herself wanting to say more. Instead she kissed Fallon again and boarded the train, then turned and waved. Her heart was pounding, and she knew it came from more than one source.

Fallon waved back. He thought she looked very beautiful. And a bit wistful, too.

9

"I EXPECT YOU'LL WANT TO START IMMEDIATELY?"

Carter Bennett smiled across his desk. "The sooner the better."

Willis Chambers sat on the edge of the visitor's chair, his position not one of anticipation or concern, but rather intended to spare the knifelike crease in his trousers. He was in his mid-thirties, tall and lank, with a sharp widow's peak that caused him great concern, a long, slender, patrician nose, and close-set, almost piggish brown eyes that, together with an unpleasant, near-permanent scowl, spoiled any chance of being considered handsome. Chambers had been a classmate of Bennett's at Princeton but, unlike his college chum, had bypassed financial studies at Wharton—viewed then as the graduate school of choice for his generation—opting instead to take an MBA at Rutgers. Yet despite this failing—in Bennett's eyes—the two had remained friends, and a year earlier, when Waters Cable had found itself in need of a new director of human resources, Bennett had lobbied to bring Chambers on board. Willis Chambers, he had reasoned, had both the nature and proclivity of a seasoned hatchet man, exactly the qualifications Bennett sought. Even more important to

Bennett, Chambers would do precisely as told without any irritating concerns of conscience. The faint, unappetizing smile that now came to Chambers's lips assured Bennett he had made a good choice.

"Where would you like to begin?" Chambers asked.

He had been summoned to Bennett's office to discuss resignations the company hoped to force, and the means best suited to achieve them.

Bennett served up another smile. "There's a certain psychology involved," he said. "At least that's my view of it."

Chambers nodded, but said nothing. In many ways he and Bennett could have been clones. Each lived with a certitude of his eventual success. Each eschewed any concern for his actions. But where Bennett did his worst with a pleasingly handsome smile, Chambers projected a certain harshness. Bennett was simply smoother, and far more clever at dissembling.

"I think we start with people high enough up the ladder so it's noticed. Visibility is key here." Bennett raised a cautioning finger. "But only a few at first, and not anyone who is currently overwhelmed with personal problems." He pursed his lips. "Heavy medical bills, that sort of thing. People like that tend to dig in and wait things out. And that's not what I want. I want people whom others respect, and who can afford to think about a voluntary relocation. That way, when those who really can't afford to leave receive similar treatment, they'll look back and see what good old Joe did, and they'll be a bit easier to push toward the door."

"Sort of the herd mentality," Chambers said.

"Exactly." Bennett raised another finger. "In that regard, our first targets should also be people who will walk away with decent pensions. That will spur them on when the pressure builds. They won't think in terms of possible buyout packages. They'll just want out. Then later, once we've set the tone, we'll go after the ones whose pensions aren't vested. By then the psychology should be set, and quite a few, I think, will be inclined to walk away with empty pockets."

"And those who don't?" Chambers asked.

Bennett shrugged, smiled. "They'll pick up some buyout money. It's unfortunate, but inevitable."

"Any particular areas you'd like to see hit first?"

Bennett nodded. "Sales and manufacturing. Both are visible, and both are overloaded with middle-aged hacks. But pick the individuals wisely. I don't know the personal facts about any of these people, so I'll let you search your records and cull accordingly." Bennett paused, thought. "People with past problems might be a good choice. Drinking, drugs, family difficulties, that sort of thing. But only if they fit the other criteria."

"The computer will do all that for me." Chambers offered up a rare smile. "Do you have any particular methodology in mind?"

"Yes. Let's start by stripping them of perks and privileges—sort of a chipping away at their prestige—the more humiliating the better. Start with small, but very tangible, very visible things. Follow that up with letters of reprimand; official warnings of impending dismissal. Things that could become part of their personnel records and impede future employment. Also very heavy, and steady, criticism of their work. Get immediate superiors to do that for you where you can, but bypass them if you sense any resistance."

"If I'm too heavy-handed some of those superiors might lodge complaints." He hesitated a moment. "I have to tell you, the mood in the building is a bit tense. People seem to sense what's in the wind. In fact, security has brought some things to my attention. . . ."

Bennett waved him off. "Yes, I expect things may be tense. But that's only going to worsen as things move ahead. I'll need you to handle it." He had spoken the words sharply, and now smiled away the mild rebuke. "I also expect some complaints to be lodged. Unfortunately for those who make those complaints, I already have a plan to deal with that. It only needs Mr. Waters's personal approval." The smile widened. "I expect to have that this week. Then, I'm afraid, any complaints will get a fair, but somewhat disinterested, hearing."

Chambers decided not to press the other concerns he had. It was obvious Bennett didn't want to hear them. And it was quite possible the security people were just being paranoid. Instead he gave off a small, mirthless laugh. To Bennett it sounded more like a bark.

Bennett stood, placed both hands on his desk, and leaned forward. He wanted to bring himself intimately closer to the man. "Down the road, Willis—when this downsizing plan moves into full gear—the company is going to need its director of human resources to manage it all. I don't have to tell you that's a plum assignment, something that's quite impressive to have on one's résumé these days." He paused a beat. "I'd like you to be the man who gets credit for implementing this plan."

"And I'd like that very much, too."

Bennett smiled down at him. "Enough said."

Thirty feet down the hall from Bennett's office, Annie Schwartz came out of the ladies' room, where she had spent the last twenty minutes with her ear pressed against a heating duct. She paused, gave her recently coiffed hair a final fluff, then threw a sharp glance toward Bennett's closed door. "Enough said, indeed, you dick," she hissed. Then she turned and hurried toward Jack Fallon's office.

Thirty seconds after Annie Schwartz left, Fallon was standing beside his assistant's desk. "See if you can get me in to see Charlie Waters today," he said. "I'll be in

Wally Green's office, then up in legal with Samantha Moore if you get an answer."

Carol Hall looked up at him; her eyebrow rose infinitesimally at the mention of Samantha's name; then she made a quick note. She was in her late forties, an attractive, very married woman with two grown sons. She had worked at Waters Cable for seventeen years, and with Fallon for the past ten.

"Do I detect a maternal sense of concern?" Fallon asked.

"Just noting a new name," Carol said. She hesitated, then asked: "How's the home situation?"

Now Fallon elevated an eyebrow.

"All right, I *am* concerned," Carol said.

"The home situation is static," Fallon said. "But I think I'm getting used to it." He grinned. "Not unpleasantly."

"That's what I'm afraid of," Carol said. "Be careful. You're vulnerable."

Fallon's grin widened. "Thank you, Mother."

Carol rolled her eyes. "Speaking of which, the nursing home just called. They said there was nothing urgent about your mother's health, but the director"— she paused; checked a note on her desk—"a Mr. Montague, would like you to call when it's convenient."

Fallon sighed inwardly; certain it concerned his mother's bill. He made a mental note to see if Trisha had made the last monthly payment. He thought: Maybe she skipped it. After all, why dilute a soon to be looted checking account when there was a goddamned condo to be furnished?

He shook his head. "If they call back, tell them I'll get in touch as soon as possible."

Wally Green's office was a glass-enclosed rectangle that overlooked a large bullpen area that housed the desks of his New York District sales force. Wally was on the phone. Fallon started to enter, then stopped when Wally's first words reached him.

"I don't care what your shyster cousin says, I'm not footing the bill."

Wally looked up, saw Fallon standing hesitantly in the doorway, and waved him in.

"Hey, F. Lee goddamned Goldberg can stick it in his ear," Wally continued.

Wally listened, his face turning scarlet. "Oh, yeah. Oh, yeah, Janice. Well, you go to court. You tell your goddamned cousin to be my guest. The company's dental plan, which you're still under, doesn't cover middle-aged women who want their teeth capped. They all fall out someday? The policy will get you a nice set of choppers you can glue in. You get a cavity? It'll pay for the goddamned excavation—they should only use a jackhammer. You want 'em polished up like goddamned pearls? Be my guest. But no capping. The policy doesn't cover it, and Wally Green, your former schmuck of a husband, isn't about to fork over four grand so some goddamned orthodontist can have Corinthian goddamned leather in his goddamned Porsche."

Wally held the phone out in front of him and stared at it. He looked up at Fallon.

"She hung up on me," he said. He began to cackle, momentarily pleased, then stopped abruptly. "Now she'll drag my ass back to court, and I'll have to pay *my* lawyer four grand, just so I don't have to pay some goddamned orthodontist four grand."

Fallon stared at him. "Is your wife's cousin really named F. Lee Goldberg?"

"Naw," Wally said. "I just say that to drive her crazy. I used to call him Oliver Wendell Goldberg, but the woman didn't know who the hell I was talking about. Then I tried Clarence Darrow Goldberg. Ditto. But F. Lee Bailey she knows. The woman spent half her life watching the O.J. Simpson trial."

Fallon shook his head. The whole world was being run by dentists and lawyers, he decided. "Hey, maybe she's going to Howard," he said. "If she is, let her go. He makes a quick four thousand, Trish might let me have some of my furniture back."

"Yeah, fat chance," Wally said. "Learn this right now, my friend. Ex-wives do *not* give back."

"You ever think about becoming a marriage counselor?" Fallon asked.

"I'd make a damned fortune," Wally said.

Fallon shook his head again, dismissing the madness. "While we're on the subject of making money, tell me what's happening with the Sprint account."

Wally let out a long breath. "Disaster is what's happening. The trials we're running just keep falling apart. Or I should say our fiber optics are falling apart." Wally shook his head and hurried on before Fallon could speak. "The shit they sent down from the plant keeps failing. We're getting electrostatic interference, which should not be happening. According to the Sprint engineers, there have to be variances in our tolerance levels that no one on our manufacturing side can explain."

"Have you brought our technical support people in?" Fallon asked.

"A whole army of those stupid sonsabitches. They fly in with their briefcases full of computer printouts that claim our tolerance levels are all within acceptable limits. But I'm telling you they're wrong. They have to be. In the meantime"—he held his thumb and index finger an inch apart—"Sprint is that far away from eighty-sixing us from any shot at a contract."

"Do we have replacement product in production?"

"As we speak, they're setting up a run for next week," Wally said.

"Why next week? Why not this week?"

"Earliest they could get to it, according to our resident geniuses."

Fallon stared at the floor and shook his head. "Okay, let's you and me and Jim Malloy take a little trip to the plant for that run. Just see what we can come up with."

"Been there. Done that. Got blown off," Wally said. "Hey, if that's what you want, I'm happy to try again. I just don't hold out a lot of hope those assholes will listen to us."

"They will if we take product right off the line, and into the testing labs, and find out it's not what it should be."

"That's gonna put their noses out of joint," Wally warned.

"Into every life," Fallon said. "Besides, we're on the balls of our ass, and I don't plan to give Carter Bennett any more ammunition to toss our overfed butts out the door."

Wally's eyes filled with apprehension. "You hear something I should know about?"

"Yeah, a little bird named Annie whispered something to me. Seems her ear was pressed to the heating duct in the ladies' room this morning, and she heard Bennett and Willis Chambers doing a bit of plotting."

"Now I know why women always go in pairs when they gotta pee," Wally said. "One's gotta be there to give the other one a boost up to the heating duct. So what did Annie find out?"

"Just that they're ready to start pressuring people to resign. Except, according to Annie, they're calling it *voluntary relocation*."

"The shits say who's first on their list?"

"Nothing definite, as far as names go. Bennett just set some parameters and left it up to Chambers. Let's just say it fit the scenario we talked about."

"Jesus."

"Don't get your tail in an uproar," Fallon said. "It's not all bad news. It seems Chambers expressed some concern about the mood he senses in the office—also about some things security has come up with. You know anything about that?"

Wally offered up a look of mock innocence. "I suppose it could be those gun magazines Ben Constantini and Joe Hartman have been leaving in people's offices." He let out a cackle. "Benny showed me one. It had a picture of a three-fifty-seven magnum on the cover. Benny had circled it in red, with the words 'Downsizing Special' written next to it." He cackled again. "If that's got Chambers worried, wait till he sees this."

Wally opened his desk drawer and pulled out a stack of photocopies. He handed one to Fallon. It was a three-page article titled "How to Make a Bomb from Everyday Household Items."

"I planned to start leaving those on people's desks next week," Wally said. "Hell, maybe I'll start tonight. I may even leave one in Chambers's office. If the little prick thinks we're turning into a bunch of militia bombers, he might decide to voluntarily relocate his own skinny ass."

Fallon grinned at him. He noted the toy dinosaur on Wally's desk. It was the one he had given him at their lunch the previous week. The others, he had noticed, also had their dinosaurs prominently displayed.

"I love it," Fallon said. "Keep it up. And tell Joe Hartman to get started on that guerrilla newsletter we talked about."

"It's already in the works," Wally said. "We're calling it *The Daily Downsizer*, even though it will probably come out only once or twice a week. And Annie's put together a memo she's gonna send out on everybody's E-mail. It tells people to call a special number in Carter Bennett's office if they're worried about their job. It's 1-800-Pink Slip."

Fallon laughed. Bennett would not be amused. "That's great. I had another idea. I think we should all get together a couple of times a week and hit the company gym after work."

"*What?*" Wally's face filled with incredulity that bordered on outrage.

"It couldn't hurt our image. And it might help work off some of the frustration. Talk to the other dinosaurs this morning. See how many are willing to show up after work on Wednesday."

"Jesus," Wally said. "I think I'd rather get canned. I *know* I'd rather get canned."

Fallon ignored him. "And get a fix on exactly when the new product is being run, then coordinate something with Jim so we can all be there."

"Jesus," Wally said again, his mind still fixed on the company gym. "Carter Bennett won't have to fire me. He can come to the company gym and watch me croak."

Fallon started for the door, then turned back. "You might be right," he said. "He's there three times a week. But maybe the next time he goes, we'll have a little surprise for him."

Samantha stared at the papers on her desk, not seeing any of the words spread across the report she was trying to read. Her mind was fixed on Fallon, her thoughts a jumble, none of them making any sense. The man was wonderful, and she couldn't get him out of her mind, couldn't wait to see him again. Maybe you've just lost your mind. And maybe you're falling into a relationship that will do nothing for either of you—serve no other purpose than to screw up two lives. She drew a deep breath and tried to drive the thought away. But it pushed its way back. Think, woman, she told herself. Just think. And look at what you're doing. You've even begun handing out privileged information, putting yourself in a situation that could get you disbarred—even telling yourself it's the right thing to do. She clenched her jaw. It is, damn it. No matter what your law professors would say.

She shook her head again, still trying to shake the arguments away. More madness. Even thinking like this is just pure, unadulterated madness.

Samantha looked up, startled to see Fallon entering her office. All her arguments shattered. She smiled at him, her eyes holding a sudden sparkle. "It must be telepathy," she said. "I've been thinking about you all morning."

"Not as much as I've been thinking about you," he answered. "You make a strong impression."

She immediately wished she could reach out and touch him, was surprised by the depth of the impulse. "Are you here for legal advice, or is this strictly social?"

"I just wanted to see you," Fallon said. The words made him feel like a schoolboy. "I also wanted to know if you'd have dinner with me tonight," he quickly added.

Her smile returned. "I'd love to," she said.

"Great. I've got an appointment with my lawyer at four. Seems he's been in touch with my wife's attorney." He rolled his eyes. "How about I pick you up at seven."

"But you'll have to travel back and forth," Samantha said.

Fallon grinned at her. "You're worth it," he said.

They stared at each other for several seconds, the heat between them slowly building.

"Why don't you bring a change of clothes, and stay at my place tonight? Then you won't have to drive back and forth a second time." She spoke quietly in deference to the open door to her office, but her tone was matter of fact, and she watched Fallon's jaw drop slightly, and started to laugh. "You're looking at me like I'm some kind of brazen vixen."

Fallon grinned again—at himself this time—then glanced back at Samantha's still open door. "I wish I had thought about closing that," he said.

Samantha rose from her chair, walked past Fallon,

and closed the door. Then she put her arms around his neck and kissed him.

"Wow," Fallon said, as she pulled back. "And to think, in all these years, I came up to legal only when I had to."

"You should come more often," she said. "It might even improve your image of lawyers." Then she kissed him again.

Samantha's intercom buzzed two minutes after Fallon had left, and her assistant announced that Carter Bennett was on the line. Reality suddenly flooded back.

"Just wanted to know how our settlement package was coming along," Bennett began. "And . . . to see if you'd be free for drinks tonight."

Samantha listened to the subtle pause in his words; she could almost see the confident smile that would be fixed to his face. Just the thought of it made her angry.

"I'm still a day or so away from finishing the revisions," she said. "But I promise you'll have it by week's end." She let a small silence play between them, then went on. "And I'm afraid I have plans tonight."

The silence played out again; then Bennett finally said: "I see."

It was a rebuke, but she wasn't certain which of her statements it referred to—probably both, she decided.

"Let's set up a definite meeting," he said at length. "How's Friday, ten o'clock, my office?"

Samantha felt the chill of his displeasure. "That will be fine," she said. "I'll have everything together by then."

"Good. I'll see you Friday."

Samantha replaced the phone and stared at it. She had become quite comfortable turning down Carter's invitations. It was not, she now realized, something he accepted with grace. But it was also something he had better get used to, she told herself. At least where any personal relationship was concerned.

* * *

Wally was waiting in Fallon's office when he returned.

"The Sprint production run was moved up. It's set for late tomorrow morning," he said. "I had my assistant book an early flight for you, me, and Malloy."

Fallon noted a questioning rise to his own assistant's eyebrows, offered only a conspiratorial wink, then continued into his office with Wally trailing behind. "You sound like a cat headed for a dog convention," Fallon said.

"I just feel like my job is hanging on the results of this goddamned test," Wally said. "It scares me shitless."

"Your job is hanging on Carter Bennett's whim," Fallon said. "The test won't mean anything."

"Gee, thanks," Wally said. "That makes me feel a helluva lot better."

Fallon picked up a paper bag from a credenza behind his desk. "Did you talk to the troops about showing up at the company gym?" he asked.

"Yeah, I did. There was a lot of grumbling—in fact, some of them think you've lost your goddamned mind—but everybody's willing to show up. I guess that tells you how desperate we all are."

Fallon tossed him the paper bag. "Tell each of them to wear these," he said. "I want to make a statement."

Wally opened the bag and pulled out a T-shirt, held it up for viewing. He looked back at Fallon. "They're right," he said. "You *have* lost your mind."

Fallon grinned at him. "See that they get them," he said. "And tell them to wear them, and to meet us at the gym Wednesday after work."

"Jesus Christ," Wally said. "Now I'm not only gonna get my butt tossed out the door, but I gotta spend my last days of gainful employment with a nutcase."

10

FALLON'S OVERNIGHT BAG SAT BY THE FRONT DOOR OF the apartment. Just beyond the bag, the well-appointed furnishings were marked by a trail of clothing that wound an erratic path toward the bedroom. A jacket and tie lay crumpled in the foyer, not far from a pair of women's shoes. Several steps away, in the living room, a shirt and blouse had been discarded near a wall, the arm of the shirt having come to rest against a well-lined bookcase, one sleeve inexplicably pointing up as if reaching for a specific tome. Farther still, a bra, low-cut and tiered in lace, dangled from the arm of an antique Windsor chair, its strap almost touching a solitary, highly polished man's shoe, and nearby, at the base of a large sectional sofa, a pair of women's panties and a man's boxer shorts lay entwined, partially obscuring the second shoe.

They had arrived at Samantha's apartment after dinner, and clothing had begun to fall away as the door closed. It had been impetuous and urgent and had surprised them. Throughout dinner each had felt budding desire; but the unexpected degree of heat, the hunger, just seemed to erupt as they entered the apartment. They had kissed, and carnality had suddenly taken hold, and they had gone at each other in a staggering, fumbling frenzy. Now, in Samantha's bed lust continued as mouths and hands moved with a wanton will, exploring and caressing every erotic treasure; first with pressing compulsion, then slowly, pleasurably, until they could stand it no longer, and they joined, blotting out all feeling but that one final rapturous delectation.

They fell back, satisfied, yet greedily wanting more. Samantha nestled in the hollow of Fallon's shoulder, her fingers toying with the hair on his chest, lasciviously straying to the line that ran from navel to pubis.

Fallon stroked her back, allowing his hand to slowly drop to the sharp curve of her buttocks. He felt himself stir under the covers. "You certainly know how to end a day," he said.

Samantha smiled into his shoulder. "Who said it was over?" She felt his hand move to the side of her breast and smiled again.

During dinner he had told her of the trip he would take the next day, the tests he would observe at the fiber-optics plant. He hadn't spoken about his meeting with his attorney, and she hadn't pressed. Now she wanted to know, and she wondered what, if anything, that meant.

"Tell me about the meeting with your lawyer," she began.

He told her what Grisham had advised earlier, and what he had done. He paused and she could feel him take a deep breath, forcing effort. "Since then, my esteemed lawyer has talked to Trisha's esteemed lawyer," he began. "The dance of the bloodsuckers has begun."

Samantha grinned at the term. "All lawyers aren't bloodsuckers," she said.

"They're certainly all carnivorous," he said. He grinned at the ceiling. "You just proved *that*."

She poked his stomach. "And vicious, too," she added. "Now tell me what your bloodsucker said."

Fallon laughed, wondered why. None of it was funny.

He drew another deep breath. "It seems that Arthur C. Grisham—my bloodsucker—has begun negotiating my future solvency with one William Greenstreet, the vampire who represents Trisha and whose fee, of course, Trisha expects me to pay in full, since I'm getting the benefit of his acknowledged wisdom."

"And what is Attorney Greenstreet proposing?"

"Much," Fallon said. "But for starters, he suggests I pay Trisha's share of the condo's monthly maintenance fee. . . ."

"She has a *share?*"

"Oh, yes," Fallon said. "It appears that Howard—a man who obviously should have forsaken teeth and gone to law school—believes that my former beloved should not suffer the indignity of feeling like a kept woman."

"How sensitive."

"Indeed."

"And how much is her share?"

"Far more than I'll ever be able to afford. Unless, of course, I sell my house and move to the YMCA." Fallon let out a soft, mirthless laugh. "Of course, my soon-to-be ex-wife's esteemed counsel also suggests that I put the house on the market immediately so Trisha can have her share to pay her half of the condo's purchase price. He claims Howard loaned her the money for the closing."

"That's cute," Samantha said. "Sounds like Howard is getting nailed at the other end, and wants you to pick up part of the tab."

"That was the view of Arthur C. Grisham," Fallon said. "He figures old Howard will get hit for about a mil in personal assets, and about a hundred thousand a year in spousal maintenance."

"Did Trisha's lawyer mention maintenance for her?"

"Oh, yes. He feels she should get about seventy-five thousand per, which is half my base salary." Fallon let out another soft, mirthless laugh. "I was thinking how much simpler it would be if I just moved in with Howard's wife. Then we could turn it all over to an accountant and cut out the lawyers completely."

Samantha jabbed his stomach again. "Don't you dare," she said.

Fallon offered up a mock grunt. "Don't like to see lawyers knocked off the gravy train, huh?"

"That's not what I mean." Samantha rose up on one elbow and stared down at him. "I have no intention of giving up your considerable conjugal talents. Just remember that I'm a lawyer, too, and there is a certain legal tenet that deals with alienation of affection."

Fallon offered her a mock grin. "Everybody wants something," he said.

Samantha jabbed him again. "You have no idea how much," she said.

Charlie Waters stared at the traffic that raced along Fifth Avenue, a satisfied smile toying with the corners of his mouth. The table he shared with Carter Bennett was set before a floor-to-ceiling window in the West Lounge of the Metropolitan Club, the sanctum to which they had retired following dinner in the club's upstairs dining room. Seated there now, surrounded by the protective opulence of the room's gilded ceilings and fine antique appointments, Waters felt the quiet arrogance that the golden age "captains of industry" like Frick and Morgan and Henry Ford must have known—men who had been allowed to look out on the daily drudgeries and tribulations of common folk, certain that those same miseries would never be visited upon them. Quiet contentment spread through him, and he appeared to noticeably swell, filled with the sense of it.

Bennett sipped his brandy and studied Waters—the puffy red face displaying all the self-gratifying pleasures that had accumulated over the years. "You seem quite relaxed," he said. "I almost hate to bring up business."

Bennett's briefcase sat on the floor next to his chair, and a collection of papers lay in his lap. Club rules prohibited business papers in the dining room and other public areas, but the lounge was otherwise empty and Carter knew the rules could be bent, providing no complaints were made.

"You never hate to bring up business, Carter. You're like a machine." Waters chuckled at his small joke, then raised his own brandy snifter in salute. "And I do feel relaxed. This is a lovely club. Thank you for inviting me." He continued to stare at the passing traffic and the southern tip of Central Park just beyond. At the edge of his vision the Plaza Hotel sat like a shining icon of affluence, its classic facade illuminated, casting its rich glow on the line of limousines gathered before the main entrance. It was a sight that filled Waters with well-being. After years of early struggle, life was now everything he had hoped for—and held the promise of becoming even more.

"Stanford White designed this building, you know," Bennett offered. He had decided to play on Waters's self-contentedness. "The club's founders—primarily J. Pierpont Morgan and Cornelius Vanderbilt—personally gave him the commission." Bennett smiled across the table, warming to his story, knowing it would please Waters. "According to legend," he continued, "Morgan proposed a business friend for membership in the old Union Club. This was back in the 1880s, and the Union Club was *the* club in those days. Morgan and Vanderbilt and everyone of consequence belonged. But surprisingly, the friend was blackballed for some unknown reason. Morgan, of course, was outraged. Then the same thing happened to William Seward Webb, who had married into the Vanderbilt family." He saw a small rise to Waters's eyebrows and knew he had him hooked. "Well, that sparked a bit of a rebellion, led by Morgan and Vanderbilt, and it was quickly joined by the Goelets, the Iselins, and the Roosevelts." He watched Waters suck in the names of those prominent New York families of old, and he leaned back in his chair, ready to deliver his punch line. "Morgan, it's said, was determined to punish the Union Club's old guard, so he summoned Stanford White to his presence and told him: 'Build me a club fit for gentlemen. Damn the expense.'" Bennett spread his hands. "And that's how the Metropolitan Club was born. Morgan and his friends spent close to a million dollars—somewhere between fifteen and twenty million in today's money. And, of course, the Union Club was never quite the same again in terms of prestige and power."

Waters chuckled softly, and nodded approval. "That's a wonderful tale," he said. "Damn. Those were the days, eh? No income tax, and money to burn."

"And a will to have things your own way," Bennett added.

Waters looked back at the younger man and gave a confirming nod. "And rightly so, damn it." His chin was jutting forward now, and together with the sweep of longish white hair, it made him appear slightly leonine. Bennett smiled at the image.

"Today, people seem to forget the men behind the businesses that support them," Waters pontificated. "And it seems to be surprisingly easy for them to do it." He shook his head. "Hell, today a man works to build an enterprise, and when he succeeds, he finds that he's providing for thousands of people—employees, stockholders, suppliers, end users. But he also discovers that it's not enough. At least not for some people." He pressed his lips together in displeasure, then jabbed a long, fat finger at Bennett. "Just as suddenly he discovers that other people think he should do more—that they expect him to be even more of a benefactor. Even to the point of doing things against his own interests." He let out a dismissive snort. "These people—a bunch of damn lib-

eral soothsayers and politicians; bureaucrats and newspaper editors and God knows who else — they want him
to solve every problem that comes down the pike, no
matter the damn cost. They tell him pollution is *his*
problem, that everyone's retirement and health care are
his concern. They even throw in problems that have
nothing to do with him, or his business. Alcoholism.
Drug abuse. *Child care,* for chrissake." He shook his
head. "But what about him? What about his needs?" He
leaned forward, his look now severe. "If you listen to the
bleeding hearts, his needs be damned."

Bennett continued to smile. God, the man was
such a buffoon, he thought. Sitting there red-faced
and beaming. He actually viewed himself in a class
with a J. Pierpont Morgan, or a Cornelius Vanderbilt.
The mighty CEO — enthroned. Just like so many of
the old fools running corporations today. Filled with
self-satisfaction and blithely taking credit for the work
of all the bright young minds whose ideas made the
wheels turn.

Bennett tapped the papers spread before them.
"Except, this time, *you* have the will to have things your
own way. And there's not a damned thing anyone can do
about it."

Waters stared at the papers as though they might bite
him. "Except sue us," he said at length.

"Possible. But unlikely," Bennett said. Despite the
bravado, Waters wanted it all done quietly, without any
public fuss.

Adjusting the papers, he smiled at Waters's still
uncertain look, then continued. "With the pressure
we'll begin to exert tomorrow — to very slowly and carefully exert — there shouldn't be any faction left that's
large enough to offer a real threat. And as people start to
leave, profitability also rises in corresponding incre-
ments."

He turned the papers toward Waters and began pointing out several names. "These are people not eligible for pensions. Close, but no cigar. Next to their names are the amounts of nonvested funds that will be left in their pension accounts when they leave." He turned several sheets of the printout and pointed to a final figure. "As you can see, the total is substantial. And quite an attractive figure to anyone looking from the outside." He let the not so subtle hint drop, and hurried on. "Add to that the people who would leave with pensions, but who in doing so would relieve us of the one and a half percent increase in cost per year"—he tapped his finger against a second figure—"and that overall saving becomes equally attractive." Bennett raised his hands and let them drop under their own weight. "So without even taking into account the savings in salaries from these surplused employees, it's a money pot for us. A pure and simple money pot."

"But I still haven't seen the final figures on what it will cost to buy these people out," Waters complained. "That's the one potential fly in the ointment."

"A very small fly," Bennett said. "Legal still hasn't come up with a final proposal." He made a displeased face, shook his head. "But as I've explained before, I've projected a worst-case scenario."

Bennett pulled another printout from the stack, as Waters leaned in close to study it. The figures were identical to the ones he had seen a few days earlier. He looked up. "These are fine. But I still want to see legal's settlement proposal," he said.

"I'll have it this week. Without fail," Bennett said.

"What the hell's taking so long?"

Bennett shrugged. "Samantha Moore is putting it together, and she's an extremely careful lawyer." He forced a smile. "Perhaps too careful, but I'm not about to fault her for that. Like you, I want this to be ironclad. And I want it pulled off without any public fuss."

"Just light a fire under her tail," Waters said.

Bennett nodded, then leaned forward. "There is one other thing we *should* do."

"What's that?"

Bennett folded his hands, prayerlike. "With our program to encourage resignations beginning, I'd like to divert pressure from Willis Chambers. I envision he'll be our front man on this, the one issuing the directives, and I'd like to make sure no division heads who outrank him can overrule any of his decisions."

"What do you suggest?" Waters asked.

"I think a simple memo like this might do the trick." He handed Waters a single sheet of paper.

"Won't this also tip our hand?" Waters asked.

"We can revise this draft, make the final memo one magnificent obfuscation," Bennett said. "I can do it myself if you wish. I'd like to get it circulated tomorrow."

"Do the necessary revisions and give it to my girl, Gladys," Waters said. "I'll tell her to expect it. But the foggier the better."

"My feelings, exactly." Bennett eyed a waiter standing by the door. "Would you care for another brandy?" he asked.

"Yes, I think I would," Waters said. "I think we've earned it, don't you?"

"Definitely," Bennett said. He felt an inner swell, and punctuated the word with another smile. "Most definitely."

11

JIM MALLOY PUT DOWN THE PHONE AND STARED AT Fallon and Wally Green. They were killing time in a conference room adjacent to the technical services laboratory, waiting to start tests on the just completed manufacturing run of fiber-optic wire. Malloy had just telephoned his office in New York.

"I just found out I don't have a secretary anymore." His face was suddenly pale.

"Marge quit?" Fallon asked.

"Hey, I'm not surprised," Wally said. "Who the hell wants to work for a Simon Legree like you?"

Malloy shook his head. It was more confused incredulity than denial. "She didn't quit. She was reassigned to marketing." He stared at Wally. "As of today, you and I are sharing *your* secretary. Excuse me, your assistant, since that's what the title is these days."

"*What!* Who the hell says *that?*" Wally demanded. "I'm not sharing my goddamned secretary, or assistant, or whatever, with you or anybody else." He turned to Fallon, as did Malloy. "What the hell is this, Jack?"

Fallon looked from one to the other. "Damned if I know." The fact suddenly registered and anger took hold. "And I damned well should," he snapped. He moved past Malloy, snatched up the phone, and telephoned his own assistant, then listened—incredulous—as she explained. "Switch me over to that smarmy little S.O.B.," he said.

When Willis Chambers's assistant answered, Fallon growled into the phone. "This is Jack Fallon. Tell Willis I need to speak to him. Now!"

Fallon glowered at the wall, shifted his weight several times, and waited. Two minutes passed before Chambers picked up his extension with a bright "Good afternoon, Jack." Fallon was certain he could hear a sneer behind the words.

He didn't wait, he simply launched. "What the hell is this crap about Jim Malloy's assistant, Willis? I'm told it was your directive."

"Costs, Jack," Chambers answered. "I've been told to thin support staff wherever possible."

"By whom?" Fallon snapped.

"The directive came straight from Carter Bennett," Chambers said smugly.

"Well, I'm countermanding it. I want Malloy's assistant back at her desk before lunch. And don't you ever usurp your way into my division like that again."

There were several long seconds of dead air. "I wish I could oblige, Jack. But there's also a second directive. This one from Mr. Waters himself." He paused, allowing the second deity to register.

"And what does *that* say?" Fallon snapped.

"Well, it seems Carter has been named by Mr. Waters to study the need for a *personnel surplus reduction*. In light of that, all department heads have been ordered to report directly to him. *I* would interpret that to mean that only Carter can countermand orders for the present. I'm sorry, Jack. I'd like to help, but my hands appear to be tied."

Fallon ground his teeth, then spoke through them. "Have your assistant switch me over to Carter's office."

Chambers let out a breath. "I'm afraid she's tied up on the other line. Couldn't you just call him directly?"

"I'm not in my goddamn office, Willis. I'm at the Plattsburgh plant. Please ask her to get *off* the other line and transfer me. Or do it yourself. It's not that complicated."

Chambers paused. "What are you doing in Plattsburgh, Jack?" he finally asked.

"Never mind what the hell I'm doing here. Just transfer the damn call."

Another silence. "Certainly, Jack." Chambers let the seconds play. "It may take a few minutes," he added, then punched the hold button.

Minutes passed again. Fallon had no doubt Chambers was trying to phone Bennett and warn him. When the woman in Bennett's office finally answered, Fallon found himself placed on hold yet again.

Time dragged once more—a full five minutes before Bennett came on. He ignored all amenities. "What is it, Fallon?" he demanded. It was the schoolmaster challenging the recalcitrant child. Fallon bristled, but held his temper.

"I'm calling because Willis Chambers eliminated Jim Malloy's assistant. Apparently, in his wisdom, he expects him to share one with Wally Green. He did this without consulting, or even advising, me."

"And you consider that a problem?" Bennett asked.

"You bet your ass I do. First, Jim is in charge of all government sales. He's running eight sales execs, and the whole group is burdened with government regs and specs. Wally's running seven men, who deal with phone companies and a shitload of private firms. Now Willis expects both of them to handle their staffs and everything needed to support them with one person. It just won't work, Carter. And what it saves in one salary will be lost two or three times over in productivity." Fallon listened to dead air, then continued, "It also pisses me off that things are being changed in my division without the courtesy of speaking to me."

"I'm sorry you're offended," Bennett said. "But let's settle it quickly. I stand by Willis's decision. We're cutting costs, and your people will have to live with it along with everyone else."

Whatever patience Fallon still had evaporated. "That's bullshit, Carter. Willis doesn't know a thing about our operation, or our needs, and he's making decisions without even trying to find out."

"Willis is following *my* directives. So let's be clear about what and *whom* you're questioning."

"Oh, I see," Fallon snapped. "And that alone is supposed to eliminate the bullshit quotient?"

"My orders come directly from Charlie Waters," Bennett snapped back.

"That still doesn't change the fact it's a bad decision, and one I should have been consulted about before Willis started fucking around with *my* division and *my* people."

"The decision stands, Fallon. If you have a problem with that I suggest you consult Waters himself."

"You can bet your bippie on that one, Carter."

"Good luck, Fallon." Bennett paused, and his malicious grin could be felt across the line. "By the way, what are you doing in Plattsburgh?"

Fallon did another slow burn. "I'm surprised Willis didn't have that information for you. He seems to know everything else about my division."

"I'd like an answer to my question."

"I'm sure you would," Fallon said. "I suggest you check with Willis. He seems to be the resident authority on everything you need to know."

Fallon replaced the phone and glared at it, as though ready to smash it with something heavy. "That goddamned snake," he hissed. He turned back to the others.

Malloy stared at him. "So Bennett's backing Chambers?"

"I think Chambers is just following orders. Bennett's orders. It seems everyone reports to Carter now. Myself included. It's all part of a study he's doing on the possible need for a *personnel surplus reduction*." He ground his teeth. "I should have seen it coming. Annie picked up something about it when she had her ear pressed to the heating duct."

Malloy interrupted him, his face ashen. "Wait a minute, Jack. What the hell is this personnel surplus reduction crap?"

"Don't get bent out of shape. You know what it is. We all knew it was coming. They're just throwing out some hints."

"Getting their ducks lined up is more like it," Wally said.

"Well, if that's what they're doing, we're the ducks," Malloy added.

Wally ground his teeth. "First they reduce our support staff. Next that little shit will have us sharing toilet paper. You think maybe Carter's trying to tell us we should look for work elsewhere? *Personnel surplus reduction*. Where do they get these bullshit terms? Why can't they just say, fired, axed, laid off, for chrissake?" He offered up an evil grin. "We oughta just turn Georgie Valasquez loose and let him shoot those Ivy League sonsabitches. Put large holes in both of them. Except he'd have to call it something else. Maybe, *involuntary ventilations*."

Malloy drew a deep breath, and Fallon could see the fear in his eyes. "I think Wally's right. I think this is the first step to get us to pack up and leave, and I've been elected to go first," he said.

Fallon had little doubt it was, but forced any confirmation away. He needed cool heads, especially his own. "Look, let's not jump to any conclusions," he said. "We'll straighten it out when we get back to New York."

Jim Malloy and Wally Green stared at him. Each looked far from convinced.

Stuart Robaire flipped through computer printouts of earlier tests, as Fallon, Malloy, and Green peered over his shoulder. Robaire was a small, slender man in his mid-forties. He had a pinched, narrow face, set off by bottle-glass lenses perched on a large nose that hooked down toward his upper lip. A protruding Adam's apple added to the picture of a man who spent his days hidden away in an electronics laboratory. The final touch was a white lab coat, replete with pocket protector stuffed with pens.

Robaire ran a finger along a row of figures. "As you can see, each run is meeting manufacturing specs. All tolerances should fall well within acceptable limits." The man's voice was high and squeaky, naturally defensive. As head of the plant's technical services department, he was repeatedly accused of failing to discover problems that affected sales.

"Could the specs be wrong?" Fallon asked. They were still in the mini conference room, just off the laboratory. It was furnished with institutional metal furniture crammed into a small space, and Robaire took a step back as if trapped in a closet.

"The specs were set by Mr. Waters himself," he said. "He spent weeks down here overseeing all the engineering that went into them."

"Well, shit. I guess we don't have to worry they might be wrong."

Robaire glared at Wally Green. "Why don't you try your sarcasm on him?" he snapped.

Wally pulled his own printout from his briefcase and a specimen of wire he had brought from Sprint. "These are the recent set of screwups we ran into when Sprint did some controlled tests of our wire," he said. "And this is a product sample. We're running into similar problems on the gyroscope tests that Jim is running with the air force. Why don't *we* run some new tests to see if we can duplicate those problems. Maybe we'll have a revelation, some little epiphany as to what's going wrong."

Fallon raised a hand, stopping the sarcasm, then took Robaire by the arm and led him to a window that overlooked the rolling fields that surrounded the plant. A light rain had fallen that morning and the meadows were wet and glistening under the sunlight that had now broken through the clouds. A quarter mile distant, a trout stream snaked through the terrain, and he fixed his eyes on it as he spoke.

"Everybody's a bit on edge, Stuart," he began. "We're getting our tails kicked, and the cause always comes right back to product. We haven't run comparative tests on end-user results. So let's do them. What the hell can we lose?"

Robaire twisted nervously. "You want to tell Mr. Waters his specs are crap?" he asked.

Fallon let out a soft laugh. Back in the early days he had done just that—he and Waters had debated engineering points endlessly. "It wouldn't be the first time," he said now. It was a pleasant memory, quickly killed. That was a long time ago, and too much had changed. Waters would not react well to being told he was wrong. Especially now. Especially by Jack Fallon. "Look, I'm not half the engineer Charlie is," he said. "And it's been a lot of years since I worked this end. But that doesn't mean Charlie can't make mistakes. All I'm suggesting is that we check. And if there *is* something wrong, *I'll* tell him. Then we'll fix it and climb out of this mess we're in. Okay?"

"You'll authorize the tests?"

Fallon held back a smile. "They'll be on my head, Stuart."

Robaire thought about it, then said, "I'll need a memo covering it."

"You got it."

Robaire hesitated again, then spoke in a lower voice. "I don't mean to be a shit about this, Jack. But we hear the rumors up here, too." He pulled a folded paper from his lab-coat pocket and showed it to Fallon. It was a copy of *The Daily Downsizer*. Jim Hartman had obviously gotten the first edition out by E-mail. "Have you seen this?" he asked.

Fallon fought back a grin. "I've seen it," he said.

"I'm not trying to be a hard-ass, Jack. But I've got a kid in college, and another ready to start next year."

Fallon squeezed his arm. "I understand, Stuart. I'll take the heat if anything hits the fan."

Robaire drew a breath. "Shit," he said. "I do *not* want to do this." He shook his head. "But we might as well find out. Let's go into the lab."

They were in shirtsleeves, huddled around a lab table, as Robaire fed the needed information into a computer. He compared the data on the screen to the computer printout Wally had provided.

"Make sense?" Wally asked.

Robaire nodded. Despite the air-conditioning he was sweating. "Some of the same questions were raised before the first gyroscope production run," he said.

"And?" Fallon asked.

"The concerns were not well received."

"So what's your best guess."

Robaire shook his head. "I *think* Sprint may have gotten the wrong product. I *think* they may have gotten stuff intended for the gyroscope research contract. But I'd have to run more tests to prove it."

"So let's run them."

The telephone rang, and Robaire went to a nearby desk to answer it.

"Yes. I'll take the call here."

He was silent as the call was transferred, then again as he listened.

"Sales requested the tests to resolve some end-user problems. We're just setting it up now."

Robaire listened again, bit on his lower lip. "Do you want to speak to our salespeople?" he asked at length. "Jack Fallon is here." Robaire stiffened slightly. "Very well," he said. "I'll tell them."

Robaire replaced the phone, let out a long breath, and turned to Fallon. "No tests," he said.

"Who the hell says so?" Wally snapped.

"That was Carter Bennett," Robaire said. "He says nothing will be run without his, or Mr. Waters's, approval. He suggests you check with him before you order anything in future."

"How the hell are we supposed to do this job?" Malloy spun toward Fallon. "How, Jack? Tell me."

Fallon glared at the top of the lab table. The muscles in his jaw danced against the bone. "I guess we're not. That seems to be Carter's message. Not unless he tells us to."

"And we're supposed to work that way?" Wally asked.

"Let's get back to New York," he said. He extended a hand to Robaire. "I'll make it clear I authorized this," he said. "With any luck we'll be back."

He could tell by the look in Robaire's eyes that he hoped that would not happen.

12

FALLON GOT BACK TO HIS OFFICE AT FOUR-THIRTY. CAROL seemed nervous, perhaps even a bit fearful. He decided that the "all-girl grapevine" that Annie Schwartz touted so highly had already passed on the news of his Plattsburgh debacle.

"See if you can get me an appointment with Charlie Waters," he said. "And stop looking like your cat just died."

Fallon entered his office and fell into his chair. Carol came in a few minutes later and found him leaning back, staring at the ceiling.

"Mr. Waters is in a meeting with Carter Bennett," she said. "His assistant said it could run late, and suggested you try again tomorrow."

"Do you know if she told Charlie I wanted to see him?" Fallon asked.

Carol seemed embarrassed—for him, he thought. "Yes, I think she did," she answered.

Fallon stared at the top of his desk. "Try again in the morning," he said.

Carol avoided his eyes. "Samantha Moore called. And Warren Montague, the administrator at your mother's nursing home, called again. He said it was extremely important that he reach you."

Fallon closed his eyes. He had completely forgotten the earlier call from Montague. He tried to picture the man; the image of someone tall, slender and graying came to mind—a well-dressed man, despite his somewhat rakish choice of combining perennially dark suits with a flowing, British-style, military mustache—sort of a cross between a *GQ* funeral director and a Parisian pimp.

"I'll call him," Fallon said. He added *tomorrow* to himself.

Carol hesitated. He had always encouraged her to speak freely with him, and she always had.

"What is it, Carol?" he asked.

"I guess that's what I need to know from you," she said. "What's going *on* in this company. We all hear the rumors, but now—with Jim's assistant being transferred, and Mr. Waters apparently avoiding you . . ." She hesitated. "And I heard what happened in Plattsburgh."

Fallon came to a quick decision. The woman had a right to know. "I think the company's headed toward a big downsizing, Carol. I think this is just the beginning of it."

"But it's not going to affect you, is it? I mean you're . . ."

"Don't count on that saving me," he said. He tried to soften the words with a smile. Then he thought of Samantha's projection—a one-third reduction in the workforce. Carol was from his own generation. And she had two teenage sons at home.

She seemed to sense his thoughts. "Does that mean I'll be going, too?" she asked.

"I don't know," he answered honestly. "I don't know who'll be hit and who won't. But I think the numbers are going to be high."

"Those bastards," she snapped. "How can they do that to people?"

"It's like a disease going around," Fallon said. "And they've obviously caught it."

Carol let out an angry breath. "If there's anything I can do, please tell me."

Fallon was touched by the generosity of her offer. He smiled at her. He considered telling her about Annie Schwartz's ladies' room listening post. "Just keep your ears open," he said. "Executive assistants usually hear things before anyone else."

"I'll do better than that," she said. "I'll talk to the other assistants and get them all to keep their ears open. If anything happens, we'll know it first."

Fallon smiled again. Add a few more dinosaurs to the club, he told himself.

When Carol retreated, Fallon picked up his phone and dialed Samantha.

"How went the trip to Plattsburgh?" she asked without preamble.

"I should of stood in bed," Fallon said.

Fallon told her about the aborted tests, and the surprise Willis Chambers had laid on Jim Malloy.

"None of that makes any sense," Samantha said. She seemed to hesitate, and Fallon jumped in.

"It does if Carter Bennett is sharpening his ax." Silence came from the other end of the phone. "Anyway," Fallon continued, "I've got no choice but to go to Charlie Waters. All I have to do now is get in to see him, and that's not proving too easy."

"I'm sure he'll listen, Jack. You go back a long way together." There was a note of genuine hope in her voice, and Fallon wished he felt it himself.

"I just wish I had something solid to hang my hat on," he said at length. "I hate like hell to go in there sounding like a damned paranoid."

There was a lengthy pause. "Are you free for dinner tonight?" Samantha finally asked.

"Sure. But are you going to the gym first? I was hoping you were. I have a little surprise for you."

"What is it?"

"Uh-uh. This is something you have to see with your own lovely brown eyes."

"Well then, I'll certainly be there. Now that you've intrigued me so cleverly."

The smile was back in her voice, matching the one Fallon now wore.

"Great," he said. "I'll see you there at six. Then we can have dinner."

"At six," she said.

Fallon was still smiling when he replaced the phone. Then he noticed the message Carol had placed on his desk—Warren Montague, the director of his mother's nursing home. The smile faded and he picked up the phone again and dialed the number. There was no sense in putting it off.

Montague had to be paged, and sounded slightly breathless when he got on the line.

"Mr. Fallon, I'm so glad I finally reached you," he began.

"Is something wrong with my mother?" Fallon asked. He felt immediate guilt that he hadn't called back earlier.

"Oh, no. No," Montague assured him. He hesitated. "Nothing physical at any rate. But it is important that we sit down and talk as soon as possible. Could you stop by tomorrow morning, perhaps?"

"Well, what is it, then? The fees?"

"No, no, no. Everything is quite current." Montague paused again. "It's just that your mother is causing a bit of a problem, one we're hoping you can help us resolve."

"A problem?" Fallon had a sudden vision of a list of complaints, or perhaps demands, that his mother had issued.

"I really can't go into it right now," Montague said. "You caught me in the midst of a tour with a prospective family, and there just isn't any privacy at the moment."

He hurried on. "Would it be possible for you to be here at nine tomorrow morning?"

Fallon thought of his need to see Charlie Waters. "Actually, a bit earlier would be better for me," he said. "Eight. Eight-thirty at the latest."

"Let's say eight-thirty then." Montague paused again. "And, Mr. Fallon, would it be possible for you to come to the rear door. I'll be there waiting for you."

"The *rear* door?"

"Yes. If you simply leave the visitors' parking lot and walk around the building, you'll find it easily. I assure you it's necessary. I'll explain fully when I see you."

"And you're sure my mother's okay?"

"Oh, yes. Yes, yes, yes. Please don't concern yourself. Her physical health is excellent."

Fallon let out a weary breath. "Okay," he said. "The rear door it is."

"I'll see you then," Montague said, an obvious tone of relief in his voice.

Fallon replaced the phone and stared at it. Jesus H. Christ, he thought. What the hell was happening now?

Samantha also found herself staring at her desk. Before her was the initial draft of the buyout proposal Carter had directed her to prepare. It was thirty pages long, but it felt pounds heavier.

Throughout the day Carter's assistant had badgered her for it, and she had forced herself to complete it. She thought about Jack, and the obstacles being thrown in his path. Her proposal included some final recommendations that she was sure Carter would not appreciate, but they had been necessary, if not legally, then to soothe her own conscience. Now they seemed even more imperative. If Charlie Waters could be convinced, Fallon and some of his men might be able to survive.

Samantha buzzed her assistant, and handed her the document when she entered the office.

"Ruth, I'll need two copies of this," she said. "One for our file, and one for me, personally. Then please deliver the original to Mr. Bennett's office. It should be in an envelope marked confidential," she added.

The assistant, a slight, bespectacled woman in her early thirties, took the envelope and started to leave. Samantha's words stopped her.

"And, please. This is highly confidential, Ruth. Make sure the office copy is locked up, and that it's discussed with no one."

"Certainly," the woman said.

Samantha sat back and momentarily closed her eyes. Now it's just a question of ethics, she thought. She sat up and pushed the problem away. But it returned immediately. Damn it, she thought. She had no doubt what her law school professors would say. But that was easy, she thought. Ethics were complex, and theory and reality were very different things.

They entered the gym behind Fallon—a group that would make any health club owner rub his hands together with the prospect of long-term profits—six sets of legs, clad in a mixture of shorts and sweatpants, each displaying oversized posteriors and protruding guts. Only Fallon looked reasonably fit. He had added morning sit-ups and painful abdominal crunches to his daily regimen, and it had begun to show some incipient results. The remaining six—Wally Green, Jim Malloy, Ben Constantini, Annie Schwartz, Joe Hartman, and George Valasquez—seemed exactly what they were: middle-aged people slipping rapidly into self-satisfied decline.

Across the gym, Samantha Moore stared at them in disbelief. All seven wore matching navy-blue T-shirts with an identical logo emblazoned in white across their chests. The logo depicted the profile of a *Tyrannosaurus rex*, encircled by the words THE DINOSAUR CLUB. The back of each shirt carried the warning BEWARE OF DINOSAURS. She stared at the shirts and fought back laughter. The Dinosaur Club had just made its public debut.

Fallon handed each of his blue-clad crew a sheet of paper bearing the exercises they would all do. Wally Green stared at his and rolled his eyes.

"Jesus Christ, Jack. Why don't you just buy a gun and shoot me in the head?"

Fallon squeezed his shoulder and felt a layer of dampness beneath the T-shirt. Changing clothes—or perhaps bending over to tie his gym shoes—had already caused Wally to break a sweat. Great, he thought. You're playing right into Bennett's hands—killing off the very people he wants to push out the door.

Fallon blew out a long breath, driving away his doubts. "Okay," he said. "They've got four treadmills and four stationary bikes. We'll divide up and do fifteen minutes on one or the other. Then the exercises on the sheet; then back for another fifteen on either a bike or a treadmill—whichever one you didn't do before."

"And then the goddamned undertaker comes and takes us all away," Annie Schwartz groused.

Fallon leaned in close and lowered his voice. "No. First Carter Bennett comes here, sees your Dinosaur Club T-shirts, hears you bitching and moaning, and laughs what's left of his skinny butt off."

Silence and six sets of stony eyes met his.

Annie broke the silence. "So, I'll do this, and later, when this gorgeous body is even more gorgeous, I'll enter the Miss Middle-Aged America beauty pageant."

"That is something I will sweat to see," Wally said. He grinned at the tongue Annie had stuck out. "Okay. Let's get moving," he snapped. As the others turned to the machines, he looked back at Fallon. "Did you at least alert the paramedics and my goddamned rabbi?" he asked.

"Get on a bike, Wally," Fallon said. "And try not to fall off."

As Fallon headed to his own bike, Ben Constantini beckoned him forward. "Hey, Jack. They had a gym like this at the Pentagon. I tried it when I worked there. I lasted two days." He widened his eyes for effect. "And that was sixteen years ago, Jack. So don't expect too much."

Fallon winked at him. "Just keep remembering how bad basic training was. This is a piece of cake, Ben."

Fallon mounted a bike between those being used by Wally and George Valasquez. "Race you to the top," he said.

Wally grabbed his crotch. "Race this, you sadist. If I drop dead, I'm suing you."

"If you drop dead, I'll fire you," Fallon shot back. "Now let me see a pool of sweat under that bike."

"Fascist," Wally growled. "I wanna join a union."

Out of the corner of his eye, Fallon saw Samantha moving across the floor. She was dressed in the same black unitard and pink thong she had worn when Fallon had first seen her. She stopped before Fallon's bike. He noticed Wally's eyes widen.

She stared at Fallon's T-shirt. "The Dinosaur Club?" she asked.

"In the flesh," Fallon said. "All seven of us." He winked at her. "You think Carter will be impressed?"

"He'll be in shock," she said. "I can't wait to see his face." She held out a copy of *The Daily Downsizer*. "Have you seen this? It was on my E-mail this morning."

Fallon widened his eyes in innocent surprise. "Everybody keeps asking me that." He studied the newsletter, then read the headline aloud. "WATERS CABLE LOWERS VOLUNTARY RETIREMENT AGE TO 35. This is fascinating," he said. "It says a lot about the company's sensitivity, don't you think? The way it keeps everyone up to speed about what's going on."

"There also were some terrific E-mail memos," she said.

"Even better." Fallon inclined his head to each side. "By the way, I'd like you to meet Wally Green and George Valasquez, salespersons unparalleled. This is Samantha Moore, gentlemen. From our legal department."

"You represent abused employees?" Wally asked. He was grinning now, desperately trying to hold in his gut, and peddling as fast as his plump legs would allow. Sweat already dripped from the tip of his nose.

"I'm afraid I'd have to represent management."

"I'm management," Wally insisted. "Represent me. Sue this sadist, Simon Legree boss I've got."

Samantha lowered her head and smiled, then looked back to Fallon. "Meet you in the lobby at seven?" she asked.

"You got it," Fallon said. "If I'm late it's because the coroner hasn't finished up yet."

Samantha turned away, smiling, and headed back across the floor. Seven sets of eyes followed her.

Fifteen minutes later The Dinosaur Club was scattered about the gym. Joe Hartman sat on an exercise bench, T-shirt drenched with sweat, eyes staring at a rack of dumbbells. Wally Green lay on the floor next to him, imitating a beached whale.

George Valasquez walked up and nudged Wally with his foot. "Come on," he hissed. "That prick Bennett will be here any minute."

"Let me die." Wally moaned. "Send for somebody to sit shivah for me."

Joe Hartman pushed himself up from the bench and picked up two twenty-five-pound dumbbells. "Come on, Wally. Georgie's right."

Wally rolled over and struggled to his knees. "I wanna beer," he said. "What kinda gym is this? They don't even have a goddamned bar."

Wally stood and stretched his back. His stomach drooped down over his sweatpants. Across the room he could see Fallon and Constantini taking turns spotting each other on the bench press. Annie Schwartz was struggling through a set of chin-ups on an outlandishly large Nautilus machine. "Outta their goddamned minds," Wally hissed as he joined Hartman and Valasquez at the dumbbell rack. "We're all gonna die. Every goddamned one of us."

Carter Bennett entered the gym at six-thirty and stared in disbelief at the logo-emblazoned T-shirts.

Wally spotted him first, and immediately began pumping his dumbbells at a furious pace. Sweat rolled down his face, and he grinned maliciously in Bennett's direction. "Watch this, you motherless bastard," he hissed under his breath. He glanced across at Valasquez. "The prick's here," he whispered.

George's eyes shot toward the door, washing Bennett with undisguised contempt. He glanced toward the others. Each had seen Bennett arrive, and each had intensified his or her own exercise. George's pinched face took on an even sharper edge.

Again, Wally increased his effort. His right hand shot up, and the edge of the dumbbell struck his chin. His knees quivered, and he groaned, sotto voce. "Shit, I'm dying," he whispered. "Take me to intensive care."

"Not now," George hissed. "Look at that prick's sweat-shirt."

Wally glanced at Bennett. He was wearing Princeton sweats with the face of a tiger set beneath the school's name.

"Beware of dinosaurs," George hissed. "They eat little pussycats."

Wally let out a weak giggle, then forced himself to pump the weights even harder, this time holding his chin out of harm's way.

"If I die, Georgie, there's a pack of glow-in-the-dark condoms in my nightstand," he whispered. "They're yours. I hereby put it in my will."

"I'll use 'em to fuck Bennett in the ear," George whispered back.

Wally giggled again. "Oh, God. Oh, God. Send for the goddamned paramedics."

Bennett spotted Samantha across the room and moved quickly to her side. He lightly grasped her elbow.

"What the hell's going on here?" His voice was low and slightly urgent.

"What do you mean, Carter?" she asked. Her face was intentionally blank as she fought down a smile.

"The T-shirts. What's it all about?" There was a bewildered look on his face, mixed with a hint of anger.

"I have no idea. I guess it's some sort of club."

Bennett digested the idea, his face darkening. "Well, I don't like it," he whispered. "It smacks of conspiracy."

Samantha put down her pair of ten-pound dumbbells, lowering her head to conceal the smile that flickered across her mouth.

When she stood, she raised her chin toward the mock newsletter that lay on a nearby bench. "Have you seen that?" she asked.

Bennett stared at the newsletter, the muscles in his jaw doing a little dance. "I saw it. I wasn't amused." He leaned in close again. "I also wasn't amused with your proposal. Especially the addendum about who *should* and should *not* be terminated."

Samantha stared at him. "I'm sorry it displeased you. I made those suggestions with an eye toward avoiding litigation. That's my job, Carter." There was an edge to her voice now that surprised Bennett.

"I've told you, I don't care about litigation. I only care about how costly *losing* might be."

Samantha fought to keep her voice even. "The best way to avoid a costly loss is not to litigate."

Despite her efforts, Samantha's tone continued to be sharp, and Bennett bristled under it. "I'm starting to wonder whose team you're on," he snapped.

Samantha had a sudden urge to snap back: Me too. Instead she bathed him with an innocuous smile. "I'm sorry you're displeased. But can we meet about this tomorrow, Carter? I'm a bit pressed for time tonight."

Bennett felt staggered by the remark. He took another step back, then turned and glanced again at Fallon's little group. The sweat-stained T-shirts gnawed at him. What the hell was going on? he wondered. Newsletters. E-mail memos. Now this. His jaw hardened. The Dinosaur Club, indeed.

He turned back to Samantha. "Tomorrow morning. First thing," he said. He spun around abruptly and moved back across the room, passing Fallon, who was now prone, well into a set of sit-ups. Bennett was surprised by the ease with which he seemed to do them.

His lips curled into a partial sneer. "Like your T-shirt, Fallon," he said. "By the way, have you seen Charlie Waters yet?" The sneer grew.

Fallon stared at him; forced a grin, keeping his voice light. "Not yet. Haven't had time. But I'll get to it, Carter."

Bennett's sneer grew. "Good luck. I believe you'll need every bit of it."

"I'd like to strangle the smarmy little creep."

Samantha looked up from her menu. Fallon's face was tight, as he stared into a glass of Pouilly-Fuissé. They were seated at a window table at Polo, an upscale restaurant on the ground floor of the Westbury Hotel, and the delicately pale white wine glimmered in the brash glow that came in from the street. It had begun to rain again, and it had darkened Fallon's mood. Outside, rain-slick Madison Avenue mirrored the lights of surrounding buildings, and Samantha thought it quite beautiful.

"You're talking about Carter, I suppose." As they had walked to the restaurant, Fallon had told Samantha about Bennett's jibe, and each word had seemed to deepen his anger.

Fallon picked up his glass and took a large gulp. He looked beaten and weary.

Samantha reached across the table and took his hand. "That's an excellent wine, Jack. And you won't enjoy it if you gulp it down. You won't even taste it."

She was smiling, teasing him, but immediately Fallon shot her a look that seemed to say: It's my wine; I'll drink it the way I want. Then, just as suddenly, he let out a breath, shook his head, and forced a smile.

"God, that rotten little bastard really got to me. I'm even ready to bite *your* head off."

"Don't let him." She squeezed his hand. "And *please* don't bite my head off."

Fallon squeezed back. "It's not just him. It's all the Carter Bennetts who've crawled out of the woodwork over the last ten years." He shook his head again. "I was thinking about it on my way back from Plattsburgh."

"They were always there, Jack."

He nodded, but it lacked commitment. "Maybe. But not in such profusion." He let out a breath. "I seem to remember a time when companies respected the guys who had been around a while—who had survived, helped their companies survive. I used to look for guys like that in the firms we sold to, because they knew so much more than the others did. They were hard, but if you could impress them, you could impress anyone."

He picked up his glass again, sipped it this time, then offered Samantha a smile of concession. "My, what a wonderful bouquet," he said. The smile turned to a grin. "Anyway, on the way back from Plattsburgh today, I was thinking how I was Carter's age when he was sitting in his little room at Princeton fantasizing about cheer-leaders."

"I don't think Carter ever fantasized about cheerleaders," Samantha said. "I think he always fantasized about money and power."

Fallon grinned again. "Yeah, you're probably right. But, anyway, I was thinking about it. And I wondered if Carter ever thought about it. I wondered if he ever visualized another little future yuppie sitting in a similar dormitory, and if he understood that fifteen years from now that kid will be dead center in the carnivorous world he seems so determined to create—but that, then, *he'll* be the meat the little bastard wants to feed on."

"I don't think Carter worries about that," Samantha said. "I think he expects to be CEO of a company long before that happens. And if he's not, then I think he believes he deserves whatever he gets."

Fallon looked back into his glass and shook his head. "Is that what it's come to? Have we degenerated all the way to accepting the idea of survival of the fittest?"

"Was it ever different?"

"Jesus, I *think* it was. I can remember going to retirement parties. I can remember the sincere affection for those people—the sense, in most cases, that they'd be truly missed." He looked across the table at her, wishing she could remember it, too. "I'm not saying there weren't people rubbing their hands together about the vacancy that was being created. Or ruthless bastards, who tried to push people out of the way. Of course there were. But they were *looked upon* as ruthless bastards. They were an anomaly. They weren't respected by their peers. They weren't people anyone wanted to emulate. And, most of all, they didn't represent the way things were done."

Samantha stared at him, but said nothing.

"I sound naive, huh? Maybe I am. Maybe Trisha is right—that I'm a guy with seventies values who's stuck in the nineties."

"When do you think it changed? This attitude toward people, I mean."

Fallon paused, as if trying to pinpoint a specific date. "It's hard to say, because it seemed to sneak up on us. I guess it started in the early eighties, with all the merger insanity, all the mindless acquisition. That's when the bottom line became king. Then it just grew. And before anybody knew it, the idea of permanence had simply faded away. All of a sudden nothing was expected to last. Not people, not companies, not even society. Only profits." He toyed with his glass. "It just sort of crept in, and then it was there. Or maybe we just ignored what was happening. Maybe we never expected it to go this far." He stared across the table at her. "Human values aren't supposed to change that way, I don't think. But they do, of course. It happened in Europe in the thirties, didn't it? A whole new set of values that lacked any humanity. Suddenly it was there. And people bought into it because it held out the promise of economic gains after some very hard times. And it also gave them a chance to blame someone else for those bad times, to ignore their own complicity. And that was important. The ability to have an easy scapegoat—people who had *caused* the problem. It gave the ruthlessness a justification."

Samantha stared at the table. "That's a hideous picture, Jack."

"You think I'm wrong? That this is somehow different? You think jettisoning people solely for the purpose of increased profitability has any moral standing, or even any humanity to it?" He picked up the cocktail napkin on which his drink had sat and began tearing at it absently. "Bad management is the reason companies are in trouble today. Years of bad management, complete with all the excessive perks that went with it. But the guys running things are never going to admit that. They want an easy scapegoat. And what better than to piously proclaim that they've been too good to people for too long." His fist closed around the shredded cocktail napkin. "And guys like Carter *feed* on that kind of thinking.

You saw those poor klutzes in the gym tonight—that group of wonderful clowns who've been labeled dinosaurs. All of them, scared to death, and even more frightened that it might show. Christ, none of them ever wanted to be CEO of anything. Their sense of worth didn't depend on that." He stared across at her, his face weary again. "Those people are everywhere, in every company. They work in labs and in manufacturing, in clerical jobs and shipping departments, because it's what they do best, and they're proud of it. But by Carter's premise they're fodder, and they're expendable because they haven't made it to safety at the top." He let out another cold laugh. "The very place everything got screwed up in the first place."

He looked away, shook his head, then turned back to her. "Have you been into a Kmart, or a McDonald's, and seen the fifty-year-olds who are suddenly all over those places doing menial jobs?"

She shook her head. "I haven't noticed, I guess."

He nodded. "I only really started to notice myself." He offered her a regretful smile, as though acknowledging his own absent sensitivity. "I guess you have to face the bear before you realize how dangerous the woods are."

He shook his head. "Christ, I watch all these companies shutting down plants and moving to Mexico, and the Philippines, and wherever. All to get cheaper labor so they can grab more profits." He leaned toward her, his face earnest. "I see them laying off hundreds, thousands of people, and I wonder what the hell is going on in their minds. Isn't anyone saying: Hey, wait a minute, if we all do this, who the hell is going to buy our TV sets and our cars and our toasters? Where's our talent pool going to come from when all those families can't afford to send their kids to college anymore? What's going to happen to our economy when those kids grow up and are never able to buy a house? And you know what's even sicker? Nobody's asking those questions. Not even guys like me. We're all too busy watching our own backs, because we're all just trying to survive this new wrinkle in the game. And the guys who are making those decisions are oblivious to it all. They're fixated on balance sheets."

Samantha was stunned by his vehemence; even more than she had been able to put aside those same concerns for so many weeks. Yet, despite the mock newsletter, the phony E-mail memos, and the T-shirt bravado, there was also a hint of surrender in Fallon's voice that frightened her. She looked into her own glass of wine. "Jack, I'm going to give you something I shouldn't." She glanced up, held his eyes. "I've given it a lot of thought, and it's something I want to do. Not just for you, but also for myself. Up until now, I just didn't think I could . . . ethically."

"What makes you think you can now?" he asked.

She shook her head. "Sometimes, I guess, one set of ethics outweighs another." She wanted to tell him she cared about him, too. Perhaps was even falling in love with him. But no similar words had come from him, and perhaps, just perhaps, he was still in love with his wife. Even the possibility of that caused her pain.

He reached out and took her hand again. "Look, I don't want you to compromise your job. I'm a big boy, and this isn't your problem."

No, but I'm very much a part of the problem, she thought. Her own boss was on their hit list—which was why she had been given the task of preparing a severance proposal—and she had done nothing to warn him. The man was a chauvinistic fool, but he still didn't deserve what was about to happen. The realization she was a party to it disgusted her.

She stared across the table, kept her voice soft. "I've been doing quite a balancing act for the past several weeks," she began. "I've been doing something I haven't liked very much, but something I felt I had to do anyway." She lowered her eyes, realized how easy it was to make excuses. "I've tried to justify it in a lot of ways. Legal ethics versus personal ethics. But I guess it all boiled down to hanging on to a job I very much wanted to keep. I've worked hard to get where I am, and it hasn't been easy. There aren't many women in my position, and I guess I valued that fact more than I admitted, was even willing to do things I wouldn't have considered a few years ago." She felt cheapened by what she had said, but pushed it aside. "But I can't keep doing it. I realized that earlier today. Part of it's you, but part of it's what I see happening around me. And *to* me." She let out a long breath, urged herself on. It was a point from which she would not be able to return. "Jack, I've finished the draft buyout proposal I told you about. No one, other than Carter and whoever else is in the loop, is supposed to know about it."

Fallon let out his own long breath. "Have they told you who they're targeting?" he asked.

Samantha nodded. "I got the names a few days ago. All of you—all the dinosaurs—are on Carter's list. But it's been designed very cleverly. It includes almost everyone close to fifty and over, with a few exceptions in the lower salary brackets. It also includes enough younger people to undermine any claims of age discrimination. If you buy into Carter's bravado, he really doesn't expect that suit to happen. Though, frankly, I think the idea makes him nervous. Still, he's hinted that the whole question of a suit might be moot—that a sizable number of people might leave before the offer is even made."

Fallon let out a derisive snort. "I think he's already started that little game." He lowered his eyes. "And I don't think there's any way to stop it."

"Probably not," Samantha said. She reached down, withdrew a manila envelope from her briefcase, and slid it across the table. "That's a copy of my proposal. Carter just got it today, and he's already indicated he's not pleased with it. Especially not the recommendations I made concerning factors that should be considered before anyone is put on their final target list."

Fallon opened the envelope and flipped to the back of the report. He read the addendum and offered her a haggard smile. "I bet he wasn't," he said. "But even with this, even if he agreed, it's still wrong."

"I know." She felt an odd mixture of emotions, moving between professional and personal. There was an underlying sense of betrayal in each.

"I don't think Carter has final approval for this, but I think he's close," she said.

"I think he has the approval that counts," Fallon said. "I think Charlie Waters is one hundred percent behind him. They may still have to sell it to the board, but it's Charlie's board. As long as the numbers crunch the right way, they'll get what they want."

"If it comes to that, the proposal will help you make a case for age discrimination. Especially if the recommendations are ignored."

Fallon nodded. "I know. And I appreciate what it means for you to give it to me. You could get in a bit of trouble, couldn't you? I mean even outside the company?"

"Believe me, I've thought about that. And, yes, it's a breach of client confidentiality," she said. "The bar's disciplinary committee would not view that lightly."

He reached across the table and took her hand again. "Being a hired gun sucks at times, doesn't it?"

Samantha let out a small, mirthless laugh. "I never suspected how much."

A waiter came to the table, ready to take their order. Samantha shook her head, sending him away. "I think I've lost my appetite," she said. She glanced out the window. The glistening street didn't seem beautiful anymore.

"Yeah, I know what you mean," Fallon said. He

squeezed her hand. "I have to be at my mother's nursing home early tomorrow morning," he said. "But I still have the change of clothes I took to Plattsburgh, and I'd very much like to spend the night here with you. I'll just have to leave early in the morning."

Samantha looked across the table and gave him a wistful smile. "I'd like that, Jack. And I think I could use it."

13

THE RESIDENCE AT WILLOW RUN SEEMED SOMNOLENT, almost still, when Fallon pulled his car into the parking lot at eight-fifteen. A few elderly denizens had already taken their posts on benches scattered near the front entrance. Otherwise, all was quiet.

Fallon sat in his car with the window down. The rain had ended during the night, and the morning was unseasonably cool, almost crisp, the still-wet foliage filling the air with a sniff of the autumn yet to come. He had left Grand Central at six-fifteen, retrieved his car at the suburban station parking lot, and had driven home to drop off his suitcase and check his mail. Then he had headed for The Residence and his eight-thirty, rear-door meeting with Warren Montague.

Fallon glanced at his watch and decided to remain in the car rather than stand outside the rear door until the appointed time. He had done this once before, he recalled. Trisha and he had come together for his twice-monthly visit. They had been arguing, and had remained in the car, spewing invective at each other until, finally, he had gone inside alone.

Had there always been that much fighting, or were those times just indelibly marked in his mind? Perhaps now they were—some necessary defense mechanism to ease the pain—the cuckold convincing himself he was better off. It was a depressing thought, the fact that the pain was still there even more so. But he knew he would never seek reconciliation, would not spend his days wondering when infidelity would again reenter his life. And renewed intimacy, he was certain, would always carry the taint of a former lover, and would crush and overwhelm all feeling. Was that some primal need for exclusivity, some perquisite of possession? He hoped not. He wondered if he was sorry she was gone or simply hurt by her decision to dump him for another man. And what about your complicity in all of it?

Fallon stared out the window, not wanting to consider any of it. Think of better things, he told himself. His mind settled on Samantha, the one, perhaps the only *better thing* in his life right now.

What she had done the previous night staggered him. He did not dismiss a higher ethical motive behind her decision. But there was no doubt her feelings had played an essential part. The end result would probably not allow him to escape Bennett's scheme, but that didn't matter. There had been little hope of that anyway. And that was something she knew, had to know. Yet she had placed herself in jeopardy. Love? The thought of it so soon after Trisha's betrayal scared the hell out of him. But how do you feel? You think about the woman incessantly, see her every chance you get. Are *you* falling in love with *her*? Everything about Samantha kaleidoscoped through his mind. She seemed so damned perfect in so many ways. Is there any reason not to be falling in love with her?

Jesus. What would she want with you? What would anyone want with a middle-aged mutt about to be tossed out of the only real job he's ever had? Add to that a divorce that's about to bankrupt you, and two kids in college with grand expectations you may never be able to meet. He glanced toward The Residence and reminded himself not to forget dear old Mom.

Fallon climbed out of the car, escaping his thoughts. He made his way along the walkway that led around the building. As he rounded the final corner, he came upon the small, man-made pond at the rear of the building. Empty benches were scattered around the perimeter, vapor rose from the surface. Five ragged-looking mallards paddled along the far shore, old ducks no longer capable of migration who had adopted the pond as a year-round home. Ducks in a nursing home, Fallon thought. Why not?

He went to the rear door and found it open, an anxious Warren Montague waiting just inside. The nursing home director was tall and slender, and he was dressed in a dapper, yet very somber, blue suit—an undertaker in waiting, Fallon thought. Montague was smiling, but Fallon thought he detected more than a little panic in it.

"I'm glad you could come." He let out a slightly weary sigh. "We have a somewhat awkward situation." Montague had clasped his hands and was rubbing the palms back and forth. Fallon had the distinct impression he was about to be shown a coffin.

"How awkward?" Fallon asked.

Montague took Fallon by the elbow and led him away from the door. There was a small sitting area in front of a picture window. They took chairs opposite each other, Montague's back to the window. Behind him a bedraggled male mallard was pursuing a female along the shore. It was not an amorous pursuit, Fallon noted. The female had a crust of bread in its beak.

"Your mother has caused a bit of a commotion, I'm afraid," Montague began. He offered a weak, helpless smile. "All of us here—the entire staff—are at a loss on how to deal with it. We were hoping you might help."

A commotion? My mother? Why am I not surprised? Fallon thought.

"What seems to be the problem?" Fallon asked.

Montague clasped his hands, rubbed the palms again. "Goodness, this is embarrassing. But I assure you it just happened. No warning at all."

"What *is* it?" A hint of concern had come to Fallon's voice.

The weak smile reappeared. "Well it seems your mother—a lovely woman . . ." Montague was fumbling now. "Everyone here just adores her. . . ."

I doubt that, Fallon thought.

"Well, it seems she's become a bit delusional."

Fallon sat forward and held the man's eyes. "Please, Mr. Montague. Just tell me what the hell is going on."

Another breath. "Well, it seems your mother has decided that she is the reincarnation of the Virgin Mary."

Fallon stared at him. "What?"

Another weak, sickly smile. "The Virgin Mary. The mother of Jesus." He studied Fallon's face, seeking comprehension. The palms massaged each other again. "She's begun dressing in a blue robe and blue veil, and she's been holding . . . apparitions, I guess, throughout The Residence."

"Is she walking on water?" Fallon asked.

"That was her son, I think," Montague said.

Fallon covered his face with his hands, shook his head.

"I'm afraid it's even a bit more serious," Montague said.

Fallon looked up. "How so?"

"Well, it seems some of our other residents—not many, but some—have taken this situation to heart." He made a face, as if what he was about to say would not be believed. "Some of them seem to be . . . venerating her. Some of the Catholics have even begun saying the rosary when she . . . appears, so to speak. I'm afraid the numbers have even been growing."

"She has a *following?*"

"I'm afraid so," Montague said. The expectation of disbelief appeared on his face again. "Frankly, it's why I asked you to come to the rear door. The staff was concerned the sudden appearance of the, uh . . . Virgin's son"—he offered a weak, apologetic smile—"might create a bit of a stir." He looked nervously at his feet. "There have even been some cures."

"*What?*"

"They're psychological, of course. But several residents have refused to use their walkers. Someone has even called the Archdiocese in Manhattan claiming a miracle. We're terrified, of course, that someone will call the press."

"What do you want me to do?" Fallon feared he would be asked to take his mother home.

"Well, we were hoping you could speak with her, convince her she's *your* mother—Kitty Fallon—not Mary of Nazareth." He twisted nervously. "I'm afraid all of our efforts have met with rebellious behavior."

"From my mother?"

"Oh, no. She's quite the proper lady—*as always*. She simply holds out her hands and looks beatific." He imitated the gesture. It reminded Fallon of statues he had seen in church. "It's her followers," Montague said. "The other day, when I tried to lead her back to her room, an elderly gentleman began chasing me in his wheelchair, screaming that I was Pontius Pilate."

Fallon stared at him in disbelief. Behind him the aging male duck had fallen on its face and was floundering in the grass. "How many followers are there?" he asked, trying not to be distracted. He could hear the old mallard quacking in frustration. The female duck waddled away with the crust of bread.

Montague tried to smile, failed. He seemed bereft of hope, embarrassed by it. Floundering like the old duck, Fallon thought.

"How many?" Fallon asked again.

"Only a few dozen, but the numbers seem to be growing each day," Montague said. "There were twelve saying the rosary yesterday, but those were only the Catholics. A few Protestants have joined in—in fact, we've had two who've declared themselves prophets. And one Jewish gentleman has become an *apostle* of the Virgin. He's even inquired about converting." He let out a sigh.

"Converting to what?" Fallon asked.

"We're not sure," Montague said. "We don't think he is either." He hesitated, looked at Fallon with skeptical hope. "Do you have any idea why your mother might choose to become the Virgin Mary? If we knew, it might give us some clue about how to deal with it. We may ask your permission to bring in . . . uh . . . a psychiatrist to evaluate her."

Fallon shook his head. "I never thought my mother was very religious." He thought a moment. They were lucky she hadn't become John the Baptist, he decided. Then she might be dunking her fellow inmates in the duck pond.

He offered a befuddled shrug. It had to be some kind of scam his mother had devised. He was still terrified he'd be asked to pack her bags and take her home. "I'm at as much of a loss as you are," he said. "But I'll certainly speak with her. I'm sure we can clear this up."

Montague brightened up visibly at the thought. "Oh, God, I hope so." He seemed suddenly embarrassed at having invoked the deity. He stood, as did Fallon. "Just one thing," he said. "Would you mind wearing one of the white coats our orderlies use?"

Fallon stared at him.

"I just think it best you're as inconspicuous as possible," he explained.

Fallon followed Montague through a labyrinth of hallways that isolated food and service areas from the residential portions of the complex. Fallon was dressed in a white lab coat that had the name, *Dwight*, stitched over the right breast. When they reached a doorway at the other end of the complex, Montague stopped and raised a finger to his lips.

"We're just outside her room," he whispered. "Let me take a peek first."

He inched the door open, peeked into another hall, then closed the door quickly. He beckoned Fallon to him, then leaned toward his ear. "There's a line of residents outside her door."

Fallon stared at him.

"She also holds some private apparitions," he explained.

"Does she charge?" Fallon asked.

Montague stared at him in horror. "God, we never thought to ask," he said.

They entered the residential hallway just outside Kitty Fallon's room. A line of elderly men and women, some propped on walkers, stood waiting outside the door. An ancient man in a wheelchair sat to one side like a palace guard. He glared at Montague as he approached.

"What do you want, Pilate?" he snapped.

Montague stiffened, then smiled. "We must go inside. Just for a moment. The Virgin needs her medication."

Montague eased himself to the door. A low hissing rumbled throughout the queue.

"No line jumping," one elderly woman snapped. She swung a cane at Montague's back, barely missing his head. He opened the door and stepped quickly inside. Fallon followed, ducking low to avoid any follow-up strike.

Fallon leaned back against the door and drew a breath. His mouth fell open. Kitty Fallon's room blazed with light. The curtains were drawn and no fewer than thirty candles sent out a luminous, beatific glow. His mother stood before the closed curtains. She was dressed in a flowing blue robe with a matching veil covering her head. Her arms were extended from her sides, palms open and forward, thumb and index finger joined. Jesus, Fallon thought. The Mother of God.

A small woman knelt before her, head bowed. Fallon recognized her at once. She was one of the women he had seen in the sitting area on his last visit—the one who supposedly drank. Fallon stared at her; wondered if she was there seeking a cure for Don Ho.

Montague went to the kneeling woman, and gently guided her to her feet. "You must leave now," he whispered. "The Virgin needs her rest."

The woman's head snapped around. "What does she need to rest for? She's been dead for two thousand years. What the hell's the matter with you? I need my prayers answered."

"You can come back later. I promise you," Montague soothed. He led the grumbling woman past Fallon. Their eyes met. Montague's were imploring. Fallon's were filled with disbelief.

The door shut behind him. Kitty Fallon leaned to one side, assuring herself they were alone. Then she lowered her arms and slumped into a nearby chair.

She looked Fallon over from head to toe, an open inspection, seeking some fault. "What are you doing here?" she finally asked. "It's not the first or third Sunday."

"They sent for me," Fallon said. His eyes roamed the glowing candles. "Because of this."

She continued to stare at him. "Sit down, John," she snapped. "Don't stand there with your mouth open like some lump."

Fallon sat on the edge of her bed, irrationally wishing she'd call him Jack just once in his life. His eyes took in the room again, and he made an all-encompassing gesture with his hands. "What is this, Mom? What the hell's going on?"

Kitty Fallon lowered her veil to her shoulders and patted her perfectly coiffed gray hair. Her powdered cheeks were pinched and severe, and she looked neither blessed nor virginal—at least not by choice, Fallon thought. She glared across the room and snapped out a reply. "I'm making sure they can't throw me out. And that's just what they'll do when you tell them you're broke." She continued to glare at him, rebuking him. "I'm not going to be sent to some hellhole just because you can't hold on to a job, John."

Fallon wanted to snap back that he'd held on to the same job for nearly a quarter of a century. He resisted the pointlessness of it. "How is this . . . this . . . religious madness going to help you?"

"Medicaid!" She glared again. "The government won't let them send me anyplace if I'm loony tunes. I know. I've checked the rules."

"But you're not on Medicaid," Fallon said.

"I will be as soon as you're fired. I've already made application."

"But you have too much of your own money," Fallon argued. "You don't qualify."

"I've taken care of that," Kitty snapped back. "I've liquidated everything and put it in trust for my grandchildren. I don't have a dime to my name. But my Medicaid application will take a couple of months, so try to hang on to your job for that long."

Fallon bristled, then surrendered. He shook his head. "You're causing chaos here," he said. He watched his mother smirk. "It's not right," he added.

"I'm providing a religious experience. I'm not hurting anyone."

A Maxwell House coffee can caught Fallon's eye. It was on a table near her chair. He got up and stared into it. It was half filled with money, a few coins but mostly dollar bills. He stared down at his mother. "Are you charging these people?" he asked.

Kitty Fallon looked momentarily embarrassed. "They make donations," she snapped. "I can't afford to pay for all these ridiculous candles."

Fallon sank back on the bed and began rubbing his eyes. "Mom, it's got to stop. Please. I'll find a way to keep paying your expenses."

She stared at him. "I don't believe you."

14

THE DINOSAUR CLUB

...

CHARLIE WATERS PACED HIS OFFICE, HIS FACE REDDER
than normal.

"What do you think it means?" he asked.

"I have no idea," Bennett said. "But I don't like it
either."

"You think Jack Fallon's behind it?"

Bennett raised his eyebrows, inclined his head to one
side. "He was wearing one, and he runs the division. It
makes sense. As far as this newsletter goes, and the phony
E-mail memos, well, this so-called Dinosaur Club is the
only hint of resistance we've encountered."

"The Dinosaur Club," Waters said. "Goddamned
T-shirts. I don't like the smell of that. It could mean
they've banded together to fight us."

"There's nothing to fight," Bennett said. "Not yet. And
by the time there is, quite a few of them won't be
around."

"Damn right they won't," Waters shot back. He
stopped in front of his desk. He was in shirtsleeves, his reg-
imental necktie lying on top of his protruding paunch.
Behind him smaller buildings dotted a path to the East
River. He placed his hands on his hips, head lowered,
deep in thought. "Maybe we should bring Fallon in on

this," he said. "Just remove any personal insecurity he's feeling."

Bennett twisted in his chair. The idea irritated him. Once they started making exceptions there would be no end. "I'd rather not," he said. He decided some qualification was needed to soothe Waters's concerns, along with his ego. "At least not now." He smiled. "I'm sure I can handle him."

Waters jabbed a finger at him. "Don't underestimate the man. He's not a pushover. Read his damned war record if you think so."

Bennett wanted to tell Waters what he could do with Fallon's war record, but he simply tried to sound confident. "I assure you, I won't take him lightly," Bennett said.

Waters returned to his desk, sat, and continued to study the younger man. Bennett was bright and ruthless, and he had his finger on the pulse of the market. He wondered if he'd really be a match for Jack Fallon. He thought about it, decided if he had to lay a bet he'd go with Bennett. Waters glanced at a note on his desk. Fallon's assistant had called that morning, again seeking an appointment for her boss. He decided he'd see Fallon, just to see what was up his sleeve. He thought about having Bennett there as well but decided against it. Better to evaluate the situation without Carter's input.

"All right, let's let things sit as they are," he said. "But find out who's behind this damned newsletter and these memos, and put a stop to it. And keep an eye on this goddamned Dinosaur Club. We don't want any ugly surprises this late in the game."

Bennett offered Waters another self-assured smile. "I'll keep everything under tight rein," he said.

"How was your mother?" Samantha asked.

Fallon had called her when he got back to his office. Now he thought of his mother's own words. "She's

Loony Tunes," he said. He explained the apparitions at The Residence and his mother's demented reasoning.

"Oh, Jack, I'm so sorry." He could hear her fighting back laughter, and fought down his own smile.

"I am sorry, Jack. I don't mean to laugh. It's just the way you said it. What did you do?"

"I talked to Montague—he's the director there—and tried to explain that she was concerned I wouldn't be able to keep up her monthly maintenance costs. I assured him I would, and suggested he counsel her with that in mind."

"Do you think they'll keep her there?"

"Yeah. I'm pretty sure. She pays the full freight, and the people who do are golden to places like The Residence. Almost two-thirds of their clientele are covered by Medicaid. They don't pay anywhere near the full monthly fee, and nursing homes are precluded from turning them out. But if she keeps up this Virgin Mary nonsense, and other families start threatening to take their parents elsewhere, who knows."

"Do you think she'll stop?"

Fallon blew out a long breath. "God, I hope so. But I really don't know. Hell, tomorrow I might get a call that she's levitating over a burning bush."

Samantha suppressed a giggle. "I'm sorry, Jack. I know it's not funny."

"Yes, it is. Except it really isn't." He shook his head, driving away the madness of it all. "Tell me how your meeting with Carter went."

"Let's just say he is not amused with his formerly favorite lawyer."

"Maybe we should celebrate our mutually successful day," Fallon said. "How about dinner at my house tonight? We could grab a train right after The Dinosaur Club finishes up at the gym. I'll pick up some wine, and we'll drink to my mother's madness and Carter's lack of amusement."

"That sounds great." He heard her suppress another giggle.

"What?"

"Nothing."

"What? Tell me?"

"Well, I was just thinking. You could just get a bottle of water." More laughter was suppressed. "Then you could change it."

Carter Bennett surveyed the well-appointed room. A look of mild satisfaction crossed his face as he took in the men and women holding power lunches that day. The majority were his age or slightly younger, as they always were now. When he had first entered the business world such was not the case. Men of fifty-plus ruled. Oh, there were still a few of the ancients scattered about, but they were fast becoming extinct. This visual proof pleased him. It told him his philosophy, as always, was on the cutting edge of business wisdom.

Bennett turned his attention to the day's lunch-mates—Les Gavin and Willis Chambers. His luncheon invitations—summonses really—had been accepted greedily as they always were.

They were seated at a round table in the Oak Room of the Plaza Hotel. The dark, wood-paneled walls gave the room a subdued sense of wealth and permanence, a feeling of who belonged and who did not. Like many other tables theirs held a large bottle of Pellegrino water at its center. Drinking at lunch, save for the occasional glass of white wine, had become passé. Power, not pollution, had become the rule. Here, uniformed waiters moved unobtrusively. No one was rushed. Power required both time and patience from all concerned. Bennett smiled at the ambiance, then turned a cunning eye on Les Gavin.

"What do you know about this Dinosaur Club non-sense and any connection it may have to these newsletters and memos we have circulating through the office?"

Gavin was caught off guard and fumbled for an answer. "Uh . . . Nothing, really. I've seen the newsletter and the memos, of course, and, uh, I heard Green and Malloy kidding each other about dinosaur T-shirts. But I, uh, thought it was just some sort of inside joke."

"Any reason to believe the three things are connected?"

Gavin looked bewildered, making it obvious the idea had never occurred to him. He tried to recover. "Nothing definite. But it does look suspicious, doesn't it?"

Bennett sat back and hooked his thumbs into the vest of his three-piece suit. "Indeed it does," he said. "And if it's more, it's something we should know about." He leaned forward and stared into Gavin's eyes. "None of us wants any unpleasant surprises down the road."

"I'll do my best to find out," Gavin said. "But I'm not exactly buddy-buddy with those old fossils." He offered an exculpatory grimace. "I don't think they trust me." He let out a small snort, as if expecting laughter from the others.

Bennett gave him a smile. There was a touch of benevolence to it, but nothing more. He wanted Gavin to know he expected results. Gavin was the type who floundered under too much personal pressure. He needed the occasional there-there to keep plugging along. But he also needed the whip.

"Payback time will come, Les. You could very well be the one to hand all of them their walking papers."

Gavin grinned at the idea. "Nothing would please me more," he said. "I keep hoping that Fallon will hit the bricks first." The grin widened. "Just so the others will be left to me."

Bennett picked up a glass of designer water and sipped. "Could happen, Les. I know how badly they've all treated you. Of course, it might be even more satisfying if Fallon was forced to do it for us. But either way, the man's history." He replaced the glass, studied it for a moment, then raised his eyes back to Gavin. "But right now, I need you to find out what's going on. Surprises are not acceptable"—he paused for effect—"and they aren't something I'll be inclined to forgive."

The gauntlet dropped, he spread his hands. "Gentlemen, we're the people who are going to turn this company around. Let's not fall asleep at the switch." He turned quickly to Chambers. Willis had seemed to take some pleasure in Gavin's rebuke, but Bennett's final words had put him on edge. It was exactly what Bennett wanted.

"I think Wally Green should be next on our list," Bennett said. "I caught him sneering at me at the company gym last night. Let's start with some sort of reprimand. Any suggestions?"

Chambers narrowed his eyes in thought, then removed his glasses and placed one stem in his mouth. "The recent sales record leaps to mind. But then the reprimand would have to come from someone senior or equal to Fallon. Your office, or perhaps Mr. Waters himself; otherwise it would lack any real force."

Bennett shook his head. "I don't want Waters involved at this point. Or at any point, if possible. And, for the time being, *I* want to remain above the fray. What about this trip to Plattsburgh, and the little test they wanted to run?"

Chambers considered it. "It could work," he said at length. "The account involved was one of Green's, so it could be assumed the request came from him. The only problem I see is that Fallon—his immediate superior— was there with him, obviously condoning it."

"Even better," Bennett said. "By reprimanding Green we indirectly reprimand Fallon."

"What do we achieve?" Chambers asked. "In concrete terms, I mean."

Bennett shook his head, a reprimand in itself. "We're not trying to achieve *anything* concrete. We don't have to. Not now. Not in future. What we want is demoralization. If we reprimand Green, his entire sales staff will get twitchy. They'll begin to wonder when management will turn on *them*." He smiled. "The handwriting on the wall, so to speak. And if any reprimand is also an implied reproach of Fallon, even better. Then all his subordinate managers will get the jumps." He leaned forward, clasped his hands together—prayerlike.

"So what we want is a great deal of *handwriting on the wall*." Bennett unclasped his hands and put imaginary quotes around the words. "We want people looking for work *elsewhere*. They're not fools. They all know it's easier to get another job when you're employed. They also understand that prospective companies prefer to go with winners rather than someone who's already been cast off." He offered up a grin. "Although nobody's terribly interested in *old* winners anymore." The remark produced the expected chuckles, but he waved a hand, dismissing it. "In any event it may also prod some to take early retirement, if that option is available. And that alone will serve our purpose. It will lower the number of people who will have to be bought off, and it will also diminish the numbers who might join in any class-action battle. And if those numbers are low enough, *that* whole issue becomes moot." Bennett's hands went back together. "And that, gentlemen, is the bottom line. It's what this whole exercise is about."

Chambers gave the table two solid pats. "I'll have a letter of reprimand out no later than tomorrow morning." He grinned. "Then we can sit back and listen to Jack Fallon howl." He hesitated. "What about Jim Malloy? He was at the aborted test as well. We could hit him with a letter, keep his pot boiling."

Bennett shook his head. "Leave Malloy alone for now. Taking away his assistant sent a pretty clear message. I have a particular endgame in mind for Malloy."

Chambers raised his eyebrows. "Yes?"

Bennett picked up a fork and toyed with his napkin. "Malloy's the weak link in the division. When we need someone to crack, he'll be the guy." He stared across at Gavin. "Did Willis tell you he's a reformed boozer?"

"No. But I recall hearing *something* about that." Gavin offered up the supporting words a bit too quickly.

"I found it in his personnel records," Chambers said.

"About five years ago, he got what was supposed to be a private warning from Fallon," Bennett said. "But word got out via the clerical grapevine, and Willis's predecessor picked up on it and stuck a note in Malloy's file. You boys should learn to talk to your assistants occasionally. Those women know everything that goes on in this company." He tapped the fork lightly on the table. "Just mark my words. Malloy's the one. We can crack him open whenever we choose."

Bennett watched the others nod mute agreement, then turned on them. He was still toying with the fork. Now he jabbed it straight down at the table. "Now, as far as these newsletters and memos go, I want some results. I want to know who's behind it. I want to be able to prove it. And I want it quickly."

There was momentary silence, then Chambers waded in. "That could be difficult. It's going out by computer. It's not as though someone's delivering them desk to desk."

Bennett stared at him. The disapproval was obvious. "There will be notes, I'm sure. Something incriminating left behind. We know who we *think* is behind it. Check their offices after work. Get into their computers. Collect their damned trash if you must." He turned to Gavin. "I've seen you skulking about on weekends, Les. You know what I'm after." He looked back at Chambers. "You both do. So just do it."

The others remained silent, and Bennett raised a hand toward their waiter, signaling an end to the conversation. "Let's eat, gentlemen. I'm loaded down with meetings this afternoon."

When the waiter had taken their orders, Chambers decided to ease the tension, turn the conversation to something that would please Bennett.

"How's the paintball tourney coming?" he asked.

Bennett smiled. "New England finals this weekend," he said. "It's being held at an abandoned military base in Massachusetts. I fully expect to come home the winner."

"Stiff competition?" Chambers asked.

The smile widened. "Not stiff enough." He jabbed a finger at Chambers. "You should have stuck with it. You had potential."

Chambers tapped his glasses. "Damned eyesight held me back." He inclined his chin toward Gavin. "You should have gotten Les involved. He's a tennis player. Great hand-to-eye coordination."

"I tried." Bennett turned a cutting smile on Gavin. "You never heard so many excuses."

Gavin twisted in his seat. "I would have embarrassed you." He thought up a quick lie. "When I was a boy I tried target shooting at summer camp. I was a disaster."

Bennett grinned at the confession, which also commended his own talents. "Just as well to stick with what one's good at," he said. "I saw you on the tennis court at our golf outing last spring. I'm not sure I could handle that serve of yours."

Gavin smiled at his mentor. Oh, yes, you could, he thought. I assure you, I'd see to it. "It's not as good as it looks," he said. His own smile widened. "Anyway, I hope you bring home that trophy. New England regional champion—that would be quite a feat."

Bennett winked at him. "Someday they'll have nationals. Now *that* would be something."

From across the room, Bennett noticed a woman staring at him. She was in her late twenties, he guessed, quite attractive and exceptionally well dressed. He smiled at her.

The faint hint of a returning smile played across her lips. Then she looked away. But the smile had been enough. All around, it was turning into a very good day, Bennett thought.

15

THEY SAT BEFORE THE UNLIT FIREPLACE, BRANDY GLASSES in hand. Fallon had moved the leather love seat out of his study to provide some furniture for the denuded living room, and Samantha was snuggled into one corner, her legs tucked beneath her. They were watching *Casablanca* on the small portable television he had brought down from his son's bedroom.

A commercial came on, and Fallon stroked her knee. "I've got this old hunting cabin up in the Adirondacks," he said. "I'm thinking of going up there this weekend to see about selling it; using the money to set up a trust for my mother's nursing-home expenses."

"I didn't know you hunted," Samantha said.

"I don't," Fallon answered. "At least not since I went with my dad as a kid." He looked away toward the empty hole of the fireplace. "I haven't touched a weapon of any kind since I got back from Vietnam." He dismissed the comment, the memories that flooded in, and turned back to her. "Why don't you come with me? It's beautiful up there."

"I'd love to. Is it livable?" she asked.

"It's rustic and a bit rough, but I go up several times a year. It's kept up. You might even say it's civilized."

Samantha gave him a doubtful smile. "Indoor plumbing?"

He laughed. "Oh, yeah. Trisha and my daughter insisted on that years ago. It cost me an arm and a leg, but it has a septic system, *and* a well."

"Bears and mountain lions?"

He laughed again. He decided he had never before known a woman who could make him laugh at least once each day. "No mountain lions," he said. "They're a bit farther west."

"You sort of skipped over bears," she said.

"They've been seen," he said. "Black bears—the smaller kind. In fact, my dad shot one years ago. The skin's on the cabin's living-room floor. But, alive, you usually only see their backsides going over a hill, if you see them at all. They avoid people." He inclined his head to one side. "Smart animals."

Samantha remained silent. There was nothing she could say.

"Do you think I'll run into any legal problems selling the place? I mean with the divorce and all?"

"Is it solely in your name?" she asked.

He nodded.

"And you say your father left it to you as a final bequest?"

Another nod.

"If you use it solely for your mother's benefit, with none to yourself—I mean if it's clear you're not selling it to hide any assets from your wife—then I don't think you'll have a problem. Trisha may object, of course, but the courts tend to ignore *faits accomplis* if there's no intention to deceive or defraud. And since circumstances have changed, it could be argued that your father would have wanted the property put to his surviving wife's benefit."

"I can't imagine Trisha objecting," he said.

Samantha held back any negative comment.

Spouses, she knew, had a tendency to grab all they could in a divorce. But he'd find that out in time. Or his lawyer would explain. "Her attorney may want to use it as a bargaining chip," she said. "He may ask that it be set up so that, in the event of your mother's death, anything left in the fund goes to Trisha, or at least becomes community property."

"If my mother knew that she'd refuse to die—out of spite."

"You could, of course, structure the trust to allow her to dispose of any remaining assets in *her* will. I think the court might insist it not be returned to you, but it would be a tough argument that it not go to your children, or some charity."

Jesus, Fallon thought, then added aloud, "She'd probably have a shrine built. To Our Lady of Willow Run." He explained, "The place where she lives is called The Residence at Willow Run."

Samantha fought back a smile with only partial success. "Anyway, expect some kind of resistance from the other side. It's a lawyerly thing. But, again, I don't think it will be successful. You should talk to your own attorney, but I think you're safe in going ahead. Selling it will take time, anyway."

"I hate to ask Grisham anything," Fallon said. "It's a hundred and fifty bucks an hour every time he opens his mouth."

"Think of what it might save you overall," she said. Samantha grinned at the expression on his face. "I know," she said. "I'm one of them."

A familiar voice drew Fallon sharply back to the television. He stared at the image. "Jesus Christ," he said.

"What is it?" Samantha asked.

Fallon raised his chin toward the set. There, a man in a glistening white lab coat was talking about gum disease. "That's Howard," Fallon said. "Hawking his bloody HMO. I forgot he advertised on this channel."

Samantha stared at the image. Howard looked to be about fifty, she thought. He had a high, deep widow's peak and a precisely trimmed mustache under a moderately large nose. He spoke through a smile that seemed to glisten at the camera. Caps, she decided. Very expensive ones.

"*That's* Howard?" she said.

"That's him," Fallon said.

Howard rambled on about a free cleaning with a first visit, as a list of his four offices appeared beneath him. His lab coat looked as though it had been starched, and a wildly patterned but clearly expensive necktie flashed beneath his chin. Samantha made some mental comparisons to Fallon; tried to imagine climbing into bed with the man and immediately dismissed the idea. Trisha was an idiot, she decided.

The telephone interrupted, and Fallon went to a phone that sat on the floor next to the staircase. The table that had once held it was now somewhere in Manhattan.

His daughter's voice greeted him; cheerful, upbeat. God, a dual assault. First Howard, now his daughter. He wondered if his son was on an extension—a triple assault. He felt guilty thinking it.

"Hi, Dad," his son's voice chimed in. Fallon pressed his thumb and index finger into his eyes.

"Hi, guys. What's up? Is everything okay?"

"Everything's fine, Dad." It was Liz, taking charge again. "The summer session ends Friday, so we'll be heading back Sunday or Monday. We both have to pack, and I have to clean up the apartment and everything."

"It'll be good to see you guys." He thought of his plans to be away for the weekend. But he'd be back late Sunday. He'd just have to drop Samantha in Manhattan first. The last thing he wanted was another confrontation with his children.

"There's a business thing I have to take care of on

Sunday"—he decided to leave the subject matter up in the air—"but I'll be back later in the evening."

"Business on Sunday?" His daughter sounded skeptical, perhaps even suspicious.

"Divorce business," he said. Technically it wasn't a lie, he decided. The words were greeted with momentary silence.

"Dad, there is one thing." Liz again.

"Tell me."

"Well, you remember how you promised to send us to Europe as a graduation present?"

Fallon's stomach sank.

"I remember . . ." He was prepared to say more, but her words cut him off.

"Well, Mike and I were talking, and, with the divorce and all, nobody seems to know what everybody's finances will be like then."

Fallon's spirits rose slightly.

"Well, there's this great foreign exchange program for the spring semester. It's in France, with opportunities to travel on to Spain and Italy. Even Greece."

Fallon's stomach plummeted again.

"And we were thinking that maybe *instead* of a graduation present, we could do that. Go to Europe this spring." Liz paused only for breath, then prattled on. "We'd get credit, of course, and it wouldn't be much more expensive than what you'd planned anyway."

Silence. Expectant on his children's side, stony on his.

Fallon drew a breath. "Liz, honey. Mike. I would love to say: Great, pack your bags. But I can't commit to *anything* right now. I mean, I can, but it's liable to fall apart before anything happens. Things are just too up in the air—with *everything*."

Silence. Then Mike. "But Mom said you have the money now. It's later—after the divorce—that it might become a problem."

Fallon envisioned Trisha saying just that. His temper flared and he snapped back: "Your mother is . . ." He hesitated, caught his breath, and changed the words that had rushed to mind. Then added, "She's just wrong." He drew another breath, calming himself, then decided to tick off a few realities. "Look. The expenses are already building on this divorce. My job has become even less secure than it was when we last talked. Some problems have arisen at your grandmother's nursing home that will require some long-term financial planning if she's going to stay there. And your tuition is due again in a few weeks. Then again in the spring, and again the following fall. Those are priorities I have to plan on before I commit to anything else. Any trips to Europe right now are out of the question. Maybe, when you graduate, they won't be. But right now, I can't even commit to that."

"Well, this is *like* tuition, Dad." Mike's words were insistent, oblivious to everything he had just said. It made Fallon's hackles rise.

"No, it's not, Mike. It's an extra. A lovely extra that I wish we could afford. But we can't. Right now you've got to settle for your regular tuition and living expenses with no frills attached."

"I thought you wanted us to get student loans for our living expenses." His daughter's voice snapped out at him, filled with sarcasm.

Fallon was dumbfounded. He drew another breath. "That wasn't *my* plan, Liz." He measured his words, trying for as much calm as possible. "I suggested you look around for some part-time jobs to cover that. *You* mentioned getting student loans, which, if you recall, I argued against. And am *still* against."

More silence. Finally, Liz continued, her voice angry now. "It seems you're going back on everything you've promised us," she snapped. "I don't think that's fair."

"I don't think I am, Liz. I very much want to send you kids to Europe as a reward for graduating. If it's possible, when that time comes, it will happen. But it's not possible this spring."

"And maybe not ever," she snapped.

"That's a reality of life, Liz. If I had dropped dead during your senior year, things would have changed, too. There are no stone tablets. If circumstances allow me to keep that promise when you graduate, I'll be tickled pink. If not, I'll tell you I'm sorry, and I will be."

He could almost hear his daughter's grinding teeth. "What's wrong with Grandmother?" she asked. Her voice still held a bitter edge.

Fallon was momentarily uncertain how to explain it. Did he say: "Nothing, she's just as wacko as she always was. Except now her madness requires money to keep her from being tossed into the street."

He decided against reality this time. Trisha's parents had died when the children were too young to remember them. So had his own father. The only grandparent they had ever known had been his mother. They probably thought all grandparents were as crazy as bedbugs.

"She's had some delusional incidents," he finally said. "She's become convinced that no one will be able to pay her nursing-home costs, and it's made her a bit irrational. The people at the home are concerned about her, and I have to find a way to ease her mind—set up some sort of guaranteed payment plan."

"Did you tell her about your job? Is that what caused it?" His daughter's voice was heavy with accusation. Fallon felt his stomach sink again.

"Yeah, that was part of it," he said. But she's also a flaming nutcase, he added to himself.

"So *she's* afraid you'll break your promise, too."

They were in a full fight now, and there was no way around it.

"Liz, that's enough!"

She wouldn't let go. She simply changed tack. "What

are you *really* doing Sunday?" More heavy accusation. Only slightly veiled this time.

"What do you mean, Liz?" Fallon's voice softened, a fuse burning toward full-blown anger.

A small hesitation, then: "I thought, maybe, you were really going to be with *Her*."

Fallon squeezed his eyes shut, fought for control, even thought about lying, then decided: Hell no. His voice remained soft, still on the edge. "I'm taking care of some business that involves the divorce, and also your grandmother's needs. If I'm also seeing someone else, I fail to see what the hell that has to do with anything."

"So you're still seeing her."

"Yes, I am. And her name is Samantha. Samantha Moore. And as unreasonable as it may sound, being with her makes me very happy. I would hope that small fact made *you* happy."

Liz was quiet for several interminable seconds. "We're going to Mother's when we get back," she said at length. "So you don't have to rush back to the house."

Fallon closed his eyes again, opened them, and stared at the floor. He could still see the indentations in the carpet where the table had once stood.

"I'm sorry to hear that," he said. "I was looking forward to seeing you both." Another deep breath. "This is your home, and you're welcome here if you change your mind. I hope you do."

"You can change *your* mind, too," Liz said. Her voice was still cool, but the sarcasm was now gone. Fallon was uncertain if she meant a spring semester in Europe, or Samantha.

He kept his voice even, equally cool. "You're pushing pretty hard, Liz. I don't respond well to being pushed."

"Someone has to talk some sense into you," she snapped.

Fallon's temper boiled. He fought it. "Thanks for the

effort," he said. "I'm glad those courses in Logic paid off."

Liz sniffled. Tears were about to flow. Fallon felt instant regret. "Someone has to try to keep this family together," she said. Now the words ended with a sob.

"Liz. Honey. I didn't break up this family. Your mother and I have separated; we're getting a divorce. I'm getting on with my life, Liz. Nothing more. Nothing less."

"You're having an *affair*," she snapped. The final word was part accusation, part wail. "Don't try to minimize it."

And what's your mother doing? Fallon thought. Getting dental therapy? An image of Howard's television commercial flashed through his mind. With effort he kept his voice soft.

"Your mother and I are doing what adults do when a marriage fails," he said. "She's getting on with her life. I'm doing the same with mine. There is nothing unnatural or sinister about it. I know it hurts and upsets you, and I'm sorry."

"I'm tired of hearing that you're sorry," Liz snapped. "You're sorry about everything. You're sorry about Mom. You're sorry about breaking your promises to us. You're sorry that you've turned things around so we can't even come home." She slammed the phone down, and was gone.

Fallon listened to the silence. His stomach sat somewhere near his throat. "Mike? You still there?" His voice sounded suddenly hoarse.

"Yeah, Dad." A pause. "Gee, I'm sorry, Dad. I didn't know everything was gonna blow up like this."

In his mind Fallon could see his son shifting nervously from foot to foot. The kid despised confrontation, wanted everything smooth and untroubled. He hated battle royals, ran from them even if he wasn't directly involved.

"Mike, I'm sorry, too. Things will work out in time.

Are you coming here, or are you going to your mother's with Liz?"

"I guess I'll go with her," he said. "I mean, I don't know what else to do. I don't want Mom to think we're choosing sides or anything."

She won't think that. She'll be delighted if you're here, he thought. Two adult kids in an East Side love nest were not part of her plan. He wanted to tell his son exactly that; knew he could not. Mike didn't deserve any additional pain. He closed his eyes again.

"Listen. If you change your mind—or if things don't work out at your mom's—please come home," he said.

"I will, Dad. I'll come by to see you, anyway. Maybe I'll call you at work and we can meet for lunch."

"That would be great," Fallon said. His stomach was sinking again. Was that what his life with his kids would be? Hi, Dad. Let's do lunch. "Listen, Mike," he added hastily. "I mean what I say. I want to see both of you. *And* I'd like you here. Both of you. Don't ever doubt it. Okay?"

"Yeah, Dad. Sure. But maybe it's better the other way for now. Okay?"

"Yeah, Mike, that's fine. I'll talk to you soon. Please be careful driving back."

Fallon stooped down and replaced the receiver. He remained squatting for a moment, staring at the floor of his empty house.

Samantha walked in from the living room. "I couldn't help overhearing. Are you okay?"

He nodded; shook his head. He wasn't really sure what he was. Then he told her about the Springtime in Europe plan, his daughter's accusation that he was having an illicit affair, and the decision to stay at Trisha's condo. He smiled faintly over the final part.

"Trish will love it," he said. "It will be another ploy in my evil plan to destroy her relationship with Howard."

"If they feel unwelcome, maybe they'll come here,"

Samantha said. She hesitated, then continued. "Jack, if I'm complicating your life . . ."

He cut her off. "You're not. You're the only sane thing *in* my life right now."

Samantha squatted next to him and stroked his cheek. "Their concern about your seeing someone else is quite natural," she said.

"I know." He smiled at her. "But I can't change my life to suit them. Even more, I don't want to."

"What about Europe? Giving in might help smooth things over."

"I can't do that." He shook his head again. "It's really my fault. I spoiled them. I never forced much reality on their lives. It was always easier, and more fun, to just give them things. Now there's no choice. And they'll just have to accept the fact that life isn't always the way they'd like it to be. It's something they should have learned a long time ago."

"So there's nothing you can do." It was spoken as fact, not a question. She stroked his cheek again.

"No. Nothing." He was quiet for several moments, then a small grin played across his lips. "Yes, there is. I'll do it tomorrow."

"What is it?" she asked.

"I'll go to The Residence, join the other lunatics, and make a novena to the Virgin." He winked at her. "Hell, maybe a pot of gold will fall from the sky."

16

FALLON AND JIM MALLOY MET UNEXPECTEDLY IN THE lobby of the Chrysler Building. Each had come down a separate marble-lined entry hall, two of three that converged at the building's central lobby and its distinctive banks of art deco elevators. Malloy held a container of coffee in his hand. He glanced at it—embarrassed; said to Fallon, "My coffeepot left with my assistant." His face suddenly flushed; his voice became tight. "I haven't had to do this in ten years," he added.

Fallon tried to keep the mood light. "There's a pot in my office," he said. "I make it myself every morning. Help yourself, Jim."

Malloy looked away, fought to lighten his own voice. "No wonder Carol worships the ground you walk on. She doesn't even have to make coffee. You're a liberated boss."

Fallon grinned, still struggling. "That's true, I am." The grin widened. "She also makes lousy coffee, so there's an element of self-preservation in it."

Malloy forced a smile. It came across badly. Fallon took time to look him over. He seemed haggard, and his attempt at shaving that morning hadn't gone well. He had missed a spot under his nose, and there were several small wounds on his neck. Fallon hoped he hadn't started drinking again.

Malloy looked about him, taking in the African marble walls, with their symmetrical butterfly pattern, the vaulted ceiling set off by marble inlays, then glanced back to the elevator door that stood before them, faced, like all the others, with its own distinctive marquetry and art deco paneling. "God, I love this old building," he said. "I have since the first day we moved in." He glanced at Fallon. "What was it? Ten years ago?"

"Twelve," Fallon said. Malloy was trying to seem calm, but the game wasn't working. He was talking about their office as though he might never see it again. "How are you hanging in, Jim?" Fallon finally asked.

The elevator arrived and they stepped inside, then turned to face the closing doors. They were the only passengers.

Malloy stared straight ahead. "I feel like they've ripped the heart out of me, Jack. My customers keep asking where Marge is. You know what I tell them? That she's on vacation. I can't bring myself to explain I don't *have* an assistant anymore. You know what else I can't do? I can't bring myself to think about what they'll do to me next."

Fallon felt a sudden rush of guilt. It was as though he had abandoned the man. "I know," he said. "But you've got to hang with it. You can't let the bastards beat you."

Malloy shook his head. "Christ, if they're going to fire me, they should just do it and stop the goddamned games." He closed his eyes, drew a breath. "When I had to tell Betty about losing Marge it was one of the most humiliating moments I've ever known." He gritted his teeth. "How do you explain something like this to your wife, Jack? Christ, I dread that one of my kids will call, or even worse, stop by. How do you explain that you're being treated like shit, humiliated in front of the whole office, just so they can force you out. Because they just don't want you anymore. Because you're too damned old." He stared at Fallon. "Christ, Jack, I'm fifty years old. I'm in my prime. I know things I didn't have a clue about ten or fifteen years ago." Tears welled up in his eyes, and Fallon looked away. "What do I do for the *next* ten or fifteen years? What do I do about the son I've got in law school if I don't get a decent buyout? Tell him to kiss his future good-bye? And what about Betty? Is this what *she* gets? Sell the house, move to a small apartment, and spend the rest of her life with a husband who works at Kmart because nobody else wants him?"

The elevator stopped at their floor, and Fallon took Malloy's arm and pulled him aside. He kept his voice to a whisper. "There's no shame in anything you're saying, Jim. Not for you. Not one bit. Even if it all happens." He let out a breath, took the man's arm again. "And it won't. I promise you. You'll be part of any damned buyout, and I'll fight like hell to see it's a good one. We all will." He squeezed Malloy's arm. "We're all in the same boat, Jim. All the dinosaurs."

Malloy lowered his eyes, shook his head. His thin face looked sunken—like someone who had just been whipped. "I don't know how much more of it I can take."

"You can take it, Jim," Fallon said. "You can take it, and you can laugh in Bennett's face when you walk out the door."

Malloy looked at him, defeat heavy in his eyes. "You don't think you can stop it, do you, Jack?"

"I'm going to try like hell. But, no, I don't know if I can. I told all of you that up front. But that's as far as I'm willing to give, Jim. Don't *you* give them more."

Malloy straightened, nodded. There was no conviction in his eyes.

They entered the reception area and headed toward the hallway that led to the executive offices. The receptionist, a pretty, young, blond woman, smiled at Fallon. When her eyes fell on Malloy a look of undisguised pity filled her face. Fallon hoped Jim hadn't noticed, but was certain that he had.

"Mr. Waters says he can see you right away," Carol said, as Fallon entered his office. "I just got the call a minute ago."

Fallon dropped his briefcase behind his desk and started to leave. Carol took his arm, stopping him.

"Before you go, there's something I have to tell you." She glanced toward the outer door, assuring herself it was closed. "Nellie Morris—she's Willis Chambers's assistant—came by a little while ago. She told me she overheard Willis talking to the head of maintenance yesterday. Apparently he wants the trash collected from all the offices in sales and brought to Les Gavin each night. He told the maintenance guy it had something to do with a breach in security."

Fallon let out a laugh, then turned suspicious. "Why would Nellie do that? Willis is her boss."

The look in Carol's eyes told him he should already know the answer to that question. "She's fifty-three years old, Jack. She has a husband who's been out of work for a year, and she's frightened out of her wits. The men aren't the only ones who are scared, Jack. And they're not the only ones who hate what these S.O.B.s are planning to do to everyone."

Yet another dinosaur. Fallon smiled at the thought. And Carol was right. He should have seen it. "Make sure Wally and Jim Malloy know about this trash business," he said. He gave Carol an exaggerated wink. "I think Wally can have the troops leave some stuff for Willis that will give him nightmares."

Fallon headed back down the hall that housed all the executive offices, including his own. It was a long row, and the offices were set in their order of importance within the company. Bennett's office was four closer to Waters's own sanctum than was Fallon's own. The message was not lost on anyone. Especially now.

Charlie Waters's suite was at the top of the hall, just off reception. It also had its own reception area in the oversized, outer office his assistant, Gladys, occupied—just so those important enough to come before The Man himself were not required to remain outside with lesser mortals.

Fallon smiled at Gladys as he entered. He liked the woman—middle-aged, always tastefully dressed, and exceptionally competent. Unlike many of the presidential assistants he had encountered in other companies, Gladys had never allowed an air of self-importance—apparently infused through some mysterious form of executive osmosis—to govern her treatment of anyone, down to the lowliest of mail clerks.

"I understand my audience has at long last been granted," Fallon said.

Gladys smirked. "You have been beckoned to the mountain. I was beginning to think only Carter Bennett was allowed inside." She picked up her telephone. "I'll tell him you're here. I *think* he's ready for you."

Gladys was right. Fallon was allowed inside immediately.

"Jack, good to see you. It's been too long."

Waters stood behind his desk, draped in a three-piece suit, bluff and hardy and red-faced. The hail-fellow approach left Fallon cold. He took a seat that hadn't been offered.

"That's true, we don't seem to see much of each other anymore," he said.

Waters puckered his lips; sat. "It's the price of running a business that's gotten too damned big," he said. "You even lose track of old friends."

Fallon sat forward, forearms on knees. He wanted the

old friend approach, even if it was phony. "That's why I'm here," he said. "There are some things going on I don't understand."

Waters offered up a false chuckle. "Hell, there are things going on that *I* don't understand." He was trying to dismiss the statement.

Fallon held firm. "For example, Charlie. I was up in Plattsburgh the other day. Just trying to have some tests run, to resolve a problem one of our customers is having. Out of the blue, Carter Bennett canceled the test."

Waters twisted in his chair. "What the hell are you running tests for, Jack? I set those specs myself. They're solid."

Fallon hadn't mentioned the test involved manufacturing specs, and that told him Charlie had already been briefed on what had occurred. He ignored it; pushed ahead. "It's just good engineering, Charlie. Even if the tests only confirm what we know. We get that out of the way at the source, then we can look for end-user problems." Waters seemed ready to object, but Fallon pushed on. "The point is, Carter didn't even consult us, or ask us for justification. I approved those tests, and he just stopped them cold. He also had Jim Malloy's assistant yanked. Malloy runs our team of government sales reps, and he was simply told to share secretarial time with the New York District manager. Again, it was just done. I wasn't even consulted. And I think it's still my division."

The last had been issued as a challenge. Waters twisted again, waved his hand. "Carter's just trying to save the company some money," he said. "Hell, that's his job. And he's damned good at it." He offered another bluff smile. "He's young and aggressive." He raised a mollifying hand. "Maybe too aggressive at times. But the lad knows what the market wants to hear, and he has a clear picture of the economic realities we're facing. I'll talk to him, Jack. Advise him to ease up just a bit. Not run roughshod over the chain of command."

Waters eased back in his chair, seemed to study Fallon more closely. "Damn, you're looking good, Jack. You look fit."

Fallon sensed he was about to be dismissed. Stroked and sent packing. He had no intention of allowing that to happen. Not before he got to the real issue. But first, he decided, he'd throw the man a curve. Charlie, he knew, was the sort who had to know what was going on around him. "I've been working out in the company gym, Charlie. Along with some of our sales crew. We've formed a club—the more senior guys, anyway."

Waters's eyes narrowed slightly. Then he offered another smile. "Yeah, I heard you boys had some kind of club. That what it's about? Getting back in shape?"

"Just a reaction to some rumors, Charlie."

"Rumors? What rumors, Jack?"

The response was openly false, and Fallon bit back a need to tell him so. "The word filtering down is that the company is headed toward some rather heavy downsizing, and that the people who are fifty-plus are on the block."

Waters seemed startled by the words—or perhaps by Fallon's frankness. He moved physically back in his chair.

"Hell, that's nonsense, Jack. I mean, sure, we're looking toward some downsizing. We need to make this company a little leaner and meaner. Economics demand it. But the idea's in its infancy, and we sure as hell aren't gearing anything to age. Christ, Jack, that's illegal. And it's certainly something I would never condone."

The man was lying through his teeth. Fallon felt suddenly sickened. They went a long way back—almost all of his adult life. He stared across the desk, sadness heavy in his eyes.

"Does Carter know that?" he asked.

Waters seemed flustered again. "Jesus, Jack, you're obsessed with Carter. Look, if you're worried you're somehow going to be affected . . ."

Fallon's temper flared. He fought it. "I'm not worried, Charlie. I'm a big boy. But I'm damned concerned about the people who work for me. And they're concerned too—right down to the assistants and clerical staff." He stared Waters down. "People who work for *you*, Charlie. And who've done a damned fine job for a lot of years." He struggled to moderate his tone, then continued, "None of them deserve to be humiliated. None of them deserve to be forced out. No matter what Carter Bennett thinks. And I can't just sit back and watch it happen."

Waters bristled. "That sounds like a threat, Jack."

Fallon drew a breath, looked down at the floor. He didn't want the meeting to degenerate into a shouting match. It would do no one any good. He raised his eyes, softened his voice.

"It's no threat, Charlie. I'm telling you how I feel about it. About what I perceive to be happening." He held Waters's eyes. "Charlie, it's *my* company, too. It has been most of my life. And I can't sit back and watch something happen that I believe is wrong."

Waters fiddled with the edge of his vest. It was an old habit that Fallon recognized. Waters's hands always sought something to do when he himself was uncertain about what to say next.

"Jack, I understand your position." Waters's demeanor had turned coldly serious—his version of false sincerity. "And I'm sorry Carter has left you out of the loop on things. But I assure you nothing disastrous is afoot. I'll speak to him; make sure he keeps you apprised."

The check is in the mail, Fallon thought.

"So I tell my people not to worry?"

Waters seemed to consider the statement, the future legal problems acquiescence might present. He doesn't trust you on this, Fallon thought.

"Jack, I can't make broad-based statements about anything right now. As I told you, we're evaluating our entire cost structure. Sooner or later decisions will have to be made." He waved a hand. "Hell, maybe we'll scrap the whole idea of downsizing." He leaned forward, intent now. "I need you to be a team player on this, Jack. Just as you've always been."

Fallon sat back. The game was over. No points scored. He let out a weary breath. "That's what I am, Charlie." He paused a beat. "So are the guys who work for me. We're all company men—a team."

"Jack, I can't tell you how glad I am to hear that," Waters said.

17

FALLON STOOD BEFORE THE WINDOW AND STARED INTO the clearing. Beyond, the forest floor seemed to run forever; the towering pines all but obliterating a distant mountain peak.

When he had come there as a boy the pines had been smaller, leaving more of the mountain visible. The real estate agent had suggested clearing some of the trees to recapture that view, claiming it might raise the value of the property. But he had decided against it. He had seen areas of Vermont and New Hampshire and Maine where timber companies had clear-cut large sections of older forest for economic gain. Here, he thought, at least while he still owned it, the trees would remain.

The Realtor had visited the cabin yesterday, and they had agreed on a listing and a price. He had been assured the cabin and its two hundred acres would sell quickly. With deer season only a few months off, the market was brisk. Fallon was surprised how the idea saddened him. The cabin was a place he visited only a few times a year, yet it now seemed an integral part of his boyhood; something, he realized, that his long-dead father had taken great pride in owning.

Samantha came up behind him, unheard. She was

wrapped in a heavy blanket; her hair tousled by sleep. She nuzzled against him, and he slipped his arm about her shoulders.

"You get up too early," she said. "I heard you moving around hours ago."

"Go back to bed. It's only seven."

"Uh-uh. I want to hear the little birds, and see the furry bunnies."

"My, aren't we feeling woodsy?"

Samantha snuggled in closer. "That's me. Nanook of the North." She shivered. "God, it's still summer. Why is it so cold here in the mornings?"

"It'll warm up later. I can lay a fire."

"Oh, please. I'll make some coffee."

"It's already on," Fallon said.

"Wonderful. I'll just snuggle up on the sofa and wait for heat."

Samantha made her way to the sofa and curled up in one corner. Even on a chill morning the cabin exuded its own singular warmth. Its knotty-pine walls, exposed beams, and well-worn floors spoke of a permanence, an ability to endure. The furnishings were simple and rustic—overstuffed sofas and chairs, tables by local artisans, made from wood still covered in bark that had been gleaned from the forest and molded for use. The bearskin rug—his father's trophy—lay before the fireplace. They had made love there the previous night, the fire blazing; the stuff of dreams, she thought.

She watched Fallon lay the fire. His broad back filled the flannel shirt, tapered down to a waist already far narrower than when they first met. In the early morning light she could see flecks of gray in his hair, and she wondered at how that now marked a man for extinction rather than distinction. The world—at least her world—was going mad, she decided. Women, to have real value, were expected to emulate eighteen-year-old anorexics; their true worth determined by their thighs. Men, though permitted some plumpness, dared not pass the age of forty without the security of a trust fund. She smiled at the absurdity. Perhaps some cabal existed—some secret group of plastic surgeons and hairdressers—that was manipulating public perceptions so face-lifts and hair dye would be required for all.

The fire now going, Fallon stood and stretched. Samantha smiled again.

"You know, Fallon, for an old dinosaur you've got a great tush," she said.

He turned to her, his expression dumbfounded; then he began to laugh. "Thanks, Moore. For a woman pushing thirty-five you've got a pretty nice tush, yourself."

"What do you mean, pretty nice? These are buns of steel. Bought and paid for in the company gym. The cabal will never get *me*."

"The cabal?" He grinned at her. "I think this mountain air is affecting your mind." He waited for her to explain. When it became obvious she would not, he winked at her. "Anyway, the veracity of your claims to a superior tush will remain in doubt as long as you stay wrapped up in that Indian blanket."

"Nice try, Fallon. But you'll just have to trust me," she said. "At least until this cabin warms up."

The old logging trail moved up a slight rise, cutting through outcroppings of rock on either side. The forest floor was heavy with fern, dotted by occasional wild laurel and incongruously delicate trillium, which sat like white jewels among a sea of green.

Samantha knelt beside one of the frail wild lilies. Her finger traced its whorl of three leaves, out of which rose a solitary three-petaled flower.

"How do they live here?" she wondered aloud.

Fallon knelt beside her. It did seem illogical—something so delicate surviving such harsh surroundings. "Must be like us—tougher than it looks."

Samantha continued to study the flower. "Are we tough, Jack? Sometimes I'm not sure."

"Maybe resilient is a better word. We endure. It's something about human beings. Surrender comes hard to us."

They continued on, moving along the ancient logging trails that crisscrossed the forest. Fallon explained that the trails dated back to a time before the Adirondacks became protected—that he, and his father before him, had hired someone each year to drive a bushwhacker along them, just to keep the forest from reasserting its claim.

They took various turns, one trail to another. It seemed a giant maze. After an hour Samantha became concerned. "Are we lost?" Her eyes begged him to say they were not.

He raised his chin to another crossing trail that lay ahead. "We turn right just up there, and then a few hundred yards on we'll hit the cabin," he said.

She shook her head. "I don't see how anyone finds their way back."

"In the winter, when there's snow, it's easy. You follow your own boot tracks. It's an old hunter's trick—knowing the sole pattern of your own boots, so you don't confuse them with others you might come across. Any other time of year you'd have to mark trees at each crossing. If you didn't, you'd be lost in minutes, and your chances of finding your way out would be pretty slim. The forest rangers here spend most of the summer searching for lost hikers."

"But you didn't mark anything," Samantha said.

"I've been walking these trails since I was nine years old," he said. "I've seen every turn more times than I can remember."

Samantha was still skeptical—the questioning attorney. "What if you wandered off a trail, and then found yourself in an area where they didn't exist?"

"I'd walk until I found a stream. Then I'd be okay."

"Why a stream?" she asked.

"Streams run downhill. Sometimes they'll connect with other streams, but they still keep moving down. You just follow the downward course. Eventually, the stream will cross a road." He grinned. "It's inevitable—a gift of civilization. Unfortunately, most people who go hiking in the woods don't know that. So they get lost, and usually keep walking in circles."

"So *you're* Nanook of the North," she said. She began to laugh.

"What's so funny?"

"I was just thinking of Carter," she said.

"How unpleasant for you."

"Did you know he enters paintball competitions?" She laughed again. "He's quite proud of it, fanatical even." She decided not to tell him that Bennett had invited her to go with him on more than one occasion.

"He showed me photographs once—even a map of one of the courses. Some have old tanks and military vehicles scattered around, and elaborate trails. They all carry their maps with them, of course, so they won't get lost. Then they dress up in camouflage clothing and hunt each other down. They even have tournaments. The person who avoids being splattered with paint wins. And he gets a trophy. Carter keeps his in his office."

Vietnam flashed in Fallon's mind—crawling through steaming heat, the surrounding jungle rank with the smell of death and decay, almost but not quite overwhelming the scent of his own fear—hunting men who were hunting you. Except those men had had real guns, and the dying that inevitably came wasn't a game. It came with screams of agony and fear.

"Bless his heart," Fallon said.

Samantha ignored the sarcasm. "I was just thinking

about Carter and all his paintball friends. About what would happen if they held one of their tournaments here. They wouldn't have any maps and they'd probably all get lost and wander around aimlessly until somebody rescued them. Carter would be crushed."

"I'd prefer it if he just stayed lost," Fallon said.

Samantha laughed again. "That's another option," she said.

They arrived back at Fallon's house shortly after five. Samantha had packed clothes for work and would spend the night. Fallon grilled steaks, and opened a bottle of Eger Bikavér—one of his favorites, a full-bodied Hungarian red wine that, translated, meant "bull's blood."

Samantha laughed at the name when he told her, and teased him about his flagrant machismo. He offered to provide proof of his virility, and she laughed even more, and he marveled at the ease and comfort that existed between them.

After dinner they retreated to the living room, to the small sofa set before the fireplace. It brought back fresh memories of the cabin, and Samantha recalled how his body had felt as they lay before the fire.

"Make a fire, Jack," she said. He turned to her, his face curious, even doubtful. "Please?" she added.

Fallon inclined his head to one side. "We're not in the mountains now," he said. "And it's summer. We'll roast if we do."

There was no resistance in his words, only humor. She could tell he liked the idea. "We can turn on the air conditioner," she said.

He laughed and got to his feet. "There's some wood out back," he said. "Let's hope the neighbors don't see the smoke and call the fire department."

They sat before the fire, the long-sleeve shirts they had worn back from the mountains cast aside, their bodies stripped down to T-shirts, each knowing those would soon be shed as well. It was eight-thirty when the doorbell rang.

Fallon glanced at his watch. His first thought brought a chill: Trisha had sent the kids packing from the condo. He dismissed it. They each had their own key. Had they returned home unexpectedly, he would already be under the baleful glare of his daughter. He offered Samantha a regretful shrug. "Probably some neighbor, who wants to make sure the house isn't burning down," he said.

He moved to the door, trying to conjure up a reasonable excuse for the fire. When he opened it, Trisha stood before him, a key clutched in her hand. She stared at him. Her chin was trembling.

"You changed the locks," she said.

Fallon was momentarily stunned. "No, I didn't." Anger flooded in as the accusation registered. He wanted to tell her that he wished he had, but simply hadn't thought of it. He stared at her hand. "You've got the wrong key," he said instead.

Trisha stared at the key. Her eyes blinked. Then her chin trembled again. She looked back at him, tears only seconds away.

"Jack, I've come home," she said.

Fallon glanced past her. The baby-blue Mustang convertible was in the driveway. His children were standing beside it. He looked back at Trisha. She had dressed carefully in off-white silk, blouse and pants. Her makeup had been artfully applied; she looked fetching, seductive. There was a suitcase by her feet. Fallon was dumbfounded.

"I asked the children to wait by the car until we talked." That said, she picked up her suitcase and stepped into the foyer.

Fallon stepped quickly in front of her, stopping her progress. "Wait a minute, Trish. Uh-uh. You don't live here anymore. Remember? You live in Manhattan with Howard."

Trisha's eyes filled with disbelief, then hurt. Her chin trembled again. "I've left him." Her voice was choked. "I've been a fool, Jack."

Fallon held up his hands. "Wait a minute. Wait a minute. The last time I spoke to you Howard was still Mr. Wonderful. You gave him all our furniture. Christ, you even gave him my bathrobe."

"The furniture is coming back." She sniffed, held back the tears.

What about my damned bathrobe? Fallon asked himself. Immediately, he felt ridiculous even thinking it. He searched for something else to say. Trisha beat him to it.

"I found out that Howard isn't the man I thought he was." Her voice turned into a wail and tears began to flow. "Jack, please don't ask me any more about it. Not now."

Fallon stared at her. He wondered if libidinous old Howard had climbed into yet another bed. If he had, what did Trish expect? Was he supposed to get a gun and avenge her honor?

He shook his head, part in rejection of what she had said, part to clear his own thoughts. "Look, Trish, I'm sorry he hurt you. I really am. But it doesn't change anything between us. You left. You filed for divorce."

Trisha choked back more tears. "Don't be cruel, Jack." She sobbed. "I was frightened by all the insecurity I saw heading our way, and Howard seemed . . . so secure . . . and he said he wanted me, was ready to leave his wife for me. It seemed like such an easy way to escape everything . . . everything that terrified me." She drew a long breath. "Now I see what a fool I was, and I want you to forgive me. I want to make it up to you."

Fallon was momentarily stunned. She was implying it had been his fault—the insecurity he had put in their lives. Reality hit, and anger simmered. She was running a game on him. Even if what she said was true, it was still a game. Men didn't offer to leave their wives for women they hadn't already slept with. No, Trish had made a bad choice, and now she wanted back in on what she had already thrown away. Fallon thought of his children waiting outside, both now part of this madness, drawn in by their mother—pawns to help her get out of her failed escapade.

"I'm sorry, Trish. I just can't buy it."

She stared into his eyes; her own eyes were filled with need and regret. He wondered if she sensed that the chance she wanted was slipping away. "I've talked to the children, Jack, and they think it's the right thing for me to do. The right thing for both of us."

"You didn't have any right to do that," he snapped. His anger flared, and he started to say more, but his words were cut off by her eyes. She was staring past him, pupils dilated, mouth open in disbelief. He looked back. Samantha stood in the doorway of the living room. The T-shirt and jeans she wore made her look younger than she was.

"I'm sorry, Jack. I heard raised voices." She started to turn away, but Fallon held up a hand, stopping her.

"It's okay," he said. He seemed momentarily uncertain about what to say next. An introduction seemed ludicrous, but what else was there?

"Samantha, this is Trisha." He turned back to his wife. "Trish, this is Samantha Moore."

Trisha continued to stare across the room, mouth still agape. Her eyes returned to Fallon. "Oh, Jack. How could you?"

He stared at her. "How could I *what*?"

Her lip trembled again. "How could you bring another woman into our *home*?"

"Our *what*?"

"Oh, Jack. This is so *tawdry*."

Fallon realized his hands were shaking. He fought to control his voice. "This is *not* our home, Trish. You left. Remember?" He drew a breath, still struggling. He wanted to shout at her; knew it was pointless. "You ran off with Howard. You had an affair with him and decided he was what you wanted. I accepted that, and went on with my life. I'm *still* going on with my life, and there is nothing tawdry about it. I'm in love with this woman. She makes me happy. And I haven't been happy in a long time. It's that simple." He paused for breath; shook his head again. "Look, I'm sorry things didn't work out with Howard, but that's not my problem. So good-bye, Trish."

Trisha took an involuntary step back, shocked. Then her face filled with rage. "If you think . . . you're going to carry on . . . with *this* woman . . . in *my* home . . ."

"It's not *your* home. You left."

Trisha stamped her foot. "The children and I are *staying*," she shouted.

Fallon felt a hand on his arm. He turned and found Samantha standing beside him. "Jack, let me speak to you." She glanced at Trisha. "Mrs. Fallon, please excuse us for a moment."

Trisha glared at her. "I want you *out* of here. Now," she hissed.

"I understand, Mrs. Fallon. Just allow me to speak with Jack, then I'll get my things." Samantha kept her voice soft, respectful.

"Your things? Your *things!*"

Samantha led Fallon into the living room, took hold of his hands. "Jack, listen to me. As a lawyer. Okay?"

He was about to object, then settled for a noncommittal shake of his head.

Samantha kept her voice low, soothingly soft. "If you stay, one of you will end up calling the police. They'll come. There will be an ugly scene. Even if the cops side with you; agree to let you stay, it won't mean anything.

Trish will call her lawyer. They'll go to court. And the judge will tell you either to surrender the house or to rent a comparable one for your wife and children."

Fallon blinked. "So I just leave? Go to a hotel? Just like that?"

Samantha lowered her eyes momentarily. When she looked back at him she said, "I want you to stay with me. If you're sure you don't want Trisha back."

Fallon blinked again. "You really mean that?"

"Yes."

He let out a long breath. "Let's get out of here," he said.

Samantha squeezed his hands. "Pack all your things," she said. "At least everything you're going to need for a while. After Trisha talks to her lawyer you won't be getting back in until the court orders her to let you get your possessions. And that could take some time."

Fallon packed three suitcases, along with his briefcase. Samantha helped. When they carried the first of the suitcases down to his car, neither Trisha nor his children were anywhere in sight.

Samantha remained at the car, while Fallon got the last of the bags. As he reached the bottom of the stairs, Trisha stepped into the foyer. "I'd like your house key," she said. Her face was rigid, and he realized she didn't look nearly as beautiful as he had thought.

He unclipped his key from a leather key wallet and laid it on the newel post.

Behind Trisha he could see his daughter staring at him, her face a mix of regret and anger. His son stood farther back, looking as though he wanted to be somewhere else.

"I'm sorry you kids got dragged into this," he said. "I'll let you know where I am when I'm settled."

Trisha drew herself up, trying to salvage some dignity, he told himself.

"Just go, Jack," she said. She straightened even more,

spoke with the conviction of all the injury that had been done to her. "Go have your younger woman. She'll make you happy for ten years. Then she'll break your heart."

They drove toward Manhattan. The Sunday night traffic was heavy with people returning from weekend escapes. Fallon took in the cars, realized he was probably unique among them. He was escaping back *to* the city.

"How do you feel?" Samantha asked. She had been silent the first ten minutes of their trip.

"Numb, I guess." He smiled at her. "It all happened so damned fast."

Samantha hesitated. There was something she wanted to say, had to say. She drew a long breath. "You know, Jack, I think some of what Trisha said is true. I think she *was* frightened. And perhaps she made some bad decisions because of it. I think you have to consider that possibility—that she may be a victim of this downsizing plan, too."

Fallon looked out the side window. He nodded almost imperceptibly. He turned back to her, then lowered his eyes. "You're probably right, but it doesn't change anything." A small smile began to form. "You know Trish said something to me when I was leaving. She told me that you'd make me happy for the next ten years, and then you'd break my heart." He looked at her, the smile widening. "And I thought: You're right, Trish, I should stay here. Then I could be miserable for the next ten years."

Samantha remained silent. Then: "Jack. Did you mean what you said back there?"

Traffic was stalled in a long line for a distant toll booth. He looked up. "You mean about being in love with you?"

She nodded, then whispered, "Yes."

"I meant it." He smiled again. "I didn't realize it until I said it. But as soon as I had, I knew."

Samantha leaned across the seat and put her arms around him. "I want a lot more than ten years," she whispered. "I love you, too, Fallon. I think I started falling in love with you the first day I met you."

18

"WHAT WE NEED RIGHT NOW IS A VISION STATEMENT." Carter Bennett extended his hands as if trying to contain something that was too big for his office. He looked across his desk at Les Gavin and Willis Chambers.

"What I'm talking about is a criterion for winning, something our younger employees will grasp as a leitmotif for success." He smiled at his own phrasing.

"It's also important that this statement come across as a clear signal to our older employees that this leitmotif does *not* include them." He gestured as if throwing out an idea that had just come to mind, although he had been considering it for days. "We might use a slogan." Again he framed the idea in the air. "Wanted for Waters Cable: Jet fighter pilots to fly us into the twenty-first century." Another smile. "How about this? We have coffee mugs made up that we can hand out to *select* people. You can read younger into that if you want, although I, of course, never said that." This time he laughed and was quickly joined by the others. He waved off the laughter, then raised one hand as if writing in the air. "I see slogans on the cups. On one side it would say: 'We're High Octane Flyers.' On the other: 'Accept the Values—Join the Vision.'"

Bennett watched the others nod approval. "The message of course will be clear to the people who *don't* get coffee mugs. And it will be abundantly clear to those who do. They'll be on our side. And that's what we want. Even among the younger people who might eventually find themselves on our list of surplused employees." He tapped the side of his nose. "But until then, I want them thinking positively. That way, if older employees start talking organized resistance, the younger ones will hear it with an attitude that says: 'Hey, don't screw up my opportunity.'"

Bennett paused and Chambers jumped right in. "It's brilliant," he said. "It sends just the right message to everyone."

Bennett raised a finger indicating he wasn't quite finished. "What I'll also need is a selection guide. By that I mean a list of criteria for those who will be *selected* to remain with the company." He waved a hand, dismissing objections that weren't even close to being broached. "I realize we already know who those people will be. Generally speaking of course. But we'll need this in case a lawsuit materializes—just to show how much careful thought went into our decisions." He paused for effect. "For that same reason, there will, of course, be no reference to age. We'll say that without saying it. Something like"—he paused as if coming up with the phrase at just that moment—"the ability to understand and effectively utilize new technology. Something along those lines." He tapped his nose again. "Make it positive, not negative, and also make it as saccharine and platitudinous as possible." He jabbed a finger at Chambers. "That will be your job, Willis. You're exceptionally good at that."

The three all laughed at the comment, and Bennett stood as if ready to dismiss them.

Gavin seized an opportunity for which he had been waiting. He jabbed a finger toward Bennett's desk. "By the way, is that the new trophy?" he asked.

Carter Bennett acknowledged the accolade with a

grin. "It is, indeed." He nodded toward his desk. The New England Paintball Association championship trophy sat on one corner. Gavin and Chambers studied it in open admiration.

"Our own Paintball Wizard," Gavin said, playing off the old rock-and-roll song. He ran a finger along the hand-painted figure that stood atop the prize. It depicted a man in battle dress, body crouched, both hands extended in a combat pistol stance. "Really neat," he added. "Was it an easy win?"

"They're all easy." Bennett smirked, then dropped into a crouch that imitated the figure on the trophy. He extended his clasped hands simulating a pistol. "They went down like ducks in a barrel," he said.

The door swung open, and Charlie Waters entered the office. Bennett momentarily froze, still in a combat crouch. Chambers and Gavin stiffened. Waters looked from one to the other, then back at Bennett.

"Good morning, gentlemen. Did I interrupt something?"

Bennett's face flushed, as he fought for composure. Had Waters not been there he would have slammed the heel of his hand repeatedly into his forehead.

He forced a laugh. "Sorry. We must look ridiculous. I was just regaling these gentlemen with stories of last weekend's paintball tournament," he said.

Waters eyed the trophy on the desk. "I see you won. Well, congratulations, Carter." His eyes moved to Bennett's credenza, where numerous other trophies stood, each somewhat smaller than the newest arrival. "Was this the big one, then?" Waters asked.

"The New England championship, sir," Bennett offered. He replayed the scene Waters had walked in on; wished the floor would open up and take him. "Next year they're talking about a national championship," he added, more to deflect what Waters had seen than to say anything of real interest.

"My God, what's next?" Waters shook his head, putting on an act of concern. "Can't spare you for the Olympics, Carter."

Bennett flushed again.

Waters glanced pointedly at Chambers and Gavin. It was an unspoken but clear dismissal. Both men started for the door, offering final congratulations for Bennett's victory.

"Sorry to interrupt," Waters said, when the others had gone. "But I wanted to fill you in on a meeting I had with Jack Fallon last week."

Bennett felt immediate concern. A meeting last week, one he had been told nothing about until now. It didn't bode well. He took a visitor's chair, while Waters took another. Bennett knew better than to place the desk between them, put himself in a superior position.

Waters gave Bennett a brief account of the meeting. "I'm particularly anxious about these tests he's determined to run. It does us no good to have our problems bandied about. Not now. Not when we're looking toward a big boost on the Street."

"I agree," Bennett said. He understood Waters's concerns. More than the man thought he did.

"And I'm also distressed that Jack seemed unwilling to commit to a team approach on this downsizing matter. He seemed resistant, even when I assured him no final decisions had been made."

So he didn't buy your lie, Bennett thought. But the man would have to be a complete fool to have done so. "There's a solution, of course," he said.

"And what's that?" Waters asked.

Bennett extended his hands, then brought them together again, feigning reluctance over what he was about to say. "We get rid of Fallon. Dump him before he can cause any trouble."

Waters shook his head. The vehemence of the gesture surprised Bennett. He had made the wrong move and now had to regroup. "That's as a last resort, of course. We may still be able to bring him around."

"We have to," Waters said. "The man's a fighter. He doesn't take things lying down. And while we'd win any fight in the long run, it's not something we can afford to engage in right now." His eyes bored in on Bennett. "We need smooth sailing, Carter. We don't want to raise any unnecessary hackles on the board. And Jack knows some of them quite well. And they respect him."

"What do you suggest?" Bennett was the full supplicant now.

"I had someone do some checking this weekend," Waters said. "Jack has some personal problems that may make him susceptible to reason if we couch an offer the right way. He's headed into a potentially costly divorce."

"I'm aware of that," Bennett interrupted, seeking to score some points.

"Good," Waters said. "I'm glad to hear you're on top of things." His eyes narrowed—the predator now. "He's also got two kids in college, and an aging mother in a nursing home. My informant tells me he may be facing some difficulties on that last front that could escalate his costs." He seemed to consider what he had said. "Jack's financially stable. Hell, he even owns a thousand shares of our stock. But he's not *that* stable. And what he does have will probably end up in his wife's pocket, or certainly the lawyers'."

Waters raised a finger. "He also knows his head is potentially on the block. He's figured out what we're planning, and he certainly knows he's not immune. What we have to do is offer a large carrot, and bring him into the fold."

Waters noted the displeasure on Bennett's face. "You disagree?" he asked.

"Not in principle," Bennett said. "But I don't trust Fallon. He's not a team player. He doesn't belong."

"Absolutely right," Waters said. "The man lives by values that no longer apply. But he's temporarily dangerous, and he has to be neutralized. After we've accomplished what we want . . ." He let the sentence die with a shrug.

Bennett smiled. Then you ax him, he thought. And you do it when the buyout package has gone by the board. It had a lovely touch to it. He nodded. "I'm sure I can pull it off," he said.

"And in the meantime, I want you to escalate your plan to force resignations," Waters added. "The more we get, the less chance we have of any organized resistance. Fallon or no Fallon."

"I just finished talking to Chambers and Gavin about doing just that." He smiled at Waters. "If Fallon comes on board, perhaps we can even get him to do some of the hatchet work for us." The thought of actually handing Fallon one of his envisioned coffee mugs suddenly pleased him. Perhaps even do it in front of the other members of his so-called Dinosaur Club.

Waters raised another cautioning finger, as if reading his thoughts. "Don't push Jack too hard, Carter. Lead him. You're an exceptionally bright young man. But, sometimes, youth lacks patience *and* perception."

Bennett nodded. He could afford to appear chastened by the old bastard. "What do you suggest? Carrotwise?"

Waters pursed his lips, pleased with his own superior cognition. "I think a nice fat raise would be a good start. What do you think, Carter?"

Bennett flashed a dazzlingly white smile. "I'd like to tell him myself. I think the man has certainly earned it," he said.

Fallon answered Bennett's summons at four that afternoon. He noted that Bennett's office was about the same size as his own—denoting their relative rank within the company—but that Bennett's, in addition to being closer to Charlie's, was much more elaborately furnished. His penchant for austerity did not extend to personal creature comforts, Fallon decided.

Bennett waved Fallon to a visitor's chair that had been placed—strategically, Fallon thought—so he would be forced to gaze at some ridiculous trophy on the front corner of Bennett's desk. Fallon obliged, taking in the crouched figure at the top—clad in fatigues, jump boots, and jungle hat, and poised for battle in a two-handed shooting stance. His eyes dropped to the brass plate affixed beneath. It identified Carter Bennett as that year's New England Regional Paintball Champion.

"Just won that this weekend," Bennett said, noting Fallon's interest. "Ever thought of giving it a try? Paintball, I mean."

"No, I don't think I ever have." Fallon's features remained serene, noncommittal.

Bennett thought he heard a faint note of derision in Fallon's voice and decided to spike it. "I know you had some military experience back in Vietnam. But I think you'd find this interesting." He grinned. "Of course, you don't get any troop support. It's strictly mano a mano. And I can tell you, those paint cartridges hurt like hell when you get hit."

Yeah, those AK-47 rounds smarted a bit, too, Fallon thought. He forced a smile. "I don't think so, Carter. I did all the crawling around I wanted thirty years ago. I'm sort of a peaceable old dinosaur now." He threw in the last, part for fun, part to leave no doubt where he stood.

Bennett seemed unfazed. He leaned forward, his face filled with sincerity. The pose reminded Fallon of his assistant, Les Gavin. "That's one of the things I wanted to talk to you about, Jack. I think you have a misperception about the company's plans for the future. I want to be sure you know that everyone in the company considers you a big part of that future."

What lovely bullshit, Fallon thought. Samantha had already told him what Carter had planned for his future. He smiled into the smoke screen. "That's comforting to know, Carter. But my perceptions—and concerns—also extend to some other people who have put in some long and productive years for this company."

Bennett's hands went up defensively. "Jack, I assure you, nothing has been definitely decided, and if and when it is, no one will be unduly hurt. When our plans are formalized—and that's still quite a way off—compensation for anyone affected will be quite liberal." He sensed Fallon about to question that liberality and hurried on. "And I'd very much like your input on that." He paused. "If and when it comes to that, of course."

"I assure you, I'll be happy to do it, Carter."

Bennett decided to stop fencing. It was hardball time. Buyout time. "Jack, we need you to be a team player on this. We all have to do what's good for the company. Above all other considerations."

Fallon sat back and crossed his legs. "Carter, I couldn't agree more. It's my company, too. And if austerity is called for, well, that's life in the big, bad world. Everyone understands that." He paused, leaned forward. "My concern—in addition to my own survival—is the selection process. I think it should be based on individual contribution and merit. Those who provide the most, stay. Those who don't, leave. Not selection based on age with salary and pension costs factored in. And I think that because it's what's best for the future of the company."

Bennett smiled. It was a warm, sincere, open smile, but to Fallon it was the expression of a hungry lion watching a gazelle. "I couldn't agree more, Jack. We—the company—need to retain top talent. And cost-efficient talent. I assure you that's my goal, and I'm going to rely on you, and the other division heads, for a great deal of input." He hesitated a beat. "But it can't become a debate based on friendships, Jack. That won't serve the company, or our purpose." Another smile. "Do we have a meeting of minds on that?"

Fallon returned the smile. He hoped it resembled a wolf eyeing a lamb. He had hoped Bennett would pick up on his expressed interest in his own survival, and he had. It was exactly what the man had been seeking. But he had still played it close to the vest, not revealing all that Fallon had hoped he would. "I think we understand each other perfectly, Carter."

Bennett stood and extended his hand. Fallon accepted it.

"It's great to know you're on board, Jack." The smile came again. Fallon returned it—wolf versus lion. "I wish we could have brought you into the loop earlier, but it just wasn't practical."

"It's nice to be there now," Fallon said. He turned to leave.

"Oh, wait one minute, Jack," Bennett said, stopping him. "I forgot one minor detail."

Fallon turned back and found Bennett grinning again. "Charlie Waters wanted me to let you know that your next paycheck will include a long-overdue raise." He jotted a figure on a piece of paper and handed it to Fallon. "This will be your *new* base salary."

Fallon looked at the figure and inclined his head to one side. "I'm impressed. And appreciative."

"Well, as Charlie said, it's long overdue. I think he regrets that business pressures have kept you two from being as close as he would have liked." He offered his own look of regret, began to sit, then stopped himself. "Oh, Jack, do me one other favor, would you? Just to make my life easier. Let's not push for any more tests just now. It really raises hell with all our cost-cutting efforts."

"That won't be a problem, Carter. We'll find a way to work around it."

"Great, Jack."

Bennett was smiling again, as Fallon left his office.

"The sonofabitch." Fallon looked at the ceiling of Samantha's apartment and barked out a laugh.

"Which sonofabitch are you talking about?" Samantha asked.

Fallon thought a moment, then gave an almost imperceptible nod. "You're right. There *are* two of them. That smarmy little shit, Bennett, and my dear old friend, Charlie Waters." A cold smile came to his lips. It was the first hint of one Samantha had seen since they returned to her apartment. The unexpected raise had left him hurt and confused, angry and uncertain.

Fallon crossed the room to the window. Samantha came to his side, rested her head against his shoulder as his arm circled her waist. "Have you considered that you may have frightened them?" she asked.

He hadn't. "With what? A few T-shirts that say THE DINOSAUR CLUB? A phony newsletter and some E-mail memos?" He mulled the idea over, tried to make sense of it. "I don't see the threat," he said at length. "Not a real one, anyway."

Samantha chose her words carefully. She turned and paced the room, the lawyer before the jury. "Jack, it's obvious *they* felt one. Why didn't they just fire you?" She returned to his side.

"Okay, I'll bite. Why?" He ground his teeth. "Because they thought they could buy me off. Right?"

"That wasn't because of you. It's the way they think."

Fallon continued to stare into the street. "You know what my first thought was, the first thing that flashed through my mind? I thought: You're saved." He drew a breath. "It was only momentary, but it was there." He faced her, placed his hands gently on her arms. "And they knew I'd think that. They knew I was that desperate to save my own hide." The words stung, and he shook his head again. His mother, his children, the upcoming divorce rushed to mind. "And damned if it isn't tempting." His voice was weary, with an overtone of self-disgust. He turned back to the window.

Samantha hesitated, still wary of hurting him further. Being treated with disdain after so many years had left him reeling. She didn't want to add to it.

"Okay, Jack. Let's accept that idea—in principle. And if you did, you wouldn't be doing anything a million others wouldn't do in your place. And they know that. It's part of their mind-set. Corporations understand only two ways of dealing with people: Buy them off or beat them into the ground. And they buy people off only to avoid problems. So let's figure out what threat you presented."

Fallon went to the sofa and sprawled in one corner. The apartment was still alien territory to him. It was comfortable, tastefully furnished, but it was still too new for him to feel he belonged there. His job of twenty-three years now felt the same way.

Samantha had taken a chair opposite him. "Think about it, Jack," she urged.

Fallon sat forward, rubbed his hands together. "Okay. They're worried I might lead a small insurrection. That it might end up in the courts, and perhaps even cost them some money." He shook his head. "Even if that happens—even if they lose that fight—they still come out ahead over time. They've already factored all that in. You told me so yourself."

She let him mull it over, work it out for himself. When he remained silent, she prodded him gently.

"You're right. In the long run they still win," Samantha said. "Unless a judge stops them. It's unlikely, but possible. More likely if a suit comes before a buyout is completed. They usually happen after the fact. That's when employees realize what's been done to them and decide to fight for additional compensation. By then they *know* it was discriminatory, and their initial fear is gone. They understand they have nothing more to lose. It's why companies make their offers lucrative and set a time limit for employees to accept them. It pressures the employees; makes them afraid they'll lose what's being offered. So they grab it, and the companies have accomplished what they want. The employees are gone, and even though it may cost them some more money down the line if the employees eventually sue, they know what they've done won't be overturned. They know judges are loath to reverse something that's preexisting."

"But *we* know what they're going to do," Fallon said. "Before the fact."

Samantha shook her head. "We know what's being considered. But even if they start forcing people out, we can't prove any connection to a definite downsizing plan based on age. After the fact we probably could make a strong case for it. But not now."

"So they're using me to buy time. And even to do some of the dirty work for them."

"And if you play hatchet man for them, what do you think happens to you later?"

Fallon gave her another cold smile. "No question about that, is there? They dump me after the buyout. They get me to play their game, maybe even swing the ax for them, and then I'm out. A nice hard lesson for Jack Fallon. Because he caused problems. Because he didn't want to lie down and take it."

"So why not just get rid of you now?" She pointed a finger at him. "Because they know you'd probably fight them. And that might delay what they want to do. It might even stop them from forcing other people out, because they know those people might join up with you and give them an even bigger fight, a bigger problem.

The very problem they want to avoid if they can." She paused, cocked her head to one side. "So what's the threat you present? Time. First, you might be able to get people to resist—to fight any attempt to force them out voluntarily. And if that happens, it raises the odds of a time-consuming lawsuit. Next, you could go to individual board members and create a minor fuss and some potential delays. They can overcome that, but they don't want to. Again, it would take *time*. So again time appears to be some major factor here. It seems to present some kind of problem for them. Why? And what is it? That's something you have to find out."

Samantha leaned in closer. "What else did Bennett suggest?"

Fallon thought back. He had almost forgotten the other point Carter had made. It had been done as an apparent afterthought, and he had almost allowed it to slide past. "He doesn't want any more tests."

"And why is that? Charlie Waters wouldn't even agree to see you before you requested those tests. Maybe there's a connection. I think you have to find out if there is, and, if so, how it plays into this entire scenario."

Fallon nodded absently. He ran through the possibilities. None of it seemed to make sense.

Samantha continued. "And you can't do any of that from the outside, Jack. You were smart—maybe inadvertently so—but still smart. You played along with Carter to see what he'd say. It didn't work, but maybe if you keep playing along with him, it will. Maybe you can find out what they're really up to. And you'll definitely be more help to your friends if you can find out the whens and hows and whys of everything."

"So what do I tell them? My friends. My fellow dinosaurs. These guys who depend on me. What do I say? Hey, guys, it may look like I've joined the other side, but I really haven't. Trust me, even if I seem to have finked out on you." He looked across at her. What would he do if everyone balked—if everyone just walked away—if they decided Jack Fallon was just covering his own tail?

Samantha seemed to read his thoughts. She reached across and took his hand. "I think you have to tell them the truth and hope they believe you."

19

SAMANTHA MET HIM IN A RESTAURANT NOT FAR FROM THE office. She had known him since her days at Columbia Law School. Stanley Kijewski had been nineteen and already working toward his doctorate in computer science. Her own computer had been causing her endless problems, and Kijewski had offered invaluable help. They had become friends, and had remained so over the years.

Kijewski was small and skinny and unkempt. His hair fell across a forehead still splattered with adolescent blemishes despite his twenty-nine years. He had a long nose and oversized lips, and he seemed to have last brushed his teeth in high school. They had yellowed, almost to the point of becoming brown. A jumbo-sized Snickers bar protruded from his shirt pocket.

He lived and breathed computers, acknowledged spending no fewer than fifteen hours a day before his personal terminal, and his thick glasses seemed to affirm that claim. He had also left his doctorate unfinished—bored by what he saw as an absence of creativity among his professors. What he meant was that they refused to condone the tireless hacking that alone inspired him. Now he headed up a three-man team of hackers who specialized in corporate computer security. In effect, he taught them how to avoid people like himself, then spent his free time deducing ways to overcome his own security systems. And he earned an impressive living doing it, the poacher turned gamekeeper.

Samantha leaned across the small table that separated them, both hands circling the glass of white wine that sat only inches from Kijewski's bottle of St. Pauli Girl beer. "I want you to do something for me," she said. "It may not be completely legal, and it's certainly not ethical."

Kijewski flashed a yellow/brown grin; his eyebrows fluttered up and down. "Any chance of getting caught?" he asked. He sounded as though he'd be disappointed if there was not.

Samantha shrugged. "I don't think so, but I can't promise that it's risk free." She watched his grin widen. "You could work out of my office, if necessary, pretend you were fixing some computer problem. But if it takes a great deal of time, it might be better if you could move off site."

"Hey, once I crack your system, I can work on the moon." He was twisting in his chair, eager to hear more.

"I remember you once told me how computer information, even when it's deleted, can often be retrieved." She watched him nod agreement. "I also recalled you saying that the same was true about E-mail, and other communications transactions." Another nod.

"Easy stuff. Time-consuming sometimes. But doable." Kijewski was grinning again.

Samantha hesitated. She hadn't told Fallon what she planned, hadn't really formulated it in her own mind. She wanted to investigate Bennett and Waters; try to find out what, if anything, of their plans had found its way into their personal office computers. Kijewski had often told her hair-raising tales about sloppy employee practices when it came to computers; how they lulled themselves into the false belief that the use of passwords and codes hid their entries from prying eyes. How they sometimes even failed to erase damning information, or when they did, failed to realize that the information could often be recovered.

A computer, he had said, was not unlike a group of employees standing around a water cooler glibly exchanging company secrets. Especially where E-mail messages were concerned. And the courts had ruled that those messages, like all other information stored on computers, were part of a company's records and were, therefore, subject to subpoena and discovery. Kijewski had made a great deal of money teaching companies how to avoid that computer pitfall. But even with that information the problem continued to exist. Arrogance often replaced ignorance—especially among company executives. It was a flaw Samantha was counting on.

What she wanted Kijewski to do was not technically illegal. She was an employee of Waters Cable and had legal access to their computer system. The question of ethics, however, was another matter. She was a lawyer working *for* the company, and as such was expected to safeguard its secrets. She had argued the point endlessly in her mind. Did that ethical obligation extend to other *employees*—Waters and Bennett—who might be acting illegally? Or did she have an obligation to uncover that illegality for the good of the company, its board of directors, and its stockholders? It was a fine line, and she had chosen to cross it.

"There are two people at Waters Cable who may be doing things that violate federal law," she said.

"Naughty boys." Kijewski grinned again. He considered it his job—his destiny, really—to break federal laws every day.

Samantha ignored him. "Their names are Carter Bennett—he's our chief financial officer—and Charlie Waters, the company's CEO and chairman."

"Lordy, you do go right to the top, don't you?" He leaned toward her until their faces were only a foot apart. "What are the rascals up to?"

Samantha moved back from the yellow grin, covered the withdrawal with a sip of wine. "I *know* they're about to stage an employee buyout," she said. "One that involves age discrimination that they're trying to hide."

"Pension costs, huh?" Kijewski said. "Dump the older slaves and pocket the savings." He had seen the game played before during strolls through the computer secrets of countless companies. "But you think there's more, huh? What's your guess? A little insider trading, maybe? Snag some heavy personal loot when the downsizing is announced?"

Samantha raised her eyebrows. Kijewski had eased back in his chair, so she leaned forward again. "It's one place to look," she said. "But there may also be others. Time seems to be a factor here. They're very concerned about any delays, and that confuses me." She told him about Fallon without mentioning his name—about the pressure being exerted to bring him on board.

"Most companies who want to pull something like this do it very methodically," she continued. "They rid themselves of opposition, then move ahead. This case seems different. I keep asking myself why Waters and Bennett didn't just fire this man and quietly deal with any fuss he raised. Then just sit on their hands for five or six months and let everything quiet down. *Then* start forcing people out. And when they'd achieved maximum results, *then* announce their downsizing plan and their proposed buyout."

Kijewski nodded. "It's a long-range program. So there's no need to rush." He tapped the side of his head and winked. "Unless something else is going on that demands a time frame."

"One other thing," Samantha added. "This executive they're trying to coerce has also been told not to run quality-control tests at our Plattsburgh plant. The company is having product problems, but for some reason it appears they don't want to know what they are. That doesn't make sense either."

"Does the company have any government contracts?"

"Yes. They've been working on a fiber-optic gyroscope for missile guidance systems, but it's purely research and development; there's no production contract in hand."

Kijewski shrugged. "Maybe they want to hide their problems until they have one. The government is notorious about letting companies get away with that. Even helping them. Then they shell out beaucoup bucks to correct production glitches that should have been corrected beforehand."

Samantha thought about it, nodded. "If that's being done, it's an attempt to defraud."

"Hey, for today's bozos that's just good business. But if it's there, I'll find it." Kijewski winked at her. "There'll be memoranda, and memoranda are something everyone gets careless about. It was safer in the old days, when everything was on paper and they just shredded the evidence. Now . . ." He waggled his eyebrows and let out a soft cackle.

Samantha looked at her watch, then asked, "What is all this going to cost?"

Kijewski gave an exaggerated shrug. "Hey, things are slow, and this sounds like it could be fun. It's also something I can do myself. If it gets more involved, and I have to bring my cohorts in, then we'll talk money. Otherwise, consider yourself obligated for one heavy dinner at the Four Seasons." He grinned and fluttered his eyebrows again. "I love to go there. I love to walk in in my jeans and sneakers, and watch them all shit." His yellow/brown teeth flashed again. "If I can walk in with a gorgeous woman, even cooler."

Samantha reached across and lightly stroked his cheek. "You're a doll, Stanley."

Kijewski's revolting smile widened. "If you think you like me now, wait'll my wizardry nails these humps. Then you'll think I'm Tom Cruise."

No, I won't, Samantha thought. But I'll hug you so hard your Snickers bar will melt. She gave him one of her best smiles and raised her glass. "To the Four Seasons," she said.

Charlie Waters stroked the ball and watched it run across the green, then veer off and miss the cup by a foot. He frowned.

Carter Bennett stood eight feet to his rear, marveling at the man's total lack of hand-to-eye coordination. Losing to Waters at golf was undoubtedly the hardest part of his job.

Waters tapped the ball in, retrieved it, then walked sullenly to their golf cart and slid his putter into his golf bag. They drove on to the next green, Waters quietly fuming over his missed shot.

"So you're certain Jack bought the package," he said at length.

"Positive," Bennett said. "When I told him about the raise, you could almost see his lawyer's bills falling from his shoulders."

"Frankly I'm surprised he bit so hard, so fast," Waters said. "I always thought he was tougher than that. But . . ." He let the sentence die, then looked over at Bennett, who was just pulling up to the next green. "Just make sure he keeps his promise about those tests. We don't want our problems finding their way to the Street. Especially when they're not on our end. I've already sent out memoranda on it, but Jack Fallon could charm the skin off a rattlesnake. So let's remain alert."

Bennett fought back a smile. Fallon was dead meat. Bought and paid for and wrapped for delivery. But if

Waters couldn't see it, he wasn't about to contradict him. "I'll keep an eye on him," he said. "In fact, I'll be escalating the pressure on one of his people next week. It should provide a nice little test of Fallon's commitment."

"What are you planning?" Waters asked.

Bennett told him.

Waters chuckled, shook his head. "Jesus, Carter, that's insidious. Even for you. That should send tremors through the whole company." His chuckle turned into a laugh. "Hell, every washroom stall will be filled. And everybody in middle management will be trying to pad their expense accounts to cover liquid lunches."

"It'll be cheap at half the price," Bennett said.

"Yes, it will," Waters agreed. "Yes, it will."

They pulled up to the next green. Waters put his hand on Carter's arm as he prepared to exit the cart. "What's happening with this phony newsletter and those E-mail memos? Have you found the source?"

Bennett had known the question would come sooner or later and he gritted his teeth. "Not yet, but I have people working on it." He thought about the gun magazines that had been found in the trash of the sales department. There had even been an article explaining how to make bombs. One of those articles had been mailed to him, together with a map that detailed the route from the Chrysler Building to his apartment. It had both shaken and angered him, and he had ordered Les Gavin to get to the bottom of it, to physically search offices, if necessary. But Gavin had failed miserably. The trash in question had been in the bullpen area outside Wally Green's office and could have been placed there by any of his salespeople.

Waters pulled some folded papers from his shirt pocket and handed them to Bennett. "Have you seen this?" he asked.

Bennett unfolded the papers, revealing the latest issue of *The Daily Downsizer*. The headline read:

WATERS CABLE BUYS NURSING HOME. EMPLOYEES OVER 45 OFFERED ROOM AND BOARD AT REDUCED RATES. The article that followed, which Bennett had already read, liberally quoted both him and Chambers. In it they explained that a fleet of ambulances would arrive at the Chrysler Building next week to move employees to the nursing home as part of a *resource relocation*. The plan, the article alleged, involved the *nonrenewal* of four thousand jobs, as a means of *refocusing the skill mix* and implementing a much needed *redundancy elimination*. What was especially painful was that Bennett had used exactly those terms on various occasions. That realization had led him to have his office swept for bugging devices. But none was found.

"I've already seen it," he said now.

"Well, you haven't seen this," Waters said. "This goddamned newsletter was mailed to my *home*." He jabbed a finger at the envelope. Arrows had been drawn, pointing to the stamp affixed at one corner. It was one the government had issued a year earlier. It depicted a large rodent, and was intended to celebrate the Chinese New Year—The Year of the Rat.

"I received a similar letter," Bennett said.

Waters looked at him in the same way Bennett often looked at Chambers and Gavin. "Get on the stick, Carter," he snapped. "We need to put a stop to this. And we need to do it now."

George Valasquez stared at Fallon, his eyes narrowed into a suspicious squint.

Fallon returned the stare. "Don't give me that look, George. If I was out to screw anybody, I wouldn't be standing here talking about it."

They had gathered at Ryan and McFaddan's, a popular watering hole on Second Avenue and Forty-second Street, only two blocks from the office. It was four o'clock, an hour before their normal gym time, and the bar was empty as expected; the lingering smell of stale beer, together with two bored bartenders, the only signs of human presence, past or yet to come.

"So why'd they hand you a raise?" Valasquez asked. They were clustered at the far end, away from the bartenders' always curious ears.

Fallon's jaw tightened. He placed his draft beer on the mahogany bar with an audible crack. "They were buying me, George. It's that simple. It's what you want to hear, isn't it?" He glanced at the others; saw some flickers of doubt.

"And you took it," Valasquez said.

Fallon wanted to reach out and grab the man by his skinny throat. He held back, fought to keep anger from his voice. The man is just frightened, he kept assuring himself. "That's right, George. I played dumb and said thank you very much. What would you have done?"

Wally Green didn't give George a chance to answer. "Hey, he would of blown Bennett's brains out." He glared at the smaller man. "You're being an asshole, George."

"Let's calm down." It was Ben Constantini. He moved his square, heavy body between Green and Valasquez like a referee in a boxing match. He faced Fallon. "So what did the little prick tell you?" he asked.

"Nothing we didn't already know. He assured me I'd have input in any final buyout plan, but there's no guarantee he'll live up to it."

"So what was the alternative?" It was Jim Malloy.

Fallon gave him a sick grin. "I think they would have tossed my butt out on the street. Just to make sure I didn't organize any resistance." He shrugged. "I think this Dinosaur Club thing is making them nervous. I'm just not entirely sure why."

"Maybe it's the T-shirts," Annie Schwartz suggested. "People always get nervous when I make one of my many fashion statements." She winked at Fallon, then turned serious. "Or maybe they think we're a lot better organized than we are." She tilted her head to one side. "Look, I think we're all being a little schmucky about this. I understand that. We're all scared." She saw some faces scowl at the word, and she let out a coarse laugh. "Oh, I know, it's only the poor, helpless women who get scared. But let me tell you big guys something. The reason some of us are ready to jump on Jack is because we're all scared shitless. We're scared that if he walks away, we won't have him to lean on. So let's screw our heads back on and get real. Okay?"

Fallon listened to mumbled agreement, as he took in his ragtag group of dinosaurs. He was grateful to Annie, but he also knew the suspicion and the fear would not go away.

"Someone I spoke to thinks the real concern for Waters and Bennett is timing," he said at length. "That they're trying to buy me off because they don't want any resistance until they've picked enough of us off."

"They've already started that game," Joe Hartman said. "Look what they're doing to Jim. I'm just wondering when they'll get down to me."

Six pairs of eyes turned to Malloy.

"Hey, don't worry about me. I can take anything they dish out." It was pure bravado. Fallon could hear it in his voice, and as eyes were slowly averted, he could see the others knew it as well.

"We better get ready for more." Fallon's words snapped their attention back. He looked at each of them in turn. "If timing is a part of this, and if Bennett thinks he's got it all under control, he'll start picking up the pace."

Malloy's face paled. "You think you'll know when he's ready to make his next move?" he asked.

"I don't know. I'm hoping. But the important thing is, we stick together. Nobody buckles. Nobody quits. We play their game and live with whatever they hand down." He turned back to Valasquez. "Whether they hand us a pile of shit or a bouquet of roses. Okay?"

Valasquez curled his lips. "Yeah, sure, Jack."

"Georgie, when we get to the gym, I'm gonna rap you upside the head with one of the dumbbells," Wally snapped.

"Come on, George. Cool down." It was Constantini again. "Let's not jump all over Jack." He turned to Fallon. "You're right, about us needing to hang together on this. But this business about the raise isn't making it easy. Annie's right. We're all pretty scared."

Fallon raised his hands. "Look, everybody's nervous. I know I am. But *they're* nervous, too. Bennett made a point about the tests we tried to have run. He wants us to back off; leave it alone. He claims it's a budget issue, but I'm not so sure. I think it may be a part of this whole thing. So I want to find a way to run those tests without his knowing."

"That's a tough nut," Malloy said. "They have pretty tight controls. Some lab tech would have to do it on his own time and not record what he did in the laboratory log. And if nobody's willing to do that, then one of us would have to request it." Fear returned to his eyes. "Either way, whoever did it could get himself canned. Hell, they sent Wally a letter of reprimand about the last test we tried to get."

Fallon had scotched the reprimand Willis Chambers had sent to Wally. He had simply sent a memo to personnel, for inclusion in Wally's personnel file, stating that he, not Green, had ordered the tests. But this was different.

"Yeah, he could," Fallon said. "*If* he got caught." He grinned at them. "But we're all going to get canned anyway, right?" He watched several of them nervously shift their weight. They still didn't want to believe it, he thought. They were terminal patients, each praying a cure would be found before they croaked. "Look, it's something we've got to do," he said. "I've got a trip scheduled to Washington tomorrow. But I'm going to Plattsburgh instead. I'm going to see Stuart Robaire and lay it all out, try to convince him to run the tests on the QT."

"He wasn't too helpful when we were up there," Wally said. "Bennett called and said boo, and Robaire wet his pants. What makes you think it'll be any different this time?"

Fallon smirked at him. "I'm supposed to be a salesman, right?" Wally rolled his eyes. Fallon's smirk turned into a laugh. "Okay, so I'm management. I haven't sold anything in a long time. So it's time I got off my ass and sold something to someone. Robaire's elected."

"There may be another way." It was Annie, and all eyes had turned toward her. "It's just an idea," she continued. "But my niece is married to a guy who's an assistant professor at M.I.T. He's a dork, but he's always bragging how he works with the best minds in the country. And he owes me a little favor. If Robaire gave us some sample wire from different runs, I could ask him to run the tests, then get one of those geniuses to check the results."

"You think he'll do it?" Fallon asked.

"I think so." She grinned at Fallon. "His name's Paul Palango, and he likes to be called P.P." She rolled her eyes. "He's a nose picker and a farter, and according to my princess of a niece, she's gotta use masking tape on P.P.'s little pee-pee every time she wants a little romance in her life. In short, he's an all-around schmuck. But he owes me money, so I think he'll do it if I ask him."

Fallon grinned, shook his head. "Sounds like nobody thinks I can sell Robaire. But it might be an easier route, and an outside evaluation would be even stronger."

"Especially M.I.T.," Wally added. "I like it, Jack."

"Why don't we cut the roundabout bullshit and just make Bennett tell us," Valasquez snapped. "If this crap about faulty wire is part of it, that bastard knows why."

Fallon stared at him. "What do we do, George? Beat it out of him? Or do we just say please?"

"We do whatever the hell we have to," Valasquez snapped back. "We stop dancing around this god-damned thing. It's not getting us anyplace. We start playing the game the way they play it. We *make* them do what we want."

Fallon glanced at the others, then glared at Valasquez. "Forget it, George. What you're talking about would blow everything. And—just in case you haven't noticed—we're a bunch of middle-aged, overweight wire peddlers. This isn't Don Corleone's crew. I don't want to hear this crap. Is that understood? We'll get through this, but we'll do it by sticking together and playing it smart." He drew a breath and glanced at each of them again, then at his watch. "And speaking of middle-aged, overweight wire salesmen, it wouldn't hurt if we hit some of those machines back at the gym."

Valasquez started to move past, then stopped. He stared up into Fallon's eyes. "What are you gonna do when Bennett sees that you're still working out with us, Jack? Say, 'Don't worry about it, Carter old buddy, we're just a bunch of fat guys getting in shape'?"

Fallon took hold of his arm, a bit tighter than necessary. He wished it was the man's neck. He held George's gaze. "I'm going to tell him that I'm lulling you into a sense of false security, George. And if he has any doubts, I'm gonna tell him to talk to you."

20

STUART ROBAIRE LOOKED AS THOUGH HE'D JUST BEEN asked to play Russian roulette with five bullets. They were seated at a minuscule conference table in Robaire's small, neat office at the Plattsburgh plant. It was glass-enclosed, and they could see his two assistants in even smaller adjoining offices.

"All this talk about downsizing and buyouts has my wife terrified," he said. "I tried to explain that to you last week. We have one kid in college, and another ready to go next year. If I lose my job, I don't know what we'll do." He glanced at Annie Schwartz as if she would understand, almost as if her sex alone could corroborate his argument.

Fallon pressed his hands against the table and stared at them. He had removed his wedding band weeks ago, but he could still see the slight discoloration that remained on his finger.

"Some things won't go away, Stuart." He looked up at the man. He was in his mid to late forties, well within Bennett's dinosaur range—one of the people who in a few short years would cost the company an additional one and a half percent in yearly pension contributions.

Robaire stared back. His pinched, narrow face

seemed suddenly more so. He had removed his glasses and was squinting to make up for his poor vision. He seemed to be gulping air, and his protruding Adam's apple bobbed up and down with each nervous swallow.

"I told you about the group we formed in sales," Fallon said. "We're going to fight this thing, Stuart. But to be successful we have to have people throughout the company who are willing to fight it, too."

"But what do these tests have to do with it?" Robaire was nervously toying with the pocket protector in his shirt pocket. He kept checking the outside flap, as though assuring himself it still covered the exterior.

"It may have nothing to do with it. I just don't know." Fallon held his eyes. "I do know that Bennett, and even Waters himself, seem determined that no one check into it." He raised a mollifying hand. "Look, I just want you to give us samples. Enough so we can have the people at M.I.T. run tests on the gyroscopic cable you think Sprint got by mistake. You won't be running any tests yourself. If anyone asks, Annie and I will say we needed the samples for a potential customer. We'll cover you completely. We'll play it as safe as you feel is necessary."

Robaire averted his eyes, shook his head. "Jesus, Jack. What do I say if anyone finds out? Christ, I've got two young guys working under me." He raised his eyes to the adjoining offices. "They've heard these rumors, too. They're just sitting there, rubbing their hands together, each one hoping he'll be the one who takes my place. I even caught one of them going through the papers on my desk the other day."

"Stuart, I've got a guy across the hall who's doing the same thing. He's even going through my trash. We're all in the same boat. And the *only* chance we have is to stick together and find out what the hell is going on."

"But you said this might have nothing to do with anything." He was almost pleading, searching out any escape.

"That's right. But if it does we need to know."

Robaire shook his head again. "If one of those bastards ever saw me and reported me for it, I'd be dead. Management would just think I was a party to this M.I.T. test. I got that memorandum from Mr. Waters a few days ago. I sent copies to my staff. If they see me, what excuse do I have?"

Fallon had already seen the memorandum. Robaire had shown it to him. It had put Robaire's entire department on notice. Put them in a box.

"You think that memo is unusual?" Fallon asked.

Robaire stared at him, incredulous. "Unusual? Christ, I've never seen anything like it. And I've worked here for fifteen years. We've never cut back on testing. Not even in the most austere of times. It's just bad engineering."

"What do you think of the tolerances?"

Robaire stared at the table. "I agree with you. Something has to be wrong. I don't know if it's something minor that can be corrected with a quick fix, or if it's something more systemic."

He looked up. "Jack, I raised some questions when Mr. Waters was here laying out the specs. I told you about that. He almost took my head off. I don't understand any of this. I'm not sure I *want* to understand any of it. I've got my résumé out now, and I'm just praying somebody out there will want me."

Annie leaned forward and smiled at him. "Stuart, Stuart, Stuart. You're worried about those schmucks next door?" She inclined her head toward the adjoining offices. "You leave them to me, while you get Jack what he needs." She winked at him. "As long as they're not gay, they'll be captivated by my charms."

Robaire pressed his thumb and index finger into his eyes. "All right." He shook his head. "But Jack, what you're asking scares the living hell out of me."

"We're all scared," Fallon said. "We're all there together. We'd have to be fools not to be scared."

* * *

An hour later, after Fallon and Annie had left the plant, one of the assistants Annie had "captivated" entered Robairc's now empty office and took a seat at the small conference table. He was a twenty-eight-year-old electrical engineer named Victor Nagy, and two weeks earlier Carter Bennett had telephoned and suggested he keep an eye out for any unauthorized testing. It was something the young engineer had viewed as a chance to send his personal corporate star into ascension.

Nagy spread some computer printouts on the table, as though waiting to review them with Robaire, then reached beneath and surreptitiously removed a micro-cassette from a small voice-activated tape recorder he had secreted there more than a week ago. He then gathered the printouts and left.

Back in his own office, a small smile played across the engineer's lips as he listened to the tape on a second recorder. His star was not only ascending, it was about to go off like a rocket. Nervously—triumphantly—he picked up the phone and called New York. The smile faded when Bennett's assistant explained he was not available.

"Please have him call me," he said. "It's very important that I speak to him. Please tell him, Victor Nagy from Plattsburgh."

They moved across Killian Court, the only open stretch of greenery on M.I.T.'s urban campus. The rectangle of grass was crowded with students; each intent on soaking up the August sun in brief respites from the summer research projects that kept them locked away in cramped laboratories. Fallon and Annie zigzagged through the sprawl of slender, half-naked bodies. Behind them lay Memorial Drive and the Charles River, and perhaps the best view of the Boston skyline to be had anywhere in the city. Ahead was the Great Dome, a white marble edifice that bore a striking resemblance to the Jefferson

Memorial, and beneath which lay what denizens of the 'Tute called the Infinite Corridor—an expanse of hallway said to be the second longest in the United States, and to which the majority of the school's buildings were connected. It was there that Fallon and Annie would hopefully find Material Sciences, known simply as Building 8, where Paul Palango had his office and lab.

Fallon had never been to M.I.T., and once inside the Infinite Corridor, he was stunned by both its dimensions and its shabbiness. Curls of peeling paint dotted the vast expanse of bland-colored walls, and the doors of offices and the walls beside them were cluttered with notices and memos and taped-up newspaper clippings, many so old they had begun to brown at the edges.

Outside the entry to Building 8 the wall held a seemingly endless supply of Dilbert cartoons. Fallon stopped to read one, as Annie looked over his shoulder.

"That's just what I'd expect in this joint," she said. "A whole wall dedicated to the patron saint of nerds." She tugged on his sleeve. "Please, let's get this over with. Being around all this brainpower is gonna give me a migraine. P.P.'s office is on the second floor. But be prepared. The place is gonna smell of stale farts."

Paul Palango opened the glass-fronted door to his office and stared out at them with what Fallon thought was the most sickly, insincere smile he had ever seen. Palango was short, in his early thirties, Fallon guessed, with a soft, slightly swollen body that hinted at the Pillsbury Doughboy he would become in another ten years. He squinted at Annie, then Fallon, as he scratched at wavy brown hair and sent a cascade of dandruff to his shoulders.

"Oh, you're here today," he said. "For some reason I thought you were coming tomorrow."

Annie rolled her eyes, then reached out and pinched his cheek. "Paulie, bubala. I called yesterday, and said we were coming *tomorrow*. Since yesterday was yesterday, tomorrow is today. Do you have any coffee?"

Annie brushed past, leaving Palango slightly stunned in her wake, and entered the cramped office, which barely had room for an institutional metal desk, two metal chairs, and two overflowing bookcases. She wrinkled her nose at the smell that indeed permeated the room. "This is Jack Fallon," she said over her shoulder. "He's vice president of sales, which means he's my boss, which means you should be nice to him or I could lose my job, which means I'd be unemployed and *poor*." She said the last as though warning that money she'd lent him in the past might have to be repaid if that unfortunate event occurred.

Palango turned to Fallon, his dull brown eyes suddenly bright. "You know, I've often thought of leaving academe for the private sector." His face became instantly offended. Then he puffed himself up and stretched his arms to take in some larger entity. "For all the brilliance that goes on behind these walls, they pay us a pittance."

Fallon grinned as he stepped past, Palango's ploy too blatantly obvious. "Don't rush off," he said. "Especially if you have tenure. Five years from now the people working here may be the only engineers in America who haven't been downsized to jobs at McDonald's."

Palango's face screwed up again. "That would be the ultimate offense," he said. "I could end up serving my all too unappreciative students their lunch."

Annie reached out and pinched his cheek again. "Well, until then, Paulie, help us appreciate your genius by doing the little job I told you about."

Quickly Annie restated the problem and handed over the wire they had brought from the Plattsburgh plant.

"I'd like to have your findings double-checked by someone else in your department," Fallon added. "It's not that we don't trust your expertise. It's just that I expect resistance to those findings, and I need the results to be as irrefutable as possible."

"That won't be a problem," Palango assured them. "I'll get the chairman of my department to do it. He's one of the top materials men in the world."

Palango led them into a surprisingly small lab. Despite the cutting-edge research for which M.I.T. was noted, the room had a World War II feeling about it, the black laboratory bench chipped along its edges and permeated with a coating of ancient dust that seemed lacquered to its top. Even the windows were coated with years of grime, and it made everything seem even smaller and darker.

Palango worked for an hour and a half without comment, checking the sample wire against the printout of manufacturing specs that Fallon had provided. When he finished he squinted up and shook his head with open incredulity.

"It's just as you suspected. Sprint received a batch of the new cable, which, I'm afraid, falls far short of any workable spec." He hesitated. "Let me ask you something. You do, I suppose, sell fiber-optic cable to aircraft manufacturers as well as communications companies?"

Fallon nodded. "We sell to most of the majors."

Palango shook his head. "Well—and I assure you I'll have my preliminary findings checked—if I were you, I'd make damned sure none of this faulty stuff gets shipped to any of those companies by mistake. I don't know who set these specs, but this cable doesn't even have the tolerances needed to meet cable TV standards. If it ever ended up in an aircraft, a good electrical storm could have those birds falling out of the sky."

Les Gavin and Willis Chambers were out in the hall when Fallon arrived at his office the next morning. Gavin had a smirk on his face, and he was speaking to Chambers in hushed tones. When he saw Fallon coming toward him, the smirk disappeared. Then he whispered a final word to Chambers, and the pair moved away.

Fallon watched his assistant retreat and decided there was one thing he'd do before he left the company. He would call Gavin into his office and summarily fire the smarmy little sonofabitch. He would do it just for kicks, even if Carter Bennett rehired the man an hour later.

Fallon entered his outer office and immediately caught the look on Carol's face. Her eyes darted to the closed door of his private sanctum. "Jim Malloy's waiting for you," she said. "And he's not in good shape."

"What's wrong?"

Carol shook her head. Her eyes were both sympathetic and frightened. "I better let Jim explain. Everything went crazy here yesterday, and I didn't know where to reach you."

Fallon entered his office and closed the door behind him. Malloy was seated on the sofa, and even from across the room Fallon could tell he'd been drinking. His face was pale and haggard, eyes streaked with burst capillaries, and his attempt at shaving that morning had left a patchwork of nicks and untouched beard. Fallon took a chair next to him and could smell the stale booze that wafted off the man. Malloy hadn't touched a drop in years, not since Fallon had called him on it, warned him that his job was at stake. He chose to ignore that now, at least for the moment.

"What's going on, Jim?" he asked.

Malloy stared at him. "You don't know?"

"I've been in Plattsburgh and Boston. You know that. Talk to me."

Malloy chewed on his upper lip. There was a cup of coffee in his hand, and Fallon could see it was shaking. "I thought they would have told you," he said. He took a gulp of coffee.

"Who? Tell me what?"

"Chambers. Bennett. All of them. I thought they would have cleared it with you."

"What the hell are you talking about?" Fallon leaned in closer. "Come on, Jim, start at the beginning."

Malloy gulped coffee again. He used both hands to keep it from spilling. "I came to work yesterday, and I found my office locked and my desk in the hall."

"*What?*"

Malloy glared at him. "That's right. Out in the hall. Right where my assistant used to sit."

Fallon envisioned it. Unlike upper management, who were provided office suites, mid-level executives had smaller private offices with assistants stationed at desks outside their doors. The assistants sat literally in a wide, well-traveled hall.

"So who's in your office?" Fallon asked.

"No one. It's empty. Locked and empty." His hands gripped the cup so tightly Fallon thought it might break. Malloy's face contorted; his eyes looked as though he might break down, but he fought it off. "I went to see Willis Chambers," Malloy continued. "I figured he's head of human resources, right? He'll know what the hell is going on." His jaw tightened in anger; his face flushed. "Well, he knows all right. My office is being redecorated, he says. It's part of an overall refurbishing, he says. They had to start somewhere, he says."

"Did anyone notify you?"

"Hell, no." He stared at Fallon. "Did they tell you?" His features filled with suspicion.

Fallon's temper flared. But not at Malloy. What else could the man think? "No, Jim. Nobody said a word to me." He sat back. His hands had closed into fists. "What else did Chambers say?"

Malloy grunted, shook his head. "I asked him how long this *refurbishing* was gonna take. Just how long I'd be sitting out in the goddamned hall. And he says he has no idea. He says he's sure it won't be *too* long. So I ask him what other offices are being refurbished, and he tells me he's not sure. He says he can't understand why I'm so upset. He says I should be pleased I'm first on the list." Malloy's face contorted again, but he pushed on. "So I ask him when the workmen are supposed to start, and he tells me he's not sure exactly. But he insists they had to move everything out of the office now, just so there wouldn't be any delays doing it when they got here. He just grinned at me, told how those guys got paid by the hour, and the company didn't want them standing around, waiting for me to move out."

Fallon looked away toward the window, simmering. "You have a key to the office, right?" he asked at length.

Malloy let out a bark of a laugh. "Oh, yeah," he said. "Except they changed the locks. Chambers said it was for security. He said the workmen would be leaving tools there, and the company would be liable if they disappeared. The *fuck!*" He stared at Fallon. His eyes were filled with a mix of fear and rage. "This is it, right, Jack? This is all part of their game. I'm the first target, the first guy they're gonna force out the door. That's the goddamned list Chambers is really talking about."

Fallon leaned in close, forearms on his knees. He kept his voice low and even. "I'm not going to lie to you, Jim. I don't know. But I'm going to find out. Right now, I want you to take the rest of the day off," he said. "Just go home and call me later this afternoon." He hesitated. "And, Jim, lay off the sauce. You've been away from it for years. Go to an AA meeting. Do whatever works for you. But don't let them beat you this way."

Malloy's jaw trembled, and Fallon thought he might burst into tears. Again, he fought it back. "Jack, I'm scared. I don't know if I can take this kind of humiliation." Malloy's eyes searched Fallon's face for some kind of answer. "Jack, what the hell did I ever do to deserve this? What kind of people are they? Why don't they just fire me? Why do it this way?"

"They don't want to fire you, Jim. They want you to quit. If they fire you, you're still part of the problem. You're another example of age discrimination that'll be added to the list when they force everyone else to take their buyout. If you quit, then it's something that was out of their control. Your choice, not theirs." Fallon reached out and grabbed his forearm, squeezed it lightly. "Don't let them win this way, Jim. Tell them to go to hell and hang tough."

Malloy's head drooped; his eyes fixed on a blur of carpet. "I don't know if I can, Jack. I just don't know."

Fallon walked into Chambers's office without waiting to be announced. He could still hear Chambers's assistant telling him he had to wait. But she wasn't doing it too vehemently. She had even given him an approving nod as he marched past. He closed the door, shutting her out. He didn't want one of Carol's covert dinosaurs pressured to be a witness against him.

Chambers was seated in his high-backed chair, and Fallon walked straight around the desk and stepped in close, not leaving the man room enough to stand.

"Tell me about this goddamned redecorating plan, Willis," he snapped. "And tell me quick."

Chambers began to sputter. Fallon leaned down, his face only a foot from Chambers's nose.

"Jack, calm down. Please." Chambers was pressed back in his chair, fighting for any distance he could put between them. His eyes were wide and terrified, and his hands had gone up to fend off an anticipated blow.

"You listen to me, you little shit," Fallon hissed. "This is the last time you're going around me and pulling crap in my division. You're going to tell me what this is all about. You're going to tell me how long Jim Malloy is going to be sitting in a goddamned hall. And if I don't like the answers, you're going to give me a key so his desk can be moved back in now."

Chambers started to sputter again, and Fallon stood, giving him some small breathing space.

"I don't have a key," Chambers pleaded. "Building maintenance has the key. And I have no idea how long it will take." He raised his hands to his sides in a gesture of helplessness. "You know what workmen are like, Jack. Who can tell?"

Fallon reached down and jabbed a finger into his chest. "Then find out!" he snapped. "Because I want to know." He straightened again, but still did not move. "Now tell me how Jim Malloy happened to be the first person on your list, and why the hell nobody told him, or me."

Chambers's hands were up defensively again. If Fallon moved, just a few steps, he fully intended to bolt for the door. "Jack, I thought you knew. I thought Jim knew. I assure you, it was just some kind of snafu, that's all."

The lie was so blatant Fallon wanted to grab him by the throat and slap him silly. He fought back the temptation and simply glared at the man. His voice became unnaturally soft, and that seemed to frighten Chambers even more. "Then you find out, Willis. Because if this is some attempt to humiliate the man, then you've got one pissed-off executive on your hands, and you better be ready to deal with it. If it's not, then I want an explanation, in writing, about why things keep happening in my division, at your direction, without me knowing about it."

Chambers sputtered again. "Fine, Jack, fine. I'll find out."

"You better, Willis," Fallon snapped. "And you better do it today."

Two hours passed before Bennett made his way to Fallon's office. Fallon wasn't certain if Bennett had been tied up and had just learned about the outburst, or if he had been wise enough to give Fallon time to cool down. He entered the office with a broad gesture—hands out at his sides, head cocked in apparent disbelief. He was in shirtsleeves, just another working stiff.

"Jack, what's going on? I just had Willis Chambers in my office, and the man was really shaken."

Fallon sat back in his chair. His tongue was pressed to the inside of his cheek. "In case you haven't noticed, Carter, Willis is an incompetent ass. I think we should fire him. In fact, I may make a formal request for his immediate dismissal."

"Now wait a minute, Jack. Willis was just doing his job. Maybe there was a little slipup here. Maybe Willis didn't touch all the bases he should have. But I can't support any talk about dismissal, and I won't."

Fallon faked sudden surprise. "I didn't realize I needed your permission, Carter. Last time I checked the organization chart, I thought we were equals."

Bennett seemed to bristle at the idea. His eyes hardened momentarily, then relaxed. "I don't want to fight you on this, Jack. It's too petty. Besides, I thought we had an understanding."

Fallon kept his voice calm. "Not about this, we didn't. This is about people going around me and *fucking* with my division, and with my people. That's not going to happen, Carter."

Bennett's jaw tightened, and he stared at the floor. Just letting you know he's controlling himself, Fallon thought. Letting you know how difficult it is for him to do it. It was a cute act, by an even cuter actor.

"Jack, this is just what we talked about the other day," he said at length. "About not letting personal friendships stand in the way of the company's needs."

"I thought we were talking about your downsizing plan," Fallon said.

Bennett seemed horrified that the word had been spoken, and he turned abruptly and closed Fallon's door.

Fallon was suddenly amused. He repeated the statement. "As I said, Carter, I thought we were talking about downsizing. Is this part of it? If it is, why don't we just fire Malloy, instead of humiliating him?"

Bennett let out an exasperated breath. "We're not firing anybody, Jack. We're redecorating offices, just as Willis explained. I can't help it if Malloy is taking it another way. He shouldn't, even though his recent performance has been poor enough to warrant that view."

"I think his performance has been just fine, given the circumstances."

"Well, then we disagree," Bennett snapped. "But let's leave that for another time."

Fallon's instincts kicked in. An all-out battle would not serve him well. Not now. "So Jim sits in the hall?" he asked instead.

"I'm afraid it can't be helped," Bennett said. "It will happen to all of us in time. Hopefully, some of us can schedule our vacations while it's going on."

"Maybe Jim can do that," Fallon said.

"I don't think this is the time for sales executives to be taking time off," he said. "In fact, I've directed Willis to withhold vacation approval for all key personnel until further notice. The company is in a rough economic position, Jack. And Mr. Waters feels we need everyone pulling their oars."

Pull this, Fallon thought. He leaned back farther and gave Bennett a cold smile. "Maybe Willis should consider those oars when he pulls secretarial help and office space," he said.

Bennett returned the chill. "That's a good point, Jack. I'll speak to him about it. But in the meantime, let's you and me stay on the same wavelength. I don't think it would serve either of us well if we worked at cross-purposes."

Fallon let the warning slide. If Bennett wanted to threaten him, he'd force him to abandon subtlety.

"That's exactly what I want, Carter." Fallon offered up a warmer, falser smile. "Wavelength-wise."

Bennett stared at him, trying to gauge his sincerity. "I'm glad to hear that, Jack," he said.

Fallon picked up a pen, toyed with it. "I hope our minions stop screwing that wavelength up," he said.

When Bennett returned to his office his assistant handed him a message. "That Mr. Nagy, who called yesterday from the Plattsburgh plant, called again. He left the same message. He said it was very important that he speak with you."

Bennett tried to remember who the man was. Nagy. Nagy. Then it connected. The testing lab. The drone he had asked to keep watch on Robaire.

"Call him back. Tell him I'm in a meeting. Just ask him if Robaire has done any unauthorized testing."

Bennett entered his own office and slid into his chair. He picked up a report Chambers had prepared, then put it down again. Dealing with Fallon was becoming burdensome. The man was still playing his little dinosaur game, still protecting his fellow incompetents. What they should do is get rid of the lot of them immediately—Fallon, Malloy, and Green. Chop the head off sales management and then deal with the rest. No, he told himself, not Malloy. Malloy at least was serving a purpose. He let out an exasperated breath. And not the others either. Waters won't allow it. Not now, at least. He's running scared. And you know why.

Bennett's assistant knocked lightly on his door, then entered. "Mr. Nagy says there's been no testing at the plant. But he reiterated it was important that he speak with you. He said he couldn't explain, that he had to speak to *you*." She raised her eyebrows and offered up a small, dismissive smile.

Bennett waved a hand reinforcing that dismissal. "I'll get to him when I can. If he calls back, tell him that."

* * *

Fallon left the office early, got his car from the company parking garage, and headed out to Jim Malloy's home on Staten Island. He dreaded what lay ahead, and as he drove across the Verrazano Bridge, he tried to formulate the words he would use. His mind seemed as cluttered as New York's harbor, with its scattering of tankers and cargo ships lying at anchor as they awaited berths.

He had called Samantha before leaving to let her know he'd be late. Then he'd talked to Wally, told him he'd be missing their session at the company gym, and filled him in on what had taken place with Bennett. He had decided not to tell anyone about the preliminary tests at M.I.T., and had told Annie to keep mum as well until the final results were in. Finally, he'd telephoned Malloy's home, spoken with his wife, and explained he needed to stop by. Betty had sounded fearful, and he had tried to put her mind at ease. Years earlier, he and Trisha had been close to Jim and Betty. They had gone out to dinner and to Broadway shows together. They had always arranged to sit together at company functions. Then they had drifted apart. Betty had returned to school for her master's degree, and had found less time to socialize. Then she had begun teaching, and time, between family and work, had become even more restricted. So she had stopped going to company functions, which she had always despised, anyway. And the friendship had drifted, had been left between the men, and as such had been limited to company matters and occasional lunches and dinners. They had simply grown apart. Fallon regretted that they had.

Jim Malloy's house was in an Irish-Catholic enclave, one of many ethnic bastions on the island. Malloy had grown up in the neighborhood and had remained—had purchased his first home there, shortly after his marriage, and had provided his children with the same upbringing he had received.

Fallon climbed the steps that crossed the small front yard and approached the modest, sturdy, brick barbican.

Betty opened the door almost immediately, almost as if she'd been standing watch for him behind a front window.

"Jim's downstairs in his rec room," she said, after accepting a kiss on the cheek.

"How are you?" Fallon asked. "It's been a long time."

She seemed uncomfortable. "I'm fine, Jack. I was sorry to hear about you and Trish."

Fallon shrugged. "I was, too. But those things happen, I guess."

She hesitated, momentarily uncertain, he thought. She had always been a strong, self-confident woman, but now she seemed haggard. There were worry lines around her mouth that came from more than age, and her once vibrant blue eyes seemed dulled.

"I'm worried about Jim," she said. "What they're doing to him is tearing him apart, Jack."

"I'm worried about him, too," Fallon said.

"I told him to quit," she said abruptly. "Just tell them all to go to hell, and walk away." She lowered her eyes. "He said he can't do that—that we can't afford it." She looked at Fallon imploringly. "But we can, Jack. If we have to we can. I'd rather have less money than watch my husband die a little each day." Her eyes filled with tears. "Those bastards. They're killing him, Jack."

Fallon's stomach tightened. Jim, all the others, were depending on him, waiting for him to do something that would resolve their lives. But there wasn't a damned thing he could do, except keep playing pattycake with Carter Bennett.

He took Betty's hand. "I'm doing everything I can to work this out," he said, silently praying it was true. "Right now, I don't know if I can." He paused a beat. "I guess he's told you about this downsizing crap." He watched her nod. "Well, there's a pot of money at the end of it. But only for the people who are still there. If those bastards find a way to force Jim out—to force any of us out—they can cheat each one of us out of it. And I don't want that to happen."

"What good is the money if he's dead, Jack? Or if he's back spending his nights with a glass of bourbon in his hand? He's just as good as dead that way."

Fallon drew a long breath. "Look, Betty, I'm not asking this as his boss. But if Jim's drinking again, we've got to find a way to make him stop. I know he was drinking last night, and I don't know a lot about this. But if he has a sponsor in AA, or anybody else, let's reach out for him. Let's do whatever has to be done."

Betty closed her eyes, shook her head. "He's been drinking for weeks, Jack. Ever since this whole thing started." She drew another breath, almost a gasp. "It wasn't very much at first, and I told myself not to worry. Then yesterday happened. He went into that damned office and found his desk in the hall. Jesus Christ, Jack. What do they expect him to do? Just sit there and be publicly humiliated? Be a joke for everybody, for the whole office?"

"They want him to quit, Betty. It's that simple. They want him to quit so they can cheat him out of what they owe him. And they want to do it to enough of us, so that when they drop the ax on the rest, there won't be enough of us left to fight them."

"Then let them win, dammit," she sobbed. "It's not worth it."

Fallon suddenly understood the truth of what she was saying. It probably wasn't worth it. The money would never assuage the toll of human misery. But neither would quitting. And maybe living with defeat you hadn't struggled against was worse.

"I can't argue with you, Betty. Or with Jim. I think you both have to do what's best for you." He squeezed her hand. "But if he decides to fight them, I promise you he won't go down in flames alone. And we'll all be there to pick each other up when it's over."

She shook her head. "I don't want him in flames, Jack. That's a male thing, and it doesn't make any sense to me. I want him whole, and I want him happy."

"I won't push him, Betty. I'll support him in whatever he decides."

She seemed momentarily uncertain, then reached up and touched his cheek. "I hope so, Jack. He's in the basement. Go talk to him."

Fallon had started away, when she reached out again and touched his arm. He turned back to face her.

"There's one thing I've got to tell you, Jack. I never liked Trisha. I'm glad you're rid of her."

Fallon laughed. It was the first bit of pleasure he had felt that day. "You know what, Betty? I'm glad, too."

Jim was in the basement recreation room just as Betty had said. He was seated in a leather recliner, his feet propped up, and as Fallon had feared, there was a tumbler of amber liquid on the table beside him. Bourbon, Fallon guessed.

A small color television set was on, and Jim was staring at it. The picture on the screen was flipping—some malfunction with the vertical hold—but he didn't seem to notice. He also failed to notice the intrusion. The man was far away, rummaging among brooding fears.

The recliner sat next to an old plaid sofa, and between it and the stairs sat a full-sized pool table. It was an antique, maybe seventy or eighty years old, with ornately carved legs and woven pouches at each pocket. Fallon picked up a stick, lined the cue ball up with the nine, and shot at the far corner pocket. He missed. The sound of balls clicking brought Malloy's eyes to the table.

He stared at Fallon, blinked several times. "When the hell did you get here?" he asked.

Fallon raised his chin toward the table. "I used to be

pretty good at this," he said. "My father warned me off pool halls when I was a kid, but I was fascinated with them, and all the badasses who hung out there. Then one day—I guess I was fifteen—this black kid took me for all my paper-route money. Didn't even leave me with carfare. I can still hear all the badasses snickering when I headed for the door."

Fallon seemed to recall he'd been asked a question. "I just got here a few minutes ago. I've been upstairs, talking to Betty." He grinned across the table. "She just told me she never liked Trisha, that she thought it was good I was rid of her." He laughed, still enjoying that small tidbit. "She doesn't know what the lawyer is costing me."

"Yeah, I know. She told me the same thing," Malloy said. "She always thought Trisha sat on a bit of a high horse, liked to play the boss's wife a little too much."

Fallon hesitated, thought about it. "I never noticed. Did you?"

Malloy shook his head. "Can't say I did. But maybe it was a woman thing, something we didn't see. She also thought Trisha liked to flaunt the material stuff you guys had, that that's what really mattered to her."

Fallon considered it. He could certainly see it now, wondered how he had missed it for twenty-four years. "That's a good lady you've got upstairs," he said.

Malloy nodded. "I've been finding out just how good the past few weeks." He picked up his drink and took another swallow. "Betty deserves better than she's getting."

"She tells me she has what she wants, Jim."

Malloy eyed Fallon with suspicion. "You here to give me the bad news, Jack?"

Fallon shook his head. "Just to tell you about the crap we're all standing in."

"You talked to Chambers?"

"Chambers *and* Bennett. It's all a big misunderstanding. Redecorating does not equal downsizing.

Chambers was horrified we thought so. And Bennett? Well, Bennett was Bennett."

"So when do they drop the ax?"

"They don't, Jim." He raised his chin toward the glass in Malloy's hand. "Unless you give them an excuse they can't pass up."

"I'll come to work sober, Jack. Don't worry." He put the drink down, as if that confirmed the fact. "You want a drink?" He said it almost defiantly.

"No thanks, Jim."

Malloy seemed momentarily embarrassed, then pushed it away. "So I guess I just sit in the hall and play whipping boy, huh? That the game plan?"

"You could take some sick leave," Fallon said. "Tell your doctor what's going on. He could back you up with a letter if you need it."

"Maybe I'll take a vacation," Malloy said. He let out a disgusted breath. "We won't go anyplace, of course. We're not about to dip into the vault at a time like this."

"No vacations," Fallon said. "Our boy Carter put a freeze on them. Seems the company can't afford to be without us now." The words dripped sarcasm, but had a more horrific effect on Malloy. His face fell, became pale—he looked like a man who'd been told about a death in the family.

"Go with the sick leave, Jim."

Malloy shook his head. "Won't work, Jack. Our family doctor retired last year and moved out west. We haven't found anybody new. There hasn't been any reason to." He picked up his drink again. "You think some new doc is gonna pass out written excuses for some guy who walks in off the street. Hell, it could be some insurance scam for all he knows."

"So just stay out, Jim. Until they push it."

"How long do you think that'll take? A week? What's the use, Jack? They want me there. They want to piss on

me so everybody can see it. Shit, if they force me to quit,
maybe some other guys will decide to walk—before the
same thing happens to them. Besides, my department
has too much going right now. And I'm involved in it up
to my neck. I take off, we'll just be in worse shape when
I get back. Then they'll say I'm incompetent. Or negli-
gent. Either way I'm screwed."

He seemed to think about it, his face becoming even
more haggard. Fallon had never seen him look beaten
before. "So what happened at M.I.T.?" he asked. "I was
so screwed up this morning I didn't even ask."

"Nothing definite yet. Annie's contact gave it a preliminary look, but we're waiting for the results of another
test."

"So Robaire sucked it up and gave you sample cable.
At least that's a plus."

Fallon nodded. "Yeah, he did. But he's scared. He
knows his head's on the block, too." He raised his eyebrows, his own uncertainty clear. "Hell, he might even
call Bennett and turn me in."

Malloy snorted. "Then your desk will be out in the
hall. We can sit there together."

"We'll all be there soon enough, Jim."

Malloy shook his head. "You know what I don't
understand, Jack? The cruelty. But, hell, I don't understand any of it, even without the cruelty." He forced the
recliner's footrest down and sat forward. "I mean, what
do they do? They sit there and crunch their numbers,
and they don't like what they see. Okay, that happens all
the time, and companies find ways to resolve those
things. They always have. Hell, layoffs are a way of life in
this country. They've always been part of it, and they
always will be. They stink, sure, and they hurt, but at
least everybody knows that someday they'll get their jobs
back. And it's based on seniority—there's always some
tacit respect for all the years people have put in." He ran
a hand over his mouth, then took another swallow of his

drink. "But not anymore. What the hell is the matter with these people, Jack? They don't think they're ever gonna turn fifty? They don't think this game they've invented will ever apply to them?"

"It never will, Jim. Not the guys who really make those decisions." He laughed. It was a bitter, cold sound. "Hell, companies lose millions, and their boards hand bonuses to the CEO and all his buddies at the top. Their pensions, when they do decide to pack it in, are so heavy they drag everybody down. And then some of them are even kept on as consultants, so they can draw a salary on top of it all."

Malloy snorted again. "So we're screwed 'cause we never got that high."

"Yeah, that's about it. We should have wielded the blade a little better; gotten ourselves up there, and looked down on everybody else."

"That's just it, Jack. They don't *see* anybody else. We're not even there. We're just numbers on some computer printout. They even take away our humanity. And when they buy us out, they don't even regret doing it. They don't even understand that it's wrong. Laid-off people have become a corporate asset. They just want us to leave quietly and not make a fuss, not hand them any grief."

Fallon was overwhelmed by the man's despair, by the blatant surrender in his voice that came through the anger. He wanted to respond, to say something that wasn't weak and ineffectual.

He tried. "Maybe this time they won't get what they want, Jim. Maybe for once we'll stick together and make them see us." He looked into Malloy's eyes, listened to his own words. They were as weak as he had feared, and Jim Malloy knew it.

21

A WEEK WENT BY WITH MALLOY SEATED IN THE HALL, AN undeclared pariah in a well-tailored suit, someone best encountered with averted eyes. It was worse than Fallon had feared, and he suggested Malloy move in with one of his salesmen, or ask two junior men to temporarily double up and use the remaining smaller office himself.

Malloy had refused, had insisted he wouldn't share the grief with anyone else, that Bennett would simply find some new torment if he did. Instead, he sat there each morning; doing what work he could in the well-traveled hall. He seldom returned from lunch.

At the beginning of the second week, workmen still failed to materialize. Malloy's office remained locked and now became the subject of whispered office humor. Fallon overheard two young salesmen sharing one such joke. He went ballistic, ordered both men out of the office, told each not to return until either his attitude changed or he had found employment elsewhere and was there to clear his desk. Both men reappeared later that day, acts of mealy-mouthed contrition spewing from their lips. "You're apologizing to the wrong person," Fallon snapped.

And the joke? It was stupid and cruel, not even modestly funny. "How many workers does it take to redecorate an office? Answer: None. It only takes one executive to see the handwriting on the wall." Fallon hoped the *humor* was not finding its way back to Malloy.

It was late Wednesday afternoon when Malloy entered Fallon's office. He was pale and drawn; his hands trembled. It was clear he had enjoyed a long, liquid lunch. He handed Fallon a letter, explaining he had just gotten it via E-mail.

The letter was from Carter Bennett—terse and cutting and morally indignant. Reports of excessive drinking had come to his attention and would be reported to Malloy's immediate superior for appropriate action. However, these allegations also created a potential liability for the company, which required prompt resolution. Malloy was therefore directed to turn in his company-owned vehicle until the matter was "adjudicated."

"So what do I do, Jack? Just turn my keys in to you? You're the judge, right?" Malloy's voice trembled like his hands, a mixture of fear and rage—directed, in part, at Fallon himself. But it was primarily fear, Fallon thought. Malloy's self-esteem had cracked and was ready to crumble.

"You don't do a damned thing," Fallon said. "You go home with your car, and you let me handle it. Nothing's crossed my desk, and I'm going to try to kill this crap before anything does."

The fissure deepened; one could see it in the man's eyes. "What's the use, Jack? What the hell is next? I won't survive long enough to take any goddamned buyout."

Fallon felt deluged by the man's fears. He raised his hands. "Jim, calm down. None of that's going to happen." He tried to put conviction in his voice, knew he had failed.

Fallon came around his desk and took a chair next to

Malloy's. "Jim, go home. *With* your car. And let me deal with it. Take tomorrow off. Just give me a couple of days."

Malloy turned his head away. His eyes were filling with tears, and he couldn't bear that added humiliation. He shook his head. "I can't let this happen to my family, Jack. I just can't."

"It's not going to happen, Jim. It's not."

Malloy shook his head again, but said nothing.

"Jack, what could I do? I have an obligation to this company. We *all* do." Bennett sat behind his desk, forced regret in his voice.

"You could have come to me, Carter. Let *me* deal with this ridiculous allegation."

Bennett extended his hands, palms up, then allowed them to fall back to his desk. "Jack, I think my letter makes it clear I intended to do exactly that. These allegations, as you call them, initially came from Les Gavin, who should be in a position to know."

Fallon stared at him. "Then why the hell didn't Gavin say anything to me?"

"I told him to, and I'm sure he will. And I don't think the allegation is ridiculous. I did some other checking myself. It's not exactly a secret. I even walked by the man's desk. Hell, Jack, I could smell the liquor from three feet." He offered up another helpless gesture. "What do we do? Wait until someone's hurt, and the company is faced with a major liability?"

"I'll deal with it, Carter," Fallon snapped. And with that little shit Gavin, he added to himself.

"That's great, Jack. I was certain you would. And I regret this came to you in such a roundabout way. I'll speak to Les about that. I'm sure he was just hoping it would all go away." He paused a beat. "But I have to be firm about the company car," he added. "I don't really have a choice about that."

Fallon stared him down. "It's my division, Carter," he said. "I'll deal with it."

Carter smiled. "Jack, I couldn't ask for anything more," he said.

"Jack, I just made a comment about Jim in passing. It was a joke, an off-the-cuff remark. I just suggested they get cracking on his office before Beefeater stock went through the roof." Gavin cringed with false regret. "Jesus, I never expected it to blow up like this." Gavin shook his head. He was contrite, horrified, and Fallon wanted to strangle him where he sat.

"Frankly, when I saw Carter was all juiced up about it, I decided to just ignore it. I still thought it would all blow over if and when it got to you. I never expected Carter to take any independent action. Jesus, Jack, I'm just beside myself about this."

Fallon stared across his desk, pinning Gavin where he sat. "So it was all a little joke?"

"That's right, Jack. I mean . . ."

Fallon cut him off. "You have no independent evidence that suggests Jim Malloy is a drunk who shouldn't be trusted with a company car. Right?"

Gavin stuttered over his next words. "Well, Jack . . . well . . . I mean . . ."

Fallon lashed out at him. "Spit it out, Lester. Do you or don't you have any solid, independent knowledge that Jim Malloy is a drunk? Because if you do, I expect you to give it to me, and be ready to back it up."

More stuttering. "Well . . . no, Jack. I mean . . . I mean I haven't been following him around. I've . . . I've *seen* him . . . when I thought he had maybe a couple too many drinks. . . . But . . ."

"I've seen *you* that way, Les. Are *you* a drunk?"

"Jesus, Jack . . ."

"All right. Enough. I want a memo from you, Lester. I want you to go out to Carol, and dictate it right now.

You don't leave her office until you do. Understood? And in it, I want you to state exactly what you just told me—that your comment about Jim was not intended in a serious vein, and that you have no independent knowledge about any real or imagined drinking problem." Fallon continued to pin him with his eyes. "If you do not, Lester, I will regard that as blatant insubordination. If you dictate anything else, I'll view this conversation we just had as a flagrant attempt to withhold the truth from me."

"But . . . but . . . Jack . . ."

"And if you change your story, and decide that Jim *does* have a drinking problem, I'll expect you to support that belief with facts. Otherwise, I'll be forced to consider it an attempt to slander a fellow executive of this company for your own personal gain. And you will then find yourself in one helluva pissing contest with me, my young friend. And win or lose that war, it will cost you dearly. I doubt that management will exactly clutch you to their bosom. They don't like these ugly little battles, Lester. And when Jim Malloy drags you, *and* the company, into court for slander, they're going to like it even less. And *I* will not like it when I'm forced to say that your observations were a crock of self-serving shit. Do we understand each other, Lester?"

"I'm worried about Jim," Fallon said. The dinosaurs were gathered just outside the locker rooms, ready to start their nightly session in the gym. Fallon had taken them aside to fill them in about the latest move against Malloy. The news had hit each of them hard.

"You think the memo you forced out of Gavin will stop them?" Wally asked.

"That, and the veiled threat of a lawsuit that I'm sure Lester passed along." Fallon looked at each man. "But if Jim keeps hitting the sauce, it won't matter. Bennett will just take a step back and start building a case against him. And it won't be too damned hard to do."

"Have you heard back from Bennett?" Wally asked.

"No," Fallon said. "But I'm sure I will."

"Have you heard anything back from M.I.T.?" It was Joe Hartman. "Or from anyplace that gives us a handle on what the hell is going on?"

"Not yet." Fallon glanced at Annie.

"Paulie said his boss—the *big* genius—hasn't finished his test yet. But he promised me we'll have something definitive in the next day or two."

Fallon looked at the others. "We'll just have to wait. But it won't be long."

"So what the hell *do* you want us to do, Jack?" It was Ben Constantini. He seemed frightened and nervous. But he also looked angry.

"For now, try and help Jim. Just reach out to him. Call him at home tomorrow. I told him to take the day off to let everything settle down. Let him know what happened and that you're all behind him. I'm afraid he's ready to pack it in and give Bennett what he wants."

"Maybe he should." It was Annie Schwartz. "I mean, how much should anyone have to take, Jack? What good will it do if he gets the damned buyout and ends up a broken-down juicer who sits in his house all day with a glass of booze in his hand."

Joe Hartman chimed in, "Nobody should have to take this shit. Nobody."

Fallon looked at Hartman, then at Annie. What she had said had hit hard. The words were almost identical to Betty Malloy's. He shook his head. "There's too much at stake to give in," he said. "For Jim; for all of us. But right now, especially for Jim."

"Why don't you tell him that, Jack?" It was George Valasquez.

The words had been snide and cutting, and Fallon turned to face him. "Because I don't think he'd believe me, George."

"Gee, that's a big surprise." He sneered. "By the way, Jack, have you seen these new coffee mugs they've started to hand out? 'I'm a High Octane Flyer' written right there on the side. I was wondering if you've gotten yours yet."

Samantha had just come out of the women's locker room as Valasquez spoke. She was dressed in a black leotard, and each man had watched her as she started past the group. Then she stopped abruptly, rounding on them. Her eyes blazed. "Excuse me for interrupting." She stared at George. "I couldn't help overhearing what you just said."

Valasquez seemed stunned. Fallon raised a hand to take her arm, to stop her. But she pushed it aside.

"So what are you saying? Jack Fallon's a hatchet man? Someone who shouldn't be trusted? Or is he just pretending to be one? For your sakes." She continued to glare at George. They were about the same size, but George suddenly seemed smaller. "Which is it?" she demanded. "And whichever it is, what do you think happens to him when everything's finished—when this buyout has come and gone?" She continued to stare George down. "Does he get a raise? A medal, maybe? Or do they toss him out on the street with nothing?" She watched Valasquez twist. "Maybe you should ask yourself who's taking the biggest risk here. And while you're at it, while you're being so concerned, maybe you should also stop being so damned stupid."

Fallon took her arm now and gently eased her away. He looked back over his shoulder, his face clearly shocked. "Do what I said, okay?" he called back.

When they reached the other side of the gym, he leaned in close. "Jesus, don't expose yourself like that. If Bennett heard about it . . ."

"I don't give a damn," she snapped, cutting him off. "What he's doing to that man, Malloy, makes me sick. What he's doing to you makes me sick. And when I hear someone suggest *you're* not doing enough—especially one of the people you're risking everything to help, it just . . . it just . . ."

Fallon started to laugh softly. "Boy, remind me never to make you mad," he said. "I thought you were going to punch little Georgie out. The man just ran into the locker room to change his shorts."

Samantha struggled for a straight face, smiled, and then began to laugh herself. She kept her back turned so the men across the room wouldn't notice. "And don't you ever forget it, Fallon," she said.

22

BENNETT TURNED INTO EAST SEVENTY-SECOND STREET at Madison Avenue. He had just put Eunice in a cab. They had dined at Le Provençal, and for once her spirits had been high. But why shouldn't they be? The company's stock had taken a substantial jump that day, and he was certain it was due to word reaching the Street that a major downsizing plan was about to be implemented.

Bennett smiled as he walked briskly toward his apartment. It was six blocks away, but it was a beautiful, mild evening, and his own spirits were high. It was due to something Eunice had said. It had surprised him, and thinking about it, even now, made his smile widen. He had told her about Fallon's tirade against Les Gavin, and his ridiculous attempt to save another decrepit fool. Gavin had come to him in panic, and both Fallon's attempt and Gavin's fear had amused him. He'd let Malloy keep his company car—for now. It had never been a serious point of contention—simply added pressure. He'd let Fallon think he'd won a round. Made a point of bowing to his wisdom. He told Eunice he might even publicly chastise Gavin. Just for a bit of added fun. Then, in a few days, he'd hit Malloy again, and the man would fold. It would be an indelible lesson that Fallon wouldn't quickly forget.

Then Eunice had said the thing that had so surprised him. She had said that his description of Fallon made her think of his brother, Edwin—his father's favorite. *Like your brother, this Mr. Fallon seems to possess a great deal of front, with nothing of substance behind it,* she had said.

He had never considered that comparison, but now he thought it apt. Like his brother, Fallon was a fool, and he wondered how the man had gotten as far as he had. He knew how Edwin had. But Jack Fallon didn't have the luxury of a wealthy and doting father.

God knows. How do *any* of them get that far? By default, I expect. Bennett considered the thought. Watching Fallon's weak little struggle against the inevitable was rather sad, actually. A slow grin crossed his face. But not *that* sad. You've never been too proud to accept an easy victory.

But then, it *was* a matter of genetics. A certain class was expected to lead. They were bred for it. It was not discriminatory, or even exclusionary, simply a fact of life. He briefly wondered about the others—the Fallon-like creatures his plan would soon displace—and how many of them would find new employment. Most, he supposed. Over time. And with what was in the offing, the people who were forced out would actually be better off. Another smile crossed his lips. If they knew what was really going to happen, they'd probably thank you.

He fought back laughter. Perhaps I should tell them, he thought. Perhaps they'd even throw me a small dinner. But perhaps not, he thought. They might doubt my egalitarianism.

He stopped at Third Avenue. There was a liquor store on the corner, and it brought a pleasant thought to mind. He could buy a bottle of champagne and stop by

Samantha's apartment. It was only four blocks north of where he stood.

His smile widened as he turned in to the store. Why not give yourself a little reward? And give Samantha one, too. When you were seeing each other she always liked your little surprises. And the job at hand has created a bit of a strain. This might be a good way to ease it.

Bennett rode the elevator up. His lips held a small smile. He had just tipped the doorman five dollars, told him he wanted to surprise Ms. Moore, that he preferred not to be announced. The man knew him from past visits, noted the bottle of champagne crooked in his arm, and happily pocketed the money.

Bennett rang Samantha's bell, then stepped aside, out of range of the spy hole. He wanted to get the full impact of her surprise. The door opened and he stepped quickly into the opening, the bottle of champagne held out before him.

"A peace offering," he said. "To make up for all the pressure I've put you under these past weeks."

The reaction was not what he had expected. Samantha seemed momentarily flustered. She hesitated, shook her head slightly. It was almost as though she were embarrassed. He flashed his best smile. "We'll just have one quick drink," he said. "The renewal of a meaningful friendship."

He started past her, but she stepped in front of him. Behind her a short entry hall led to the living room. It was too narrow for him to move past. He stared at her, unable to keep his irritation hidden.

"I don't understand your attitude," he said. "There was a time, not too long ago, when my little surprises pleased you."

"I'm tired, Carter. And I'm occupied."

The remark puzzled him, but he brushed it aside. The smile returned. "You can ignore your work for just an hour," he teased. He started past her again, but she put a hand up, pressing it against his chest.

"Carter! Please!"

He was stunned. Then, behind her, a shadow filled the narrow hall. At first he couldn't make the person out, and he felt a momentary rush of embarrassment. Then the figure became clear: Jack Fallon standing there in a T-shirt and pair of shorts.

Bennett stared at him. Slowly the clothing registered. His eyes snapped back to Samantha. "What *is* this?" he demanded. Thoughts of betrayal flooded in: Fallon and Samantha; all the well-guarded secrets she held. Then weeks of subtle rejection returned—the way she had begged off each time he had suggested a drink, or dinner. She had been with *him*. It was all too apparent now. And there was no telling what she had told him. He wasn't sure which infuriated him more—the threat of disclosure or her obvious preference for this aging fool.

"Carter, I think you're completely out of line," Samantha said. She had kept her voice soft, and he considered her tone blatantly condescending. His anger flashed.

"You do, do you?" He glared at her. "And what am I supposed to think about *this?*" He jerked his head toward Fallon. "When I come here and find *my* corporate counsel in *this* situation."

Bennett's peripheral vision caught Fallon coming toward him. Samantha seemed to sense it as well, and she moved slightly, keeping herself between them.

"Carter, I think you should go. Now." Her voice was commanding, and that, too, shocked him. He had always enjoyed a hint of subservience from this woman, had always told himself that it came not only from his superior position in the company but from himself as well.

"Don't you dare speak to me like that," he snapped. "I

expect some answers, and I expect them now." His eyes went past her and riveted on Fallon, only a few feet away. "You're both on very dangerous ground."

Fallon grinned at him. It sent Bennett's rage up another notch.

"The lady asked you to leave, Carter," Fallon said. "Be a good boy and do it now."

Bennett spun to face him again. "Don't you *ever* tell me what to do, Fallon. You're pathetic, an impotent laughingstock to everyone around you."

Fallon stepped around Samantha so quickly Bennett had no time to react. When he did the bottle of champagne hampered him, and when he finally dropped it, it was too late. Fallon had spun him around, grabbed him by the seat of the pants and the collar of his shirt and yanked upward. The move drove Bennett's trousers into his crotch, and forced him onto his toes. He felt himself propelled forward as Fallon threw him into the hall.

He hit the far wall and immediately heard a mild rebuke from Samantha: "Jack. Please don't." She was concerned—afraid Fallon might hurt him. *Him! Hurt him!* He spun around and found Fallon filling the doorway. In the T-shirt and shorts he looked fitter than Bennett would have suspected. His bravado surged past doubt. He wasn't sure exactly what he'd do if Fallon came after him again. At that moment he didn't care. He jabbed a finger at the man's face, intending it for Samantha as well.

"You're both finished," he snapped. "Neither one of you will survive this. I promise you."

Fallon stared at him. He seemed infuriatingly amused. Bennett felt as though he might explode.

"Kiss my ass, Carter." Fallon spoke the words with contempt.

Bennett stormed off toward the elevator. Fallon closed the door and picked up the abandoned bottle of champagne, held it up and inspected the label. He grinned at Samantha. "Not a terrific vintage," he said. "But it *is* chilled. Let's have a drink."

Samantha stared at him. "You're feeling quite proud of yourself, aren't you?"

Fallon's grin widened. "Actually, I haven't felt this good in years," he said.

23

SAMANTHA ENTERED BENNETT'S OFFICE AT EIGHT-thirty. She knew he always arrived early, well before his assistant—to set the tone, as he liked to say. She left the door to his office open and walked straight to his desk. Bennett stared up at her; a smirk seemed to be hiding behind a coldly indifferent countenance. He thinks you're here to plead for your job, she thought.

"I'd like to discuss last night," she began. "Specifically, your behavior." There was an edge to her voice that seemed to re-ignite his anger. She could see him struggle to keep it in check.

Bennett turned back to the papers spread across his desk. "There's nothing to discuss," he said. "You'll be gone by the end of business today. And your friend Fallon won't be far behind."

"You told me *that* last night, Carter. I heard you, Jack Fallon heard you, and I'm certain several of my neighbors heard you. There's an elderly woman across the hall who hears everything." Samantha placed her hands on his desk and leaned forward. "So I doubt I'll have any difficulty proving the suit I intend to file against this company on Monday."

Bennett sneered at her. "What suit? You don't have a suit."

Samantha offered up a small, cold smile. "The suit will charge sexual harassment, and it will name you as the offending party."

Bennett laughed in her face. "Good luck," he said. "You're being terminated for gross insubordination and ethical misconduct—all of it involving your disclosure of privileged information. I don't think the company will have much trouble proving it. I don't think the bar association will either."

Samantha kept her smile in place. "That should be an intriguing defense, Carter. Let's see. Your attorneys will argue that I was dismissed because I told one of this company's executives that Waters Cable intends to violate federal law by initiating a plan that eliminates all its older employees." She raised her eyebrows. "Well, confession is good for the soul, but no, I don't think so, Carter. It certainly wouldn't be my advice. In fact, I'd tell them to settle, and settle quickly. And if the plaintiff wouldn't agree—which, of course, she won't—I'd advise them to drop any downsizing plan they had, so they could deny its existence in court, and then to deal with the charges directly." Samantha leaned closer and hit him with the smile again. "And those charges, Carter, will consist of you showing up at my apartment, champagne in hand. Of you bribing my doorman, so you could arrive unannounced. Of you then seeking sexual favors similar to those you had enjoyed in the past. And finally, of you finding another man there, and feeling rebuffed, making loud, verbal threats against my employment, which you subsequently carried out. Yes, I think the company's defense will be interesting. Especially after I bring up your downsizing proposal as a way of showing the previous faith and confidence you had in my abilities. And when I also point out that you fired the man you found in my apartment, well, I don't think the outcome will be much in doubt."

Bennett's hands began to tremble with rage, and he clenched his fists to hide it. She was right. The company would respond exactly as she predicted. He could see his downsizing plan sailing out the window. He could see Charlie Waters's plans sailing along beside it. A lawsuit— especially this type of suit—would have the media salivating, and the public glare would be too bright to allow anything else to take place. Bennett clenched his jaw. *And you haven't even begun to assess its effect on your own career.*

Bennett drew a breath and eased back in his chair. "Well, Ms. Moore, you don't paint a very pretty picture. It would seem I may have miscalculated." He gave her another cold, sterile smile. "And you know how I hate it when that happens." He pushed himself forward, and again began to study the papers on his desk. "So please forget any personal disagreements we may have had. They, of course, have no effect on your position within the company." He rearranged some papers, tightened his hands into fists again. "And, also, please be advised that no further work will be required of you regarding the proposed downsizing of this company. I want to be sure the company is in full compliance with federal law, and I'm afraid your suggestions failed to provide that assurance." He glanced up with a horrible attempt at a smile. "I'll send you a memo to that effect later today. Is there anything else?"

Samantha waved her hand in a gesture of dismissal. "No, Carter, that will do nicely."

Bennett watched her leave. He had unclenched his fists, and his hands had begun to tremble again. As the outer door to his office closed, he rose from his chair, grabbed a paperweight from his desk, and hurled it across the room. It hit the opposite wall and fell to the floor, leaving a deep gouge just below a photograph he had hung that morning. The photo showed Bennett, attired in camouflage, his paintball gun held in the air, as he accepted his trophy as the New England Regional Paintball Champion.

Bennett fell back into his chair. His breath was coming in gasps. There was a light rapping on his door and his head snapped toward the sound.

There was another light knock, then the door swung open and a man stepped tentatively into the office.

"Mr. Bennett?"

"Who are you?"

The man swallowed, seemed to summon up his courage. "I'm Victor Nagy, Mr. Bennett. I'm from the testing lab at the Plattsburgh plant." Nagy's eyes drifted to the gouge in the wall, then the paperweight on the floor. He turned nervously back to Bennett. "I'm sorry if I came at a bad time, sir. But I've been trying to reach you for over a week. It's truly important, Mr. Bennett. So important I decided to take the day off and try to see you personally."

Bennett glared at him. He spoke through gritted teeth. "My assistant told you I'd call when I could."

Nagy seemed to freeze in place, then again draw from some hidden reserve—perhaps courage, perhaps unabashed ambition. "Mr. Bennett, it's about Mr. Robaire and Mr. Fallon, and some unauthorized tests they're conducting."

Bennett's eyes widened. "Tell me!" he hissed.

Nagy fumbled a hand into his coat pocket and withdrew a micro recorder. "Mr. Bennett, if you'll only listen to this tape, it will explain everything."

Wally stared across his desk, a cup of coffee growing cold before him. "So what the hell does it mean?" he asked.

Fallon was seated in Wally's office. He had just given

him a rundown on the earlier tests conducted by Paul Palango, and the confirming results he had just received from Palango's boss.

"Damned if I know. But two separate scientists at M.I.T. are certain. And I keep telling myself that Charlie is too good an engineer for this kind of screwup. There's no question Sprint received cable intended for the gyroscope research project. And there's no question the production tolerances set by Waters were off. The error was infinitesimal, but enough to cause static-electrical breakdowns in the gyroscope system we're developing. Christ, they weren't even adequate for less demanding communications. And they sure as hell never would have sustained laser impulses over the distances set in the government's gyroscope specs."

"So I guess we go to him and tell him what we found," Wally said.

"How do we do that without putting everybody's head on the block?" Fallon asked. "Charlie's directive was clear. No unauthorized tests. Period. If I'm right about this, I think he'll bounce anybody who was even on the periphery of having those tests run."

"But, for chrissake, we're bailing the company out of a bind. If it hadn't been for this foul-up—if Sprint hadn't got the wrong cable—we never would have known." Fallon just stared at him, and the lightbulb went off over Wally's head. "Jesus, Jack, you think it was intentional?"

Fallon shrugged. "I think you have to consider the possibility. What if management is angling for some cost overruns. You know how the government operates. Technical problems come up, and the government bears the freight to resolve them. Look, the Defense Department wants us to have this contract. The last thing they want is to yank it. It's ours, and the procurement guys want it to stay that way. Hell, the only viable competition is foreign, and they want to avoid that route.

They don't want critical parts for their missile systems dependent on foreign suppliers. They learned that lesson when they handed the Japanese a similar advantage on computer parts used in F-Sixteen fighters. Now, if the Japanese withhold those parts, our planes don't fly. And nobody's geared up to take their place. The boys in the Pentagon don't want to find themselves in the same position with the Germans, or Koreans, or whoever."

Wally stared at him. "Hey, my friend, I understand all that, but you're talking fraud here."

"Look at the record, Wally. Defense contractors have made defrauding the U.S. government an art form."

"But we've never pulled that shit."

"We've never had the opportunity. We've never been *in* that money pit before. We've always been subcontractors. We provided product to the companies who manufactured the end-user item—the aircraft, or tank, or missile, or whatever. This time we're developing a new system based on our product alone."

Wally considered what he'd been told. "If this is true, Jack, then we've got a hammer. And we can use it to whack Charlie Waters right between the eyes."

"*If* we can prove it," Fallon said. "Hell, my suspicions may be completely off the wall, and I'm not even sure I'll be around long enough to get to the bottom of it, one way or the other." He steepled his fingers and stared through them. The potential effects of last night's debacle slowly settled in. "I had a little set-to with Bennett last night." He explained the confrontation at Samantha's apartment, then added, "So I just might find myself on the street by the end of this week."

"No, you won't."

Both men turned to the sound of Samantha's voice. She closed the door to Wally's office, then took a chair next to Fallon. "Your assistant told me where to find you. I just left Carter's office."

She quickly reviewed her meeting with Bennett.

"Jesus," Wally said. "Oh, to be a fly on the wall, a worm in the woodwork at that little séance."

Fallon laughed. "So we won't be fired until *after* the buyout. Of course, if I insist on taking it, he won't have to fire me at all." He held Samantha's eyes. "You, on the other hand, won't be on his list. But you'll follow us out the door in short order."

"I may insist on being part of it," Samantha said. "If the company refuses, it might make another interesting lawsuit."

Wally Green let out a low, maniacal cackle. "Leapin' lizards," he intoned. "That'll make you not only the youngest but definitely the best-looking dinosaur in the club."

"And certainly the meanest," Fallon added. He reached out and took her hand. "When this is over, I'm going to fire Arthur C. Grisham and hire you."

Wally leaned across his desk, part in camaraderie, part to get a better look at Samantha's crossed legs. "Now that she's a full-fledged dinosaur, tell her about the M.I.T. results."

Fallon watched her eyes widen as he explained.

"Jack, that's wonderful—providing we can prove it."

"Yeah, that's definitely the rub. And I'm not quite sure how we do that."

Samantha's face broke into a smile. "Maybe I can help." She told them about her computer wizard, Stanley Kijewski, and what she had asked him to do.

Fallon grinned at her. "Christ, you're just full of delightful little surprises today," he said.

Samantha brushed the compliment aside. "The important thing is, if he *knows* what he's looking for it makes it easier. He might overlook something technical about the product line, thinking it has nothing to do with the buyout. But if we tell him what we suspect . . ."

"You'd better fill him in right away," Fallon said.

"I'll call him now," Samantha said. "Better still, I'll go

and see him. I wouldn't put it past Carter to have my phone tapped." She smiled at the idea. "Besides, I don't have much work to do. Not after being relieved of duty as Carter's favorite hatchet person."

A knock on Wally's door ended the banter. Carol entered quickly, her face streaked with tears.

Fallon got to his feet and went to her. His first thought was that one of the other assistants she had recruited to help them had just gotten the ax. Then the look on her face really hit, and he had a sudden foreboding that something far worse had happened. "Carol, what's wrong?" He took hold of her arms. "Calm down. Tell me, please."

She began to sob. "Oh . . . Jack . . . It's Jim . . . Jim Malloy . . . I . . . I . . . just . . . got . . . a call. He's . . . he's dead, Jack."

24

"I'M NOT SUGGESTING WE FIRE HIM. I'M SUGGESTING WE demote him and reassign him as a district manager at one of our Midwest or West Coast offices."

Bennett studied Waters's face for some hint of agreement. When he had come to Waters with news of the M.I.T. tests, the reaction had been shock and anger, with something close to fear just below the surface. Now his suggestion seemed to have added a hint of contempt.

He tried to push his argument. Samantha's threat of a lawsuit still hung heavily in his mind. But if Fallon was demoted by Waters, and if the reason was unrelated to her, then that threat would evaporate. "I think the man will resign if that happens," he added. "I don't think he'd have any other viable choice. Especially if the directive came from you, rather than me," he said.

Waters placed both hands on his face and rubbed once. When he looked at Bennett again there was a glare in his eyes.

"Sometimes I wonder if you ever really listen to me, Carter." His jaw tightened; then he continued. "I explained it once before. Jack Fallon has friends on the board. Not many, but some. And those people not only know him, they respect him. If he raises questions about product reliability they'll listen, and our plans will be delayed. Not stopped. But delayed. And I don't want that."

Bennett gritted his teeth. He understood the man's concern—his real concern—and it had nothing to do with their plan to downsize the company.

"Then what do you suggest?" he asked.

"I suggest you let me handle it. *I'll* take care of Jack Fallon." He drummed his fingers on the desk. "You say this test wire was handed over more than a week ago, correct?"

Bennett twisted in his chair. "That's right."

"Then I think we can assume that either the tests have not yet been run or Fallon hasn't gotten any results. Otherwise he would have acted. That means we have some time. Not much, but some."

Bennett noted that Waters had ignored one other possibility—that the tests had come back negative. But then he knew that wasn't possible.

Waters stood behind his desk. It was a signal of dismissal, and Bennett rose as well.

"I'm only suggesting what I think best for the company," Bennett added.

Waters leaned forward, his fists now resting on his desk. "But it's not, Carter. That's the goddamned point."

When Bennett had left, Waters fell back into his chair. He felt a slight tremor in his hands. Fallon has gone too far. He's left you with no other choice.

He reached out for his private phone, one that was not connected to the company telephone system. He glanced at his watch. It was ten o'clock; four in the afternoon in Germany. He punched out the overseas codes and the number.

"I have a problem," he said, when his party came on the line. "A serious one." He quickly explained what had happened, then added, "You once told me you had someone here in the States who could deal with this sort of thing."

He listened again, his face suddenly turning bright red. "No, I don't want the man killed, for chrissake. I'm not a murderer. I want him out of action for three or four months. That's all the time I need."

He listened again, then said, "Please get your man here quickly. I can't afford any delays. I'll explain what's needed when he gets here."

Waters replaced the phone. His head dropped back against his chair; he closed his eyes. He could feel the tremor in his hands again, even stronger now.

I'm sorry, Jack, he thought, but you haven't left me any other option.

The automobile accident had occurred at one in the morning. Jim Malloy's company car had been traveling on the interstate just south of Baltimore. It had veered off the road and struck a bridge abutment. He was alone, and he was driving fast—at least eighty miles an hour, the police had said.

Fallon stared at the E-mail message on his desk. Carol had found it an hour ago. It had been sent from Jim's home, from his personal computer, and it had been written at seven the previous night, six hours before he had died.

Carol entered his office, carrying coffee in Fallon's personal mug. She never got him coffee. It was a firmly held conviction—she was a colleague, not a servant. Fallon had never found any reason to disagree.

"Thanks," he said, as he accepted the offering. "Were you able to reach Betty Malloy?"

"Yes. She's very grateful." Carol's eyes were still red, and her voice was thick and hoarse from crying. Fallon had sent Ben Constantini to Baltimore to do whatever was needed to get Jim's body released, then find a local funeral director who could handle the transportation back to New York.

"She asked if you could meet her at the funeral home

at two. It's called O'Brien's, and it's not far from her home. I have the address."

"You told her I would?"

Carol nodded. "Wally said he and Annie Schwartz would go with you."

Samantha entered the office as they were speaking and took one of the visitor's chairs. She had returned to her office when they had learned about Malloy's death. She had wanted to contact the authorities to find out what legal problems Ben Constantini might encounter. "I'd like to go with you, too," she said now. "It might help to have two women there, and I can answer any legal questions she might have."

Fallon turned back to Carol. "Tell Wally we'll all leave around noon, and that we'll get some lunch on the way."

Carol turned to go, but Fallon's voice stopped her. "I want you to delete that E-mail message from our computer," he said. "And make sure there are no copies lying around." Carol nodded. She looked as though she might begin to cry again. Fallon had already asked her not to speak about the message. The look on her face told him he didn't have to repeat the warning.

Samantha watched Carol leave. When the door had closed behind her, she turned to Fallon. "E-mail message?" she asked.

Fallon handed her a printed copy.

The message was terse, almost cold, but Samantha could feel the emotion hidden in the words.

Jack,
Please make sure Betty gets my pension, and the insurance she's entitled to. Don't let them take that away from her.
Jim

"He sent the message last night," Fallon said. "Six hours before the accident." He looked away. "He was convinced they'd never stop pressing him to quit, and that he'd never get a chance at the buyout. He was certain his family would be financially devastated if that happened."

"But it wouldn't have," Samantha said. "He could have fought it and won."

"I know. I told him that." Fallon turned back to face her. "Jim was covered under our executive insurance plan. It's a one-hundred-thousand-dollar life insurance policy, with double indemnity for accidental death. Triple indemnity if the employee dies while traveling on company business." He held out his hand, took the E-mail message back. "Jim told Wally's assistant that he needed to be in Washington this morning to see a customer. He even had her call and make an appointment, and hotel reservations. He told Betty the same thing when he left last night."

Samantha closed her eyes. "Oh, God."

"Do you know anything about the policy?"

Samantha nodded. "I've reviewed all our different coverages." The policy Fallon referred to had a standard suicide clause—no payment if the insured took his or her own life within two years of inception. That two-year period had passed. But proof of suicide would nullify any accidental death benefits throughout the life of the policy.

"You're not going to tell anyone about that message, are you?"

Fallon shook his head. "I hope you won't either," he said.

Samantha let out a breath. Being a lawyer, and being around Jack Fallon, was an ethical nightmare. But it also made her feel very good about herself.

"My computer friend told me that even deleted material can often be retrieved from a computer's hard drive. He said it just sits there for a couple of months, and if you know how, you can find it and bring it back. I'll ask him to make sure this message is really gone."

* * *

They returned to Betty Malloy's home at four o'clock. The visit to the funeral home had been indescribably grim. Late that morning, Samantha had arranged to have Jim's body released by the coroner. The state police had found nothing to contradict an accident. The death had all the earmarks of vehicular suicide, but there had been no note, no indication of intent. Perhaps most important to Betty, there was no evidence Jim had been drinking. Perhaps most disturbing, the funeral director that Ben Constantini had found in Baltimore had recommended the casket not be opened. Betty had shown both fortitude and strength. There would be no visiting hours, she had said. Only a time before the church service when she and her children would be alone with their husband and father.

"I'll make some coffee," Betty said. She went into the kitchen, Annie Schwartz and the two Malloy children trailing behind—a boy, the law school student Jim had spoken about, and a girl, still in high school. Like their mother, the children were still in deep shock and denial. Annie had taken them on as her own special project. She had helped them select the clothing they would wear to the funeral. She had done it gently, had even gotten one small smile from the girl. Fallon had been surprised by her sudden burst of motherly instinct. She had never let him, or anyone at the company, see it before.

When Betty returned with the coffee, Annie and the children weren't with her. "Annie took the kids to my sister-in-law's house. She lives on the next street," she explained. "Jim's whole family has lived in this neighborhood their entire lives. I used to think it was crazy, that they were all in some sort of rut. But, at times like this . . ." Her words trailed off. She had been babbling, and seemed to recognize it. Now she stared at Fallon, almost as though Samantha and Wally weren't there.

"I think he killed himself, Jack. I think he did it so we'd be financially secure, because he thought he couldn't give that to us anymore."

Fallon felt his stomach sink. Betty was Catholic, and he knew from his own similar upbringing that suicide carried a terrible burden for her. "It was an accident, Betty. He had an appointment in Washington. He had Wally's assistant set it up yesterday." He let his eyes go to Samantha. "Samantha talked to the police. They investigated. They think he fell asleep at the wheel."

"There was nothing to indicate anything else," Samantha said. "They said so, and if there had been, they wouldn't have released the body so quickly."

Betty sat back and stared at her hands. They lay in her lap like wounded birds. She looked up and tried to smile. "You're good people, and I know you mean well. Thank you." She hesitated, her eyes still on Fallon. "Why did they have to do it, Jack? Why did they have to do it that way?" She drew a deep breath, holding back tears. "There've been days over the past few weeks when I thought there had to be something vicious working right there beside all of you. Some animal none of you could see, just waiting to devour you." She closed her eyes tightly. "Oh, Jack, I just don't understand. It would have been so much kinder if they'd sent someone with a gun."

The dinosaurs met in the locker room at five-thirty. Other employees drifted in. As rumors about downsizing grew stronger, more and more seemed eager to take advantage of the company's gym. Fallon wondered if they somehow hoped their fitter bodies might save them. Or perhaps they merely wanted to seize an opportunity before it was taken away. A pleasing thought toyed at the corners of his mind. Maybe there were dinosaur clubs forming all throughout the company.

When they went out into the gym, Samantha and Annie were already there using one of the stationary bicycles to warm up. Samantha, too, now wore a Dinosaur Club T-shirt. Fallon climbed on the bicycle beside her.

"I had a message from my computer guy," she said. "He thinks he may have found something and wants to stop by the apartment around seven. I'm going to leave early to meet him. Try to be there as soon as you can."

"Did he say what he'd found?" Fallon asked.

"I didn't speak to him. I just had my assistant call him back and say seven was fine." She hesitated. "I also found out something else. Legal has been asked to get a copy of the police report on Jim's death."

Fallon's face darkened. "Why?"

Samantha shook her head. "The request came from Willis Chambers, which means it came from Bennett. My best guess is that they want to see if he was drinking before the accident. Apparently, under the executive insurance agreement, it could be considered contributory, and could allow denial of the accidental death provision. I didn't know this, but the insurance carrier is responsible only for the double indemnity portion. The triple indemnity—the part that covers accidental death while traveling on company business—is picked up by Waters Cable."

Fallon ground his teeth. "Sonofabitch," he hissed.

"But they won't find anything," Samantha said. "There's nothing in the police report, Jack. I know. I talked to them. Legally, according to his blood alcohol level, Jim was sober when it happened."

Fallon glared at the wall. "That won't stop them from holding up payment," he said. "They can drag their feet and force Betty to hire a lawyer."

"Yes, they can," Samantha said. "And I'm sure that's the legal advice they'll get."

Fallon turned his glare on her, almost as if she were to blame. She felt as if all the sins of her profession were being dumped on her. "I'll represent Betty myself," she said. "Pro bono. I plan to quit, anyway." She tried a weak smile. "Before Carter fires me," she added.

Almost on cue, Bennett entered the gym. He had already changed. Given the growing tension, he now avoided the gym's locker room and used the executive washroom instead.

Samantha and Fallon were only a few feet to the left of the gym entrance. Wally and George Valasquez were working at a bench-press station to its right. They formed a gauntlet through which Bennett had to pass.

Bennett glared at Fallon, then Samantha, his eyes burning with open hatred.

"Hey, killer. How's it going? What's the body count today?"

The words stopped Bennett in his tracks. He turned his glare on George Valasquez.

"What's that supposed to mean?" He stared down the length of his nose, viewing George like some fly he had found in his soup.

"You know what it means, you prick." George had started to rise from the bench, and Wally stepped around him quickly, placing himself in George's path. Fallon slid off his bicycle, and came around the other side. The other dinosaurs, sensing the confrontation, had begun to move across the room.

Bennett didn't seem to notice, or perhaps didn't care. He continued to stare at George with contempt. "If you're trying to affix blame for the actions of some drunk . . ."

Wally spun around, ready to launch himself at the man. "You sonofabitch," he snarled. He heaved himself forward, but Fallon looped an arm around his neck and pulled him back.

Bennett cocked a fist, and Fallon's anger flashed. He pushed Wally aside and moved quickly inside any swing

Bennett might attempt. His hands shot up, grabbing Bennett's shirt beneath his chin, twisting it, and driving him back against the wall.

Bennett struggled, but Fallon had twenty-five pounds on him, and his weight was forward, his face only inches away from Bennett's.

"You better get out of here, Carter. And you better do it fast," Fallon growled. "*Before* you have six people pounding the living hell out of you."

Bennett's eyes darted toward the others, then back to Fallon. Samantha had come up beside him.

"Seven people," she snapped.

Bennett's eyes suddenly became fearful, and he looked back at Fallon. "Let go of me," he said. But there was no command in his voice. The words came out sounding like a plea.

Fallon released him, and he spun away and hurried out the door.

It was raining when Fallon left the Chrysler Building, and he quickly gave up any hope of finding a cab. Instead, he ran across Lexington Avenue and into the east entrance of Grand Central Station. The IRT subway would put him only two and a half blocks from Samantha's apartment on East Seventy-sixth Street. It wasn't the best of choices, but he felt pressed to get there rather than miss the unexpected meeting with her computer wizard.

As he descended into the bowels of Grand Central, Fallon realized he hadn't ridden a subway in almost ten years. But it was as good a time as any to get reacquainted. When the company tossed his aging butt into the street, and when Trisha's lawyer plucked what was left, traveling with the unwashed might be the only mode of transportation he could afford.

But despite his trepidation, the ride was surprisingly pleasant. He had missed the rush hour, and the train seemed far less grungy than those he remembered from the past. Perhaps the city's boast of a cleaner, safer subway system hadn't been all hype and bluster after all.

When he climbed out of the exit at East Seventy-seventh Street, he found that the rain had intensified. But one of the city's other wonders had miraculously appeared. Straight ahead, only a half dozen steps away, stood a man selling cheap, collapsible, two-dollar umbrellas for only five bucks a pop. Fallon had often pondered the appearance of these men throughout the city. He had decided that they, together with their umbrellas, lived somewhere below ground, and that they simply materialized whenever two or more rain-drops struck the pavement above their heads.

Five dollars lighter, and umbrella in hand, Fallon turned the corner and headed down East Seventy-sixth Street. He had gone no more than a dozen steps when the rain abruptly stopped.

"This is *not* your day," he hissed to himself, as he folded and collapsed the umbrella into its eighteen-inch length.

Fallon had taken only a dozen more steps when he felt a prickling at the back of his neck. He turned his head just in time to see an arm descending toward his head.

Instinct took over. He ducked and threw his body to the left. It was enough to save his skull, but not his shoulder, which flashed with sudden pain as he staggered against the wall of a building.

The man lunged toward him. He was tall and blond and fit, and the lead sap in his hand was raised again for another blow. Fallon ducked again and the sap chipped a brick above his head.

The collapsed umbrella was in Fallon's right hand, and with all his strength he jabbed it toward the man's face. The blow caught the man on the bridge of the

nose, and he staggered back, uttering a rage-filled curse
in what sounded like German to Fallon.

Pushing himself away from the wall, Fallon took a
quick step forward and kicked out at the man's testicles.
The blow missed, catching him in the stomach. Still, it
was enough. The man crumpled halfway to his knees;
Fallon grabbed his hair and, pulling his head forward,
drove a knee into his face.

The man fell back, the sap clattering to the pavement, and Fallon reached out and grabbed it. But by the
time he turned, the man was up and running toward
Lexington Avenue.

Fallon drew a deep breath and watched him race
away. Twenty years ago you would have chased the
sonofabitch, he thought. But that was twenty years ago.
Now you just want to get the hell out of here. He
glanced at the folded umbrella still in his right hand.
He thought he just might have that sucker cast in
bronze.

Fallon was still shaken when he met Stanley
Kijewski, but struggled to hide it, not wanting to muddy
the waters with his own near disaster.

"Sam tells me you may have found something," he
said.

"Could be." Kijewski gave him a wide grin; it was self-
satisfied, almost smug. He views himself as a man who
knows the secrets, Fallon thought—everything that
everyone else *should* know. Yet there was no sign of personal arrogance. In that one small way the man
reminded Fallon of his father. He recalled the slight,
knowing nod his dad would give when issuing his pro-
nouncements about world events. It had been defensive,
a way to obscure his all too visible inadequacies, and
invariably it had produced a sneer from Fallon's mother.
He wondered what his dad would think now if he saw
the "Blessed Virgin" in action. He would probably just

nod, Fallon thought. Let everyone know he had known she was mad all along.

"First, there's nothing in the computer system to indicate any hanky-panky on your government contracts," Kijewski said. "In fact, as far as Charlie Waters is concerned, the only thing that's been deleted from the hard drive is some correspondence with some people at Strube Industries, which, I gather, is a competitor of yours based in Germany." Kijewski tapped a file that lay on the cocktail table before him. "Anyway, I printed all of it, and have it here. It's also back in the system's hard drive, although no one will know that unless they go looking for it." He gave another yellow grin. A man who appreciated his own cleverness—*and* the fatal arrogance of others.

Kijewski turned to Samantha and wiggled his eyebrows. "As far as your friend Bennett goes, there's some very solid stuff that he also thought he'd deleted." He spoke the words with mild contempt and offered up yet another grin. "Seems the man has been setting up some shell corporations in the Caymans and in Curaçao. Over the past few weeks those outfits have been issuing buy orders for Waters Cable stock." He let loose with another exaggerated eyebrow vibration. "Has the sniff of a little insider trading to me—a definite no-no as far as the SEC is concerned. Especially if anything's about to happen that could send Waters stock up a few notches."

Samantha smiled. "What a naughty boy," she said. "By the way, Stanley, there is something I need *you* to delete—permanently." She told him about Malloy's message to Fallon. Kijewski assured her he could erase the apparent suicide note, both at the office and on Malloy's home computer.

Fallon reached for the folder that lay between them. "Let me see what you have on Charlie," he said.

"I've heard of Strube Industries," Samantha said. "They're a major competitor, aren't they?"

Fallon continued to read. "Just about the biggest, worldwide," he said. He appeared fascinated by what he was reading, and his answers seemed distracted, distant. "We're bigger in sales here in the States, but in the world market they clobber us in every area. But lately they've been gaining here, too."

Fallon finished reading, then sat back. There was a look of mild amazement on his face. Mixed with disbelief, Samantha thought.

"What is it, Jack?" she asked.

"I know these people Charlie's been in touch with," he said. "I know what they do for Strube."

She reached out and took the file. "What are we talking about? Price fixing? Collusion?" She began reading rapidly.

"Yeah. But not the kind you think," Fallon said.

Samantha read through the E-mail correspondence, then went back and reread some of it again. "Is it what I think it is?"

Fallon shot a wary glance at Kijewski. "You bet it is," he said.

Kijewski grinned again. "So they *are* screwing old Uncle Sam, after all, huh?" he said.

Fallon returned the smile; decided this was one secret the man didn't need to know. He nodded. "You bet they are. Listen, you did a great job. I really appreciate it."

"Hey, man, nothing to it," Kijewski said. "Computers are the most dangerous things in an office. But the guys who buy them never understand that." He nodded toward the folder Samantha now held. "By the way, Waters's and Bennett's passwords are listed in that folder. They should change them periodically, but I'll bet my tush they never do." He offered up another grin. "And if they do . . ." He grinned. "Just give me a call."

When Kijewski left, Samantha and Fallon settled in on the sofa, the papers spread out before them. They were ready to review the real subject—the one they had not wanted Kijewski to hear.

"So how do we prove it?" Samantha asked. "We know what's going on, but we're still faced with a big deniability factor." She tapped a finger against the papers. "If we go to the media—say *The Wall Street Journal* or *Business Week*—the whole scheme could go up in smoke. *If* it ever finds its way into print." She shook her head, thinking it through. "But those people aren't going to accept our word, not if it's just based on some purloined correspondence. They'll want corroboration, and Waters and Strube will just deny it."

"When you combine it with what's going on in Plattsburgh, maybe they will believe it," Fallon said.

Samantha shook her head again. "No, it's still too speculative. Their lawyers will tell them they need confirmation, and if they can't get it they'll back away. Then Charlie Waters will just wait it out—wait for everything to quiet down. Six months. A year."

"What about Bennett?" Fallon asked.

"Carter's a different story," Samantha said. "We've got Carter by the proverbial short hairs."

Fallon looked up at her. "Then Carter's the key to the rest of it."

"You think he knows." She spoke the question as fact.

"He has to know," Fallon said. "Look at the number of shares he's bought through his phony companies. He's risking a lot of money. Too much."

"But the company stock *will* go up when the downsizing is announced."

"Yes, it will. But not *that* much. Not enough to risk millions. But this other thing, that's Carter's chance of a lifetime. It's as close as you get to a sure thing. And he wouldn't be risking that much money if he didn't know about it."

Samantha sat back. Her feet were curled beneath her, and her hair was pulled back. Fallon thought she looked a bit like a schoolgirl. "So what do we do?" she asked. "How do we go about proving it?"

"We have to make Carter tell us," he said.

She gave him an uncertain, slightly quizzical look. "Why would he do that, Jack? Why wouldn't he just realize he'd been caught, then sell off his stock and try to cover up the insider-trading violation?" She offered a look of regret. "If Carter bails out before anything happens, the SEC may not even go after him."

"Why?" Fallon asked.

"If they claim the downsizing proposal was just a study, not something really being considered—and if Carter pleads ignorance of what Waters had planned, the SEC might consider it too hard to prove. You'd almost have to have him on tape, admitting he *knew* something was going to happen and had made his stock purchases to take advantage of it. Either that, or a confession, and I don't think Carter is foolish enough to let either of those things happen."

Fallon sat back, a stunned look suddenly coming over his face.

"What is it?" Samantha asked.

"Something you just said. About getting Carter on tape." He stood abruptly. "I have to make a phone call."

When he returned Samantha stared at him. "Well?"

"We have to wait. I just talked to Stuart Robaire. He's driving over to his office to check something." Samantha started to speak, but Fallon raised a hand, stopping her. "Somebody tried to mug me tonight," he said. "At least, that's what I thought it was." He took the sap from his pocket and placed it on the table between them. He let out a bitter laugh. "I was able to fight him off, and while it was happening he cursed at me—in *German*."

Samantha stared at the sap as though it were something from another planet. She blinked several times; then her eyes widened as the connection was made. "German," she said. "Strube Industries."

"I think Charlie knows about the M.I.T. tests. I'll know for sure when Stuart calls back."

Twenty minutes later Fallon replaced the phone for a second time. "Charlie knows," he said. "There was a tape recorder hidden in Stuart's office."

"Oh, God. Then Charlie Waters tried to have you killed."

"Or put in intensive care for a good long time."

Samantha shook her head. "What should we do?"

"I don't think we have a choice," Fallon said. "We play the cards Charlie dealt, and we make Carter tell us what we need to know."

"But he won't do that. He'd be crazy to tell us anything."

"I think he will. I think he'll give us just what we want," Fallon said.

"Why? What makes you think he will?"

A small smile flickered at the corners of his mouth. He felt like Stanley Kijewski. "Something else you said—about Carter's paintball tournaments."

"And what was that?"

He told her.

Samantha stared at him; incredulous. "Have you lost your mind? That's a federal crime, Jack."

"Only if someone can prove it," he said. "And if it works, I don't think Carter will want anyone to prove anything." He hesitated a moment, drawing her in. "Of course it won't work," he added. "Not unless you help."

25

FALLON MARVELED AT BETTY MALLOY. SHE BUSIED HER-
self about the house, putting aside condolences to tend
to her guests. She gently brushed away offers of help,
kept her children busy instead, and in doing so drove off
the burial of husband and father—if only for a short
time.

The innate strength of women always amazed Fallon.
He thought about the lions of the African grasslands, the
males who would certainly starve if the females of their
breed did not gather the food they were incapable of
capturing themselves. Among humans it was only
slightly different. Women were the cohesive force—
much more capable of enduring pain and suffering—so
eager and capable of tending to the physical and emo-
tional needs of all who surrounded them. Left to their
own devices, men, with their endless competition and
conflict, would have rendered the species extinct. And
as that end approached, Fallon suspected they would
have drowned in their own tears.

The dinosaurs gathered in Betty Malloy's rear yard. It
was small and neat, and at present deserted. Fallon
explained what he and Samantha had discovered. Then
he told them about the tape recorder in Robaire's office,
and the subsequent attack on him. Incredulity, then

anger approaching rage, came from the others. He explained how he proposed to prove it and stop it.

Disbelief, then wary uncertainty, descended. Hartman and Constantini shook their heads.

"But, Jack," Constantini said, "you told us . . ."

George Valasquez cut him off. His eyes blazed; his voice was a low, angry hiss.

"What is the matter with you people? Don't you see what they're trying to do to us? They're killing us. They're grinding us into the goddamned dirt." He jerked his head toward the house. "They already killed Jim. They tried to get Jack. And we're next. Maybe not all the way to the grave. But goddamned dead, all the same. And God knows how many others there'll be after us." George glared at each of the others in turn. His small, slender figure and pinched face seemed to rivet each of them in place. It was almost as if he were saying, Look at me. I'm so small, but I'm the only one of you who isn't afraid. His eyes continued to blaze until the others looked away. "What are you worried about?" he demanded aloud. "Do *they* worry about what they're doing? Do they give one shit if it's legal?"

Fallon stepped up next to George, creating a bond he hoped the others would join. "Only the first part will be dangerous." He waited, let the idea, the threat, settle in. "If we screw up there and get caught, it's over. But we'll do it right, and I only need two people to help me. The rest of you won't be anywhere near it. You'll be off setting everything else up. If the three of us are caught at the start, no one will ever know the rest of you were involved. And once Carter knows what we know, I don't think he'll ever let it get that far. Even if we do get caught."

"You got one person," George snapped. His eyes roamed the others, challenging them.

Wally let out a heavy sigh. "You've got two," he said. "If we get caught, what the hell, at least Janice will get screwed out of her maintenance check."

Annie Schwartz started to laugh. "God, I never thought I'd feel like a jock. My hairdresser will be horrified. But count me in. I just hope you have a blow-dryer. If we get caught I'll blame it on seeing that Bonnie and Clyde movie when I was a kid."

Silence followed. Then Samantha stepped up next to Fallon. "I think it would be better if you had three people helping you at the start," she said. "I'd like to be the third."

Fallon looked at her. She was one tough lady, he decided. It seemed to have the same effect on the others. Everyone agreed.

"It's crazy, Jack," Constantini said. "But what have we got to lose?"

"I'm in too," Hartman said. "Just tell me what you want me to do."

Fallon turned to Samantha. They had worked it out earlier. It was time for her to provide the glue that would either bind them together or push them apart.

"Let's understand one thing," she began. "What Jack is proposing *is* a crime."

"Jesus Christ," Annie Schwartz said. "It *is* Bonnie and Clyde."

Samantha smiled at her. "Almost. But if we get caught at the beginning, I intend to tell Carter that we're making a citizen's arrest for his SEC violations."

Joe Hartman cackled. "He'll wet his Brooks Brothers pants."

Samantha nodded. "Yes, I think he will."

"But it's still crazy, right?" It was Constantini again.

"Oh, yes, it's crazy," Samantha said. "And as a lawyer I'd have to advise you against it." She gave an exaggerated shrug. "But do I think it will work?" She glanced at Fallon. "Yes, I think it might. And, if we get caught, I don't think anything will happen to us." She let out a small laugh. "Except, of course, we'll probably be fired."

"So how do we start this life of crime?" Annie

Schwartz asked. "And what do we wear? I hope it's not going to be something embarrassing."

"We'll be wearing fatigues. Give Ben your sizes."

"Oh, God," Annie said.

Fallon fought down a grin and hurried on. "It's Friday. We'll all go there tomorrow, get the lay of the land, and get everything set up," Fallon said. "Those of you who aren't part of the initial operation here will stay there and finish up, and the rest of us will come back and do it on Monday." He pulled a list from his pocket and handed it to Constantini. "I want you to use that lovely background in military procurement to get us this stuff. Joe can help you. All of it will be available up there, so it shouldn't be a problem."

"I'm going too," Annie said. "There's got to be *someone* there with some fashion sense."

26

FALLON SAT IN WATERS'S OFFICE. IT WAS ELEVEN O'CLOCK
Monday morning, and he knew he should be tired from
all the preparations he had put in over the weekend. But
his adrenaline was flowing. Even more so as he took in
the look on Carter Bennett's face. He was seated at
Charlie Waters's right hand, smug and self-assured.

"I can't have it, Jack." Waters sat on his office sofa,
arms spread in a gesture of benevolence—a man who
has tried to be fair and who finds himself on the brink of
failure. "One executive becoming physical with another
is something I view as intolerable."

Fallon had a sudden urge to spit in Waters's eye. He
wondered about professional goons wielding saps. Did
they count?

Fallon noted the expression of moral indignation on
Bennett's face. It seemed genuine, and Fallon decided
he didn't know about the German Charlie had sent after
him. Either that, or he was not only a good actor but also
a sociopath.

"You're absolutely right, Charlie. No matter the
provocation, there's no excuse. But in fairness to Carter,
I can't be certain he actually intended to hit Wally
Green. It just appeared that way at the time. I only
grabbed him as a precaution."

Confusion flooded Waters's face. "What the hell are you talking about, Jack? You attacked Carter. That's my understanding."

Fallon raised his eyebrows. "Really?" He turned his gaze on Bennett. "Is that what you told him, Carter?"

"You know damned well what happened, Fallon." Bennett's face had turned scarlet; his teeth were clenched, and his eyes spit unconcealed hatred.

Fallon let out a weary breath and turned his eyes back to Waters. "Charlie, there were six other people standing right there." He ticked off the names. "This isn't even worthy of argument. Just check with each of them."

"Sure," Bennett snapped. "Your goddamned *dinosaurs* and your *mistress*. No one's about to fall for that, Fallon."

Fallon stared at him, putting as much regret into the look as he could. "Is that what this is about, Carter? The fact that I'm living with a woman you once pursued?"

Waters's head had been snapping back between the two. "Just a minute," he demanded. "What are we talking about here?"

Fallon explained, as Bennett sat and fumed. He thought Carter might leap from his chair and come after him.

Waters shook his head as if fighting off a bad dream. "This is all getting ridiculous," he finally snapped. He glared at Bennett. "What's the root cause of this damned foolishness?"

Fallon didn't give Bennett a chance to answer. He'd been called on Waters's carpet and fully expected to be unemployed when the session was over. He intended to go out with all guns blazing. "Jim Malloy," he said. "If you want a reason, Charlie, Jim Malloy is it."

Waters turned to him and blinked. "Jim Malloy is dead. How can he be the cause of this problem?"

Fallon wanted to grab Waters and shake him. His mind raced with everything he wanted to say: A problem, Charlie. Of course Jim's not a problem. He's dead. And we can sure as hell ignore the fact that you and your boys drove him to suicide—just so you could line your goddamned pockets.

Fallon said none of it. Instead, he glared at Bennett. "Word has gotten out that Carter is looking to withhold Jim's accidental death benefit. It's raised some tempers among his friends." His eyes went back to Waters. "I think that's quite understandable. Frankly, I'm surprised it hasn't caused greater problems."

Waters's face hardened. He doesn't care what Carter's done, Fallon told himself. He hears only one word: *problem*. And that's the one thing he doesn't want. It scares him. It's the same reason he hired that blond thug with the sap.

Carter's tone immediately turned defensive. "The man was a drunk," he snapped. "And the company is *not* liable for accidents that involve the victim's culpability. Malloy was even driving a company car he'd been ordered to turn in because of his drunkenness."

"I countermanded that order." Fallon locked eyes with Bennett. "And I was acting *for* the company. The man was not a drunk. The accusations were a crock of shit. I have a memo from the man who made them that proves it."

Before Bennett could respond, Fallon withdrew some papers from an inside pocket and dropped them on the table that sat between them. "That's a copy of the state police report," he said. "It's quite clear. There was no evidence Jim had been drinking." He watched Waters pick up the report, and begin to read it. "Charlie, Jim was one of the first people I hired after we got our feet on the ground." Fallon's voice was lower now, becoming steadily sonorous. "He was with this company twenty-one years, and in that time he did us a lot of good." He raised his chin toward Bennett. "Now Carter wants to dick around with his death benefit. Maybe even force his widow to go to court, which she can ill afford to do. And people who work here—the people who worked with Jim—know all that. They see the injustice in it. And, Charlie, it's making them very angry."

Waters folded the report and placed it gingerly on the table. "I'll look into it, Jack. I assure you we won't be creating problems we don't need." His voice was stiff, filled with irritation. He raised his eyes slowly, tried to stare Fallon down. "There's another matter I'd like to discuss, Jack. It's about some tests I hear you're having run at M.I.T."

Fallon offered up his most boyish grin, one that would go well with the lie he was about to tell. "Already had them run, Charlie. They came back negative. I'm sorry I doubted you."

Waters nodded. "I'm glad we cleared the air on that." The words were friendly, intended to imply satisfaction, but Waters's eyes were full of suspicion. In twenty-four hours all his suspicions wouldn't matter, Fallon told himself.

Waters tried to regain control. "I need you to be a team player, Jack. All else aside, I need and expect that." He shook his head slowly. "I cannot have you openly opposing other executives. I cannot have you publicly choosing sides that make that opposition apparent. And I can't have you raising groundless concerns. We need solidarity here if we are going to move this company ahead. Do I make myself clear?"

Fallon wanted to laugh in the man's face, but merely gave him an acquiescent smile. "There's nothing I want more than to move this company ahead." He extended his hands, brought them back together with a clap. "I've been working toward that end for twenty-three years. And I have no intention of stopping now."

Waters kept his eyes locked on Fallon. "Then we're agreed." His words were a command; his eyes were still filled with suspicion.

"Indeed we are," Fallon said.

* * *

Fallon dropped into his chair and glanced at his watch. It was a quarter to five. He was due to meet Wally and Samantha in thirty minutes. They would go back to Samantha's apartment and change, then get in position to confront Bennett as he jogged through Central Park.

Samantha had assured him a Monday night jog was an unwavering part of Bennett's routine. He never socialized on Monday nights. Monday was set aside for his weekly run—something he refused to vary. Even the route remained the same. He would start on the walk-way near the Metropolitan Museum, head around the lake, past Bethesda Fountain, then on through the Mall, and out again at Seventy-second Street. Samantha had assured them he was so fixated with the route, he even carried a stopwatch to compare his time to previous efforts. Fallon hoped she was right. They would wait for Bennett in the parking area between the fountain and the Mall. If he kept to his routine it would be over with before Carter had time to wet his shorts.

But first there was one other matter. Perhaps the last bit of business he would do for the company. Les Gavin was waiting in Fallon's outer office, had been waiting there—cooling his heels—for the past half hour. Fallon reached for the intercom, ready to summon the man, when Carol entered his office.

She closed the door behind her. "Jack, your daughter's here," she said.

"Liz?" he asked in amazement.

Carol smiled at his bewilderment. "She says she has to talk to you."

Fallon glanced at his watch again. He had a helluva lot to do in the next few hours. He thought, Jesus Christ, Liz, your timing stinks. "Okay, send her in," he said. "Tell Lester to wait."

Liz entered, tall and young and beautiful. Her blond

hair shone, just as her mother's always had. She was dressed in a green silk blouse and tan slacks, and had a matching tan jacket draped over her shoulders. She had become the personification of her mother in style and manner. He loved her, but he hoped her values were better grounded and that her life would follow a far different path.

Fallon came around his desk and kissed her cheek. "Honey, it's great to see you. But you caught me just as I was headed into a meeting."

Liz raised an eyebrow, and he immediately surrendered. "But sit down. Tell me what's up."

Liz settled into a chair, as Fallon took the one next to it. "I want to talk to you about your life, Daddy."

Fallon felt an inward shudder. The fact that she had used the term *Daddy* made it even more intense. It was a signal he had learned to recognize over time. This would be an impassioned plea for something she wanted badly. And it would continue, he knew, until it ended in either acrimonious argument or acquiescence.

He stole another glance at his watch. He had time for neither. Nor had he the stomach for it. His nerves were already becoming frayed.

"That sounds like a long, serious topic," he said. His mind raced. How do you tell your daughter you don't have time for this? Do you say, Listen, I'm sorry. Let's do this another time, dear. Maybe on the next visiting day at Sing Sing?

"I certainly consider it serious," Liz said. She hadn't caught his tone, had gone right past it. She adjusted herself in her seat. "Let's face it, Daddy. You're going through a midlife crisis."

Fallon thought, Oh, shit, we're off and running. "Is that what you think?" He inclined his head as though considering it.

"I think it's obvious." She twisted in place again, clearly uncomfortable. Fallon wondered if she felt slightly foolish doing this. He loved her, felt sorry for her if she did. He also wanted to get rid of her as quickly as possible.

"I'm afraid it's not obvious to me," he said.

Liz let out a breath. It was a mannerism she had employed since the age of three. "Daddy, look at the facts. Mom has come back to you. She realizes she made a mistake. She was just frightened by all the sudden insecurity in your lives. She's accepted that, and admitted she was wrong. But now you're involved with . . ." She paused, then continued, "A younger woman, let's say." Fallon started to say something, but Liz hurried on. "I can understand it. I can accept the attraction an older man feels for a younger woman. I see it in school all the time. Professors having affairs with their students."

Immediately, Fallon wondered if his daughter had been hit on by some lecherous professor. If she had he would engineer the man's ruin. The thought was interrupted as Liz continued to prattle.

"Daddy, a younger woman may make you happy now. But eventually it will all come apart, and you'll just be hurt. It's inevitable. You deserve better than that. And so does Mom."

"Your mother already took her shot at better." Fallon kept his voice soft, as nonconfrontational as he could manage. "Howard was better. Filing for divorce was better. Moving all the furniture out of the house was better." He raised a hand, stopping a forthcoming objection. "Liz, all of that hit me like a ton of bricks. But I shook it off and got on with things. And I'm happy. Maybe I won't be happy forever, but that's the way life works." He reached out for her hand. "Right now, just be happy that I'm happy."

"But what about *Mom*?" Tears had welled up in her eyes.

His telephone interrupted them. Fallon reached out and picked it up. Carol's voice came across the line.

"Jack, Ms. Moore and Wally are here. They said you were supposed to meet them."

Fallon made a point of looking at his watch. "Jesus, yeah, that's right. Tell them to go down to Wally's office and I'll meet them in a few minutes."

He replaced the phone and turned back to his daughter, praying he'd been saved by his fellow conspirators.

"Honey, I have to go. We'll have to finish this later."

Liz stared at him in disbelief. "Daddy, there's so much more I have to say. What about us? What about Mike and me? This is creating havoc with *all* our lives."

Fallon felt burdened with guilt. He pushed it away. "Honey, we *will* talk. I promise you. I don't promise you you'll hear what you want to hear, but we'll talk it out." He took her arm and guided her out of her chair. "I have to go out of town tomorrow, but I'll call you when I get back. I promise."

Liz's mouth worked soundlessly, as he led her toward the door. He stopped before opening it and hugged her. "If there's any way I can make things work out, I will."

He stood in the doorway and watched his daughter leave. Then he glanced down at Gavin, still flying one of the chairs in Carol's office. "Come on in, Lester," he said. "This won't take long."

Gavin took the same chair Liz had just occupied. Fallon leaned back against his desk and stared down at his assistant VP.

"Lester, I'm very unhappy with your work," he began. "I'm even more unhappy with your complete lack of loyalty."

Gavin shook his head. He had gone slightly pale. "Jack, I . . . I don't understand."

"It's simple, Lester. Your little game as corporate spy has not gone unnoticed. You've been going through people's trash. Looking through their desks. Making false accusations. In short, you've been a disloyal, self-serving little shit. And so you're fired. Clean out your desk today. You have one month's severance, and it won't be necessary for you to come back into the office. I've already notified security. They're waiting for you in the hall. Carol will forward all the paperwork to the proper people, and they'll no doubt be in touch with you."

Gavin's face flushed. "You can't fire me!" Like Liz, he stared at Fallon in disbelief.

"I can't?" Fallon grinned his own disbelief. "I'm confused, Lester. Seems to me my business card reads: Jack Fallon, vice president, sales. That, I believe, makes me your boss. And as your boss, I'm firing your backstabbing little ass. So take a walk, Lester. And have a nice life."

27

THE VAN THEY HAD RENTED SAT IN THE SHADOW OF a large tree only a few short yards from the roadway Bennett would hopefully use. It was eight-thirty, fully dark, and the portion of the path on which Fallon stood was thirty feet from the nearest streetlight. Fallon was dressed in camouflage fatigues. His hat was equipped with a pull-down face net that was now tucked under the brim. Wally and George Valasquez, dressed in the same mildly ridiculous attire, were crouched behind a nearby bush. Samantha, also wearing identical gear, waited in the rear of the van.

Fallon heard the slapping of Bennett's running shoes before he saw him. He stepped out into his path and grinned. "Carter, glad I caught you."

Bennett staggered to a stop. He stared at Fallon, at his clothing. He blinked several times. "Fallon," he said. His voice held a clear note of disbelief. "What is this?"

"I wanted you to know I fired Les Gavin today," Fallon said.

More blinking. "You *what*?"

Fallon grinned. "I fired Lester."

"Why are you dressed like that?" Bennett's eyes roamed Fallon's attire yet again.

"I'm going to a little paintball tournament. Wanna come?"

Wally hit Bennett from behind, knocking him to the ground. He immediately grabbed one arm, while Valasquez grabbed the other. Fallon scooped up his legs, and all three began running toward the van.

Bennett screamed, and began kicking his legs. A sudden jerk of his body sent Wally to the ground. George threw a roundhouse right that grazed Bennett's head. "Prick," he snarled.

Wally quickly grabbed Bennett's arm again and struggled to his feet. "Hit him again," he hissed. George swung but missed.

When they reached the van Bennett was still screaming. Samantha threw open the rear door, and slapped a piece of duct tape across his mouth. She wound it quickly around his head, then stepped aside as the others threw Bennett inside.

Wally hurtled in behind and pounced on Bennett's back, pinning him to the floor, while George grabbed his wrists and duct-taped them together. He immediately did the same with his ankles.

Bennett thrashed about the back of the van, his feet slamming against one side.

"Keep him quiet," Fallon snapped. He was behind the wheel now, Samantha next to him, and he was pulling the van out of the parking area.

Wally pivoted, and slammed his buttocks down on Bennett's back. A whoosh of air escaped Bennett's nose, then he became still.

Fallon's adrenaline-driven heart thudded in his chest. He drove across the park, keeping well within the speed limit. An unmistakable aroma assaulted his nostrils. He sniffed at the stench that suddenly seemed to fill the van.

"What the hell is that smell?" he demanded.

"I think I fell in dog shit," Wally answered. He studied his pants. "Yeah, I did. It's all over my leg."

"Jesus H. Christ," George snapped.

"Well, take the pants off and throw them out the window," Fallon ordered.

"Hey, I'm not gonna sit here in my goddamned underwear."

Samantha turned around and began to giggle. It was part relief, part what she saw. Bennett, dressed in an orange Princeton T-shirt and jogging shorts, looked like an Ivy League turkey trussed up for Thanksgiving dinner. Wally sat atop him, the leg of his camouflage trousers covered in dog shit. "Take off your pants, Wally," she said. "None of us are going to peek."

28

CARTER BENNETT AWOKE AT FIVE THE NEXT MORNING. Wally and George had dragged him from the van only a few hours earlier and had dropped him on the floor of the cabin. They had removed the duct tape from his mouth, but his arms and legs had remained bound. A pair of new camouflage fatigues had been placed under his head.

Constantini, Hartman, and Annie Schwartz had hovered nearby spitting invective. Bennett had lain on the floor, surrounded and terrified. It had gone on for nearly a half hour before it finally stopped. Emotionally drained, Bennett had finally fallen into an uneasy, fitful sleep. Now, the first vision to greet his eye was the specter of Wally Green again hovering above him. There was an Indian blanket wrapped around the waist of his camouflage shirt, a black cowboy hat perched on his head, and a shotgun cradled in his arms.

"Good morning, Mr. Bennett. Did we have a nice little nippy nap?"

Bennett blinked; a sense of confused terror rushed back. He couldn't believe this was happening; wasn't sure what he should or should not say. He stared at the shotgun. It was insane. They couldn't be doing this.

"I'm thirsty. And I have to use the bathroom." He heard his voice come out as a croak.

Green grinned at someone behind him. "Hey, Georgie, Carter has to go pee, and you get to hold it for him." He let out a cackle. Bennett twisted around and saw George Valasquez standing at the kitchen counter. He had just poured a cup of coffee and was taking his first sip. Ben Constantini and Joe Hartman were standing behind him, waiting their turn at the pot. All three were wearing fatigues, and they all sneered at him. Bennett's head snapped around. Annie Schwartz was seated in a chair by the fireplace, nursing her own mug of coffee. She, too, was wearing camouflage, but she had tucked a Hermès scarf stylishly in the neck. The same look of contempt filled her eyes. And all of them—*all of them*—had a weapon close at hand.

Bennett felt a tremor course through his body. It *was* insane. They couldn't be doing this. He heard footsteps and turned his head again. Valasquez was coming toward him, and there was a long-bladed hunting knife in his hand.

Bennett cringed as Valasquez knelt beside him and slipped the blade under the duct tape that held his ankles. "Turn over," he snapped. When Carter obliged, he did the same to his hands.

"Please don't cut his throat," Annie said. "Not in here, anyway. The blood will never come out of the carpet."

"I'd love to take him outside and do just that," George said. "But Jack has first dibs."

"Screw Jack," Hartman said. "I wanna see the sonofabitch bleed."

Bennett turned back and stared at the man. He knew his eyes held all the fear he felt, but he couldn't help it. He turned quickly back to George. "Can I go now?" he croaked.

"You can piss, if that's what you mean." Valasquez raised his chin, indicating the rear of the cabin. He turned to Wally. "You better go with him." He grinned. "You can blow his kneecaps off if he tries to climb out the window."

"Where's he gonna go?" Hartman asked. "If he goes in the right direction there's a couple hundred acres of woods before he hits the road. If he goes in the wrong direction there's a couple of thousand."

"Yeah, that's true," Wally said. "But Jack will be *very* upset if he hurts himself." He let out another cackle.

"I hope he tries," Constantini said. "Then we can hunt the sonofabitch like a goddamned jackrabbit."

Bennett turned to Wally. His legs were shaking so badly he doubted he could stand, let alone run. "Where's Fallon?" he asked.

"That's *Mister* Fallon to you, creep." Wally began to indicate the others in the room with an elevation of his chin. "And this is *Mister* Valasquez, and *Mister* Hartman, and *Mister* Constantini, and *Mizzz* Schwartz." He jabbed a finger against his chest. "I'm *Mister* Green. We're a bunch of useless old dinosaurs. Remember? So show a little respect for our age."

Bennett licked his lips, fighting the dry taste in his mouth. "Where's Mr. Fallon?" he asked.

Wally shrugged. "Who knows? Outside someplace, I guess. You want him to watch you pee, I'll go get him."

Bennett shook his head, more in despair than as an answer. He struggled to his feet, then turned and shuffled toward the bathroom. His legs still felt numb. He flexed them, then his hands and wrists, trying to restore some circulation.

Wally stood against the open door as Bennett relieved himself. The butt of the shotgun was on his hip. He turned back to the room, where the others stood watching. He extended his free hand, his thumb and index finger only inches apart. "Hey, our hero's got a wing-wang that's only about this big," he said. "It is truly a pathetic thing to see."

"Aw, don't say that," Annie pleaded. "All the girls fantasize about Carter. About what a stud he is." She let out a giggle. "When nobody's around to hear us, we call him old donkey dick."

Wally let loose with another cackle and Bennett ground his teeth against the sound. The humiliation wasn't necessary. They didn't have to do that.

He spun around and faced Green, forced every bit of bravado he could muster. "I want to see Fallon," he snapped. "*Mister* Fallon." He added the last with heavy sarcasm.

Wally stared into his face, and Carter's resolve dipped.

"We don't care what you want, donkey dick." Wally jerked his head toward the large open living area. "Get back in there, and sit down, and shut up."

Fallon sat on the steps of the front porch. His arms were draped on his knees and he held a cup of coffee in both hands. Samantha sat next to him watching the first faint glimmer of sunrise through the trees.

"I can hear them cackling inside," Fallon said. "Carter must be awake."

Samantha started to speak, hesitated, then forced herself to continue. "Jack . . . why don't we change the plan? We could just sit him in a chair and intimidate him; keep after him until he tells us what we want to know." She listened to his silence. "The man's terrified. You could see it in his eyes last night. It might work."

Fallon smiled. "You mean beat it out of him?"

"No. Of course not."

Fallon nodded. "We'll just reason with him?"

Samantha remained silent.

Fallon sipped his coffee. "I'm not making fun of you. It's just that it's not enough," he said. "Not for any of us."

"Why? What difference does it make, so long as you get what you want?"

"It matters." He turned to her. "We've come this far. I think we need to finish it."

"But what if he gets hurt?"

"I'll do everything I can to see that doesn't happen." He smiled at her again, a bit regretfully this time, she thought. "No one has live ammunition in their weapons. Just blanks," he said. "The pellets have been removed from the shotgun shells. They'll make a helluva lot of noise, but they won't hurt anyone."

"But something could still happen."

He let out a breath and stared into his coffee.

"What if *you're* hurt?"

He shook his head, kept his eyes averted. "I can do this. I've done it before."

"Jack . . . that was . . . a long time ago."

Fallon let out a soft laugh and looked at her again.

"What?" she asked.

"I thought you were going to say it was a quarter of a century ago." His face broke into another smile. "Actually, it was closer to thirty years."

"This isn't a machismo thing, Jack. You don't have anything to prove."

Fallon nodded—slowly, faintly. "Yes. I do." He turned to the waxing sunrise. "We all do. Otherwise we still lose. Even if we get what we want."

"I don't see it, Jack. I just don't. And the risks are too great."

Fallon nodded again. He continued to watch the clearing in front of the cabin. More of it gradually became distinct as the sun continued to rise. His father had been a great admirer of sunrise, preferring it to the sunsets that captivated most people. He had told Fallon as a boy that a sunrise was life, the start of something new and exciting and unknown. Later, Fallon had decided that preference had been related to his father's own life, which had always seemed in perpetual sunset.

"You've gone this far," Fallon said. "A lot farther than I ever expected. But now I need you to go the rest of the way. I don't think it will work without you."

Samantha surrendered to it. She wasn't certain why; questioned if it was the wrong choice. But he was right. She had come this far. Backing away now would only confuse things; perhaps even make everything more dangerous. "When are you going to start?" she asked.

Fallon pushed himself up. "We might as well do it now," he said.

Bennett's eyes snapped from Samantha to Fallon as they entered the cabin, then settled on Samantha again.

"Thank God you're here," he said. "Will you please talk to these people, explain that they're breaking the law?" The words tumbled out, filled with fear and uncertainty.

Samantha looked away, feigning disgust. She actually felt some pity for Bennett. Sitting on the floor in his orange Princeton T-shirt, his running shorts and shoes, he looked very frightened; almost ridiculous. And he seemed to comprehend—perhaps for the first time in his life—how vulnerable he was to forces outside himself.

"They've *already* broken the law, Carter." She looked back at him. "But no one will ever know that they have."

Bennett's eyes widened, and he seemed to take in her own camouflage attire for the first time. "What do you mean?" he finally asked.

Fallon stepped forward and squatted in front of him. "What she means, Carter, is if you survive this—*if* you do—you'll never want to tell anyone about it."

Bennett's face twisted; a nervous tic hit the corner of his right eye. He glanced about. The others had crowded in on every side. "Why? Why won't I?" he asked.

Fallon stared at him for several long moments.

"Because to survive, Carter, you're going to have to kill me. And if you do—if you get *that* lucky—and if you then decide to go to the police, there are six witnesses who already have a story worked out that will put you in jail."

Samantha moved up and squatted next to Fallon. "And if the authorities don't buy that, Carter, they will buy your insider-trading scheme." She patted some folded papers protruding from her shirt pocket. "We have all the evidence we need to prove that part of it."

Bennett stared at her. Everything was slipping away. *Everything.* And now, if Fallon was telling the truth, they even wanted to kill him. He felt his legs, then his arms, quiver. "Then why this?" The croak was back in his voice, and he fought to control it. "Why this?" he demanded. "You already have what you need to destroy me." His mind was racing, searching for a way out. Any way out.

Fallon smiled at him. "Because we want to see if you're as good as you say you are. We know all about you, Carter. We know you're a tough, hard businessman. We know you like to grind people down. Right into the dirt. And we know you're a paintball champ." He paused and withdrew a knife from a sheath in his boot. It was a double-edged K-bar combat knife with a four-and-a-half-inch blade; razor sharp. "Now I want to see if you can do it all for real. With one of these."

Bennett stared at the knife, then at Fallon. "You're insane," he said.

"That's right," Fallon said. "Just a crazy old dinosaur who hasn't done anything like this for almost thirty years." His smile returned, then hardened. "But I did do it, Carter. And I still remember how." He inclined his head to one side. "But maybe you'll be too quick. Too young. And too clever. We'll just have to see."

"You can't make me do this." Bennett's eyes had

grown wild, and he was struggling past the fear, struggling for defiance.

Fallon kept his voice soft, almost soothing. It was more frightening than a shout. "Yes, we can," he said. "We can't make you stay alive, but we *can* make you do this." He leaned in closer, still squatting, the combat knife still in his hand. "We're going to take you out in this forest. You'll have camouflage clothing, and you'll have a knife just like this one. You'll have an area of thirty acres to work in." Fallon raised his chin, indicating the other dinosaurs. "These people know those thirty acres. They've been up here all weekend learning it. And they'll be stationed at strategic points around its circumference. They'll also be armed with shotguns, and if you try to slip past them, they're going to blow you to hell. If you stay in the area, you won't have to worry about anything but me. And I'll only have a knife. Just . . . like . . . you."

Fallon slipped the knife back into his boot, and his voice became light, almost nonchalant. "If you kill me, you walk away. No one will touch you. If you don't . . ." He finished the sentence with a shrug.

Bennett stared at him. His face was slack, and his eyes were filled with wondrous incredulity. "Why? This is madness. Why?"

"Because you killed Jim Malloy." Fallon let the words sit momentarily. "Oh, you had help. Charlie helped you. So did Willis Chambers and your other lackeys. Just like I'm going to have help now. To keep you under my thumb, just like you kept Jim under yours. Except we'll be a bit kinder. You won't be helpless."

"But it was an accident." Bennett's voice had a whine to it now. He seemed to sense it, and stopped himself.

Fallon shook his head. "No, it wasn't, Carter. Jim killed himself. He sent his suicide note to me, and no one else will ever see it." Fallon lowered his eyes, then raised them slowly. Now they held all the fierce anger he felt. "You see, he wanted to make sure his family got all the benefits he was sure you planned to take away from him. He was scared to death, Carter. He had worked his whole life, and then, in just a few weeks, you and your boys turned him into a failure. But his only failure was living to be fifty-one."

Bennett sat on the floor, his knees drawn up, arms wrapped about them. The others hovered over him as Fallon spoke. They kept a tight circle around him. Bennett looked up toward Samantha, but she had turned her head away. He wanted to say something, but the words refused to form. Fallon's voice broke the silence.

"After Jim killed himself, I sat with his wife. Her name is Betty, in case you're interested. I've known her a long time, so she asked me a question. She asked me why the people who killed her husband hadn't just sent someone with a gun. She said it would have been kinder."

Fallon stood and looked down at Bennett. "So I'm coming after you, Carter. The way Betty would have preferred it. It won't be with a gun, because I want to be real close to you. And that's when I'll decide whether to kill you, or just cripple you. But before I do, I want to watch you run. Because, either way, before it happens, you're going to feel everything that Jim Malloy felt. And you're going to know what a sorry piece of shit you really are."

Fallon turned to Wally. "Get him dressed and bring him outside."

Wally came out ten minutes later. The Indian blanket was still wrapped around his waist, and with the camouflage shirt above, the combat boots peeking out below, he looked totally bizarre.

"Couldn't you find another pair of pants?" Fallon asked.

Samantha turned away, trying to hide the smile that

filled her face. Wally eyed her, then Fallon. "Nothing fits," he said. He caught the amused look in Fallon's eyes. "Hey, is it my fault?" he asked. "Did I put the dog shit there? Did I decide to commit the crime of the century in a place every dog in New York uses to poop?"

Fallon raised a hand Indian style and said, "Ugh."

"Very funny, Jack."

"I think you look terrific, Wally." Samantha had turned back to face him.

"You think *I* look good. Wait until you see Carterbaby. He looks like a poster boy for the Montana Militia."

"Is he ready?" Fallon asked.

"Just about. He's shaking like a leaf in a bad wind." Wally grinned. "It's nice to see after all these weeks of taking his crap." Fallon thought he detected a hint of sympathy beneath the bravado. "Anyway, I wanted to check with you one last time before we brought him out," he added.

"We could still try to make him talk now," Samantha said.

She was still hanging on to a final hope of altering their plan. Fallon touched her arm lightly. "It won't work if we do," he said. "He'll know it's a game and he'll button up, and we'll never get a second shot at him."

"You sure you can force him to move in the direction you want?" Wally asked.

Fallon nodded. "The terrain will take care of it. And if I let him see me at certain points, he won't be left with many choices. Just remember that I'll whistle when he's getting close to any of your positions, so you'll have to be ready to drive him back. And remind everyone that as soon as they hear the first shot, they start moving in, tightening the circle. If we play it that way, he'll end up right where we planned." He turned to Samantha again. "That means he should be right in front of you and Wally and Annie, when we finish it."

Samantha felt a chill, the final words disturbing her. "Please be careful," she said.

Bennett was brought out a few minutes later. He was dressed in the same fatigues and boots as the others, but his eyes were blindfolded. Yet, even with the blindfold, he did resemble some outlandish militia model. But if the tremors in his arms and legs were to be believed, a very terrified one.

They led him along one of the logging trails. Everyone remained silent, as agreed. Fallon had insisted on it. He claimed it would further unnerve Bennett; keep him on edge, ready to panic. With equal quiet, the dinosaurs began dropping off after the first two hundred yards—first Samantha, then Wally, then Annie Schwartz. Six hundred yards into the forest, they reached a small clearing, and Constantini, Hartman, and Valasquez moved off silently in separate directions. All the positions had been chosen carefully the previous weekend. They would each be several hundred yards out from the clearing, but less than a hundred from each other. It was a large circle, but hardly the huge area they had described to Bennett, and there were clear lines of sight between each position. Bennett would have no chance to slip through unseen or unchallenged.

Now Fallon stood alone with him in the clearing. He could see a slight tremor in Bennett's hands, and he felt momentary regret at what they were doing. He forced himself to think of Malloy, and pushed it away. "Just stand here until I tell you to take off the blindfold," he said. "If you take it off before that, I'll cut your throat. And remember, if you try to leave the killing zone, someone will blow your head off. Understand what I'm saying. Don't doubt it for a minute. But if you get lucky, and manage to kill me, they'll let you walk away."

Bennett twisted nervously, ready to run but afraid to try. "How do I know that? How do I know they won't kill me anyway?" he demanded.

There was a flutter in his voice, and Fallon ignored the questions. Just worry about it, he thought. He removed a sheathed K-bar knife from his webbed belt and dropped it at Bennett's feet, then moved silently back into the thick, heavy foliage.

Bennett stood in the center of the clearing listening to every sound; expecting to feel Fallon's knife slice his flesh at any moment. His arms and legs were trembling, and he suddenly felt the need to urinate.

"You can take off the blindfold."

The words swirled in on him, seeming to come from several directions at once. Bennett pulled the blindfold free. His head snapped left and right, and he turned quickly to look behind him. He could see no one, only the forest rising above a waist-high ground mist.

"Take the knife at your feet and run."

The voice swirled in again. At first he thought it came from behind him, and he spun quickly. There was nothing, no one. His head snapped to his right, then left again. He looked down at his feet and through the rising mist saw the sheathed knife lying there. He picked it up, spun around and ran into the forest. His heart was pounding in his chest, and he could barely breathe.

Fallon watched him run. He was on the ground, his body flat and still, no more than twenty-five yards from the clearing. He rose slowly to his knees, eyes fixed on the retreating figure; then reached down and took a handful of dirt and smeared it across his face. Then he lowered the camouflage netting from beneath his cap and moved silently off to his right. It had been almost thirty years, but he still remembered the moves—the gut-tightening fear of hunting other men who wanted to kill you—the two things that kept you alive: patience and silence.

Bennett crashed through a clump of heavy brush, stumbled, and fell. He pulled himself to his knees and quickly crawled to a fallen tree. He slid behind it and fought to recover his breath. The scent of the forest filled his nostrils, mixed there with the smell of his own fear. He felt cold, but he was sweating.

He glanced over the tree, searching the forest behind him. There was nothing. He held his breath, listening for some telltale sound of movement. There was a rustle of leaves to his right, and he stared in that direction. The mist had begun to clear and he saw a red squirrel race across the forest floor, then up a distant tree.

He thought, Maybe you've already lost him. Maybe you can lie here and wait for him to pass, then double back the way you came. Bennett thought of the others who'd be waiting for him with shotguns. He'd have to find out where they were to have any hope of getting past them. But first he had to elude Fallon. Think paintball, he told himself. You're the best. The best in New England. Think it. Think it. His arms and legs continued to tremble.

The voice, faint and hissing, swirled in again. "Don't make it easy, Carter. Don't just lie behind a tree."

The voice was ahead of him, slightly to his left. He rolled over the top of the fallen tree and fell to the other side. He was about to crawl back the way he had come, when the voice came again—this time from the opposite direction and to his right. "You're easy," it hissed.

Bennett pushed himself up and, crouching, ran off to his left. Brush tore at his arms and legs; a branch snagged his hat and pulled it free. He left it behind, kept moving for another fifty yards, then dropped behind a large boulder. He was shaking badly, and he fought to control it. He told himself, You're doing exactly what he wants. You're running, and you have no idea where you're running to. The realization struck him. He also had no idea where he was. He tried to recall the directions he had traveled, but found he had only the vaguest idea how to return to the small clearing where it had started.

Something hit the boulder he was crouched behind.

Then, a moment later, something else struck it. He recalled his own ploy in his last paintball tournament, the rock he had thrown to draw out his opposition. Fallon was out there, only yards away, and he was mocking him. Hatred, mixed with fear, surged, as he backed away into the brush again. He had gone almost thirty yards before he realized he might be moving toward the man, right into the knife that awaited him. He stopped; fell to his knees.

Why were they doing this? Even if he escaped, everything he had hoped for was gone. They had destroyed him, all his hopes. There would be no choice now but to quickly sell off the stock he had purchased. Then go to his father and brother and beg for a job, any job. And if these madmen knew about him, they must know about Waters as well. He'd have to go to Waters, tell him what had happened, and Waters, too, would be forced to abort his plans. No, to hell with that old fool. Let him save himself. Or let him fall.

The stupidity of what he had just thought rushed at him. None of it mattered now, would never matter unless he escaped with his life. Bennett felt his arms begin to tremble again, then his legs. He bit down on his lip. He couldn't understand how he'd become turned around so quickly, all sense of direction lost.

He heard a noise behind him and spun to face it. Fallon rose from a clump of brush fifteen yards away. He just stood there, staring at him. The camouflage netting covered his face—a specter.

Bennett turned and raced away from him. He dodged rocks and deadfalls. There was a small clearing ahead, and he headed toward it, praying it was a road, or trail, or anything that would lead him away. His ears filled with a steady, choking sound, and he realized what he heard was his own strangled sobs, desperate and filled with fear.

He reached the small clearing and found nothing leading from it—no path, no trail, only more forest beyond. He started across it at a run, desperate to reach the cover of the other side. Then the ground gave way and he fell, crashing down on one shoulder and driving the breath from his body.

He recovered in moments, and found he was in a long, shallow pit, perhaps waist high at its deepest point. He struggled to his knees. The voice swirled in on him again.

"In Nam the VC put punji stakes in the bottom of their traps. They liked to see their enemies impaled on them. I don't think you would have lasted very long."

Bennett crawled from the hole. Fallon stood about thirty yards behind him, partially obscured by brush. Bennett turned and raced directly away again. When he glanced back over his shoulder, no one was there.

Fallon watched him run. The man was hopeless, easier than he had thought. But, then, he'd never had to fight this way, never been forced to survive anything more than a social gathering or boardroom meeting. Even his paintball tournaments had been a game played by grown children.

He saw Bennett veer to his right, headed toward Constantini's position. Bennett was pitiable, and it was time to end it. Surprisingly, he found no pleasure in the man's fear. He only found his own sense of worth diminished. Samantha had been right.

Bennett raced ahead. Behind him he heard a long, sustained whistle. Thirty yards ahead, Ben Constantini rose up on a rock face. His shotgun snapped to his shoulder and he aimed down. Bennett froze, then threw himself to his left as the weapon erupted. He heard himself scream, but only in fear. Then he scrambled away, keeping low, running back the way he had come, then veering to his right again, when he was sure he was out of the weapon's range. Constantini's voice chased him.

"Run, you little rabbit. Run."

Bennett kept running. He had gone another fifty

yards when his foot struck a trip wire, and he fell forward, skidding on his chest. A loud whooshing sound filled his ears, and he looked up and saw a block of wood descending in a wide, falling arc. It was another twenty yards ahead, the block attached to a long pole that swung down from a tree, and it had sharpened stakes protruding from all sides, each capable of impaling him. He watched, terrified, as it reached its apex, then began the swing back, then forward again.

The voice came to him again, seemed to swirl in from several directions. "Just a warning of what could happen, Carter."

Bennett pushed himself up, trying to decide which way to go. Constantini was somewhere to his right; the sharpened stakes and perhaps still more traps lay straight ahead. He cut to his left, running again, knowing he should slow down to avoid the noise he was making, but unable to stop himself.

Then two figures appeared fifty or sixty yards away: one to his left, the second straight ahead. Each carried a shotgun.

"Keep coming, Carter," Valasquez shouted. "Keep coming, you miserable little shit."

"This way. Right this way," Hartman countered. "Give me one clear shot."

Bennett spun away from both, their voices trailing after him, taunting, threatening. He realized he was sobbing again, and tears streaked his face. Ahead lay two large outcroppings of rock with a path cut between. He pulled the knife from the sheath he had attached to his belt, and raced into the tunnellike passage, headed toward another small clearing he could just make out on the other side.

He broke into the clear. Wally Green and Annie Schwartz stood at opposite ends of the clearing. Both had weapons raised to their shoulders.

"Whoops. I think you made a wrong turn," Annie said.

"You're dead meat. Just like Jim Malloy," Wally shouted.

Bennett spun around to race back the way he'd come. Fallon's leg struck out, smashing into his knee, and Bennett's feet flew out from under him. He fell heavily; the knife flew from his hand. Fallon dropped on top of him, pinning his back to the ground. The knife in his hand pressed against Bennett's throat.

"It's all over, tough guy," he hissed.

Bennett stared into his face. It was cold and pitiless, filled with a mixture of contempt and hatred.

"Don't, Jack. Please don't." He could hear himself begging for his life, and only prayed he'd be given time to beg even more.

Wally and Annie moved up, and hovered over him.

"Kill him, Jack." Wally growled the words. His face seemed obscenely twisted.

"No, don't kill him. Just cut something off." It was Annie this time, glaring down at him.

The knife twitched in Fallon's hand. From the corner of his vision, Bennett could see Hartman and Valasquez and Constantini move into the clearing.

"Tell me about Charlie, and maybe I'll let you live," Fallon hissed.

Fallon knew about it. He knew everything they'd been doing. Bennett's father flashed into his mind. Then his brother. There was a look of contempt on each of their faces, just as there always had been. He didn't care. For the first time in his life, he didn't care.

Bennett fought for breath—just enough to let him speak. "Charlie's selling the company to Strube Industries." The words wheezed out, barely intelligible. "No one knows. Not even the board." He swallowed, felt his throat constrict. "Charlie owns seventeen percent of the company, and he'll get about twenty million in Strube stock." He fought for breath again, felt the knife pressing harder against his throat. "I'm sure he'll get even more, that Strube will sweeten the deal under the table if he can pull it off without a fight."

"Is that where Plattsburgh comes in?" Fallon's voice was low and cold and filled with hatred.

Bennett felt the tremors in his arms and legs. He tried to nod, but the blade of the knife stopped him. "Yes. Charlie wants the board to believe we're about to lose the government gyro contract. They all know we'll flounder without it; probably never regain our market position in fiber optics. When they understand that, they'll grab the deal and take the quick profit that's being offered."

"And the downsizing is supposed to sweeten the pot for Strube, right?"

Bennett swallowed. His mouth and throat were dry with fear, and the effort hurt him. "Strube's going to sell off the company, and they want as many people as possible gone before they're forced to buy them out. Waters Cable is a young company, and there are tens of millions in nonvested pension funds that we could never touch. But Strube can when they divest us. Any money that's left is theirs. With that money, and when they sell off our equipment and real estate, they'll have bought us for pennies. The only thing left will be a research facility. Waters Cable will exist only on paper, and Strube will have the gyro contract under that wholly owned subsidiary. They'll have it all to themselves."

"Charlie doesn't know that you know all this, does he?"

"No. He knows about Strube's plan to divest, but he doesn't know that Strube came to me and offered me a deal to handle it for them."

"And that's when you set up your own little side deal, to make a nice killing in the market."

"Why shouldn't I?" Bennett's voice rose; he was close to hysteria now. "Waters is walking away with millions. And he was going to leave me holding the bag. No job, nothing. So I took what Strube offered, and I was going to take some more for myself."

Samantha came into the clearing, and Bennett's eyes darted toward her, pleading for intervention. The others stared at him with a mixture of contempt and—he thought—something close to pity. Their weapons were slung over their shoulders now. Wally Green turned away, shaking his head. "This is the guy we were so afraid of," he said. "Look at him."

Fallon sat back and removed the knife from Bennett's throat. He reached into his shirt pocket and removed a small voice-activated tape recorder. Samantha stepped in close and he handed it to her.

"I'm surprised you had time to terrorize your employees," she said. "You were all so busy stabbing each other in the back." She continued to stare at Bennett. "Did any of you ever think about the lives you'd be destroying? All those people? All those families? How could you be such bastards? How could you try to make me help you?"

Bennett just stared at her. He heard Fallon expel a long breath.

"We're going back to the cabin now, Carter. There's a laptop computer there, and Samantha is going to put together a document that you're going to sign. Then she's going to work up a special buyout package for each of us. You'll sign that, too. If you do those things, you'll walk out of here alive." Fallon's eyes held the unspoken threat, and Bennett's face told him he still believed; still saw his life hanging in the balance. "When you've done that," Fallon continued, "you're going to take it all back to Charlie Waters and explain it. You can tell him we'll be in his office at one o'clock tomorrow to pick up our checks." He gave Bennett a cold smile. "Cashier's checks, of course. And if they're not there waiting for us, tell Charlie we'll be headed straight to the SEC with the documents you signed and this little recording. If they

are waiting, the documents and the tape are his."
Another cold smile descended. "What'll it be, Carter?"

Bennett swallowed, grimaced against the pain it
caused. "Whatever you want, Jack," he said.

Fallon nodded. "There's one other thing, Carter."

Bennett stared at him. There was no resistance, only
a will to survive.

"Lester Gavin stays fired," Fallon said. "And I'd like
you to fire Willis Chambers, too."

Bennett let out a breath. "That won't be a problem,
Jack."

29

FALLON ARRIVED AT THE RESIDENCE AT WILLOW RUN AT seven o'clock that evening, still dressed in his fatigues and combat boots. His face was covered by a day's growth of beard.

Samantha had changed clothes in the car, insisting she was not going to meet his mother "dressed like Fidel Castro's gun moll."

Fallon didn't care. He had stopped at the real estate office and picked up a copy of the broker's listing on the cabin. He wanted to lay it before the Virgin's feet and, hopefully, put an end to her veneration.

The line outside his mother's room was even longer than the last time he had visited her shrine. The acolyte guarding her door glared up from his wheelchair. Fallon opened the door and entered. His mother was standing before the drawn curtains, as before; draped in blue, veiled, her hands extended in the same beatific pose. Again, the room was ablaze with candles, and there was an old woman standing before her, propped up by a walker. The old lady's head was bowed.

Kitty Fallon glared at her son. Then she whispered something to her supplicant. Without a word, or a look back, the elderly woman began plopping her walker about, until she had turned completely around. Then she shuffled forward until she was out the door.

Kitty Fallon eyed Samantha with suspicion. "Who is this, John?" she demanded. "You haven't hired a psychiatrist, have you?"

"What did you tell that old woman?" Fallon asked.

"Never mind what I told her. *Who* is *this?*"

"My name is Samantha Moore," Samantha said. "I'm a friend of Jack's."

Kitty turned her gaze on Fallon. "A girlfriend already, John?" She shook her head. "I hope you have better luck this time."

Fallon lowered his eyes. When he looked at his mother again, he was smiling. "You never ease up, do you, Mom?"

Kitty ignored him. "Why are you dressed like that?"

Fallon walked across the room and kissed her cheek. "Sit down, Mom," he said.

Kitty moved to a chair, and Fallon took a seat on the edge of her bed. He handed her the real estate listing.

Kitty studied it, then looked up, still suspicious. "What is this?" Her voice sounded uncertain, even a bit nervous.

"It's Dad's cabin," Fallon said. "I'm selling it, and I'm going to use the money to set up a fund to cover your bills here." He inclined his head toward Samantha. "Samantha's a lawyer," Fallon said. "She's going to draw it up for me."

Kitty's jaw quivered, but she fought it off. It was the nearest to tears that Fallon had ever seen her come. "Thank you, John," she said.

"I prefer Jack, Mom."

Kitty blinked. "Why didn't you ever tell me that?" she asked.

Fallon lowered his head again and laughed. "I guess I never thought to," he said.

Kitty blinked again. She seemed to be drawing herself up for something. "Thank you for doing this for me, Jack," she finally said. "I know how much the cabin meant to you."

Fallon reached out and took her hand. "It meant even more to Dad," he said. "And he's the one who's doing it, Mom. It's what he would have wanted."

Kitty Fallon's jaw quivered again, but again she fought it off. "He was a good man," she said. "Your father was a good man."

"Yes, he was," Fallon said.

"And so are you, Jack. So are you."

They entered Charlie Waters's office at one o'clock the next day. Waters stood behind his desk, his face red and angry. Bennett stood beside him, refusing to meet anyone's eyes.

Samantha was dressed in a simple but elegant black dress. The others had worn their best business suits.

"I won't waste your time, or mine, by expressing my disappointment, Jack," Waters began. He seemed ready to say more, but Fallon stopped him.

"That's good, Charlie. Because I'd hate like hell to end twenty-three years by laughing in your face."

Waters's jaw tightened, and his color turned a deeper red. "Carter has the buyout agreements ready for your signatures," he snapped. "As agreed, each of you will receive three years' annual salary, plus fully paid-up pensions, just as if you had all worked until age sixty-five. The company, as stipulated, agrees to make your contributions as well as its own."

"And Jim Malloy?" Fallon asked.

Waters's eyes grew even harder. "Carter has checks covering each of your demands concerning Malloy. His pension is paid up to age sixty-five, and will be paid to his widow. She also gets a check for all death-benefit coverages, totaling triple indemnity. And she receives an additional check for his *pre-dated* buyout agreement totaling three years' salary." He paused, glared at Fallon again. "Is that satisfactory?"

Fallon grinned. "As long as Lester Gavin isn't working here anymore."

Waters ground his teeth. Bennett studied the carpet. "He is no longer employed here," Waters said. "Neither is Willis Chambers. Nor will Mr. Bennett be, once this matter is concluded."

"Strube Industries will be disappointed," Fallon said. "I think they liked Carter's style."

Bennett's eyes shot toward Fallon. "Don't worry about me, Fallon," he snapped. "People of my class always survive."

Fallon nodded. "That's true, Carter. Pity though, isn't it?"

Waters seemed disturbed by the exchange. "I'm afraid the deal with Strube won't be going through," he said.

"That's a pity, too," Fallon said. "I guess all the other people here will just have to go on working for you."

Waters glared at him. "Why don't you all sign your agreements and pick up your checks," he said. "And of course you'll then turn certain documents over to me. Correct?"

"Right on the money, Charlie." Wally Green spoke the words, and grinned at Waters. He had never before called the man Charlie. He rather liked the sound of it.

Samantha removed the documents from her bag and held them up. "We'll review and sign the agreements first, of course," she said. "*And* take possession of the checks."

Waters turned his glare on her. "Of course," he said.

The high fives started in the elevator and continued out on the street. The dinosaurs beamed, laughed like schoolboys, and hugged each other. Samantha gave Wally a particularly hard squeeze, and he grinned in appreciation.

"We gotta have a reunion at the cabin," he said. "We could even kidnap Carter again, and run him around the woods one more time."

Samantha smiled. "I don't think so, Wally. I think this was a one-shot deal."

George Valasquez came up to Fallon and took his hand. "I'm sorry I doubted you, Jack. I feel like a jerk."

"Don't," Fallon said. "I had a lot of doubts myself."

They stood on the sidewalk and watched the others leave. Samantha slipped her hand into Fallon's, looked up at him and smiled. "So what does the mighty Jack Fallon do with the rest of his life?" she asked.

Fallon gave a small shrug. "First I get this check to a bank," he said. "Then?" Another shrug. "I don't know. With the buyout check, I've got enough to live on for a while." He winked at her. "Especially if I hook up with a talented lawyer who can bring in an extra paycheck."

Samantha inclined her head. "That has possibilities," she said.

He grinned at her. "Well, then I just might buy a charter fishing boat in Florida, take people out on nice balmy days to chase sailfish. It's an old fantasy my dad and I had when I was a kid, and according to my daughter, I'm definitely suffering from midlife crisis. You think you could practice law someplace where there are palm trees?"

"It could happen," she said. "But what about right now?"

"Right now?" He glanced at his watch. "Well, in about an hour, I've got an appointment with a guy at the SEC." He reached into his pocket and removed a copy of the microcassette that held Carter's confession.

Samantha raised her eyebrows. "That's dirty pool, Jack."

"Yeah, it is. And it gets worse. I'm meeting a couple of our board members for dinner. I'd like you to come along." He smiled at her. "Something tells me old

Charlie may still try to salvage his deal with Strube. And that could put a lot of people out of work. And then, of course, there's Carter. He's been a naughty little boy, and he just might decide he should continue being naughty."

Samantha slipped her arm around him and they started down the street. "When the board realizes what's been going on, and that you're the one who stopped it, they just may decide they want you back to run the company."

Fallon grinned at her. "I can't say the idea hasn't crossed my mind."

"Would you ask the others to come back, too?"

"In a flash. But let's not get ahead of ourselves. Let's keep that fishing boat in mind. It sounds awfully good to me right now."

Samantha lowered her eyes and smiled at the sidewalk. "I still can't believe it worked," she said. She raised her eyes. "But it did." She tightened her arm around Fallon's waist. "I don't think I really understood. I didn't realize how much all of you needed to show Carter you could beat him. Beat him in *every* way. But when I saw the look on everyone's face today, I finally did."

Fallon nodded. "The money wasn't enough. I don't think the money alone would have done it."

"Done what?"

"Saved us," Fallon said. He started to laugh. "I think I'll start sending Carter a card every time his birthday rolls around."

Samantha hugged his waist again. "What will it say?" she asked.

"Just three words," Fallon said. *"Beware of Dinosaurs."*